CW01022032

CRASHING OUT

MAXIMILIAN VAN DEN BOSS

Grosvenor House
Publishing Limited

This book is published by
Grosvenor House Publishing Ltd
Link House
140 The Broadway, Tolworth, Surrey, KT6 7HT.
www.grosvenorhousepublishing.co.uk

A CIP record for this book
is available from the British Library

ISBN 978-1-83975-009-0

Dedication

The darkened corridors and dusty rooms of my mind palace were unlocked after the death of my mum. I dedicate the enjoyment, the laughter, the tears and the hope that I experienced by writing this, to her.

I also acknowledge all the dedicated members of staff who have worked tirelessly and sometimes thanklessly for the National Health Service in the United Kingdom over the last seventy years, keeping the great British public on their feet and many of them in the pub.

Here's to the next seventy years!

Contents

Foreword

'*Crashing Out*' is a moving, confronting and vivid depiction of walking the sticky road of a career in the National Health Service, a poignant reminder of the hazardous lives of junior doctors and the emotional turmoil that ensues.

This is a highly topical novel, based on a true story. It is for the reader to decide between fact and fiction as frontiers are forever changing and rarely policed.

Ruth Reed - International Reviewer and Focused Patient

Prologue

The following story, if you can call it that, is a work of fiction but entirely inspired by actual events.

The usual disclaimers about people or characters resembling anyone living or dead, or indeed any of the dead resembling other dead, sort of applies and is purely coincidental but the names have been totally made up to protect the so-called innocent.

Having worked for the National Health Service for almost twenty-five years, I have seen a lot of changes, some good and some not so good.

Governments come and go, policies come and go but a common denominator seems to be that the politicians, notably successive Health Secretaries, want to make their indelible mark on the NHS, like when you go out for a nice Italian dinner wearing a new white shirt, then you order Spaghetti Bolognese.

Some would even argue that the now seventy year old institution that is the NHS, the biggest employer in the United Kingdom, the pride of the British people and the envy of other countries around the world, is being actively set up to fail. Bring in the private sector, run it like a business. There's money to be made out of other people's misery.

In the end we, as loyal staff, slowly sink into the quagmire of bureaucracy, incessant pointless paperwork and number crunching that is not uncommonly detrimental to the patient.

League tables, quality scales, mortality statistics, tick boxes, guidelines, updated guidelines, pointless acronyms, commissioners, committees, federations, quality this, QALY [1]that, lies, damned lies and sometimes (often) it all boils down to a lot of statistical tricks and utter nonsense.

Now, I'm not averse to change, efficiency savings, heath care improvement, value for money and streamlining the patient pathway in order to lead to the best, evidence-based clinical care; don't get me wrong, there have indeed been some excellent and long overdue changes over the years.

I have been a hospital consultant for over ten years and I'm not about to disclose which specialty I currently find myself in. I qualified in the mid nineties all bright-eyed and bushy-tailed, as they say.

"Let's change the world and make a difference," we say.

It's what we all say at the start.

We were called House Officers, Senior House Officers, Specialist Registrars, Consultants; now it's F1, F2, ST1, CT2, PS3, PS4, Nintendo 64! Whatever. I've actually lost track and don't really care anymore.

Well, at least you still have 'Consultant'. But hold on, you've also got locum doctors, staff grade doctors and specialty doctors too.

---

[1] The quality-adjusted life-year (QALY; arguably a pointless acronym) is a generic measure of disease burden, including both the quality and the quantity of life lived. It is used in economic evaluation to assess the value for money of medical interventions.

I think someone tried to invent the *Junior* consultant and that way your specialist training could be fast-tracked. You'd have far less clinical experience than the usual consultant but we could then tell patients that they've been seen by a consultant. Cunning, indeed. Is this still even a thing now? I don't know.

We used to wear white coats, we were allowed to wear wrist watches and ties, and we had radio pagers. We had to write patient notes on actual paper, we requested actual tests on actual paper forms and, oddly, we had to know all about our own patients; we looked after them from the time they were admitted to hospital to the time we discharged them. We guided *our* patients through their diagnostic and therapeutic journey.

We knew how to fully examine our patients without having the luxury of using high-end, high resolution medical imaging and scanning technology to give us the answers. We didn't have virtual imaging, complex 3-dimensional imaging or forms of artificial intelligence to augment image analysis.

We didn't have minimally invasive surgery; keyhole surgery was in it's infancy and the world of interventional radiology or 'pinhole' surgery was in relatively early stages of evolution.

Now, I'm not saying it was better but... *The Art of Medicine* lived! Whether this *Art* was better or not, is up for debate.

We didn't really have the internet in those early years either and iPhones were certainly a thing of the future.

Now, staff in the NHS work bloody hard, often to the detriment of their personal and family lives. Looking back, I think that working in medicine has continually wrecked my personal life... well, it was certainly a major contributor to the wreckage.

Would I do it all again? Studying, training and personal sacrifice? No, I don't think that I would, but I wouldn't discourage anyone else from doing it either if they really wanted to, nor would I actively encourage them. But try and go into it with at least a little perspective.

Medicine is a vocation, a selfless way of life, a life changer and an eye-opener. It can be joyous, rewarding, life-affirming, challenging, stimulating, massively interesting, intriguing, perplexing, frustrating, annoying, cripplingly tiring and genuinely soul-destroying.

Can I say that I am now glad that I did all this work to get here? Yes, I think so.

Have I made a difference to hundreds, probably thousands of people's lives? Probably.

Have I saved lives? Yes, many.

Have I made mistakes? Yes, occasionally, it's normal and we all share and learn from them.

Have people died under my care? Yes, it's a way of medical life, it's normal and we must all learn to deal with it and move forward.

Sometimes it all gets a bit too much for some. 'Overwhelming' might be the understatement of the year. Nurses are currently quitting in their droves. Doctors are increasingly leaving medicine often for the Southern Hemispheric pleasant pastures new where, as I can vouch, are indeed quite green.

The nature of the work means that staff need to be valued and morale should be high. Governments should *not* just pay this lip service!

A healthy workforce should equate to a healthy economy. You know, the commonest reasons for work absences are migraine, back pain and work stress?

Now, we certainly don't all do it for the money, we do it because we care but we can't always give incessant extra hours for free, we still have bills to pay and families to feed.

But do we really care? Well, yes and 'no'. Of course we do 'care', but can we really, fully and genuinely care? If we did, I believe we'd certainly all be emotional wrecks. So is it all an act then? Are medical staff actors and actresses? To a certain degree, yes we are. Well, one CEO I am told, actually was an actor! How he got the chief executive officer's job I'll never know, but he certainly plays the part well enough.

Becoming a newly qualified junior doctor at twenty-three years of age is like a baptism of fire to say the least.

You are involuntarily exposed to life and death in ways very few others, if any, outside of this profession are at that age. You have to grow up very quickly; some do, some don't, some quit and some even die by suicide - a painful and unpleasant truth.

You witness extremes of disease, extremes of life, extremes of death and the extremes of humanity. You treat those that want to live and those that would rather die. You treat those that want your help to live but are simultaneously, blissfully and actively killing themselves in some way or another. They just won't take our expert advice to help themselves.

What a waste of money, what a waste of life, what a waste of NHS resources but you have to treat everyone the same: a good person, a bad person, a child, 'granny/elderly/old-crumbly/old duck' (many interchangeable and sometimes derogatory terms used by some to describe our older and respected generation), disabled, less-abled, mentally-ill, terminally-ill, pretending-to-be-ill, ethnic minority, ethnic majority, convict, lawyer, another doctor, a total arsehole... *the patient*. You cannot judge them. The patient comes first. *You*, do not.

The hospital has on many an occasion become home: living, working, sleeping, eating, loving. One can easily fall into a shallow and superficial existence whilst trivialising the joys of life and nurturing an unwanted cynicism and sometimes a necessary crude and darkened existence.

The usual filters of normal social interactions can become blurred or disappear in their entirety. The concept of 'political correctness' becomes an unwelcome annoyance to be ignored at your peril.

It is easy to suppress anger and resentment for the work or maybe for the journey and the sacrifice it took to get where we ultimately get to. Perhaps this is all part of self-protection or self-preservation.

You may have a relationship with that special person outside or indeed inside of work (perhaps even both) but sometimes you just never get to see them. Sometimes, I can't just drop everything and get home for supper on time, or meet you for lunch, plan a holiday, or just have an evening drink at the local pub. Sometimes, I get home so late you're already asleep and I wake up and leave for work again before you're even awake. Sometimes I haven't seen you for days. Sometimes work just squeezes and drains out every ounce of enthusiasm.

Saturday comes and if I am not rostered to work, all I want to do is sleep. Suddenly, it's Sunday and the weekend is almost over. Monday begins and it all starts again.

Looking back now, I have had a great career to date and have reached a pinnacle in my speciality and am truly regarded as a leading expert in my field. Should I knock that? Of course not. I am very proud of my achievements and I continue to achieve. But at what cost?

I completed several series of post-graduate degrees, diplomas and other exams until I was thirty-seven years of age. Then, one of my colleagues died suddenly not long before their retirement on a holiday to South East Asia, I think. Someone later remarked to me, "nice C.V. - R.I.P."; paradoxically, this has a nice rhythm and ring to it but it's a phrase that now hits home in my mind and might ring true for all of us if we're not careful.

I am now in my forties, divorced with no children. This is not my choice. Do I blame the job? I want to because it had a lot to do with it. Life right now, compared to many people, can't be seen as 'that bad'. Can it get better? Well, you'd bloody well hope so!

As they say, "it'll be alright in the end... and if it's not alright, it's not the end." I'm sure you've heard that before and I'm also very much looking forward to meeting '*they*' one day.

But what the hell happened anyway? A whole bunch of crap that you'd never believe.

Honestly, you just couldn't make it up...

Chapter One

A 'Fortunate' Arrest

The Night Nurse

A high frequency, high-pitched, high tempo... BLEEP! The noise that causes every doctor to momentarily look down at their waistline as if programmed by some robotic cerebral implant.

I thus looked down to check my waistline. On my belt hung two devices, the cardiac arrest or 'CRASH bleep' and the standard issue hospital pager.

"*SCHHHCHHHCH* CARDIAC ARREST WARD ELEVEN *SCHHHCHHHHCH!*" screeched the radio-distorted woman's voice from the hospital switchboard through my beloved arrest bleep.

The last relieved senior house officer who gleefully handed it over to me like a baton, had also dropped it in the loo from surprised panic when it last went off during his long shift; always unfortunate timing. I think it was just drying out and it smelt funny too.

"Aw, for fuck's sake!" The words slid exasperatedly out of my mouth after having not had any sleep for over fifty-six hours straight... or a 'natural break' either for that matter, as far as I could remember.

"Sorry, Mrs Migginski! I'll have to examine your back passage when I get back."

She let out a small, undignified fart and sighed.

Mrs Magorzata Migginski, of second generation Polish decent and in her late eighties, was dumped in Casualty by the younger members of the Migginski family who just couldn't be bothered looking after her for the weekend; they already had eight children between them, the oldest of whom at fifteen years old was already six months pregnant.

A social admission we'd call it; diagnosis - acopia, the inability to cope with the activities of daily living.

The Migginski Family were always showing up in hospital with apparently nothing really the matter with them. A bunch of malingerers and attention seekers, we thought. The hospital food isn't even that great in this place.

"Theez 'arsespital beds ar naat very cumf-rtubbl," she garbled in her West Country accent whilst groaning with fairly vague, non-specific abdominal pain. She'd forgotten to put her false teeth in.

"They're trolleys," I muttered under my breath. They weren't designed to be used in a hotel.

I ran out of the Accident and Emergency Department, my white coat flailing behind me. I was wearing my blue scrubs and a pair of decent black *Nike* trainers underneath, so running was fairly easy in my 'uniform'.

The Infirmary was a really old hospital with long corridors, still with some old Florence Nightingale-type wards. Although, there were plans afoot to have some kind of 'phased renovation strategy' which would ultimately culminate in just sticking some shitty facade over the front of the place to give the public the fake 'impression' of excellent patient care and keep the staff from seeing daylight ever again.

To be honest, they just needed to blow the whole fucking thing up and start again. Soon the government ratings would be 'good' twenty-odd years from now, in about 2020; like anyone really gave a rat's backdoor about that anyway.

I ran up an old stairwell thinking I'd just take a shortcut to Ward 11; well, I took three to four steps at a time and yanked myself upwards using the handrail, trying my best to feel like a superhero with my white cape. After all, I was supposed to be in a rush.

3

I hoped that the rest of the crash team would turn up and perhaps had had a bit more sleep than me in the last three days.

Ward 11. Didn't I catch sight of that hot nurse there a few days ago on the ward round? Chance'd be a fine thing. Nurse Jessica Totten.

I allowed my mind to wander in mid 'flight'. Long, dark hair in a luxuriant ponytail, blue eyes, luscious, raspberry-glossed lips and a rather undersized staff nurse uniform that perfectly contoured her fabulous ti…

"JEEZUUUSS!" I tripped on the last step and almost fell over my own imagination.

"FUUUCK! Who fucking closed this coded fucking door for fuck's sake?!"

I slammed it with my arm and kicked the bottom of it. I didn't know the push button code and swipe cards hadn't yet been invented. It was nearly 3.00am, it must've been the security guys; they got well paid to piss me off.

I peered through the metallic wire grid in the reinforced fire door window and could see the entrance to Ward 11 a few metres ahead. Dr Fiona Feelwell, my registrar, thrust open a fire door on the other side closely followed by Dr Robert Banks, the anaesthetist, and Dr Dave Dewani, the house dog.

The house dog, or house officer to be a little more accurate, is a newly qualified doctor who is still learning to distinguish his gluteals from his olecranon[2] and also hoping not to kill anyone… at the moment.

I banged on the door again.

"Hey, Fi!"

---

[2] His arse from his elbow.

"Fucking hell! Why did you go that way? It's always locked!"

She opened the door from the other side to let me through. Fiona was rather pretty, in a sort of plain and understated way.

"I know it's locked... *now*... and you're fucking *soaked*!" I panted.

"I was in the shower when this *fucker* went off!" she retorted whilst angrily waving the crash bleep around, pulling back her hair and wiping some shampoo from her eyes. Yet another smart and impressive pseudonym for the cardiac arrest bleep was eloquently coined.

She clearly had no time to towel herself dry and her scrub-top was damp and plastered down revealingly over her chest.

"Well, at least you're wearing scrub pants... and have *had* a shower."

"Yeah, but my knickers are still back in my on-call room."

I half-managed to suppress myself.

She was the sort of slightly over-weight, mid twenty something that looked amazing without make-up and always a little attractively bedraggled.

"Christ! Just let me do the defibrillation then or you'll electrocute yourself to hell... you've still got another night on-call and I ain't covering for you if you die!"

"Fuck off, Jace!" She grinned and winked at me.

As we ran down the long ward between the rows of patient beds, each divided by a set of dark blue curtains, we could see the distant commotion.

There was a small gaggle (for want of a better collective term) of nurses banging into one another trying to wheel in the crash trolley, move away clutter to clear some space, whilst simultaneously drawing the curtains of the adjacent patients who were witnessing this debacle in the dimly lit ward.

Dave, short for Davinder, was trying his level best to run but this merely resulted in a sort of wobbling forward momentum. He tripped over Mr Jones' urinary catheter whilst he was wandering off on a 'midnight' stroll to the toilet. Davinder went flying forward onto his face and sort of bounced using his belly to come to a slippery halt at the foot of another patient's bed.

Urine washed all over the floor and Mr Jones, the poor old codger (like I've said before: inappropriate and interchangeable terms), wailed in pain as his catheter tube was yanked rather roughly out of the end of his already swollen penis. His unbuttoned pyjama bottoms cordially fell to the floor whilst journeying over his pale, arthritic knees and sagging skin. They settled in a small heap over his slippers and began partially mopping up the piss.

What an absolute debacle.

"Oooooo-aaarrrghhhh! Nurse!" he yelled, suddenly clutching his manhood and it's one remaining loyal testicular companion.

Fresh blood now oozed out of him. The fully-inflated, almost squash ball-sized catheter balloon had not enjoyed the unexpected and premature eviction from the bladder via his unprepared and rather surprised urethra to the outside world.

The only two trained nurses on the ward were otherwise somewhat occupied.

I looked back at Dave on the floor. 'Twat' was the word that abruptly came to mind; a moderately accurate term it appeared to be.

Dave had a low centre of gravity, so to speak. His glasses had come off and he fumbled about also trying to locate where his stethoscope had fallen.

He sported a 1970's, thick but well groomed Indian moustache, not that it should affect his balance or anything but Dave *was* a clumsy oaf though.

Nurse Jessica Totten was performing chest compressions on Mavis. I almost tripped on Mavis' chest drain bottle whilst noting Jessica as she rhythmically bounced leaning forwards and backwards in a mesmerising pendulum of delight to the beat of '*Staying Alive*'. I could almost picture the blindingly white teeth of the bearded *Barry Gibb* of the *Bee Gees* right now... in soft focus.

"Whether you're a mother or whether you're a fucker, you're staying alive, staying alive... ah-ah-ah-ahh... staying alive, staying alive..."

I snapped out of this mini trance. I was so incredibly tired.

Now, you're no doubt wondering about my lackadaisical choice of language at this point, so I must explain that I'm not usually so potty-mouthed but when you really are bordering on madness, needs must.

Fiona took charge of the crash trolley by taking it off the health care assistant and barked some orders at Dave to take bloods and stick a line in. The elderly folk always seemed to rip out their intravenous lines which were, of course, usually absent when you needed them most.

Intravenous adrenaline may be required.

Rob, the anaesthetic registrar, was a slim, athletic, quite polite and well-spoken guy. Like most of us, he'd developed a very black sense of humour to deal with all the shit we had to go through on a daily basis. You grow up very quickly as a junior doctor.

Plus, with a name like Rob Banks, how could you take him seriously?

He ambled over towards the patient's head end where another nurse was frantically 'bagging' in some oxygen in the general direction of the patient's nose and mouth via the emergency bag-and-mask kit. He calmly took the specially moulded mask off her, rotated it the correct way up to fit snuggly and air tight over the face, and turned *on* the oxygen supply from the wall. The nurse looked rather sheepishly away, took a small step backwards, closed her eyes and tried her best to become invisible.

"What's the history, Nurse?" I asked, trying to sound commanding, authoritative and in utter control.

Nurse Totten looked up. She smiled in vague recognition of me and whilst continuing chest compressions, I noticed her briefly looking me up and down as I approached.

"Mavis Mervin, ninety-six or ninety-seven years old, metastatic bowel cancer... suddenly became unresponsive and collapsed on the commode," she drawled in her West Midlands accent.

There was a small puddle of poop on the floor next to us with a bed wheel track through the middle of it.

At least they'd managed to get Mavis back on the bed.

"Jeez, what the fuck?!" I moaned under my breath. "Erm, very good work, Nurse, how's she doing?" I immediately complimented.

"She's only been down for about five minutes. I put her on the commode before going off on my break about twenty minutes ago."

Jessica looked a little uneasy but I continued to listen intently, nodding appropriately and watching her pouty lips as she talked.

I wasn't really paying that much attention to what she was saying to be honest through my intense fatigue and vaguely inappropriate lustfulness.

Rob had put an endotracheal tube down Mavis' throat whilst Fiona went to charge up the 'defib'.

"There aren't any beds on ICU you know," he commented nonchalantly, "I think there's a bed in the mortuary though."

He kept a very straight face. Nurse Totten just rolled her eyes at me and shook her head slightly.

"So, she might have arrested long before?"

Ward 11 was understaffed, as was this whole godforsaken place, so who knows how long Mavis had been dead for?

"Fiona, you're still dripping wet!" I firmly reminded her in the nick of time.

"Oh yeah, shit... here, Dave, you need the practice."

Fiona handed Dave the defib paddles and tried to cover up her dignity with her oversized and slightly dirty white coat.

Davinder had piss soaking in all over his pants and you could now see his hairy navel, but at least his top half was dry.

"What's the rhythm?" Fiona sniffled, water still falling over her nose and face from her shampoo soaked mane of darkened blonde hair.

Nurse Totten paused to apply two rectangular, fluorescent orange gel shock pads to Mavis' elderly chest and multitude of now very cracked ribs and slightly depressed sternum.

"Asystole!" Nurse Totten said astutely.

You don't shock that. That's zero electrical activity in the heart.

"Erm, could be fine VF?" I said, cleverly - ventricular fibrillation but so electrically fine you can barely see it, but... a shockable rhythm nonetheless.

Plus Dave would get some practice in.

"You'd better stand back, Nurse!" I said again with confidence and authority, hoping I'd be interpreted as ice cool but clearly giving the impression that I was probably a total knob-head.

Nurse Totten stopped chest compressions again and came over to stand by me.

"I'll just stand here out of the way," she said whilst brushing against me as she passed. "I don't really know what I'm doing anyway," she whispered, "I only qualified about six weeks ago."

She had an unusually calm exterior given the shambolic scene before us, not really revealing her evident inexperience.

She smelt really good. *Somethingorother* by *Calvin Klein*. Well, I think it was. The floor was swilling with smelly piss now because Dave had managed to kick it all over the place upon his less than graceful arrival.

"Chargings to 360!" Dave informed us in a slightly effeminate, yet loud voice, as he should.

A high-pitched crescendo squeal was heard as the defibrillator charged up.

"Please, standings clear!" Davinder lightly lisped with his beautifully clear Anglo-Asian accent.

Wet-Fiona stepped well away. Rob let go of the bag and mask, checked his watch, absent-mindedly picked his nose and flicked something towards Davinder who eagerly awaited the full charge of the defibrillator.

THUD - Mavis was shocked. But, unlike in *Casualty* or *ER* on television, she didn't reflexly launch two feet upwards into the air.

No rhythm. No pulse. No breathing. No nothing.

"Go on, Dave, do it again," I encouraged.

"Chargings!"

"Charg*ing*, Dave... it's just the one charge... look just, whatever, hurry up will you?"

THUD. Nothing.

"Can I do it again?"

"Fucking hell, Dave, okay, but I think it really is asystole now. But you can't make her any worse I suppose. Did we give that adrenaline? Could probably bang in some atropine as well? Bretylium Tosylate anyone? No?"

"Yeah, I've done all that," said Rob, generally just a bit bored. "Anyway, that Bretylium[3] *toss* doesn't work anyway. It's the drug of the desperate used to make you sound a bit clever but you just sound like a dick."

Nurse Totten grabbed my arm.

"Oh my god! Do you think she'll make it? I only went on my break. I've never had anyone die on me before."

She sounded a little panicked. Nothing should stand in the way of a nurse and her break. Nor should it.

Mavis lay on the bed not breathing (obviously), looking a little bit waxy and pale but also quite blue

---

[3] The Class III antiarrhythmic potassium channel blocker - I've only ever tried it twice in desperation. It didn't work. It is no longer recommended in the cardiac arrest protocol.

around the lips. Hypoxia does that. Both of her pupils had now fully dilated and her skin was also a bit purple and mottled.

"Well, she was on the commode, probably straining and she's got cancer everywhere. She's probably had a massive pulmonary embolism."

A huge blood clot to the lungs is enough to cause a cardiac arrest and the proverbial 'curtains'.

"How old was she again?"

"Ninety-seven," said Nurse Totten.

"Ninety-seven?!" Fiona interjected, sounding more than just a little annoyed.

Although, if you looked carefully, Mavis did look half-decent for her age, under the circumstances.

"What the fuck are we doing?! I'm calling it." Fiona gladly conceded. "Time of death... 3.37am... 3.37?! I'm fucking exhausted. I'm going back to the mess to put the kettle on and have some toast. Dave, you write up the notes... and put some new scrubs on! You're covered in piss."

"I'm going back to the Unit," yawned Rob, "I'm knackered. I've only had four hours sleep and I'm off work from tomorrow and I need to pack. I'm flying to Orlando for an anaesthetic conference."

"Fuck off, Rob. Prick!" I muttered, following the pattern of our usual teasing exchange. "Get me a *Mickey Mouse* T-shirt will you?" I asked hopefully.

He smiled as he flicked me the middle finger and wandered off back to the Intensive Care Unit.

Anaesthetists had it good; one day on, two days off. The way forward is 'gas'. I had another twenty-four hours or so on-call because someone's off sick and there's no locum cover.

"Do you need a hand clearing up?" I asked.

Nurse Totten smiled at me again whilst re-buttoning her attire; the middle one reluctantly reunited. Chest compressions can take their toll on a tight nurse's uniform.

"No, that's alright," she said. "You look really tired."

Her Brummy accent really grated at times, but she smelt nice through her recently minty-tainted cigarette breath.

"Seriously, I could fall asleep right here," I said, feeling utterly knackered and a little bit disappointed that I hadn't looked better for her.

"I'll make some tea. Go and sit down over at the nurses station."

Dave was sat down, illuminated only by a small desk lamp. He'd virtually fallen asleep now on a set of case notes and his thick-lensed glasses had slid halfway down his little, brown, sweaty nose.

"Honestly, I'd love to but I've got to get back to A&E. I'm still in the middle of clerking patients in, it just hasn't stopped... but erm, maybe you'd fancy getting a drink sometime? I'm Jacen."

"Jess. Hi." She smiled coyly. "Maybe... thanks for your help tonight."

She looked away and wandered off to the ward sluice to empty the contents of someone's stoma bag that had just been handed to her by a nursing auxiliary on work experience.

The sluice was stacked with used urine bottles, commode bowls, vomit bowls and other odd bits of kit that needed a good clean; it was full of washing machinery and was generally rather malodorous.

The dead of night was beginning to return to the darkened ward. An old boy snored loudly at the other end of the ward and muffled cries of "Nurse! Nurse!" could be heard from various directions. Someone clambered out of bed over their metal side rails and unceremoniously slumped headfirst to the floor. That'll be more paperwork and a CT head scan. If only you could just pop them back into bed and ignore it for now.

Mr Jones, now disorientated, accidentally got into bed with Mrs Jacobson whilst coming back from the loo (we had mixed wards back then too!). He still hadn't put his pyjama bottoms back on and his willy was rather exposed and still bleeding a little.

Mrs Jacobson was quite deaf and suffering from moderate dementia so, on balance, probably didn't mind that much. Well, patients doubling-up might be a way to increase bed numbers, I suppose.

The two night nurses, both newly qualified, had their hands full. Only four more hours to go for them and they could go home and struggle to get to sleep in the middle of the day before their next night shift.

There was a half-eaten tub of *Quality Street* at the desk and an almost empty box of doughnuts also meant for the day staff. That would've gone well with a cuppa. No wonder many night nurses are on the more rotund side.

I needed to get out of there before something else happened. Dave could deal with the rest. I sensed that he was fairly smart deep down but, like most newbies, his white coat still weighed about half a tonne for all the pocket guide text books stuffed into it.

'How to deal with this, how to deal with that.'

Do they tell you how to deal with all this shit and the piss all over your pants whilst barely functioning on zero sleep? Nope, they don't.

"Better call the porters to come and get the body… and, *Dave*," he jolted back into life, "don't forget to write in the notes! See you back in Caz… actually," I paused turning briefly back towards him with my forefinger in the air, "just go to bed after you're done with that, mate. I'll deal with the last few admissions."

The state he was in meant Dave would've just got in the way anyhow. He'd only been qualified a couple of months. Just a poor, non-cynical, virgin doctor.

He will be turned. Oh yes.

I left the ward, slipping momentarily on Mr Jones' little pool of pee and wandered slowly back to Casualty where, in her cubicle, Mrs Migginski had conveniently fallen asleep on her left side.

I popped on a latex-free rubber glove and smeared some *KY jelly* onto my right forefinger.

"Right… I just need to pop a finger in, Mrs Migginski."

It's like a disused quarry in there.

"I think you need an enema," I sighed.

That reminded me, when did *I* last go… ?

Chapter Two

The Morning Round

Unexpected Surprises

Mrs Migginski was sent to the admissions ward for some emergency hotel care after I'd ordered a few basic blood tests and organised someone else to give her an enema.

I saw a few more patients: a possible heart attack turning out to be a bit of acid reflux, a 'query meningitis' that was actually just a hangover and an 'overdose' of six Ibuprofen with several *Jagermeister* chasers and a *Red Bull*.

Jeez, the overdoses... when you start doing this for the first few times, you have all this sympathy for them. You start to take a full psychiatric history as you've been taught in medical school, trying to determine the predisposing, precipitating and perpetuating factors involved, trying to empathise with the patient and sounding like you really care.

Self-inflicted crap is not so easy to have patience with at 5.00am!

"What did you take? How much? When? Are you gonna kill yourself if we let you go home?"

Antidote available? Give it. If not, make 'em sick or pump their stomach. Refer to Psych in the morning.

BED!

The long walk back to the on-call room when you're dead on your feet is like a marathon; not ever having run one, I'd just have to imagine.

My head was thumping, every muscle in my legs ached, I was thirsty, I was way beyond hungry, I had some weird tinnitus in both ears, my reddened eyes burned with fatigue and my dried up contact lenses had fused with my corneas.

Where am I again? What's that over there in the corridor?

It looks like a nice, red, fully-loaded laundry bag invitingly sat just outside one of the wards waiting to be collected by the morning porters.

I'll just sit on there for a minute... just... a minute. So, sooo comfortable.

The release of pressure from my heels was like bliss, the blood flooding back like a tidal wave of pleasure. I sank lower and lower on that sweet, soft, stinking bag of old sheets and hospital gowns.

My tinnitus got louder, my vision faded to black.

Blackness.

"ALROYT, DOC!" I felt my shoulder suddenly shake.

"What the fu...?!"

"Doc, you alroyt?" Another broad West Country voice poked my semi-consciousness.

I looked up to see a bulbous but very jolly man in a pale blue, short-sleeved shirt and dark blue pants. He had tattoos down both of his hairy arms and a gold chain around his neck; but one mustn't judge a book by it's cover, especially on so little sleep.

His balding upper scalp was flanked by a long, dark and slightly greying pony tail which also gave chase to bushy sideburns and a dishevelled beard.

I could smell cigarette smoke and stale sweat on his shirt.

"I'll be needin' this 'ere sack." He gave it a small kick whilst I was still slumped on it.

"Aw, shit I'm sorry, man, I must've nodded off!"

"I can see thaaat!" He nodded. "Busy noyt was it? Been up all noyt with them lovely nurses again was it?"

"Yeah. No. Sorry." I mumbled. "What's the time?"

"Just gone six, Doc."

"Day?"

"Mundee," he said, now looking a bit more inquisitively at me. "Hard shift was it?"

I'd been awake since Friday morning, all Saturday, all Sunday and it's now Monday morning. Just got to get through today and tonight, then I'm off for a few hours.

Maybe I'd ask Nurse Totten out on a date? Can't think about that right now though.

I glanced down and noticed a bit of dried blood on my left trainer. I also sensed my morning breath. What a mess.

"Bollocks, it's the consultant ward round at eight. Better have a shave, shite and a shower... and I'm shtarving." I accidentally alliterated.

He helped me to my tired feet, I swayed a little and got a bit of a head rush as my blood pressure realised that I was no longer asleep. I staggered back to my on-call room.

There was no hot water left in the doctors' showers but at least that served to wake me up a little. I had stuck my glasses on because my contact lenses had long since deoxygenated my eyeballs.

I didn't have time to shave. Aside from this, I made the ward round in a slightly more presentable state with trousers, shirt and a tie on. I was also considerably lighter by about four pounds, smelling of *Lynx Africa* and chewing on a banana.

As usual, we did our rounds starting with the patients in Casualty who hadn't yet been allocated a bed, followed by the medical wards and then the 'outliers'.

The medical outliers were the poor sods that were borderline ready-to-go-home or were awaiting some form of social care; they ended up being moved off dedicated medical wards, where they were privileged to have specialist nursing care, and transported to the magical far reaches of the hospital where beds were rumoured to exist, such as in the Eye Hospital or, God forbid, on an orthopaedic ward.

If these folk were lucky, we'd get to see them on the ward round during normal working hours. That way, should the team decide that they were finally fit for discharge, the ball of administration could begin rolling and they'd be out of here, freeing up another precious bed!

When our team got to Ward 11, the scene was a rather more tranquil hustle and bustle as if the tsunami of the wee-hours had never occurred. There was the typical, curiously controlled chaos to morning ward life.

Sun flooded the ward through the tall windows. Some patients were sat up in bed eating breakfast, some remained semi-conscious on intravenous fluids and some were sat on their commodes surrounded by the sound-proof, odour-proof, flimsy NHS curtains that 'closed' ever so perfectly well around them.

Dignity and Privacy chuckled to themselves as they looked on.

Two nurses were doing the drug round, leaving little, plastic containers with the morning poisons (as we liked to call them) that had been prescribed, just out of arms reach of several patients.

"Aw, did you not want your breakfast, Doris?" enquired one young nursing auxiliary, another one who looked like she was on work experience and bored already.

Doris Jacobson looked on forlornly as her solidified porridge and cold, soggy toast, with a small sachet of melted butter on top, was taken away from the table at the foot of her bed. It had been sat right next to her full jug of tap water.

"Never mind, lunch'll be here soon," the young nurse reassured Doris.

Doris tried to formulate the first syllable of a word but ran out of energy and allowed her shrivelling, wrinkled eyelids to fall closed instead. She'd had little sleep what with all the commotion and then Mr Jones having helped himself to half of her single bed.

Dr Cleeve Bodman, our Firm's consultant and glorious leader, was taken by Fiona from patient to patient.

Fi pretty much knew everything about everyone and she generally took the lead on the ward rounds like a puppet master. She was also studying for her MRCP, the specialist medical exam, and was therefore usually on tip-top intellectual form.

Dr Bodman liked to lie next to the older female patients almost sharing their bed with them. All the patients really warmed to him.

He was in his mid-fifties, rather portly and pompously jolly almost all of the time. He gave all the patients his full attention and really gave the impression that he truly cared about them.

He did, however, have a bit of a squint and we all had to remember to focus on his left eye when he spoke to us, as that was usually the one actually looking at you.

Dr Bodman never carried his own stethoscope, he just wore a clean, starched and very empty, thus lightweight white coat; actually he did have a single fountain pen in his top pocket just next to his name badge that wrote in a weird orangey-brown ink.

His writing was also massive, so if you knew he was going to write in the case notes at some point (which he particularly enjoyed, an event almost like writing on medieval parchment and sealing it with a waxen stamp), you had to get in there first because the file would invariably run out of 'continuation sheets' and you could never find more paper quickly enough in the wards woefully inadequate filing system.

"Doris, you're very dry. You need to drink more. Stick out your tongue for me?"

Doris kept her eyes closed but did partially protrude a crinkly, red and very dry tongue beautifully laced with oral candidiasis.

"Dr Dewani, pass me the fluid chart, please?"

Dave, virtually saluting and knowing that he'd need a good reference at some point in his career, unclipped it from the end of the bed and handed it briskly over with a straight and outstretched arm.

"And you haven't been for a wee since yesterday morning. Temperature normal, pulse a bit high, BP a bit low."

Someone has probably forgotten to record the volume of Doris' last few pees, but to be fair, she was as dry as a crisp. Her sheets were a bit damp as well but that could have been more to do with last night's visit of Mr Jones.

Dr Bodman sat Doris forward to listen to her chest.

"Might I borrow your stethoscope?" He turned to simultaneously look at Fi... *and* I who were stood at opposite sides of the bed.

We both reached out to lend him our stethoscopes just to be on the safe side.

"Thanks." He took Fi's from her.

I put mine back around my neck like the symbol of doctorly authority it represented.

"Okay, I think we should put up some intravenous fluids but encourage oral intake. Change the antibiotics to oral, keep a close eye on fluid balance and she needs some *Nystatin* for that tongue."

Dr Bodman, the consultant, pulled the wheeled patient table from the foot of the bed and back in front of Doris. He proceeded to pour her a glass of water and pop a straw in.

"Here, drink this down and take your tablets," he said, holding the glass up to Doris' mouth.

Doris sucked down the water like it was the last drop on Earth.

"On second thoughts, leave the IV fluids for now," he said.

As the ward round went on, Dave, who still smelt a bit pissy, hurriedly wrote in the all the patients' case notes trying to gain the vague essence of what Dr Bodman had said, the new clinical details that each patient had cunningly saved up and suddenly decided to reveal especially for the consultant (which generally accompanied an entire change in their clinical histories, making the clerking junior doctor look like a total numpty), what today's clinical examination revealed, what the patients' chart observations were, writing all the new blood test request forms for the day, the necessary radiology requests, trying to answer every detailed question the consultant kept firing at him about the blood test results, the microbiology results, the immunology results, the imaging test results and documenting the new clinical decisions and overall management plan, all whilst his pager kept going off from other wards wanting the loyal services of the house dog... and *breathe*!

I, on the other hand, tried to suppress a yawn and leaned against the notes trolley. I looked down and noticed that my flies were undone.

As I subtly zipped myself back up, there was a tap on my shoulder.

Ward Sister Edna Sledge stood sternly next to me dressed in her dark blue uniform; she was in her early sixties, about five feet one inch tall and bordering on equally as wide. She had grey hair cropped quite short and had a rather permanently flushed, pink face. She clasped her arms beneath her mighty bosom providing the added support that was clearly demanded.

Surprisingly, I sensed a faint whiff of minty cigarettes.

"I know you're currently rather busy, Dr Manson, but Mr Jones needs re-catheterising and I'd like it if you'd show Nurse Totten how to do it. She's only done female catheterisations."

Jess stepped out from behind the solidly stumpy silhouette of Sister Sledge, also looking a little tired but her lips were still quite glossy and her uniform was still doing it's level best to remain buttoned up.

She'd been asked to do a double shift as one of the day nurses had called in sick and she didn't look too pleased.

"Sure, no problem. Can you set..."

"The trolley is set up by his bed with everything you need on it. If you need anything else you let me know but I doubt it."

"Thanks, Sister."

She ran the ward like a ship's captain, just like one of the mythical hospital matrons of old. She was the ward oracle.

She gave the impression of being quite scary to most people, especially to the other nurses, but would sort of soften if I playfully flirted with her a bit; she quite liked that.

"Oooh, if I were thirty years younger!" she'd say to me.

As a junior doctor, if you didn't know something or had any doubts, the advice was always to ask the nurses first, especially the ward sister; they were gold mines of information and invaluable experience.

But 'don't ever piss off the nurses because they can make your life hell'. A fact, not a rule, to never forget.

Jess followed me into Mr Jones' bed area, whilst the ward round continued on without me. The curtains were drawn and Mr Jones was lying in bed under his sheets with his arms folded and looking more than just a little bit grumpy.

The urinary catheter trolley was set up as promised.

[*To insert a urinary catheter, it is important to ensure that it is as pain-free for the patient as possible. The male catheterisation, as one might expect, has a clear and usually fairly obvious target; conversely, the female catheterisation... well, as a novice, it is perhaps easier to blow up the Death Star[4].*

Special, clear, lubricating jelly mixed with local anaesthetic needs to be squirted in the end of the penis and down into the urethra whilst carefully holding the penis with the other hand keeping everything as straight

---

[4] To all those non-Star Wars fans, in the original 1977 movie, the Death Star was a space station, the size of a small moon. To destroy it, whilst avoiding enemy fire, small spaceships had to manoeuvre down a narrow trench on the station's surface and fire proton torpedoes into a small, heavily guarded thermal exhaust port not much bigger than two metres wide. "That's impossible, even for a computer!" I hear all you Star Wars fans exclaim.

as possible, thus allowing the free passage of a soft, flexible tube. A small balloon is then inflated at the end of the tube once it is within the bladder to prevent it falling out or being pulled out, before connecting the tube to a drainage bag.]

"Okay, Mr Jones, we just need to expose you for a short time." His face contorted somewhat.

I stood on the opposite side of the bed to Jess whilst I instructed her as to what we were going to do.

Mr Jones' expression changed to one of more pleasant surprise.

"So, you're not doing it then, Doc?"

"You're in very, very good hands, sir. Nurse has done a fair few of these."

I tickled Truth under the chin, then tapped her gently on the cheek.

"I certainly *am* in good hands, Doc!" His tone distinctly softening as Jess carefully grasped his penis in her smooth, slender and as yet ungloved, left hand. But it was only his tone that began to soften.

"Jess, you'd better just pop those gloves on... for better... erm, grip."

"Oh, of course, sorry, yes!" She flushed a little, clearly a tad flustered.

"Now inject the jelly from that syringe into the end of Mr Jones. Nice and gently... gen-tly... *gennnntly*!"

The jelly exploded triumphantly out of the syringe flowing liberally all down Mr Jones' now ever-so-slightly hardening shaft.

"Oh my god, I'm so sorry, Mr Jones!"

The panic in her voice hit the accelerator and went straight into third gear.

Jess began frantically trying to rub off the voluminous cascade but only succeeding in producing a tremulous, friction-free upwards and downwards motion as her gloves got further covered in the clear, slippery jelly.

I really had very little to add now, in my fatigued state, but couldn't quite bring myself to actually assist.

Mr Jones had laid himself back a little more deeply into his three pillows. He had his eyes closed and a wry smile was now etched in a tapestry of satisfaction.

"Oh no, oh my god, oh my god, oh... my... *god*!"

Nurse Jessica Totten, Dudley Town's[5] pride and joy right there.

"I think we'll come back later." I sighed, sort of wishing that I was Mr Jones right now.

I covered up Mr Jones' obvious 'enthusiasm' with a blanket, much to his evident disappointment. I ushered the crimson, blotchy and perspiring Nurse Totten out from behind the curtains. The middle popper button on her uniform had freed itself again and her dishevelled, dark pony tail had dragged through the lubricant jelly; several large, wet globs were soaking into the lapels and front pockets of her uniform.

"Oh, how did we get on, Staff Nurse?" enquired Sister Sledge, looking up from her clipboard, her eyes wandering up and down Jessica.

"We're going to take a short break," I interjected.

Sister caught a brief glimpse of Mr Jones through a narrow gap in the curtains.

"I see," she whispered. "I think we'll ask Dr Dewani to come back and do it after the ward round."

---

[5] Dudley is a large town in the West Midlands of England, 6 miles south-east of Wolverhampton and 10.5 miles north-west of Birmingham.

Chapter Three

Orthopods and Outliers

Curious Cancellations

By the time Dave went back to see Mr Jones, catheterising him was really not a problem.

It probably had less to do with the fact that Dave was a man, smelling of Mr Jones' very own excretion, but more to do with the fact that Mr Jones' penis would now be numb until about Thursday afternoon.

The medical admissions continued to arrive throughout the day while we continued the ward round and intermittently took it in turns to peel away from Dr Bodman's pearls of wisdom and see a potential new guest in our glorious House of Fun.

I had counted that our Firm was looking after almost one hundred and twenty patients scattered all around the hospital. Needless to say, this was taking a while!

Finally, we arrived to see our final 'outlier' on a distant orthopaedic ward in the far reaches of the galaxy. We actually hadn't planned to go there at all, but Dave received a page from the ward to ask why Morag McPhlinket, 74, hadn't been reviewed for four days and would we be going round today?

Coffee and a bun would have to wait. In fact, a decent meal in general was but a distant fragment of a thought.

Mrs McPhlinket had been moved there by one of the bed managers a few days before and, in all honesty, we had clearly lost track of her.

Funnily enough, losing track of patients had happened before and mapping moving targets isn't easy. They sort of vanished like socks in a tumble drier.

She was being treated for a chest infection and was evidently much better. She was shuffling around the ward with her Zimmer frame, kept warm by her thick, floral dressing gown and with thromboembolic deterrent stockings pulled up to her knees. She was chatting to other patients about her budgie, Hamish.

Dr Bodman examined Mrs McPhlinket. Her chest sounded beautifully clear and the sputum pot by her bed was empty.

"I think we're ready to go home now," he said exuberantly.

"It's 9.15pm, Dr Bodman, pharmacy is shut so we can't get her take-home meds and we'll never get hospital transport to pick her up now." Dave tapped his watch face and frowned. It was fifteen minutes slow.

Mrs McPhlinket looked deflated and she shrugged. She lived alone and had no nearby relatives to come and get her and all the food in her fridge would have gone off anyway by now, she thought.

"Ach, well," she concluded with a relieved Scottish smile, "every one here is so lovely. One more night won't hurt."

"We'll check you back in at reception, Mrs McPhlinket. Just need to confirm that housekeeping have cleaned the room and changed the towels and bedding. Will you be needing a newspaper with breakfast in the morning or a wake-up call?" I joked.

Mrs Morag McPhlinket didn't have anyone at home to chat to, aside from Hamish (who died six months ago), so a hospital stay was like a European mini break given the number of agency nurses the Trust now needed to hire.

We were increasingly reliant on the expert services of trained nurses from Europe and beyond, including the Philippines and India. The problem was that the numbers of nursing recruits was diminishing and retaining the already fully-trained British staff was becoming increasingly difficult what with the poor salaries at home, the lure of tax-free income in the Middle East and the magnetic pull of that idealistic, sun-kissed work-life balance that Australia was boasting.

So, another bed bites the dust.

Staff Nurse in charge made arrangements to cancel one of their routine hip replacement patients who otherwise would have occupied Mrs McPhlinket's hospital 'suite'.

The team began to dissipate, Fi to the mess and Dave to another ward where he was needed to re-write some drug charts, re-site some intravenous cannulas and prescribe some sleeping pills.

Dr Bodman was off home.

"Thank you, Team! Great work today. I hope tonight isn't too busy and remember... I'm always available if you need to discuss anything."

He always showed his appreciation to everyone, regardless of how good or bad he may have thought we were.

"But just don't hesitate to cope!" He winked and left. He still had Dave's stethoscope around his neck.

BLEEP, BLEEP - my pager spluttered into life. I think the battery was running down because the numbers were fading and it was more of a *FART, FART* now. I'd better change it... or perhaps not.

The number came from Casualty, probably with another admission for us.

[*Oh yeah, and at some point Accident & Emergency (A&E, if you will) or Casualty, as we also called it, became the Emergency Department or the ED, or ER, the Emergency Room - too American for my liking and nowadays they don't like us calling it Casualty. Better change the name of the long-running TV show then!*

But to be honest, you might as well just call it the 'Not Really an Accident but a GP Surgery Department' because in reality, no-one seems to really give a hoot when they turn up and for what reason.

After all, everyone's problem is their own little emergency.]

"Look, just before you go," Alice Sharples, one of the student nurses, stumbled up behind me, her soft Southern Irish accent giving her added charm, "could you just take a really quick look at Mrs Granger? She had her hip done yesterday. I know she's not one of yours."

She looked a little embarrassed.

"Can't you bleep the orthopod on-call? I think it's Dr Johnny Winterson-Waring who's on today. He's probably in the doctors' mess watching the telly anyway," I said, moving slowly towards the ward exit in a relaxed hurry.

I couldn't really muster anything more convincing than that whilst my brain fought me for a time-out.

"Oh, but I didn't want to bother him... and to be honest, I'm not sure he'd really be able to help."

"Okay." She *was* lovely and it would've been difficult to disappoint her.

"Oh, thank you... here have a chocolate," she grabbed a box of *Ferrero Rocher* from the nurses station.

The unspoken law of professional bribery.

I really needed some proper food. I took two, slipped one in my pocket and chomped the other down whilst I followed Alice to Mrs Granger's bed across the other side of the orthopaedic ward via the notes trolley where I updated myself with her case notes of the day.

There was a typed up piece of crisp white paper stuck rather perfectly in the notes from yesterday morning not long after Mrs Granger, 86, with a history of heart disease and previous coronary bypass surgery, had returned to the ward after her hip replacement surgery.

-FROM THE HIP POINT OF VIEW, MRS GRANGER IS PROGRESSING SATISFACTORILY-

It was signed by Mr Raymond Branston, the consultant orthopaedic surgeon. He dictated all of his notes on his handheld dictaphone. He had waltzed from one of his patients to the other of his two patients as if sent there by God himself (he probably delegated to God in the first instance, who was otherwise too busy doing other things). He then had his secretary/personal handmaiden type his great knowledge up and then stick it in the case notes later in the day whilst he nipped up to the private hospital for the afternoon.

What an absolute total and utter... anyway, that's going to set me off again if I think too hard about him.

We barely had the time to scrawl anything intelligible in *our* patients' notes because we were just too god-damned busy as physicians.

Ironically enough, I first met Mr Branston during a third year medical student careers fair. I remember telling him that I was keen on a career in orthopaedic surgery.

"My BOY!" he boomed. "It's a jolly hard job. You have to have the utmost dedication, the utmost commit-ment... and," I remember him pausing for dramatic public school effect, "you'll have to wave goodbye to any social life you might have."

He looked down upon me over his half-mooned glasses, the whiff of a smug smirk on his face and stroked his chin in the knowledge that he had probably put me right off.

"Fuck that then…" I hissed under my breath whilst walking with interest to the plastic surgery stand instead.

Alice was a slim, blonde and elvish-looking girl with a fresh air of naive exuberance about her. She wore a pale blue uniform with little, red lapels. She turned around and lightly, half-trotted and half-skipped on the balls of her feet toward Mrs Granger.

As I followed on behind her, I realised that my intense fatigue was causing an unwanted pervert to rise to the surface again and with rather unwelcome frequency… was I just missing having a social life and grabbing yet another cheap moment?

As we approached, I could see that Mrs Granger was lying flat on her back and had migrated towards the foot end of the bed.

She looked grey, sweaty and clammy and her breathing gurgled with pinkish froth which formed small bubbles around her lips as she exhaled. One of the bubbles momentarily left her lips and floated gently upwards for a few centimetres before suddenly vanishing with a magical… *pop!*

"Fuuucksssake! She's in acute congestive cardiac failure, Alice! Help me prop her up on these pillows and stick some oxygen on… do some obs and get a 12-lead ECG… bleep Dr Feelwell back from the mess and I'll get a line in and take some bloods. We need to get some drugs drawn up too, I need some IV diuretic, some nitrate, diamorphine… and get that Johnny Orthopod up here… and Alice…?"

"Yes, Dr Manson?" she trembled, looking paler and more than a little petrified.

"Hurry up!"

She turned and ran away… to get help. Hopefully.

"Mrs Granger! Hello! Mrs Granger!" I shook her shoulders a little, not really expecting much conversation.

Mrs Granger frothed a little more and coughed a deep, fruity, hollow gurgle, drowning in her own secretions as she washed in and out of semi-consciousness, her breathing ever more laboured.

Sweat poured off her poor, ashen face, her eye balls rolling back with every panicked and exhausted gasp.

"Shit, she's crashing!"

She's not even my patient.

With that, her breathing ceased. I checked her pulse… nothing.

"I NEED SOME HELP HERE! CALL 2222!"

I started CPR.

I sensed *The Brothers Gibb* wouldn't be able to help us *this time*.

The rest of the crash team rocked up. Fi, at least, was now dry, Dave wheezed in, sweating more than Mrs Granger; he was in dire need of an exercise regime and had 'run' from the other side of the hospital. His thick glasses were lop-sided, his shirt hung out and his navel had also made another unwelcome encore.

Dr Matt Dundee, one of the other anaesthetic registrars, arrived with barely a bead of sweat on his brow. He'd taken over from Rob who was now probably having dinner with *Snow White* and if he was really lucky, *the Seven Dwarves* as well.

Matt was Australian; he was tall, had shaggy, brown hair, was always slightly tanned being a seasoned surfer and tanning salon user, and usually fairly chilled out.

"G'day, havin' fun here are we?" His whiny inflection enquired. "Struth mate!" He followed up, after seeing our latest challenge.

He was a fairly stereotypical Ozzy, although to be honest, I always thought he put most of it on for effect… and to pull nurses. I'm convinced that he made his name up as well.

"What do you think, Doctor Dundee?! Got a knife? Haha!"[6]

I explained what was going on to him and Matt gave Mrs Granger that quick, astute end-of-the-bed assessment.

"Well, maybe we'll avoid sticking a tube down for now… she doesn't look good, mate, and if she makes it, we'll have to take her to ICU and she'll be there for weeks and we need the beds for some major elective surgical cases this week." Matt garbled to us, not that we really cared about his problems on the Intensive Care Unit right now.

It didn't matter anyway, for at that moment, Mrs Granger signed that divine form against medical advice and 'self discharged'.

Her hip replacement scar looked good though.

"Oh… well, I suppose we can get that cancelled 'routine hip' back in for tomorrow now," staff nurse in charge said, whilst walking towards the ward telephone again.

---

[6] My 1986 *Crocodile Dundee* action-comedy movie reference set in the Australian Outback and New York City, dissipated on deaf ears.

I let out a frustrated and exhausted sigh, leaned against the wall and stared briefly at the ceiling. I started to unwrap the other *Ferrero Rocher* from my pocket and looked down again at Davinder.

"Don't forget to…"

"… yes, Jacen… writings in the notes," finished Dave.

Alice, bless her… fainted.

I dragged myself off to Casualty. Fi joined me.

Only about eleven more hours to go.

Chapter Four

The War Zone

A Helping Hand

Casualty was like a war zone.

Now, I've never actually worked in a war zone but I now know people that have. Had I ever worked in a war zone, however, in my head it would look like the scene before me.

[*Having said that, at this appropriate juncture, it is also curious to reflect on the current status of the NHS in the present day (that being 2020). If my future self could tell myself of the past and those that I worked with then, that the clock of misery would be turned right back… how many would just call it day there and then?*

It really is incredible how many of the problems we complained about and indeed foresaw worsening over twenty years ago are persisting to this day.

Striving for better, state-of-the-art care will inevitably result in better therapies and surprise sur-bloody-prise… people will live longer and require better care, attention and social support in their later years.

I think the government would rather us pay millions into the Treasury pension coffers, work till we're 80, retire, then die shortly afterwards without becoming a 'burden' on society.

Anyway, I rant and digress… I must be sensing the fatigue of my past self!]

Patients lined the corridors in their trolleys like human skirting boards, hanging on to dear life in a variety of ways, from various heights with various strengths, whilst their safety ropes slowly frayed above them.

Casualty cubicles were filled and staff ran about frantically trying to prioritise, stabilise, diagnose and admit or discharge.

The waiting rooms were bursting at the seams, the reception staff were unable to cope with the irate and angry patients hurling abuse at them, unable to comprehend potential waiting times of several hours. Well, at least they were breathing and had a pulse I say. They would have to wait.

One man, dressed in overalls and looking rather grubby, shouted, "I'm bleeding to death, it just won't stop bleeding! I've been here for four hours already!"

He slammed his heavily bandaged forefinger on the receptionist's desk, who recoiled in fear of his unacceptable aggression towards her.

In an attempt to pacify the situation, the triage nurse took him aside to take a look. "Perhaps you'd like to take the bandage off, sir?" she calmly requested.

He reluctantly obliged and unravelled it, forming a small, dirty, blood-stained mound on the floor.

"See!?" He shoved his finger towards her.

"Looks like it's stopped bleeding now, sir. I think you can go home."

"WHAAATT?! I've been here four hours... for *this*! Bloody NHS!"

He stormed out, kicking the automatic doors as he left.

Lines of ambulances with teams of paramedics stood by trying their best to keep their patients as stable and painfree as possible whilst more emergency calls were being received by Ambulance Control. They were going nowhere.

Gridlock.

A pang of guilt wafted through me as I remembered the bed that Mrs McPhlinket now occupied up in orthopaedics for one more night. There was no way that 'routine hip' was getting an operation tomorrow either; they'd get cancelled... again.

As for leaping into someone's freshly-formed grave, they will have probably cleared out Mrs Granger to the mortuary by now, if the fridges weren't full as well.

'Bed blocking' we called it... affectionately.

Of course, it wasn't that long ago that we'd finished our mammoth ward round and I had lost count of the number of times Dave was asked to write in the notes:

"ISQ (In Status Quo), requires no medical input. Await social care."

"Await stair lift."

"Await social worker."

"Await nursing home."

"Await transfer."

"Await hospital transport."

It went on and on.

All of these patients fell under the umbrella of bed blockade, like tanks on the horizon preventing an escape. Meanwhile back in the trenches, the result of all this lay before me now.

The War Zone.

"Doctor! Are you going to just stand there gawping or are you gonna help us shift this lot?"

Sister Kate Ellis was in charge of Casualty. I'd first met her when she was a junior staff nurse and I had been a medical student on my first clinical placement.

She stood in front of me with a stern look on her face, a flimsy plastic apron on and her latex gloved hands on her hips. I noticed a splash of blood on the side of her left cheek.

A wry smile developed on her face as she blew a strand of blonde hair from her smooth, pale forehead.

"Hi, Jacen, nice to see you again!" She looked at me in a manner that suggested to my inner shallowness that this was indeed my lucky day... luck in the sense that I'd hang on to literally any glimmer of a dying ember of potential good fortune.

I barely had time to utter a word when she grabbed me by the arm and took me to a patient cubicle.

My heart fired off an ectopic beat in anticipation that there would be an empty cubicle and...

"This... 'piece of work' is in a post-ictal 'coma'."

There lay on the trolley a young caucasian man in his early thirties, a little scrawny lying flat on his back with his arms folded and crossed over his chest in a *Dracula*-esque pose.

For effect, he also had a dribble of dried blood at the corner of his mouth where he must have bitten his tongue during his so-called seizure.

"He's been in several times this month with grand mal seizures... but I think he's faking," Kate whispered close to my ear.

As the soft vibration of her voice gently disturbed my tympanic membrane and the quiet moistness of her breath washed around my neck, the intense commotion of the casualty department momentarily vanished and I felt a definite tremor inside my chest like sherbet dissolving in a little pool of crystal clear water.

"Ah! Pseudo... seizures," I managed to stumble, not only absolutely knackered but also kind of aroused. Her refined and beautiful face remained close to my ear. Her long, blonde pony tail was clipped upwards on the back of her head and in her slightly disheveled state, she looked like a small peacock.

"We can't get him out of his 'coma', he won't talk, he won't open his eyes, he won't react to anything, he won't move at all, he's actually faking GCS 3![7] So we can't get him out of here!"

To get the minimum of 3 points, you needed 1 point for each of 'eyes', 'verbal' and 'motor', that is you don't open your eyes, you make no sounds and you don't move. Tick, tick and... tick again. I had to admit, this was impressive, most impressive!

"I presume you've done all the usual bloods, glucose and all that?" I said.

"Of course..." she paused for playfully sarcastic and dramatic effect, "Doctor!"

She smiled whilst faking a subservient tone.

"They are all *normal,* as are all his observations."

"Right then," I sighed, considering my next vital move. "So he didn't even flinch to the pain of a needle?"

"Nope."

"While taking arterial blood gases?!"

Because that really hurts stabbing someone in the wrist directly into their radial artery with a not especially tiny needle.

"Nope."

"Okay." I frowned.

[*Now, if you're ever asked to go and see a dead person, to confirm that they are in fact dead, even knowing that the person, usually a nurse, who has asked*

---

[7] Glasgow Coma Scale (GCS) is a neurological scale which aims to give a reliable and objective way of recording the conscious state of a person. A patient is assessed against the criteria of the scale and the resulting points give a patient score between 3 (indicating deep unconsciousness) and 15.

you to go and confirm the aforementioned death, knows full well that the dead person is in fact already dead, you still have to go and confirm the death anyway. A bit of a waste of time, I agree, but paperwork is paperwork.

I guess there are instances when the suspected dead wasn't in fact dead at all and perhaps just sleeping deeply, in some kind of metabolic coma or just watching 'Match of the Day' having a beer.

Although the process is relatively simple, ensuring you apply a methodical approach to both the assessment of the patient and the documentation is absolutely essential.

From the usual feeling for a pulse, listening for heart sounds and respiratory effort (some guidance suggests a minimum of five minutes and one suspects that the living ought to show signs of both within this time), one must also test for a pain response.]

"So, he didn't even flinch when you took blood?"

"Nope."

So, there are several ways I can do this, I thought.

There's pressure on the finger nail with the shaft of my pen...

NOTHING

There's squeezing the trapezius muscle... kind of like one of those pressure point karate moves on the shoulder.

NOTHING

There's supraorbital pressure... that always looks nasty pushing hard with your thumb on the upper part of the eye socket near the top of your nose... try it!

NOTHING... or maybe something...

I'm sure I sensed the vaguest flicker of an eyelid. Was I breaking him? It was a battle of wills now. We were getting this guy out of here. We need the trolley.

There's the clenched fist with the middle knuckle slightly protruding, then you drill it with focus into the centre of the sternum.

I pushed with verve into the centre of his breast bone.

NOTHING... wait...

A small gasp of air left his tightly close lips as I'd pushed upon his lungs.

A small bead of sweat released itself from his expressionless forehead, unwilling to be a part of this charade any longer.

Kate's eyes widened a little in expectation.

"Kate, give me a green needle?" I mouthed to her pointing at the small equipment trolley just outside the cubicle curtains.

Slowly and purposefully, she handed me a needle about four centimetres long and about one millimetre wide with a short bevel at the end; it had a green plastic hub as one fully expects of a '21 gauge green needle'.

I gently peeled opened the small, clear packet as if preparing to load a magazine full of rounds and clipping it into my *Glock 17* sidearm.

I held the needle up to the light. The bevel glistened momentarily.

Kate began to smirk.

My top lip flickered as a purposeful grimace began to form.

Our young cubicle blocker and time-waster's bare feet projected from beneath his patient blanket at the foot of the trolley.

I rolled up my right sleeve on my white coat just a little more and, as if in slow motion, I placed the needle tip just in front of his left big toe, hovering expectantly above it, aiming with a steady hand beneath the toenail and the soft, pulpy, sweaty and slightly musty-smelling flesh beneath it.

Kate creased her eyes, winced and recoiled a little.

I closed one eye and focused with the other as if looking down the sight of my weapon and the target.

SQUELCH... the needle penetrated in by not more than a centimetre right beneath the nail bed, drawing the merest trickle of blood.

"AAAAARRRRGGGHHHH!!!!MOTHERFU*
KEEEEEERRRRRRRRRRR!!"

Our friend sprung bolt upright, threw off the blanket, leapt off the trolley and hobbled quickly out of the door heading for the exit, still with the needle in his toe.

"There... pseudoseizure!" I said triumphantly.

"Shall we get one of those little old ladies in from the corridor now?"

"Absolutely, Doctor!"

Kate's eyes widened and glazed a little with admiration and wanton desire - my consciousness played humorous games of overt misinterpretation.

Well, I liked the sound of it.

"And I guess you can move those ambulances up one place now too?" I suppressed yet another yawn.

The little old lady who replaced our temporary guest, turned out to be one of my favourite patients and one I'll always remember with huge fondness. I think partly because she reminded me of my own grandmother.

Nana - Sweet as Pie.

We'd looked after her several times before, and each time she became our most favourite patient who we'd often leave until later in the ward round so that we could spend a little more time chatting with her, sharing stories whilst sat on the side of her bed.

She was so sweet, that you actually just wanted to take her home and allow her to bake you a home made apple pie. You could almost smell and taste it.

Almost.

When we left her, she'd always give us a warm and lovely smile, her slightly puffy red cheeks filling out and her sparkling white and perfect false teeth glinting in the ward lights.

"Bye-bye," she'd wave, "bye-bye." Just like the end of a children's television programme. "Bye-bye children, be good for Mummy and Daddy now. Bye-bye."

Her soft tones were an elixir.

It always refuelled me with a little happiness and a little energy to continue on through the seemingly never-ending demands of the insatiable animal that was the hospital.

Mollie also had a slight purple rinse to her grey and lightly permed hair, rather like her namesake *Mollie Sugden*, the actress and TV comedy legend. She was also a little plump which was compounded by the fact that she had come in with gross fluid retention.

This time, her legs were swollen right up through to her abdomen and her lungs were filling with fluid. She was another patient in cardiac failure perhaps pre-cipitated by a heart attack or rhythm disturbance.

Perhaps Mollie 'almost' Sugden, had just forgotten to take her vital medications at the right time, or not at all. That wasn't uncommon with elderly people and they became regular attenders for a medical MOT and drug re-evaluation.

'Non-compliance' we called it.

But to a degree, one should sympathise. I find it hard to keep up with taking antibiotics on time three to four times a day during chest infection season, never mind the enormous lists of drugs many elderly people had been prescribed.

There were drugs for their ailments, there were side effects of the drugs for their ailments, there were drugs for the side effects of the drugs for their ailments, and drugs for the side effects of the drugs for the side effects of the drugs for their ailments... or something!

'Polypharmacy' we called it.

'Poison' we unofficially preferred it.

I liked treating patients with heart disease. It felt like proper medicine, magically and mysteriously manipulating human physiology, proper pharmacology.

Alchemy if you will.

[*Digoxin or Digitalis comes from the Foxglove. Aspirin, comes from Spiraea, a biological genus of shrubs containing the key ingredient of salicylic acid. This acid can also be found in jasmine, beans, peas and clover.*

The ancient Egyptians used willow bark as a remedy for aches and pains. They didn't know that what was reducing body temperature and inflammation was the salicylic acid.]

Little tweaks in doses here and there making real clinical differences.

Making people feel better.

It felt less like the '*if in doubt, whip it out*' philosophy of many a surgeon!

Things sort of seemed a little 'cleaner' for want of a better word unlike those patients with gastrointestinal problems who usually presented with vomiting or diarrhoea.

Although, I did like the idea of playing with those endoscopes where you'd go on a voyage of discovery through the human colon or the oesophagus and stomach with a big, flexible, snake-like camera that you could steer like a video game.

After planting an oxygen mask on Mollie 'almost' Sugden, I called in Dave to do the usual clerking and patient workup with me. I prescribed some further immediate therapy on the drug chart and left it with him.

By the time we'd arranged for Mollie to be transferred to one of our medical wards to review later on, she was already breathing much more easily.

Acute cardiac failure was often surprising like that; patients could present virtually at death's door, in fact banging loudly on Death's door, ringing his doorbell and shouting through the letterbox, "ANYBODY HOME?!"

Fortunately for Mollie 'almost' Sugden today, Death was somewhere else in the department.

In fact, Death had just wandered into the resuscitation bay and he promptly flat-lined a young motorcyclist who had come off his bike so fast that the front of his helmet and indeed the lower third of his face had ripped straight off.

The nurse with that tragically unfortunate biker, switched off the cardiac monitor and unplugged the oxygen tubing from the endotracheal tube that now projected from what little remained of his mouth and throat.

I'd just passed my bike test last month and had recently purchased a lovely metallic blue 600cc *Honda* with an awesome chrome exhaust on the side that swept upwards close to the black leather seat; it made an incredible sound whilst you accelerated from 0-60 mph in under four seconds.

The sight I caught in resus was a sight that burned itself into my ever-flagging consciousness.

My head was thick with fatigue and I was desperate to lie down. I headed for the mess to take a break.

"Jacen?" Kate hollered and came over.

"Please just see this one last young man before you go?"

She placed her warm, still gloved hand on my upper arm.

I, of course, couldn't refuse her sincere but subtly flirtatious request.

"Okay... one more, just one more."

I looked desperately at the ceiling wondering if I was having some kind of out-of-body experience with my inner self looking down at me wondering what the hell was going on. I almost lifted up a hand to wave at myself.

I almost waved back.

The poor young lad was gasping for breath too. His chest x-ray, previously arranged by the young casualty officer, showed a markedly enlarged heart shadow but for one so young, this was unusual.

His pulse was rapid and his blood pressure low.

I listened intently to his heart sounds which were very quiet and his ECG showed very small electrical impulses.

A large pericardial effusion - fluid in the sac surrounding and compressing his heart preventing blood from filling the chambers properly.

Kate prepared a trolley for me with all the equipment I needed to drain the fluid off and free his heart of its deadly embrace.

As I pierced the long, thin needle under the front of his ribcage and into the pericardium, rather than the straw coloured fluid I was largely expecting, the syringe filled rapidly with deep black fluid and some debris.

Malignant melanoma - the as yet undiagnosed skin cancer had spread dramatically. The source could not be immediately detected; it eventually turned out to be a small black 'mole' on the sole of his foot. He wasn't even a sun worshipper.

Kate connected up the tubing and drainage system and we admitted the lad to a cardiac ward but it was going to be a short and palliative stay, we suspected.

Fi wandered in, still looking decidedly bedraggled, having been reviewing some 'sickies' on the wards and having managed to sneak a cheeky hour of shut-eye on the doctor's mess sofa, whilst watching a re-run of *Friends*.

"Oi, Jace!" She called over lifting up her dark framed glasses.

"Look, why don't you just bugger off back to the mess or better still, will you just go and lie down for a bit? You look utterly shite. I'll take over from here," she urged.

"Thanks!"

'Utterly shite' probably looked rather more attractive when compared to me right now.

My glasses were slipping down my nose revealing my darkening and more deeply reddening eyes.

I felt relief beginning to wash all over me at the thought of some starchy, stiff and scratchy hospital sheets, a flimsy duvet and a lumpy pillow to finally crash out on in my on-call room.

A pillow, nonetheless.

Chapter Five

Sleep Deprived

Keeping Things Real

On my way back to the on-call room, I picked up a new set of royal blue scrubs and chucked them on the bed when I got in.

It was about 2.45am, Tuesday morning.

Switching on the light, the old sixty Watt bulb crackled momentarily but cast a most welcome dimly lit, shadowy hue in the old, cold room that smelt just a little a bit musty, delicately infused with stale sweat.

A few cobwebs hung from the old ceiling tiles, some of which were loose and cracked. I suspected a particle of asbestos or two had settled somewhere up there but it was best not to focus too much on that right now.

There were no pictures on the bare white walls with just an old, brown cloth easy chair in the corner which had certainly had it's better days. A rusty spring and a broad strap of dried up elastic support dangled down beneath it.

I took off my tie, the knot of which was already half way down my shirt, kicked off my shoes and ripped off my socks; my aching feet breathed in the room's cold air. I wriggled my toes against the worn, dark green carpet to try and resuscitate them a little.

I threw my glasses down on the mattress next to my little pile of folded fresh scrubs.

The old sash window by the headboard let in the sound of the late night traffic and perpetual ambulance sirens re-greeted me in an almost mocking tone whilst instilling a brief guilt that I should still be out there working.

I took a quick, cold shower in the small afterthought-of-a-cubicle in the corner of the room, trying not to wake up my snoring neighbours, likely the orthopaedic or ENT[8] team on-call; the walls were thin enough to hear them.

Dermatology on-call would of course be at home; you don't often get acute sunburn or dandruff admitted overnight... yeah, yeah, *acute bullous pemphigoid* I hear you retort?!

I cleaned my teeth at the old sink by the bed, my mouth now desperate for that foamy, minty revival provided by modern toothpaste.

I avoided looking too closely at my face in the mirror. Fiona had already alluded to my less than desirable appearance.

Sitting down on the side of my bed, I arranged my trainers side-by-side on the floor with the laces lightly tied, then concertina'd my scrub pants on top of them; this was my genius method that, in the event of a cardiac arrest, I could efficiently slip into my trainers, pull up the trousers, then run. I'd deal with throwing on the white coat in mid-flight.

I turned to put on my scrub top, yawned and went to place my glasses over on the bedside table along with my stethoscope, pager and ever-failing crash bleep.

"Shit, *where* are my glasses?!"

Yes, as glorious luck would have it, on this my 'lucky' day, you will have guessed that they were now right underneath me and adopting a newfound shape by closely following the contours of my tired buttocks; the frames had bent backward over the arms and both lenses had popped right out of the front along with the screws.

---

[8] Ear, Nose and Throat - not many people suffered acute ear attacks if you exclude tinnitus.

"Dammit!"

I tried to bend them back and tighten the screws with my finger nails.

I had nothing to repair them with and my monthly contact lenses were long gone.

"For fuck's sake... if there's a cardiac arrest, I'm screwed."

I could see very little without glasses being short-sighted and I certainly wouldn't be able to find my way to any ward, reliably, without them.

Ah well, I must have resuscitated the entire city over the last three days.

"If it goes off... tough shit," I muttered indignantly under my breath.

I got under the duvet and kicked up the tightly tucked, stiff, cold sheets so as not to feel like I was involuntarily strapped down like some psychopath in a mental asylum.

An asylum.

I flicked off the light from the switch on the wall by the bed and lay back on the lumpy pillow.

I could feel a soft, cold breeze sneaking its way through the gaps in the old window frame and swirl around my aching face as I began to slip swiftly and satisfyingly into a deep, deep, slee...

BLEEEEEP, BLEEEEEP - the pager. What else?

I opened my eyes with the startled hatred of someone whose prospect of desperate sleep had been stolen, yet again.

One of the ward numbers.

I turned the bedside light back on and answered the call on the phone next to it.

"Hi, Dr Manson, you bleeped?"

"Hi, Doctor. Sorry to disturb you, I know you must be busy but we need some sleeping tablets prescribed on a couple of patients."

The night shift nurse sounded fresh and bright.

Jeez, sleeping tablets?! It's 3.00am. I had enough sleep in me for the entire hospital for a week.

"Look, can't you just take a 'verbal', I've just got into bed. I'll sign for it in the morning on the ward round."

"Okay, Dr Manson, just this once. Don't forget or I'll get into trouble with Ward Sister."

I ended the call and settled down once more, and flicked the light back off.

I almost immediately returned to that relaxing... sinking... falling...

BLEEEEP BLEEEEEP

"Nnnddaaaa, whhaaa, *noooo...*"

The number...

"Yeah?"

"Hello, is that a doctor?" a clear, youthful, yet slightly coy voice said on the other end of the phone.

"Yeah, it is... why?" I could barely formulate a syllable.

"Oh, good. It's Student Nurse here and I'm just seeing whether I can bleep a doctor, sorry to disturb you."

She hung up.

"What the fu...?! Bleep a, Christalmighty, who the hell let her do...?! Wait what's your name?"

I let the receiver slip through my fingers onto the floor. The momentary bounce and recoil of the springy wiring took the rest of the phone with it. There was a clatter of plastic, minor splintering and a brief crackle of static noise.

Torture!

They might as well just bloody waterboard me or electrocute my testicles and be done with it.

SCHHHFFAAARTTTT SCCCHHHFARRRTT - the failing, fading crash bleep made an exhausted effort to attract what little attention I had left.

"*SCHHHKK CARDIAC ARREST WARD 15 SCCCHHHK*"

"Aw... please, PLEASE, give me a break?!" I seemingly begged for some form of divine intervention to make it all stop as a wave of numb panic and a surge of adrenaline infused through me.

I leapt into my trainers, pulled up the trousers, grabbed my white coat and ran out of the door.

"Shit, I can't see..."

Dashing back into the room, I grabbed one of the bare lenses from my glasses, held it up to my right eye and closed the left one.

I ran down corridors and up stairs trying to find my way to the ward, as best as I could remember in some form of autopilot mode, whilst pathetically holding the lens up to my face.

Ridiculous.

I burst through the main doors on Ward 15. Most of the lights were off apart from one bedside light.

"Where's the arrest?" I had no real energy left for speech.

"It's just *there*!"

One of the nurses on night duty stared at me weirdly and pointed as I held up the solitary lens to my eye again and spun around to my right to see all the commotion gently bathed by the light of that lonely lamp.

Fi, Dave and Matt Dundee were already there and also in autopilot mode.

A very old and frail man was lying naked and flat on his bed in a thick, sticky, purple lake. He'd woken up profusely vomiting fresh blood and had then arrested.

Dave was doing chest compressions and not wearing any gloves, Fiona was inserting a venous line and Matt was just shaking his head sullenly.

"I'm not tubing him," he groaned.

His Aussie sixth sense was telling him that this was a non-starter.

Nurse handed me the notes.

I quickly flicked through.

"Hang on... he's ninety-four, stomach cancer... NOT FOR RESUSCITATION!"

"Ahhh, *Christ!*" Fi hissed. "Stop, stop, just *STOP!*"

Everyone ceased what they were doing and stared at the carnage before us.

Dave turned his palms up towards him and grimaced at the blackened blood on them, much of which had seeped in between his fingers and under the nails.

That is really *not* the way anyone would wish to go. The poor old man's eyes and blood-soaked mouth were wide open forming a face of perpetual terror.

His pyjamas were drenched in the same lumpy, clot-ridden vomit. A broken rib had protruded through his skin from Dave's chest compressions.

"Oh god, I'm so sorry, I'm so *sorry!*"

The student nurse, who was doing her first night shift and, as it happens, the one who had paged me not long ago disrupting any vague opportunity I had of sleep, burst into tears of remorse.

"I picked up the wrong notes," she sobbed. "I didn't know that he wasn't for resus. I thought I was doing the right thing!" She almost began to wail.

I put my hands on my knees, leant forward and slowly shook my head.

My head pounded, my eyes pulsated and burned, my ears were ringing again and my nose was filled with the odour of 'warm, wet iron' from the sheer volume of blood that had soaked everything around us.

Haemoglobin.

All I had the energy left to do was lie down right beside this awful mess and close my eyes.

Fortunately, my vision was currently impaired and the surreally sanguineous scene before me was in a very hazy, soft focus.

"I'm off back to bed," Matt whined in his nasally Antipodean drawl.

"Can someone phone the relatives?" Fi asked, looking directly at the teary-eyed student nurse. "I'll speak with them when they arrive and write up the notes. Dave, Jacen, get out of here. You're no use to anyone right now. We need to clear all this shit up."

Fi appeared in total control, whilst clearly exasperated, her mind was alert and fully prepared to deliver a deluge of bad news. She'd seen this all before but instinctively knew that Dave and I had had enough.

We walked back to the on-call rooms. Well, Dave physically guided me back like a wounded soldier because I felt so disorientated that I could barely focus on anything before me and neither could I stand up straight.

"Thanks, mate," I croaked, when we arrived back.

"Horrible shift wasn't it?"

"You're not kidding, man," I mustered a whisper back. "See you later for some breakfast before the round?"

"My god, I cannot be waitings to get out of this place."

I couldn't find the volition to address Dave's unique turn of phrase, but having said that, I could not agree with him more.

I fell on top of my bed fully clothed. There were dried bloody finger prints on the sleeve of my white coat where Dave's hands had been.

Everything went black.

My consciousness drowned, heavily sinking to the bottom of an infinite abyss, the light above faded, the dull, slow sound of my heartbeat boomed and reverberated inside.

My breathing slowed as a dense cerebral fog engulfed every neurone in my mind.

I'd finally *crashed out*.

"SSSCCCCHHHHHHHHCCCAARDIACCCC AAARRESSSSSTSSSCHHHWWWAAARRDD... SCCCHHH"

"MMMNNNOOOO, I CAN'T... AARRGHH!"

Abruptly my eyes opened in astounded, frightened disbelief and my adrenal glands whipped up another hormonal frenzy that forged through me, inducing a profound and fierce tachycardia as my chest above was pounded from within.

Had *any* time passed at all? Had I actually slept for even a moment?

Every muscle in my legs was shocked unwillingly and desperately into life as if a bolt of lightning had energised me with one thousand volts.

My brain crackled and squealed into life accompanied by a thumping, aching pain as blood was hammered back into every capillary bed.

I ran. I had no glasses on. I had no clarity.

I banged open doors, bounded up another stairwell, careered down empty corridors.

I sprinted and staggered into the walls, trying my best to hand-off each attack.

I panted as my lungs burned.

"Where the fuck am I going?"

I had no idea where the cardiac arrest bleep had ordered me to run.

Half way down a dizzyingly-lit corridor, I stopped next to a phone on the wall. They could be seen scattered about the hospital to allow us to answer pagers promptly should we be in transit between wards.

I squinted in the brightness and allowed my breathing to settle momentarily.

I peered at the blurred numbers and dialled the switchboard, my face centimetres away from the phone.

"Hospital switchboard, how can I help you?" came the musical tone of a voice.

It was after 5.00am. I could still sense the darkness outside.

"Dr Manson… Crash Team," I almost whispered.

Speech was still doing it's best to elude me.

"The arrest… where did you say?"

Silence.

"What arrest?!" said the perplexed voice.

I let go of yet another phone receiver allowing it to dangle by its coiled cord and bounce off the clinically white corridor walls as I slumped slowly to the floor with my head in my hands and tears in my eyes.

They're breaking me.

Chapter Six

Home at Last

Now What?

So, I seem to recall being sent home not long into the following day's ward round.

Like being red-carded and sent off for an early dangerous tackle.

Aside from the fact that I had turned up looking like Death had actually climbed into bed with *me* last night, told me to budge over then snored all night, I'd bent my glasses back into some resemblance of a pair of glasses and stuck the lenses back in the frame with micropore[9], which I must confess looked utterly ridiculous and totally unprofessional. But what choice did I have if I was expected to find my way about?

Having said this, I think it was the blood-stained hand prints on my white coat that clinched the deal.

Well, I'd only been on duty for almost ninety-six hours straight, so getting sent home a bit 'early' wasn't the end of the world... for me at least.

Dave was sent home by Dr Bodman too, once he'd realised what we'd been through. Well, I think he did.

"Go home," he had said looking at both of us, come to think of it... simultaneously.

"Fi and I will handle the ward round today."

Of course they would. Fi would have grabbed a couple of hours sleep after finishing up last night. She would have broken the desperate news of last night's horror show to the relatives with utmost professionalism and in her usual 'caring and empathetic' manner.

---

[9]   Micropore - Hypoallergenic paper tape is a lightweight, breathable paper tape that is gentle, yet offers secure adhesion especially on sensitive skin. Micropore tape works well on frequently changed bandages and on 'at risk' skin. Micropore paper medical tape is the number 1 paper tape used in hospitals... so they say.

Today, again, she'd just get on with it.

Dave and I both left rather quickly without giving anyone the time to dispute our departure.

Honestly, Dr Bodman was a legend. He was so supportive when the time came. Although he had a penchant for the private sector, he did at least give a shit about *us*, unlike some other consultants I could name.

Dr Fiona Feelwell had a couple more years of experience than me but she'd established way more mental stamina than you could imagine in that time, the art of delegation and the ability to successfully power nap were also useful adjuncts.

I went home and took a long, hot shower whilst trying to simply and quickly eradicate the mental assault of the last few days, not least the literal blood, sweat and tears that encased me.

It was now mid-morning and I tucked into a bowl of cereal and slurped a mug of strong and milky tea when the phone rang.

It was Karen. On this particular occasion, her voice was eminently recognisable.

My girlfriend.

Did I not mention her?

Looking back into this dim and distant past, she was probably someone I'd met at the wrong time of my life. Who knows?

The reflecting, recollecting mind can play curious tricks if you forget to look ahead of you with clarity and optimism.

She was my first long-term girlfriend, my 'first' and someone I'd dated almost all the way through medical school. Some people would say that she 'blunted' my University experience a little.

Well, I'd kind of disagree because we were always in a rather 'on and off' kind of a relationship which was not of *my* choosing and because of this, I occasionally gained an appetite elsewhere and didn't always eat at home.

"Hello, Dr Mans…" I should really get out of work mode.

"Er, hello, Jacen here."

"Hi, it's me," came Karen's dulcet and slightly breathy tones.

Her voice perfectly complimented her beautiful, fresh and lightly tanned face. Her long, lavish, blonde hair, blue-grey eyes and succulent crimson lips completed the revitalising picture in my head.

I paused to inhale the moment.

"Hey. Wow, it feels like I haven't heard your voice in weeks."

"You haven't," she confirmed, deep disappointment displaying its innate ability to transcend the telephone line.

"Shit. I'm so sorry. How have you been?"

"I've missed you."

"I've missed you too." I inadvertently sounded very convincing.

Whilst of course I missed her, in truth, I'd had had little chance to miss anything, in fact, I'd had little chance to even think about anything outside of the hospital prison walls.

But I enjoyed hearing the words.

"Look, I know you're busy and I know you've been on-call… and I didn't want to make you feel more stressed, but… I love you."

Weirdly, at that point I hardly knew how to respond.

What did love even feel like?

My adrenal glands and limbic system[10] had long since emptied themselves of the evidence to be able to give me even the merest hint of love's ingredients.

"I love you too."

I knew that I did but all of my emotions seemed like they were encased in Kevlar.

"My mum's cancer has come back," she said, rather flatly.

"Oh, shit. I'm sorry." I repeated for want of a more original response.

"She's really sick and I don't think they can do anymore. She's going into a hospice."

My eyes began to well up with more tears. I loved her mum too. She was always so welcoming and had almost became a second mother to me.

In fact, it was me that persuaded her to go to hospital in the first place when I'd noted her abdomen swelling up. I knew it was fluid, she wasn't an alcoholic and being in her fifties, you had to consider the 'c' word given that she was otherwise fit and well.

Do I *ever* switch off? No... of course not.

Sometimes, being a doctor when those around you become sick or worried can be a challenge. We are trained to recognise clinical signs and formulate a list of diagnoses.

But you sometimes get cornered with:

"Could I just ask you about [such and such]?"

"Do you mind if I show you this [lump, bump, rash, discharge]?"

---

[10] The limbic system (emotional motor system) is responsible for the experience and expression of emotion. It is located in the core of the brain and includes the amygdala, hippocampus and hypothalamus.

"What do you think I should do about this [chest pain, blood I coughed up, weird numb feeling I get in my arm]?"

"Well, you're a doctor, I thought it'd be alright if I asked you about [my haemorrhoids, my genital warts, this breast lump, my testicles]"

Delete as appropriate.

Inevitably, one has to consider the most life-threatening conditions first and exclude them before settling on irritable bowel syndrome, psychosomatic disorder, chronic fatigue syndrome or hypochondriasis.

But when you're talking to those that ask, you have to say things like:

"Well, it's probably nothing but..."

"Better see your GP just to be sure."

"Well, we'd better just wait for the test results to come back."

Occasionally, you just knew immediately.

Whilst it is a kind of privilege that people feel that they can put their trust in you outside of the hospital environment, it can get embarrassing if you've only just met or it's around the table at a dinner party.

Yes, that happens.

I knew I'd get a call like this from Karen. At this point, I'd got no idea what to do. Ironically, I was on the verge of telling her that the relationship wasn't working, or more to the point (and not that I didn't want it to work), it couldn't work because we just weren't physically seeing each other for it to actually work!

Through no fault of our own... well through no fault of hers at any rate. Well, it *was* (probably) my fault and I, in turn, blamed the job.

The job made me feel this way, the job was stopping me nurturing my relationship. The job was clouding all of my emotional judgements.

I felt so lucky to have found Karen and I was ruining it. Sorry, the *job* was ruining it.

"Look, I'm so exhausted right now, I'll come and see you when I can... very soon. We'll talk properly then."

I wished that I was there with her but my thoughts were being fractured.

"Okay, I love you." She reinforced it and almost said it with a questioning tone.

"Bye for now." I said, inadequately.

I wished I'd told her that I loved her again before she'd hung up.

The emotional margins of major life events in my personal life and the major human events in the hospital were regrettably and recurrently blurring.

I should have better prioritised my time and devotion in dealing with life outside of the hospital but once you tell yourself that work has to come first, that philosophy regularly comes under massive assault.

One of my major coping strategies to deal with the stress, frustration and fatigue of hospital life has always been training at the gym.

It's about mind and body focus, aggression release, escapism, mental recalibration, endorphin release, not to mention that exercise is great for your cardiovascular fitness, a great anti-ageing therapy and keeps you fit for when you do need to run up and down stairs and down corridors at great speed to help save lives!

It's also about switching off from work entirely.

I don't go to there to meet women or chat, I wear headphones and listen to music which usually deters any conversation, especially with people you might see that you also know from work; I'd much rather avoid them. Although, on odd occasions you do meet the odd one that you fancy chatting to!

However, when you're knackered and full of freshly found sleep deprivation, the mind can again conjure up some curious deceptions.

I snapped out of my brief daydream and realised I'd been holding a spoonful of softening, soggy cereal to my mouth.

I finished my breakfast and got changed into my favourite gym kit, consisting of an old, slightly holey and vaguely malodorous, grey *Everlast* T-shirt complimented by the latest black *Nike* accessories.

I was just finishing a warm-up jog on the treadmill when, on this occasion, I did spot a rather slim, athletic and very attractive blonde girl doing stretches on a yoga mat.

I thought that I recognised her.

Now, despite what some people said about my looks back then, I was utterly rubbish at approaching women, becoming tongue-tied, clumsy and generally talking shite.

To be honest, I think that I'm misunderstood! Yeah, we all say that.

On this occasion, and most likely fuelled by a new found confidence, or more likely a fatigue-induced suppression of inhibition, I actually went over to where she was stretching, sat on the mat next to her and... err... started some stretching whilst trying to *look* like I was stretching.

There were other very empty mats further away, so I guess it was fairly obvious to her that I wasn't there to stretch.

"*Ah... hang on,*" I thought, "*I know where I know you from...*" I continued to think, keeping those exact thoughts in my head, as specifically thoughtful thoughts, purely for thinking only and not for sharing aloud.

"Hi!" I blurted.

"*Shit!*" I thought.

"Hi!" She smiled radiantly. Her perfectly white teeth glistened and the pupils in her clear blue eyes dilated just a little.

"How are you doing? Busy weekend wasn't it?" I said.

"I'm good thanks... why what do you mean?"

"*Ah... that's it, I knew I knew her from somewhere.*" My brain's filing system presented the answer.

I was feeling far less anxious now because I already knew that I knew her and the penny had now confidently dropped into whatever cerebral receptacle pennies drop into whenever thoughts find their way into the mind's 'Eureka' box.

Sometimes it is tricky to put a name to a face out of work when someone isn't wearing the uniform that you're used to seeing them in and they're all 'out of context'.

"The hospital... I'm a doctor. Which ward are you on again?" I half-flirted, half-genuinely enquired.

"Oh, I'm not on any ward," she said, a little surprised.

"Ah sorry, Casualty?" I corrected myself.

I'd spent far too long in Casualty for my liking over the last few days.

"Not... exactly," she said softly, an amused smile beginning to appear.

"O-K" I slowed my thoughts backing up a little now, not quite turning on the vehicle reversing warning peeps.

"I'm *not* a nurse."

"Ahhhh, mmm—okay?!"

A perplexed and furrowed frown began to form on my prominent frontal bone, followed by a slow, surprised widening of my gaze which was being chased from a reasonable distance by embarrassment; embarrassment was frantically waving it's arms at my surprise and saying, "*you'd better start feeling very embarrassed because I'm here now… and I AM GOING TO ROYALLY EMBARRASS YOU!*"

"I'm an… actress. I'm Claire," she said holding out her hand.

Her smile widened, recognising the mistake I had made.

I shook hands with her.

"Jacen, hi… oh, god, I'm so sorry! What a numpty. You must get this all the time. You're off *Casualty!*"

Embarrassment did indeed kick confidence in the 'proverbials'.

So, I had indeed seen Claire in a nurse's uniform… on the bloody TV, on a Saturday night!

What an idiot. *TV* nurse. Idiot.

I don't think she minded in the end really, as we did chat for a short while which was good of her. I suppose she felt sorry for me.

What if she'd actually fancied me though? I wish I had asked her out for a drink in my less inhibited state - but there we are, life could have been so different… in my dreams.

Was I secretly craving fame, fortune and stardom?

So, I tend not to approach people at the gym and keep myself to myself now. It doesn't stop me being approached though, which actually rarely happens.

"So, I saw you looking at me?" The voice came from directly in front of me, this time.

I wasn't wearing my contact lenses and the world, that day, was in glorious non-focused techniblurredness.

"Erm, was I?"

Perhaps I was? I didn't confess that I couldn't actually see properly, given that such a remark might have caused *her* some particular embarrassment as a woman approaching a man.

I sort of wished that would happen more often so that us heterosexual men would not need to put our heads on the chopping block all the time.

"I'm Victoria. I recognise you from work. Jacen, right?"

You see, this is why it's best to pick a gym several miles from work as then you wouldn't keep bumping into people that knew you.

They keep telling us not to piss in our own backyard - and when I find 'they'... I'll... never mind.

"Oh, you, er, you do? Er, yes, I'm Jacen," I stuttered.

The slim, athletic brunette before me was rather attractive in a 'soft focus' kind of way.

An inner voice screamed "Stalker!"

But what did my inner voice know anyway?

"Yeah, I'm a nurse on the acute admissions unit. You wanna get a coffee after your workout?"

"Erm, sure, why not?"

I was mid pectoral fly and my chest was glistening with sweat, clearly an attractive quality. Probability also dictated that I stunk of sweat too but that obviously hadn't dissuaded Victoria; clearly an attractive kind of sweat.

Perhaps a tiny tinkle in the backyard would be okay. Just this once.

Well, a coffee turned into going out for a drink and then a meal, as such circumstances occasionally demanded.

The night went smoothly, we got on well but I couldn't help but realise that relationships in the workplace might not be such a great idea.

But how else do you meet anyone? I never normally go out anywhere, not even to see my on-off girlfriend.

That really isn't working either. I live in the hospital.

I really should go and see her.

At the end of the evening, she kissed me on the cheek and we both went home. We hadn't made specific plans to see each other again after that evening.

One morning, about a week later, following a relatively innocuous weeknight on-call, I was sat with Dave and Fi in the hospital canteen having a Full English hospital fry-up, which were pretty decent to be honest; the sort of fry-up that causes every artery in your body to cry out in terror... and then suddenly clog.

My pager went off.

"Looks like an outside line." I peered at the fading numbers.

"But you're having no friends out of here!" Dave poked. He had a blob of *Ketchup* on his little chin dimple and a bit of egg in his moustache.

"Fuck you, Dave! You haven't any friends 'full stop'." I smiled at him and the food that was stuck to his face.

Fi just shook her tousled mane of straggly hair, rolled her eyes, pushed up her glasses on her nose and shovelled in another mouthful of baked beans and a bit of sausage.

I got up to answer the pager and rang switchboard.

"Hi, Dr Manson."

"Outside line for you, Doctor," said 'switch'.

"Who is it?"

I always liked to check in case it was a GP or a medical rep... or Mum or Dad.

You could then prepare your tone of voice and the level of professionalism that was best required.

"Ooo, Doctor, I think it's a young lady!" 'Switch' gleefully pronounced.

We never saw the ladies on switchboard but they always sounded lovely. They usually recognised my voice and I often ended up having a bit of a natter with them.

I bet they were right gossips as well. They probably knew the biggest flirts in the doctors mess!

"Mmm, alright..."

CLICK

"Hi, it's Victoria."

"Er, hi, how are you?"

"So, why haven't you called me?" *Kerboom*. Right across the bow.

"Well," I hesitated, feeling kind of freaked. "I've been working and we didn't really make any plans to..."

"I can't believe you didn't call me, I've been waiting for you to call!"

She sounded very angry and just a little bit... psychotic!

My two months of medical student psychiatric training kicked in.

I instantly knew that if I had a fluffy rabbit at home, it would surely be bubbling away in a pot of boiling water on my stove... if she also had a key for my flat... which she didn't, because we'd only been out for a coffee, a drink and a meal. Perhaps I'd have given her a key if we'd shared a dessert?!

A close shave. Maybe its just me?

She hung up. I never saw her again.

Don't piss on your own doorstep... or your backyard.

Not even a little piddle.

Chapter Seven

Totty, Fags and Ginger Beer

Coping with Days Off

A week or so later, after a relatively more mundane week at work… well, I say mundane…

I did succeed in intercepting one junior nurse who was doing the morning drug round with Sister Edna Sledge, who had nipped off to check on another patient.

She was slowly counting out the same pill into several small plastic tablet pots. They were all Digoxin tablets and they were *all* to give to our lovely Mollie 'nearly' Sugden for her cardiac problems.

Mollie was sat up looking much better and reading a copy of the *Daily Mirror*, which was a curious sight.

… the tablets, not the *Daily Mirror*.

"Good morning, Mollie!" I smiled at her and she looked all apple and cinnamon bunny back at me.

"I've asked my daughter to bring in some freshly baked apple pie for you doctors. She's going to use my very special recipe which includes a thick shortcrust pastry and home grown apples. Would you like that? You do keep telling me how you love apple pie."

She smiled again and tilted her purple head to the side looking quizzical yet hopeful.

I began salivating and felt myself licking my lips as I imagined such a delight.

"Oh, yes please, Mollie, that would be wonderful!"

You're not really supposed to accept patient gifts but this couldn't hurt and my stomach wanted to join in the party and began to rumble some background beats.

Each tablet of Digoxin or Digitalis (if we are to hark back to the days of experimental herbal remedies, henbane and deadly nightshade…) is 125 micrograms but if inadvertently prescribed by either a tired junior doctor or one whose handwriting has long since deserted him and been replaced by a tremulous arachnid scrawl, micrograms can be very easily and unsatisfactorily transform into milligrams.

Many drug doses are in milligrams (MG we would write) and few in micrograms (MG we must *not* write, MCG is better!).

So a single 125 mcg tablet is alchemically transformed into one thousand tablets!

Really?! Well, when the drug trolley runs out at four hundred tablets, one needs to ask some *very* serious questions.

She shall now be known as Nurse 'Nightshade'!

Sister Sledge pottered back to the drug trolley to see me counting the Digoxin tablets back into their rightful place and well out of reach of Mollie, who was now turning to the Sports section at the back of the *Mirror*, oblivious to this near death experience but happy that she could at least have her way of thanking us for looking after her so well.

She sipped some of her tea and nibbled upon a slice of marmalade on toast.

She looked up again whilst chewing and gave me a little apple pie wave accompanied by a tiny, toasty, soldier-fingery salute. I am certain that we would not have been thanked with freshly baked apple pie should we have poisoned Mollie 'nearly' Sugden by Digoxin overdose.

"Hmmm," hummed Sister Sledge, "I need to call the porters to come and collect Joan."

Joan was a few beds down and had a form of Muscular Dystrophy.

She was a frail lady and we were treating her for a recurrent bout of pneumonia and to be honest she was doing really well.

She had slipped gently off to sleep on her side, curled up in the foetal position with a beautiful serene smile on her face, looking blissful and calm... at peace, in fact.

Now we knew all this to be true that morning because she'd adopted this exact position last night at around 9.30pm and the current problem, was that it was almost 9.30am and she evidently hadn't really moved much.

Not even slightly. She hadn't even started her breakfast.

Doesn't anybody check up on patients during the night shift anymore?

Well, the hospital was yet again in the midst of short staffing, understaffing, skeleton staffing or whatever you'd like to call it; it just amounted to the fact that we never had enough nursing staff to take care of the huge inpatient burden. We should be operating at about 70% most of the time with the ability to upshift when the pressure rose; if you're operating at full pelt all of the time, what does one expect is going to occur?

Take a guess.

Or maybe the night shift just didn't want to wake her up. After all, Joan wasn't bothering anyone.

About ten minutes earlier, Nurse 'Nightshade' had left Joan's medication in the usual small pot beside her bed with a cheery smile.

"Aw, you look so peaceful, I won't disturb you. I'll pop back later."

She had given the bed sheets a token brush with the palm of her hand and continued on.

Joan, on the other hand... was rock solid.

Rigor mortis[11] had perfectly preserved her blissful passing like a beautifully sculpted statue, a vision of tranquility.

The porters arrived with the usual long, steely metal box on a trolley, with a lid. I recognised the porter with the greying ponytail who had woken me from my laundry bag slumber.

This was going to be tricky.

Anyway, like I was saying, it was a relatively mundane week and unusually for a Friday, I decided to go to the pub just up the road from the main hospital building rather than hitting the gym.

I didn't really want to run into Victoria again so soon for fear of having my own personal taste of rigor mortis.

The Carpenter's Arms... probably named after some 17th century agricultural farming incident.

I wandered over there with Fi and Dave.

Dave didn't drink alcohol and was a bacon and fish-eating vegetarian, not that it matters when you're off to the pub.

Sometimes it's good to socialise with your work colleagues but I didn't normally make a habit of it out of normal working hours.

Popping out for lunch and a coffee was okay occasionally, but as you hardly had time to scratch your own proverbial posterior most of the day, an uninterrupted lunch with the team was a rare luxury.

---

[11] Rigor mortis (Latin: *rigor* "stiffness", *mortis* "of death"), the third stage of death, is one of the recognisable signs caused by chemical changes in the muscles post mortem; it causes the limbs of the corpse to stiffen with the peak of rigor mortis occurring approximately 13 hours after death. A dead body holds its position as rigor mortis sets in.

That 'socialising' rule of mine remained fairly dusty.

It was difficult maintaining the work persona versus the 'actual me' persona. I do accept that they should be one and the same but it didn't feel like that inside anymore.

How should I behave? Remember what I said about acting?

Although, the 'actual me' persona was progressively becoming a figment of my own imagination day-by-day.

"First round is on me!" I generously offered.

I was generally generous like that.

"What you havin', Fi?" I asked, feeling increasingly happy to be out of work and by the bar.

Dave stood next to me and leant his elbow on the bar in a small pool of beer spilled by the last patron, which also dripped off the edge and onto the front of his trousers. He didn't notice and absent-mindedly took a small handful of peanuts from the bowl at the bar.

Fi noticed his increasingly wet crotch and just smirked.

"I'll have a G'n'T" she said, "a double please?"

"Hey, Dave, you know that, biochemically and microbiologically-speaking, those public peanuts are covered in piss and E.coli?"

He stopped chewing and let what was left of his nuts dribble back into the palm of his hand and he placed them in the little pool of beer, checking around him to see if the barmaid had noticed.

"What are you having, Dave?" I smiled.

"Ginger Beer please."

"Okay, that's a double G'n'T, a pint of Haemoglobin for me and a *rum* 'n' ginger beer for Dave."

He had to start sometime.

Haemoglobin was my medically fun and witty interpretation of *Hobgoblin* beer; I found it funny anyway, which was the most important thing... to me!

We picked up our drinks and went to find a seat.

The Carpenter's Arms wasn't that full and thankfully you could hear yourself chatting to the person next to you.

We spotted Rob Banks who had returned from his anaesthetic conference in Orlando. He was sporting a red baseball cap with *Goofy* on it.

The conference had clearly been interesting.

"Oi, Banksy! Where's my *Mickey Mouse* T-shirt?"

"At home!" he lied. "Come over and sit here."

As I was about to sit down with the others, my way was suddenly blockaded by Nurse Jessica Totten and Nurse Nightshade (I think her real name was Becky) who were also off duty now.

Again, it was kind of weird not seeing these people in uniform.

Jess was wearing a short denim jacket and a tight, slightly shiny, burgundy lycra top which was stretched over her ample assets like a second skin.

She also wore a short, black skirt and heels. A far cry from the nurses uniform, lovely as that could be... from time to time.

I could smell that familiar minty cigarette breath also now augmented by a decent whiff of alcohol.

She'd clearly been in the pub with Becky for a while now.

"Alroyt, Jayce?!" she twanged in a now amplified and more confident West Midlands accent.

I think my attraction towards her waned momentarily.

"So, you still fancy me do yer?"

Now, I don't remember disclosing this fact to anyone else other than to ask her out for a drink over that cardiac arrest.

"Well, there goes the mystery," I conceded.

She grabbed me and kissed me fully upon the lips, simultaneously trying not to spill all of her wine on me. Half of it remained in the glass whilst I tried to shake my right arm dry, still in a lip-lock.

Becky 'Nightshade' looked down, partly in embarrassment and partly because she knew that she'd been caught almost overdosing our Mollie on Foxgloves.

"Come 'n' sit with us." Jess stumbled over her words a little.

I waved over at Fi just to let her know I'd been sidetracked. She rolled her eyes again, as she does, and stuck two fingers up at me.

Jess lit up a cigarette and took another swig from her rapidly emptying wine glass.

It was the days before the blanket public place smoking ban, which I totally approved of. I hated coming home stinking of fags when you'd gone out having just showered and put clean clothes on. Not to mention coughing up lungs full of glob the following morning from breathing litres of other peoples fumes. Plus, you can't really preach to your patients the health benefits of not smoking if you yourself stunk of cigarettes and wheezed like a burns victim... secondarily minty though your breath might smell.

I took a sip of my haemoglobin and inhaled Nurse Totten's recently exhaled, tarry blend of carbon monoxide and hydrogen cyanide.

She smiled as I tried to suppress a burning cough.

I noted some nicotine staining on her teeth and her finger tips; she was clearly a bit of a chain smoker for a twenty-three year old.

Becky Nightshade was next to us chatting to someone else I didn't know, although he looked like one of the younger porters who had come to collect Joan from the ward. He was a bit skinny, had very hollow cheeks and a shaved head.

"So…" she began with less of an enquiry and more of an inevitable ensnarement.

I felt a bare foot beginning to slide up my calf under the table and work its way up to my thigh.

"So…" I replied, cleverly sensing that something was amiss.

She gently squeezed her shoulders together a little which plumped up her two rather willing companions.

I let out a loud cough as her toes gripped my zipper.

"Come back to moyn," she purred, "but no funny bizniss."

What precisely that was supposed to mean, I think, was open to a certain degree of interpretation.

"I'd better just let the others know."

I paused in my seated position to allow her to remove her pretty, bare foot from my groin and allowed Nature the work of a few moments to pull herself together, take a deep breath and close down some of the capillary beds that she had momentarily dilated.

It reminded me of being at school; there was a *totally hot* (which is how my peri-pubescent self would like to recall her), brunette, tall, slim chemistry teacher who also used to teach us swimming. She had gorgeous, piercing-blue, wide eyes, long eyelashes and always sported a moderate tan which exaggerated her toned physique.

An image of pleasure indeed.

"So, who'd like to come up to the board and write down the answer to balancing this chemical equation?"

She scanned the room noting that, as always, I had a blank yet thoughtful expression on my face, which had little to do with chemical equations and more to do with me mentally undressing the fabulous specimen before me.

That's adolescence for you. That's also adulthood, I hear you retort.

"Jacen?" She flashed a perfect, white smile in my direction.

"Err, no, not right now, Miss." I broke out of my trance. "Ask Ludwiko."

At that age, Mother Nature had her work cut out to shut down this particular peripheral capillary bed.

We had a very diverse ethnic group in A-Level chemistry class, which I liked, being of mixed racial decent myself. I'd experienced intermittent bouts of racist remarks and bullying at previous schools before, so this new environment was somewhat comforting.

Ludwiko was a self-proclaimed Austrian Count. At this moment he had his right hand down the front of his trousers and also politely declined the offer of sharing his chemical knowledge.

Also, who'd want to use the white board felt tips after Ludwiko had been feeling his own... felt tip?

Anyway, I digress again...

I stood up from the table, as Jessica slipped her foot back into her stiletto, and wandered over to where Fi, Dave and Rob were chatting.

Rob was in the middle of trying to persuade Davinder to become an anaesthetist. Well, the thought of an annual trip to *Disney World* was of course totally selling it to Dave.

Fi, in the meantime was just in a vacant daze watching Rob talk; she clearly had a crush on him.

"Hey, guys, I'm just off home." I tapped Truth on the bottom and pinched lightly.

"Oh yeah, Jacen, you slut!" joked Fi.

"Slut yourself."

She reddened a little, accepting the grain of truth in my expert retort.

"Remember, if you can't be sensible, don't be forgettings to be safeties!"

Davinder advised in his usual pluralising nonsensical style, now looking slightly drunk given the fact that I'd ordered him alcohol for the first time ever. His rum and ginger beer was almost gone.

I guessed that Dave was probably also a virgin, so sexual advice from him had to be taken with a pinch of salt. He'd read the books though, he was smart like that.

"Yeah, yeah, thanks bar-stards!" I smiled feeling like my luck was changing.

As I wandered towards the door of The Carpenter's Arms, a scrawny guy ambled a little drunkenly up to me.

He was scruffy and wore tattered jeans, an old leather jacket and sported a stubbly face but the sort of patchy stubble that would evacuate and float gently to the ground if ever he sneezed - proper 'bum fluff'.

"Hey, hey, Doc?"

He pointed and waggled his finger with this sort of friendly, yet aggressive certainty and I sort of recognised his country bumpkin accent.

"Hey, oy know you don't oy!"

"Er, I don't think so."

"Oy do, don't oy".

He was persistent and attracting the attention of others at the bar and of his mates who were sat at a table beside him.

Jess was by the door rubbing one bare calf against the other and beckoning me to follow her with one hand and supporting her frontal contours with the other forearm.

"Look, mate, no I don't think you do know me. I really, *really* have to go!"

The conflict of irritation and red hot desire was building.

The scrawny young man before me paused, he looked thoughtfully to the ceiling as if questioning his own sanity.

"Wait… no… oy *do* know you!"

With that, he unzipped his trousers and pulled them and his underwear down to his ankles in the middle of the now much more busy public house.

"You operated on my bollocks!" He stood there proudly.

There was an audible gasp, a few female screams and much hilarity.

Now during my early surgical jobs, I did partake in a 'lumps and bumps' surgical list, where we removed skin lesions, tags, a gamut of benign lumps, cysts and all that.

I glanced very briefly at the man who also had a distinctive tattoo of a very naked and very exaggerated *Samantha Fox*, the buxom lesbian model, on his upper thigh.

"Ohhh, *YEAH! Now* I remember," I said nodding, acknowledging my unforgivable mistake.

Well, you can't remember *all* of your patients now, can you?!

I grabbed Nurse Totten by the arm and we left.

Chapter Eight

A Nurse's Lair

Not all is as it seems

Jessica didn't live too far away.

She lived in the basement floor of an old four storey Victorian terraced house which was one of the few left in the city that hadn't yet been converted to flats.

Because of this, she lived with seven other housemates, so a peaceful place, it was not, especially since her bedroom was right beside a large kitchen.

There was an accountant, an IT trainee, a teacher, a budding model and actress, one unemployed girl who mostly stayed at home to bake and clean up after the others, two other newly qualified nurses and Jess.

She inserted her large key into the lock of a tall, brightly painted but flakey orange door which opened with a groan. The bare floorboards did not make for a subtle, silent entry, especially from Jess's stiletto heels.

"Let's see if they're all upstairs," she said, grabbing me by the hand.

We walked up three to four flights of stairs to a large attic room that had been converted into a large communal lounge. The stench of stale cigarette smoke and marijuana invaded my airways and I struggled to disguise a choking fit.

"Haven't you never not smoked before?" Jess treble-negatively announced as if I might as well have had leprosy.

"No, never." I tried not to pull a face of repulsion but one of blasé nonchalance.

There were several old, secondhand sofas scattered around the room and a large glass-topped coffee table in the middle. There were two large sash windows on opposite sides which afforded great views over the city.

I sound like an estate agent now.

There were about ten or twelve people strewn in various poses and states of consciousness across the room, either on the sofas, on bean bags or just lying on the floor.

Presumably, some were her housemates and some must have just been friends or boy- and girlfriends.

The TV was humming away in the background playing the *MTV* music channel. The floor was littered with empty beer cans, some crushed, some half-filled and some doubling as ashtrays. Numerous half empty wine and vodka bottles also decorated the carpet which, at some point in it's existence, must have been a version of cream-coloured. It now resembled something from a volcanically active nature reserve.

The glass-topped table was another scene: there were several semi-smouldering roll-up cigarettes scattered amongst small higgledy-piggledy piles of recently ground tobacco leaves, most of which I presumed had a larger proportion of weed. There was a large bong, an old charred spoon, a candle, a clear packet of white powder, some half-rolled five pound notes and an old credit card... on closer look, it was an old supermarket rewards card - sensible; you wouldn't want to wreck your credit card now would you? Plus, money off your shopping bill was smart, economically speaking... *every little helps*! That slogan could also be adopted by our NHS.

Jeez, is this how nurses and teachers spent their down time?! I clearly hadn't lived.

"Fuckin' hell!" Jess exclaimed, "they're all 'monged' out!"

I was repulsed by that terminology given it's blatantly controversial disability discrimination flavour.

Depressingly, even as a recently fully-trained nurse, she'd used it in such a carefree manner. Perhaps, it was a reflection of her naive and relatively junior status. Perhaps I was reading too much into it and she just didn't have a clue what she was saying... she was a bit drunk after all.

Clearly, a party had taken place that Friday evening. Or maybe that's what happened every night.

I suspected the latter.

Jess quickly rolled up one of the five pound notes, dug a small mound of the white powder from the bag and slightly shakily tapped out a short linear mound with the rewards card.

She sniffed it up through her right nostril, screwed her eyes up and rubbed the end of her nose with the sleeve of her jacket.

"Want some?" She held out the slightly unfurled note in my direction.

"No... I'm cool." She was certainly full of disturbing surprises. I felt like a right 'square'.

"Fuck it! Let's go to my room."

Her stilettos clopped and echoed on the wooden floors as she walked unsteadily down several flights of stairs to the basement. I followed her into her large room with a huge double bed in the middle and a TV at the foot of it.

She closed the curtains, lit some candles by the bedside and put on some music... *Morcheeba,* the mixed influences of downtempo, rock and folk rock. The candles emitted a perfumed scent of Ylang Ylang.

The room was being transformed into a lair of seduction.

Jess grabbed me and we started to kiss, her tongue performed a teasing dance of cat and mouse.

I pulled up her short, black skirt to reveal a very flimsy thong which barely covered anything. I allowed the elastic to flick and snap under my fingers.

I hadn't got my toothbrush and dental floss, I suddenly realised. An overnighter was on the cards.

She took off her tight Lycra top. I slid my left hand up her smooth back and with a very brief click of my thumb and middle finger, her bra was unceremoniously unclipped which duly released her fabulous, firm...

"So, you've got me tits out then?!" Dudley's finest exclaimed.

"Err, sorry... I wasn't... erm."

My sleek slight of hand was impressive. I was always better using my left hand.

I smirked whilst kissing her neck.

"Don't be scared, they won't bite."

It genuinely was difficult to understand how the hospital uniform department could find a dress to fit over her assets whilst simultaneously figure-hugging her narrow waist and wide hips. I gently shook my head and smiled, affording them the appreciation that they rightly deserved.

She pushed me onto her bed on my back and proceeded to unbutton my trousers and remove everything she could.

Momentarily, I thought of Karen and a distinct pang of guilt dropped firmly upon me.

Jess's long, now unrestrained and sumptuous dark hair cascaded over my head and chest and the warm, soft and slightly sweaty feeling of smooth, bouncing, glandular flesh, tapping either side of my face popped that thought instantly.

I psychologically, and indeed physically, made myself at home.

"Oh, Doctor!" she teased, "you shoulda brought yer woyt coat."

I could still smell that minty, cigarette breath through her perfume-ladened neck and chest. There was still a trace of white powder on her nostril.

Her aggressive, rhythmical and pendulous motion generated an ever increasing mammary-momentum, resulting in a forceful, repetitive soft tissue impaction right in front of my face, precipitating a potentially concussive impact.

"Knock yourself out!" I thought.

Experiences indeed to behold. I beheld them!

She closed her eyes tightly, groaned loudly, let out a short high-pitched scream and her face and neck became suddenly red and blotchy. She collapsed on top of me still writhing and grinding slowly.

I felt a sudden final surge of excitement, my vision blurred accompanied by a sea of flashing lights, my heart pounded hard, then suddenly I shared my sweet explosion of ecstasy with Nurse Totten.

She breathed deeply.

The track playing in the background changed. The candles flickered.

"Don't wurry, oy'm on the pill," she added.

"Oh... yeah, er, cool."

Perhaps I should have considered that earlier.

"Oy theenk," she followed up.

At that moment, it didn't seem to matter for suddenly, I heard a slow and steady hissing sound, like there was something wrong with the central heating.

Nurse Totten had stopped breathing and had a somewhat strained expression on her face.

"Oh my god, I'm sow sorry... oy get *really* gassy after using coke."

She sounded bizarrely uninhibited and not especially apologetic given our recent exploits.

"Ah, don't worry about it." I lied whilst trying unsuccessfully to hold my breath long enough to avoid inhaling what was truly a repugnant wave of deathly stench filling the room.

Seriously, I'd smelt better cadavers in dissection class.

Classy.

Dudley's advert for the historic Black Country metropolis.

Chapter Nine

Introduction to Death

You've Got to Learn

On the subject of cadavers… if you are dead, you are a corpse. Of course, you might have guessed that but if Doctor Frankenstein digs you up to use your body for research or for dissection purposes, you become a cadaver.

Cadavers are surreal things when you encounter them for the first time. When people donate their bodies to medical science, many end up on the cold stainless steel or ceramic slabs in medical school anatomy labs for the young doctors of tomorrow to explore. There they are preserved with formalin and carefully covered in white plastic sheets at the end of each teaching and demonstration session.

The skin is ashen and a little leathery, the faces expressionless and the eyes closed in a forever undisturbed sleep. It was strange to think that these, usually more elderly, bodies had once had a life of their own, full of experiences and stories, love and sadness. Now they were little more than objects for the purposes of our learning.

They were dissected with precision, layer by layer, by 'anatomy demonstrators' who were usually trainee surgeons.

After having done background reading each week, we would gather round in small groups to study the intricate and fascinating connections, workings and relationships of the human body part by part, system by system, limb by limb.

Sometimes, it was fairly bizarre when body parts were viewed quite remotely from the associated structures they had spent so long being intimately attached to.

We used to do weekly 'spot' tests where we would rotate in turn from station to station having to identify smaller structures of different body parts that had a little pin in the them with a tiny flag on the end and then answer some associated questions.

It was kind of surreal being confronted with these carefully presented dishes such as a grey face on a plate with a pin in one of the small facial muscles, a detached formalin-inflated penis with a pin in the corpus cavernosum, a forearm seen only from the elbow to the hand with a pin in a tendon that you could tug on a little to see a dead finger flex at the tip, a slice through a human brain with a pin in a particular neural tract or portion of grey matter, or perhaps a detached leg with all the muscle groups carefully exposed.

I used to enjoy anatomy classes; it felt like you were really training to become a proper doctor and one had to develop a somewhat macabre curiosity, should it not have been present already.

It was not a place for the faint-hearted, or perhaps it was, which was why some of our 'guests' were there in the first place.

Now, this may sound strange but sometimes, guiltily, I'd feel a pang of hunger when faced with a cross-sectional slab of muscle particularly right before lunch; imagining taking a large bite out of the specimens was a thought that had to be instantly rejected.

Even to this day, the smell of arterial blood with its moist, metallic scent is enough to make my stomach rumble. But strangely, I can't eat foods such as liver or kidney without being able to recognise the anatomical structures within them, such that they no longer appear as foodstuff but as specimens; this has the opposite effect on my stomach.

These days, anatomy teaching is more confined to using models or simulators and now virtual three-dimensional and cross-sectional scan images help medical students to understand human anatomy or allow a surgeon to practice an operation in advance.

I think that there is a certain technological sterility to that.

Now, I'll always remember my first real experience of patient death. I was in my third student year and first clinical placement year, and we were encountering real patients for the first time.

We had to pluck up the courage to actually go and talk to a real person, take a full clinical history and practice our full body systems examination.

I remember how it took me hours to gain that courage and then take hours to chat with the patients. We all took ages when we were first trying it.

Most people were absolutely delighted to have a young 'student doctor' to sit and chat with them, which would help the dull hospital hours pass a little faster.

"You've got to learn," they'd often say.

Or, "you look too young to be a doctor." Well, at that stage we were only about twenty years old, so we were.

But because we hadn't yet learned any refined skills of efficient and artful patient communication, we'd often spend far longer than necessary gleaning those vital pearls of information that allowed us to make a diagnosis.

The open questions, the closed questions, the leading questions, the focused questions, just let the patient tell you the story; listen and the patient will tell you the diagnosis. Ignore the patient at your peril.

But you had to learn to be savvy and it was a definite art to direct a patient in answering your searching questions accurately without disappearing off at seemingly irrelevant tangents.

"Well, it all started back in 1942…"

"Well, I'd gone down the shops, me and Ethel were chatting about the weather and…"

"Oooh, funny you should say that. Well, before I say anymore, I'll just show you my crochet/my knitting/a picture of my goldfish/my budgie/the dog…"

When you're in the middle of an on-call and taking acute admissions that were arriving every twenty to thirty minutes, you soon learned to be far quicker by practically putting the patient's story into their own mouths. You'd memorise almost every word of the history and all the details you'd elicited in the clinical examination and then go away and record it all with focused precision in the case notes like clockwork.

Make your diagnosis and get on with starting emergency drug therapy or whatever was needed, order some vital investigations and on to the next one.

A privilege it was though.

After about three hours, I'd been sat with a clipboard of paper chatting with a chap in his late fifties who had vague abdominal pain, I had recorded every word he'd said and written reams.

He hadn't yet been seen by any 'real' doctors who at that time were too busy, so we student doctors were able to make ourselves vaguely useful on the ward rather than getting in the way of the nurses or clumsily knocking over vases of patients' flowers that had been left on their owner's wheeled bedside tables.

It didn't take much for a nervous klutz of a medical student to kick one of those over, or trip on a recently used commode, knock over the crash trolley or a patient's chest drain or wound drain bottles; they were always left right behind a closed curtain invisible from view, like a booby trap!

Dropping a huge brick of patient's cases notes, that had been carefully yet flimsily filed, onto the floor was also a neat and common trick.

Patients' notes were a nightmare at the best of times. They were vital legal documents so everything had to be recorded accurately; the history sheets, the test results, clinic letters, operation notes and all that, were filed precariously in there. So you can imagine the particular upset it causes when these, often rather heavy, worn and dog-eared tomes fell to the ground in the middle of a ward, split apart and then resembled some kind of post-apocalyptic, post-hurricane aftermath.

So, I got around to examining my first patient. His story sounded like he was suffering from a gastric or a duodenal ulcer that I had, far from confidently, concluded.

I followed the usual procedure of starting with looking at the patient's hands for subtle clinical signs (you can tell a lot from people's hands, fingers and nails), examining the heart and lungs, the central and peripheral nervous system and of course an abdominal examination.

This involved carefully palpating the abdomen in a slow methodical and logical way with care to feel for enlargement of abdominal organs or abnormal lumps, bumps and masses.

The rectal examination was a vital part of the abdominal examination but as this was my first patient and the fact that I would have absolutely no idea what I was feeling for or what it felt like should I have felt something abnormal in the first place, I would spare the patient... and myself... the agony of even contemplating doing this.

The decision would be made with the common mantra of *"if you don't put your finger in it... you put your foot in it!"* in the forefront of my mind.

My patient had winced a little when I had palpated his epigastrium, the space beneath the ribs in the upper tummy. Once I had finally finished, I thanked my first ever guinea pig and wandered back up to the doctors' mess to gather my thoughts and have some lunch.

Fortunately my patient was 'nil by mouth' since the meal trolley had long since been and gone.

I had not long been in the mess when one of the nurses paged me.

If we were helping out whilst on-call, some of us would get a student bleep; this made us feel like a real doctor; what a great feeling to hold a doctors' bleep.

Believe me, that feeling does *not* last long once you're qualified.

We also had to wear short white coats that only went to below the belt line, which sort of ruined the illusion. I also wore my stethoscope with pride; that vital symbol of the medical profession was like brandishing a wand at *Hogwarts University*.

"Hi, Jacen?" crackled the voice on the phone.

"Hello," I replied tentatively. This was my first ever legitimate page by a nurse. What on earth could she want from *me*?

"Your patient that you've clerked in and just examined…" she said rather matter-of-factly.

"Yes?" A small wave of perplexed concern bathed my response.

"He's vomiting blood… quite a lot of it actually. Did you want to come back to the ward to see him?"

Did I want to come back to the ward?! Oh shitly shitness of the shittiest order! What had I done?!

I ran back to the ward.

The nurses had clearly also bleeped the actual real, proper, non-pretending doctors with the *long* white coats as well because there was a small army of attendees surrounding my patient.

Guilt accompanied me to the ward just as fast as I could run, then proceeded to sit in the corner out of the way to watch the unfolding scene and point a guilty looking finger at me.

"Look what *you* did!" said Guilt, in a guilt-inducing tone of voice that only I could hear.

"Pissing… *hell*!"

The scene before me might as well have been precipitated by a chainsaw. In fact, the writers of the *Texas Chainsaw Massacre* were probably on the ward at the time getting ideas for a sequel.

I really did *not* feel hungry anymore.

My patient was not only vomiting blood, but literally hosing blood in a rather high pressure, pulsatile way. There was complete and utter terror etched across his face as he exsanguinated in front of his very own eyes.

Fresh, bright red arterial blood.

Arterial blood has a higher oxygen content than venous blood which is somewhat more purple in colour. This blood was certainly rather red.

The anaesthetist quickly sedated and intubated the man and several intravenous drips were set up to attempt to replenish his rapidly diminishing circulating blood volume.

I was sent running to the blood transfusion lab to collect as much O-negative[12] as I could get and bring it back directly to the theatres where my man would be cut open in an attempt to try and stop the bleeding.

Having been a 'speed merchant' on the athletics track and rugby field as a sprinter and a winger, I sprinted to the blood laboratory and collected a large polystyrene box filled with several cooled units of blood and then sprinted up and down stairs and along corridors to the main theatres.

Out of breath, I delivered my vitally important package and was invited by the operating surgical consultant to scrub-up with him.

This was a real privilege and a learning opportunity not to turn down; my first operation where I actually got to help.

I will always remember the scene that unfolded; the surgeon made a large incision down the middle of the patient's abdomen, the *laparotomy*, only to be greeted by an ocean of blood. We could not see anything, not even the internal organs.

To help clear a visible field, suckers can be used to drain the blood whilst the surgeon clipped or tied off any bleeding vessels to allow finer and more precise cutting and repairing to be performed. At worst, maybe two or three sucker tubes would be used.

We used *five* and could still see nothing.

---

[12] O-negative blood is the 'universal' donor blood only carried by about 7% of the population.

Despite us pumping blood in, we were losing this battle and fast.

The heart rate monitor was getting faster but the blood pressure was not coming up.

The anaesthetist looked despairing and just shook his head.

The surgeon kept exclaiming, "I just can't see a thing, I'll just have to clamp the aorta... well, if I could see it!"

Sweat poured off his brow.

I held two of the sucker tubes whilst they consumed the man's life force from within him. He just looked as white as the driven snow now.

I was only chatting to him about half an hour ago.

"I'm stopping," said the surgeon, "this is useless! Does anyone object?"

None of us in there could refute this. The scene before us was a bloody catastrophe, a literal blood bath.

I remember how we all took a pace backwards from the patient and watched the electrical rhythm on his heart monitor in front of us gradually begin to slow... slower...... slower…....... and then…........... *STOP*.

Flat line. Dead.

The sound of the five suckers continued hissing and slurping in the background for a minute or two until the scrub nurse realised that they slurped through deadening silence and switched them off.

Dead silence.

An 'aortoduodenal fistula', the post-mortem said; the man did have a very bad ulcer which had eroded into his upper abdominal aorta.

I had recorded in my recently acquired history that he had been having pain for a few weeks.

The high pressure major arterial tube, feeding the whole body below the chest, had been drilled into by an adjacent large, inflammatory ulcer causing a rather large short cut, forcing pulsatile blood out backwards into the stomach, up the gullet and violently out of the mouth.

I could not believe what I had just witnessed.

My first ever clinical examination. My first operation. My first death.

How am I going to do this job?!

Shit.

Chapter Ten

Morning Chatter

Taking the Mickey

I sat in the doctor's mess having a morning cup of tea with Davinder.

Well, he'd actually made us a chai or masala tea as he liked to call it; he'd boiled up some water and milk added a couple of tea bags and dropped in some cloves, cardamom and cinnamon sticks.

And a sack of sugar!

It smelt and tasted great though.

Dave was a little hungover from his single shot of rum and boasted a vague headache.

A few of the other junior doctors were milling around, making toast and eating cereal, some just starting a normal day and getting ready for the daily ward round or an outpatient clinic, some finishing a mammoth shift and all in varied states of fatigue, irritability, anger, cynicism and hunger.

Fi wandered in and began to stuff her overcoat and her handbag into her locker.

She was wearing a *Mickey Mouse* T-shirt and the rest of her clothes from the day before.

"Alright, Fi!"

"Mor—-ning!" She practically sang.

"So… someone got lucky last night then, did they?"

She looked down at Mickey, who was smiling back up at her with his big, black ears and red underpants.

"Shut up." She blushed, flicked her shaggy hair from her eyes, slipped on her white coat emphatically covering Mickey's little mousey face and slung her stethoscope around her neck ready for action.

"Is Rob well this morning then is he?" I enquired with further sarcastic concern.

"Fuck off! He's got a day off so he's still in bed."

Dave and I chuckled to ourselves and slurped our masala tea.

"You cannot be talkings," Dave reminded me.

Fi wasn't the only one to have got lucky last night. Although, it depends how you define 'lucky' of course.

Dr Isaac Ali wandered in.

Isaac was Nigerian, about six-feet tall with a truly insane cackle of a laugh and had a real tendency to be an extremely lazy gynaecology registrar.

The nurses really didn't like him that much because he was so infuriatingly frustrating. He didn't like them much either because they just pestered him with 'crap' that he didn't regard as remotely important and with 'stuff' that they should just use a bit of common sense to sort out. To be honest, I think that they feigned a certain level of pseudo-stupidity just to annoy him.

Like I've said before, don't piss off the nurses or they'll make your life miserable.

If the rest of us ever managed to get time to sit in the mess, Isaac could usually be found lounging across the three person leather couch in front of the TV watching re-runs of the *A-Team* and other old seventies and eighties cop shows.

As he sidled past us to sit down, Davinder looked up from behind his large mug of tea, and while taking in an eye-full of Isaac's black trousers plastered tightly over his large continental African backside, his little face momentarily flushed his otherwise brown complexion.

"Dave! You dirty, diggerty doggerty perv..." I blurted with surprise.

"Shutting up, Jace!" he whispered and punched me in the arm.

Well, I say punch. Dave couldn't even form a fist, never mind inflict a punch.

"Alright, mate!" I conceded. "Your secret's safe with me… but Isaac?!" I whispered back, loudly.

Isaac sat down on a chair near Dave.

"What eez dat, Dev? Eet smells good."

"Masala tea. You like? I'm making some more."

"Yes pleez, Dev!"

Dave put down his cup on the table and got up from the sofa to make Isaac some tea. As he did so, one of his shirt buttons popped open under the stress and it leapt in the air seemingly to free itself, only to reveal Dave's little, hairy navel… again. The button landed in his mug of tea with a tiny 'plop'.

So that was that for the day; that button's work was done.

Isaac's eyes followed Dave to the kitchen. He noticed me noticing him notice Dave and upwardly nodded in my direction in his non-verbal code as if to say, "good morning, how are you?"

I upwardly nodded back, then gave him a knowing flicker of raised eyebrows and a widening grin.

Isaac let out a burbled gasp of air, flubbered his full lips and changed the unspoken subject.

"I haf gat cleenic tooday… a whole day of lookeen at faginas. Faginas, faginas… faginas aaaaallll daay!"

He cackled in a high pitch with a wide open-mouth, flung his head backwards, banged his hands repeatedly on his big thighs and stamped his big feet on the floor.

"Lucky you," I had to say.

"Well, you git totally bored wid dem hafta ay while," he sighed.

"Seen one, seen 'em all is it?"

"Eet is not evreeting eet eez cracked up to bee Jayceen."

"Well, better than dealing with the old 'Ducks 'n' Dorises' all day, Isaac, like we have to."

Taking care of our large cohort of elderly folk on the medical wards was probably more of a challenge than Isaac could possibly handle.

Dave brought over Isaac's tea and they took a slightly prolonged look at each other.

"Hey, tanks, Dev... do *you* like faginas?? AAAAAhahahahahahaaaa!"

He cackled again, flinging his head back with such force that he could have considered suing Dave for the whiplash.

He spilt some of his hot masala tea on his trousers after having performed this chaotic manoeuvre. Dave just stared at him and didn't really know what to say.

I'm sure Dave would have never seen a vagina outside of medical school... or a penis for that matter, outside of his very own underpants.

Fi came over and sat down with us as we all worked up the collective courage to begin our day. She was a bit of a 'laddette', so she didn't mind the usual crudity of conversation and generally just looked at us in a condescending way, knowing that men just never grow up.

I think that it was just another coping strategy we had; that was my excuse anyway.

"Our team is on again today," she reported to us and yawned with that post-coital glint in her eyes.

"Yeah, I know. I hope it's nothing like the other week."

"I am an-call az well too-night," said Isaac.

I was certain that acute gynaecology would be fairly quiet.

"Lots of acute vaginas then?" I offered.

"Only sum of dem are *cute*! Aaahahahahaha-hahahahaa!"

Again, he flung his head backwards and fell about into fits of juvenile hilarity.

More tea was spilt.

Fi just stared at him aghast and shook her head.

"Isaac, we'll need to put you in a neck collar if you're not careful," she said.

"You do dee acute angina... and I do dee cute faginas! Leave dem to me!"

His pearly white teeth gleamed against the backdrop of his exotic, velvety, dark brown skin. This time he managed to control himself and simply chuckled, his shoulders bouncing up and down gradually dissipating the nonsense.

"So, you and Rob then, Fi?" I revisited my curiosity.

"Look, it's just sex, nothing serious. I can't be doing with a relationship right now. No time and I've got the exams coming up."

"Yeah, I know what you mean about having no time for a relationship."

"Just sex for you too then?" she nodded, clearly empathising.

"Yeah, although that Nurse Totten is not quite what you'd think. Totally different out of work."

"Most people are like that, especially the nurses Jace," she said. "They go through so much shit at work, get treated like shit, paid like shit, clean up shit... shit, shit, *shit*... it isn't surprising that they all quit in the end with all the shit they have to put up with."

"Yeah, I mean if you paid nurses, occupational therapists, social workers and all that lot much more money, they'd all stay. You'd get more recruits and they'd probably put up with more shit because at least they were getting paid properly."

I did wonder where the money came from to buy cocaine though. Perhaps the struggling actress? No. The accountant? Maybe.

"But they doing it because they're carings," Dave contributed.

"Well, yeah, but they'd give more of a shit if they didn't have to take as much shit. Plus renting a flat is frickin' expensive nowadays too. Anyway arseholes," Fi looked at us both, "we have a ward round to do and we're taking GP calls today. So, Dave, get your fat ass off that sofa and Jace, get that cute ass over here to *me* and let's go,"

Dave momentarily looked somewhat short-changed with what was clearly an unfair remark. He gave his own right buttock a brief squeeze, subconsciously checking for the truth.

Fi winked at me again and pursed her lips making a brief, fake air kiss.

Just innocent workplace flirting.

Just sex.

Dave got up and followed on. Isaac confidently slapped him on the aforementioned posterior. Somewhat shocked over this sudden verbal and physical assault on his crudely moulded 'behind', Dave skipped sideways a little and stumbled whilst looking back at his perpetrator.

"Aaaaahahahahahahaha!" Isaac squealed and flung his head back yet again.

There were a few small audible cracks as his cervical vertebrae clicked across each other letting out an orchestra of tiny little vacuum pops.

"Oooh, argh!"

Isaac went suddenly quiet, frowned and rubbed the back of his neck.

He should really exert more self control.

Chapter Eleven

Cheese, Chocolate and Custard

Round Two

The team wandered on to our main ward where a fair percentage of our full cohort of patients were kept, sorry, cared for.

Sister Edna Sledge was there to greet us with her buxom, authoritative stance and thick calves pressed so tightly together that they barely left a gap at the ankle. A stern frown bridged her slightly bulbous nose and thin, tight lips.

There were three mugs of hot tea waiting for us, a plate of yummy, freshly-baked, warm chocolate chip cookies and soft pillows filled with rose petals, unicorn mane and fairy dust upon which to rest our tired heads... yes in my imagination, but I could almost smell it.

Almost.

It was no longer 1968 when the nurses would bring breakfast to the doctors in the morning and even (in no particular order) polish their shoes, iron their shirts, trousers and underpants and leave them outside of their on-call rooms in readiness for the consultant ward round.

"First off, Dr Dewani, can you please re-write all these drug charts."

An order not a request.

Back to Earth with an administrative splat.

No cookies then. Or pixie poop.

She handed him a pile of about fifteen charts, each patient being on about ten different drugs, not to mention all the PRN[13] medications like painkillers, anti-sickness, sleeping pills, anti-night cramps pills, skin

---

[13] p.r.n.: Abbreviation meaning "when necessary" (from the Latin "pro re nata" for an occasion that has arisen, as circumstances require, as needed).

creams, oral anti-fungals, anti-diarrhoeals and laxatives - not all of them were always for the same person.

That would take a while for Dave. He would have to go AWOL and take this one for the team.

"When you've done that, there are seven cannulas that need re-siting and you need to write up some more intravenous fluids. Oh and Mrs Migginski *still* hasn't had a bowel movement."

Is she *still* here?!

Dave's face sunk with disappointment. His bottom still stung from where Isaac had spanked him a few minutes ago. He also knew that he had to go and take the daily bloods from most of our patients, especially the ones on fluids or diuretic medication, to make sure that we weren't poisoning them by causing concerning swings in their vital electrolyte levels.

"... and there are two accident forms to sign and you need to review their head injuries please."

Two more attempted elderly overnight skydives. I'm not sure if they were from the same plane though.

"I guess we should start the round without Dave for now then, Fi?"

"Fksssake..." she muttered, "yeah, come on. Go and get the notes trolley."

I wandered off to fetch it, trying not to smash into anything on the way back, as the coaster wheels were no more accurate than your average shopping trolley.

"Oh and Dr Feelwell, Student Nurse Alice Sharples will be joining you on the ward round now that she has rotated to us from orthopaedics. She will make a list of any nursing tasks that you may require as we are rather short-staffed today, so you can't have a trained member of staff joining you, I'm afraid. Please have some patience with her."

Sister Sledge introduced Alice to Fi, who nodded and let out a prolonged exhalation of not particularly disguised disapproval.

A petite Alice looked a little intimidated by Fi, who was about a foot taller than Alice and could occasionally, well often, look menacing to student nurses being a successful woman and doctor.

I returned with the notes trolley and was delighted to be reacquainted with Nurse Sharples who I had last seen having fainted in a heap on the floor by, the recently deceased, Mrs Granger.

"Hi, Alice!" I gently tapped her on the waist as I stepped past her with the trolley.

Alice turned her head and her blonde pony tail swung around to join us. Her pretty face lit up and she smiled at me warmly with, I think, some relief that she wouldn't be doing the ward round all alone with Fi the Menacing!

"Oh, hi Jacen, how are you?" Her eyes gently fluttered.

"Can we postpone the flirting and date night planning until *after* the ward round please?"

Fi glared at us, with what seemed like more than just a pang of jealousy in her tone.

You may have noticed that my imagination has a penchant for misinterpretation.

"Sorry, Dr Feelwell," I smiled.

Alice vibrantly blushed and her face and neck went geographically blotchy and warm. Was that Antarctica or the Archipelago of Atlantis I could just about make out?

Her right hand accidentally brushed against mine and I felt a brief inner fizz.

Fi, couldn't pretend to be annoyed at me and she smirked back.

"Okay, Miss Anderson, how are you today?"

Alison Anderson was in her mid-twenties. Her dark, naturally-permed, pseudo-Afro hair was matted down across her forehead which framed her slightly sunken, disappearing facial features that were flanked by puffy, red cheeks and embellished with a slight fluffy moustache.

She was morbidly obese[14] and had suffered a fairly sizeable pulmonary embolism.

I was surprised at how almost everyone I'd encountered up until now called Alison, Doreen or Jennifer (outside of Hollywood) is particularly overweight; it's probably just a statistical quirk - the incidence of obesity is soaring and they are popular women's names... anyway, I'm rambling... but with a surname like Anderson[15], you kind of hoped for better.

The offending blood clot had insensitively and rather selfishly formed in her right leg; this was likely due to her profound inactivity due to excessive TV watching, a gargantuan doughnut-based eating habit, a full fat *Coca-Cola* addiction and her moderate chain smoking... whilst on the oral contraceptive pill.

The thrombus had broken off from its deep venous home and taken a little abdominal road trip up her

---

[14] Although with political correctness gone mad and for fear of upsetting the sensitive millennials, this was now Class III obesity according to the World Health Organisation. Still really fat though.

[15] For all you 90's TV show *Baywatch* fans out there, this is Pamela Anderson. Or for any *X-Files* fans way out there... Gillian Anderson. Each to their own I suppose.

inferior vena cava, into her right atrium, avoided paying the toll at the tricuspid valve and then again at the pulmonary valve after having bounced of the walls of her struggling and panting right ventricle, then settled snuggly and occlusively in her distal right pulmonary artery.

"Still... quite... short of... breath... doctor," she puffed, heaving her shoulders up and down whilst slowly and carefully annunciating every word.

Paradoxically, her oxygen saturation levels were 99% without an oxygen mask on and her pulse and blood pressure were normal and stable.

"Just need to examine you. If we can just lift up your gown a little at the front?"

I closed the curtains around the bed space.

Fiona was careful to maintain Alison's dignity and kept her as covered as possible, with the limited size of the overlying bedsheets, and tried to lift up the exceedingly tight hospital gown. Even the extra large size was way too small and its coarse, faded, floral NHS material hugged Alison's every fatty fold of skin in a moistened, humid ecosystem of sweaty, white flesh.

"Give me a hand, Jace? I need to listen to her heart and lungs."

I went to the left of the bed opposite Fi and gave the gown a very hefty and prolonged yank.

Scchhhhhhtt.

"Okay... a bit hard but, well, we now have exposure."

Fi shook her head, flicked her eyebrows up and down and crumpled her top lip, totally unsurprised at the outcome.

The gown had shredded. I should really tone down the weight training.

"I'm just going to feel for your heart first."

Fi went to palpate the apex beat of the heart and tucked her hand beneath Alison's extraordinarily large and pendulous left breast.

Fi's right hand slipped beneath and immediately skied almost frictionlessly laterally and out the other side. She hadn't put any gloves on and it was now too late.

"Alice, come here and help me lift this breast up."

Alice skipped lightly over and next to where I stood and was just about to grab two hands full of bosom to crane it up, when I quickly thrust a pair of latex gloves in her direction from a box on a ledge next to me.

"Oh... yes of course, thanks, Jacen."

I winked at her smugly.

Fi and Alice hoicked up Alison's left breast to reveal not only a complex fungal excoriation of erythema but also a new variety of cheese, a piece of yesterday's ham sandwich, some softened crisp flakes, a few large smears of melted chocolate... and a *Mars* bar wrapper.

Not to mention the most repugnant stench I had ever smelt.

"Blllooik!" Puffing out my cheeks, I took a step back next to the bed's headboard and, out of patient eyeshot, I tried in vain to suppress a wretch and instinctively thrust my left hand in front of my face to filter as much of this particulate-laden odour that I could.

Alice's face contorted, she looked away at almost one hundred and eighty degrees with her eyes scrunched tightly shut and I saw her trying to hold her breath whilst she strained to keep this magnificent portion of adipose tissue aloft.

"I'll just have a quick listen instead."

Fi placed her stethoscope on Alison's chest and listened to the heart sounds.

Squelch and ssssuckkk.

"Okay, sounds normal."

I don't know how she heard anything, given that Alison's heart was probably a foot down from the surface of her skin.

Alice let go of the breast leaving the *Mars* bar wrapper and the other flotsam and jetsam to be cleaned more thoroughly later. She made a note on her 'to do' list... for someone else 'to do' I presumed.

"Jace, seeing as you are feeling strong today, help me sit her forward a bit so I can listen to her lungs."

I bent forwards and put my left knee on the side of the bed, tucked my left arm under Alison's armpit, immediately wishing that I hadn't and we heaved her forward. Fi tried her best to squeeze the diaphragm of her stethoscope down Alison's back and in front of the pillow and back of the bed. It was a tight squeeze.

It was just as warm, moist and sweaty down there and the pillow covers were soaked.

"Give me some deep breaths in and out."

Everything was clear, as best as one could tell, with the ear of faith.

"All sounds good. Your Warfarin blood thinner levels are all good and stable."

"Oh, I'm not sure I'm ready to go home yet Doctor you see there's no one at home and I do like it here everyone is so nice and I do like the food and I don't normally get out much and I don't mind staying as long as I'm not in the way as I don't really feel that well and I just couldn't bear it if I had to come right back here again!"

She then took a breath.

The initial exchange was clearly for effect.

Alison had been in hospital for over a week and had adopted a certain level of the 'sick role'. The attention-seeking patient actress.

It took about six paramedics and the fire brigade to help get her admitted in the first place.

"I think we should be arranging for her to go home. Alice, can you please get this sorted out and get Dave to do the TTAs[16]?"

Alice nodded. Sister Sledge *would* be pleased as Alison was a nursing and manual handling nightmare.

The dense, mouldy, cheesy smell lingered in the air like a thick cumulo-nimbus cloud of spores.

My pager went off.

I went to answer it.

"Hi, Dr Manson, this is staff nurse on ward sixteen, can you please come and certify a lady please?"

"Is she dead?"

"Yes. She hasn't eaten her breakfast either, but *you'll* have to confirm it."

"Okay, but we've just started the ward round and I'm on-call today, so I probably won't have time for a while."

"Well, okay, do it when you can because we can't do anything until you have."

She hung up, sounding frustrated that I couldn't do this quick and simple task that was the most important thing for that nurse to attend to today.

---

[16] To Take Away discharge drugs from the pharmacy, also known as TTOs, To Take Out.

At the moment, dealing with the living was taking priority over those that had already given up the ghost, so to speak.

Mr Peter Clementine was an overweight, fifty-something alcoholic who'd been admitted with alcohol-related pancreatitis about two months before. He was jaundiced and had become a beautiful, vibrant, English Mustard, custardy yellow with sclerae to match, which gave his eyes a demonic quality.

His legs were oedematous and his abdomen was swollen with fluid, *ascites,* we called it. His cirrhotic liver was contemplating downing tools and cancelling all protein production once and for all, which would also include clotting factors.

Peter could drink two bottles of whiskey a day before he'd even begin to start feeling drunk. That amount would kill Fi, myself and Dave five times over... each.

His wife had left him about ten years ago, he'd lost his job as an accountant, he lived alone, could no longer afford to pay his rent and was being threatened with eviction.

Despite all this, he did his best to remain cheery on the ward and always greeted us with a smile and the occasional dirty joke, I think because we gave the impression that we cared about what happened to him... which naturally, we did.

We also enjoyed the odd dirty joke.

"Morning, Peter, I see that you've had your intravenous vitamins? Make sure you take this anti-withdrawal medication as well."

In Peter's state, even total abstinence was unlikely to allow his liver the time to recover and his time, we suspected, was therefore rather limited.

"My tummy is very swollen again," he grimaced whilst hugging his firm, inflated abdomen like an eight month pregnant belly.

"We'll up the water medication," said Fi, "but we'll probably have to drain some more of that off. Make a note will you Alice to set a trolley up for Jace or Dave to do it later?"

Peter nodded. He'd had this done before and gave us the thumbs up and a special yellowy smile in Alice's direction.

She blushed pinky-red again.

I felt like the crumble in rhubarb and custard.

BLEEEEP, BLEEEEEP

Alice handed me the cordless receiver we took with us on the notes trolley.

"Yes, Dr Manson here?"

"Hi, Jace, it's Kate in Casualty."

"Hi, Sister Kate, we're just on the ward round at the moment."

"Sorry, we've got one for you. Needs admitting and we need the cubicle. Mrs Blaise Laflamme, sixty-three, exacerbation of congestive cardiac failure. You can't miss her, she's got fiery ginger, red hair!"

"Okay... is she stable?"

"Yes, Jace, she is but that doesn't mean you can use your usual delaying tactics... we *need* the cubicle, my lovely." She sounded a little croaky today.

Ah, Kate knew just how to charm me with her lovely, sexy, and today slightly husky telephone voice.

"Will there be *Jaffa Cakes* waiting?"

"As usual, Jacen, there will be indeed, and a welcoming reception made up of our finest and most beautiful, semi-naked nursey-nymphs who will shower you with petals and compliments as you arrive. I will even play the harp for you."

She lied... obviously. I doubted they'd be semi-naked.

"M'kay... I'm on my way."

I gave the phone to Alice who looked a little grumpy after hearing the clear flirting on the other end of the phone.

"Sorry, Fi. Sorry, Alice. Gotta shoot!"

I was kind of glad to bunk the ward round. Lesser of two evils. I'd join them later as they'd probably still be going round at midnight.

"Okay, bugger off then... ah-haa, Dr Dewani! In the very nick of time."

As if by the most fortunate of magic... Davinder appeared, like the Indian sugar-plum genie from a lamp, ready for (his version of) action.

Dave dropped his new stethoscope.

Three wishes would have to wait.

Chapter Twelve

Shockingly Certifiable

Never a Good Time

For once, I wandered casually down to Casualty.

As I walked in… BLEEEEP! BLEEEEP!

Jostling for a place in line for one of the incessantly engaged phones by the nurses station, I noticed that the admissions 'white board' was filling up very fast.

I could see the name of 'Blaise Laflamme' in cubicle 9.

I felt a vice like grip on the underside of my left gluteal muscle.

"Oiiii… ooo… ah!"

"Welcome back, Dr Manson!" A soft, crispy, husky voice dallied with whether to allow syllables to create either an actual sound or a sexy breathy exhalation.

"Hey, Kate!" I smiled, relieved that it wasn't buttock cramp after all.

Her blonde peacock hair had since fallen into an equally attractive ponytail. I felt a sudden warmth and a vague flush.

I didn't really flush that much being of a genetically tropical persuasion.

"Mrs Laflamme is…" Kate began.

"… in cubicle nine, yes I saw."

"… has been moved… into cubicle seven, Doctor." She corrected me, smiled and winked.

The first syllable of 'seven' became intertwined with a sheer pleasurable breathy delight… to my ears, anyway.

"Oh right, well let me just answer this bleep."

Kate folded her arms, the corner of her mouth turned up just a tad.

I turned away.

"Hi, Dr Manson here?"

"Hi, yes, it's staff nurse on ward sixteen. Could you please come up and certify this…?"

"Look someone's just called me up about that. This isn't a good time!" I retorted, clearly a little irate.

"Sorry, it's just that we can't…" came the inevitable challenge.

"Look, I *know*, but I'm in Casualty dealing with the living at the moment, I'll be up later."

I hung up and wandered to cubicle 7.

The curtains were drawn and I popped inside. There was no-one on the bed but just behind the curtain stood Sister Kate Ellis. She grabbed me by the waist, stood on her tip toes and planted a very soft and very wet kiss right on my lips and I suddenly felt 'cramp' in both buttocks.

"Right, you can go to cubicle nine now!"

She pushed me out of the closed curtains and off I went.

In cubicle 9, on the trolley, lay Mrs Blaise Laflamme. Now, her name clearly made her sound rather exotic, however, at 63 years of age, she could quite easily fool you into assuming she was 83. She had become rather plump, deeply wrinkled from her endless cigarette smoking and increasingly short of breath, not just from the severe emphysema that had ravaged her lungs but also because her heart was failing her too.

She sat upright with an oxygen mask on, the elastic strapping holding down her shoulder-length, fiery, reddish ginger hair that stood on end in a whole variety of directions making her look something like a children's toy troll doll[17]. She had rather vibrant green eye shadow

---

[17] A Troll Doll (Danish: *Gjøltrold*) is a type of plastic doll with furry up-combed hair depicting a troll, also known as a Dam doll after their creator Danish woodcutter Thomas Dam. The toys are also known as good luck trolls.

on and had painted vivid, thick, red lines around her mouth where her actual lips should have been resident.

Her teeth were in a small pot on a chair by her trolley.

"Hello, Mrs Laflamme."

I tried to sound vaguely cheerful. After all, I had just been unexpectedly and passionately accosted by a nurse. What was not to be cheerful about?

"Call... me... Blaise... Doctor," she panted.

"So you're obviously short of breath, Blaise? Listen, to save you some effort, stop me if I am wrong..."

She nodded.

"You've been getting increasingly short of breath, it's been much worse in the last day or two, leading you to come in today. I notice that your legs are very swollen, so that's been getting a lot worse too and now you can't really walk around very much. You're now having to sleep more upright in bed because lying flat is making you more short of breath and occasionally in the night you've slipped down flat and woken up in a panic? How am I doing?"

She nodded in the affirmative.

"Have you had any chest pains?"

She shook her head.

"Good. Are you taking your water tablets?"

She nodded.

"Anything else?"

She shook her head.

Diuretics were important when people suffered with fluid retention in the context of heart failure and it was also important to moderate their oral fluid and salt intake.

"Are you coughing up any nasty sputum?"

She shook her head.

"Good, again. I just need to listen to your heart and lungs."

Placing my stethoscope on the front of her chest, her heart was galloping ten to the dozen; the 'gallop rhythm' was a lovely and rather accurate term to described an additional third or fourth heart sound secondary to impaired left ventricular filling or forceful atrial contraction, respectively.

The visual image in your mind's eye of that majestic, black stallion's galloping hooves across acres of green fields, through trees against the backdrop of cloudless, blue skies with rays of sunlight causing a vibrant sheen on that intense, velvety coat and flowing mane, accompanied by the thunderous rapture of the theme to 'Black Beauty'...

My mind paused in wonder as I allowed the sounds through my stethoscope and the visions in my head to blissfully blur.

The cerebral cinematic experience acutely expired to be replaced by an old donkey clippity-clopping to the theme of 'Only Fools and Horses'.

Blaise, let out a rattled, fruity cough, quickly pulled off her oxygen mask from her face and spat out a large globule of frothy, slightly blood- and lipstick-stained sputum into a piece of old, damp tissue she'd whipped out from under her wrist sleeve.

Honestly, how many elderly people do that?! I'd lost count.

I also listened to her back. What did her life-giving bellows have to say for themselves? Her lungs were also filled with fluid.

"Let's take some bloods, put a little tube in your vein and get a chest x-ray. Are these all your drugs in this bag over here?"

She nodded again and coughed up more cappuccino-like froth.

"Okay, I'm going to borrow them to write up your drug chart and we'll probably need to adjust your medication a bit."

I think I'll stick to drinking tea for a few days.

BLEEEEP BLEEEEP

I looked down. Not bloody ward 16 again?!

"Hi, Dr Manson here, look stop calling me to certify that lady, I told you I'd come up and do it when I had time!"

"Sorry… I didn't realise anyone had let you know, we've just finished handover."

I hung up… *yet again.*

Nurses 'handover'. That sacrosanct time that successive shifts of nurses would pass on all the vital clinical information and management plans about all the patients on the wards to one another, to ensure a totally seamless transition from one shift to the next. What was not mentioned in handover, was not worth mentioning at all.

Never ever interrupt this aliquot of time.

I have, on occasion, wandered into a Sister's office during handover.

Nurses would abruptly stop all conversation, their scribbling pens ceasing all activity, they'd simultaneously look up and stare at you as if you'd just wandered into a local yokel pub or more accurately… stepped on a landmine, realised you'd stepped on a landmine, looked down and then reluctantly accepted that you now can't move and really, really wished you hadn't stepped on said landmine in the first place.

"Someone's died, so why the hell didn't they hand *that* over?!"

Two paramedics came thrusting through the main outer electric doors with a man on a trolley. At first glance he looked like he was in jolly conversation with the younger paramedic, Freya. The other paramedic, Phil, was clearly more senior, balding, older and infinitely more portly.

Freya Williams was about five feet two inches tall. She always looked very fit and muscular, like she'd hit the gym five times a week with those 'guns'. But she actually did no weight training at all, she just shredded fat by doing lots of cross country running and rode horses which probably explained her firm-looking thighs. Neither did the paramedic dark green overalls truly do her bottom the justice it genuinely deserved.

She had piercing blue eyes and absolutely golden blonde, thick, wavy hair and she always managed to maintain a glowing, heart-warming, white smile. Everyone just loved her. You couldn't help but love her. Her positivity in life was infectious and it almost didn't matter what was wrong with you as a patient, Freya would make you feel ten times better without a single drop of a drug or a whiff of oxygen.

"Malcolm Magee, fifty-two year old man, previous history of heart attack complicated by ventricular tachycardia, implantable cardioverter defibrillator[18] in situ, observations are stable... ICD malfunctioning."

---

[18] An ICD or automated implantable cardioverter defibrillator (AICD) is a device inserted under the skin of the upper chest with an electrical lead fed through a vein in the shoulder and down into one of the heart chambers.

Sister Kate and I went over to greet him, given that this was clearly a medical problem, so I might just as well go and sort this out myself before the casualty officer did. The patient would be coming my way anyway.

The 'Cas Officer' was a relatively junior junior doctor (yes I know it sounds silly but if you are below Consultant grade, you're a 'junior doctor'), most of whom went to work in Casualty, as an SHO, after only one year as a newly qualified doctor.

You kind of learned on the job as a Cas Officer. Whilst patients weren't generally presented to us for entertainment value, the job could be described as 'good fun', as you saw a whole variety of conditions both 'major' and 'minor'. But the bottom line was, you had to accept that you were generally a bit shit when you first started out, but you did get the chance to make real decisions and do lots of therapeutic practical procedures for the first time.

"ICD malfunctioning?!"

The ICD can give the patient an internal shock straight to the heart if it detects an abnormal and 'shockable' rhythm; truly a life-saving little fellow.

So, now I'm imagining this thing firing off willy nilly, continually and inappropriately shocking the poor man.

"Aarright, Doc?" came the broad, Liverpudlian Scouse accent, spitting out the 'c' of 'Doc' as if clearing the phlegm from his mouth.

He held out his hand to shake mine.

"Good afternoon, sir. So, let's take a look at y…."

BZZZT

"Ooooarrgh!"

He clutched his chest and jerked a little.

"Sure, Doc, no problem," he said calmly.

"See you later, Mr Magee, they'll take good care of you," said Freya bouncily and waved at him. Another job beckoned.

"Hi, Jacen. Bye for now, Jacen!"

"Hi and bye, Freya. Maybe see you later?!"

We took Mr Magee into the resuscitation area which still had a free bed space in the corner.

"So, what's been going on…?"

I started to take a thorough history but what began to unfold was a bizarre crescendo of torture, expletives and a desperate urge by Mr Magee to maintain some kind of linguistic decorum.

BZZZT

"Nrrrgh, damn it."

He clutched his chest and held his breath expecting another shock… nothing came.

"Well, I've been fine for almost two years since me 'art attack and then…"

BZZZT

"grrrrghhhargh… Jeeee-sus Chri… *God*…!"

He tensed again, getting a little more red-faced.

"Hmm, I see. So have you had any…"

BZZZT

"MMMMRRRGHH… pissing arghhh! For shit's… since my 'art attack and then suddenly in the last coupla days it's started to go off and today it's…"

BZZZT

"SSSSSSSSSSTTTAAAARRRTTTed… *shittting pissing bollocks*… getting a lot more frequent, Doc. It musta gone wrong."

"Blimey, that looks pretty uncomfortable Mr Magee! We'll get you plugged into this monitor and give you something to help you relax a bit."

"Okay, Doc, you reckon you can…"

BZZZT

"… FFFFFIIIXXXXXXXX… nnnnrrghhh, fer fkkkksaaaakkeeee, bollocks bastard… fix it please, Doc?"

This was clearly escalating out of control as were the shocks being delivered to his poor ticker.

Kate attached the monitoring stickers and leads.

"Ah, *see* Kate, he keeps going into fast VT!" I pointed smugly at the ECG trace.

And right on cue…

BZZZT

"FFFFFFFFFFFUUUUUUUCCCCCKKKKKKSSS SAAAAAKKKEEEEE… it's really get'n a bit much now, Doc. Ad really appreeceeayte some help ee'er!"

Mr Magee gasped and gripped his chest, then held his breath, clenched his teeth hard, went a deep crimson shade and threw up over his, now matching, Liverpool football shirt.

"Okay, let's sedate him a bit and bleep the anaesthetist to take him to the coronary care unit as he's probably gonna need slightly more 'poison' than I'm prepared to give."

I attached him to some oxygen, inserted a cannula and gently gave Mr Magee some intravenous Midazolam to ease his obvious, yet paradoxically polite, attempts to not be quite as vulgar as he would have really liked.

This is a wonderful drug of the benzodiazepine class which is not only sedating but also has fabulous amnesic qualities.

The last time I'd used it was after finally and successfully inserting a large central venous cannula into the internal jugular vein of a middle aged, very grumpy female patient with renal failure. It was proving to be a difficult procedure and it'd taken me several attempts including one gentle and rather brief carotid arterial puncture with my needle.

You'd try and keep your fingers on the pulsation of the common carotid artery, in the neck, to help judge the location of its intimate venous neighbour, but it could occasionally get in your way; you knew you'd made a slight misjudgement if the syringe attached to your needle rapidly filled up with the pressurised arterial blood that was otherwise making its merry way in the opposite direction to the brain before being rudely diverted.

The woman complained incessantly during the procedure, would not keep her head and neck still, saying it was the worst experience of her life and told me she'd sue.

Clearly, this was quite unreasonable since I was adequately experienced, knew exactly what I was doing and, in fact, was trying to save her life, if only she'd stop wriggling about.

Just a drop of Midazolam then.

The complaining stopped, her eyes gently closed, she started snoring a little and her oxygen saturations remained at 98%. You can stop someone breathing if you overdo it.

I completed the line insertion and nicely dressed it ready for the nurses to use. I administered a dash of the antidote to reverse the sedative effects.

"Hello, again." I had said, cheerfully, as she slowly woke up again.

"Hello, Doctor," she replied dopily.

"How are you feeling?"

"Oh, I'm okay. Is it done?"

"Yes, of course it is. All finished," I said softly. "You did ever so well."

"Oh, that's a relief, I was so worried. I thought it'd be more painful."

"Do you remember much of what happened?" I had tentatively enquired.

"No nothing… you *are* good, Doctor."

"That's good then." I was sure she'd now forgotten the number to her solicitor.

Dr Rob Banks turned up to collect Mr Magee. He was on a later shift, had obviously had a nice sleep in after Fiona had left his place.

"Alright, *Goofy*?!"

"Fuck off!" said Rob, under his breath, as if his vulgar mind had been suddenly tapped with a tendon hammer.

"Oh, I'm sorry, sir!" He looked at Mr Magee and put his foul-mouthed hand in front of his skinny little Disney face.

BZZZT

"Thaaaaaaaaattttsssss nnnnrrrrghgghhhhhhFUUUU CCCKKKKKKING HEEELLL.. okay, Doc. We *all* do it."

Clearly, Mr Magee had more of a reason to swear but certainly needed better sedation from Rob.

Rob set about drawing some more anaesthetically-orientated drugs up into syringes like the wizarding alchemist he was.

"Hey, Jace, I bought a new car… an *MGF*, British Racing Green."

"Cool, man, you'll have to show me."

"It's got red leather seats too. Really good example."

"Oh yeah, soft top too? You and Fi been out in it?"

"How do you know about that?"

"I work with her, you dick. She tells us everything. Well, we usually grill her unceremoniously and she *eventually* tells us everything... well... she turned up to work with, presumably, your *Mickey Mouse* T-shirt on... and we did the maths."

BZZZT

Malcolm Magee had run out of satisfactory expletives and just stiffened up momentarily and then then let out a groaning sigh.

The Midazolam had at least begun to have some effect.

BLEEEEP BLEEEEP

"Jesus Christ! Ward sixteen again?"

I used the phone in the resus area next to where Rob was finishing the preparation of his special sedatory cocktail.

"Looks good, man," I admired.

"Would sir be needing it on-the-rocks with a twist and a decorative umbrella perhaps?"

"Shaken, not stirred."

Rob held up a small cardboard tray with a series of syringes all labelled carefully and side-by-side. He smiled smugly out of the corner of his mouth.

Malcolm Magee was in safe hands.

I punched in the ward number in a manner that the phone could have been forgiven for thinking that it was under attack.

"Yes, Dr Manson... *again!*"

"Look, I'm really sorry to disturb you yet again, Doctor, but we really *need* you to certify this dead lady."

"I will do it *later* when I have some time. Please *STOP BLEEPING ME!*"

Chapter Thirteen

Death and Epistaxis

Got an Itch?

The admissions kept streaming in at a thankfully steady and handleable rate. Dave and Fi eventually joined me in the fun house. They hadn't had the time to see all of our inpatients who would have to wait. I needed help on the frontline.

Ward 16 continued to pester me which, funnily enough, coincided with each nursing shift change and yet another handover.

When you are on-call or on-take, as we call it, you are taking calls from other specialties but mostly GPs who have been called out to see patients at home or during their daytime and evening clinics.

As a junior hospital doctor, you'd generally hope that the GP had given sufficient time and effort in taking a history and fully examining a patient before referring to the most appropriate junior hospital doctor, whether a surgeon or a medic. But in reality, the GPs are so busy that they rarely have sufficient time to do that and, as the accepting doctor, you'd often be in receipt of a very rapidly scribbled letter of referral with a paucity of clinical detail and the patient would just rock up or be delivered by the ambulance crews for us to sort out.

Sometimes you'd get a very convoluted story of some tentative suspicion of an unusual disease and in a rather sneaky, cheeky, yet clinically acceptable way, the GPs could slide their patients under the locked office door of the hospital when they could no longer cope at home with their illnesses.

That 'social admission' again.

Experienced general practitioners deserve a great deal of credit because, even without the same level of detailed clinical assessment, they often just 'knew' whether someone was truly unwell or not and needed hospital admission, especially if they'd been caring for that patient over many years.

Although, the occasional GP had a reputation for being, for want of a better word, shite. They'd refer absolute bollocks (in our expert junior opinions) and sometimes entirely to the wrong specialty; maybe this was due to lack of time and increasing workload, emotional pressure from relatives, the inexperience of a more junior GP, the out-of-date opinion of an older GP, or just plain old uncertainty.

Once we'd received the patient, we'd then have to go through the usual 'turf war' of trying to palm off the punter to another more appropriate specialty, usually the surgeons or the orthopods, in a way that required the minimum of clinical effort.

You'd also spend time trying to prevent these 'turfs' coming back the other way.

I'd already received a call that day from Mr Raymond Branston, the consultant orthopaedic surgeon, from the local private hospital, The Tower, via the golf course.

His SHO, Dr Johnny Winterson-Waring, who also played some golf with Mr Branston (being up his arse and licking his way up for most of his orthopaedic career to date), had complained to him that a GP referring a ninety-three year old woman, who had fallen at *Waitrose* with a 'query fractured hip', was utterly inappropriate and tried to palm her off on *me*.

The cheek of it!

Johnny had had a wholesome public school education since he was four years old, even starting at an expensive fee-paying nursery with a waiting list to join and probably a Masonic ceremony to include a fattened goat sacrifice on his first day.

I had five years of public school education from thirteen to eighteen years old.

Johnny was a total knob-end (so to speak), for want of a more accurate urological term. Mr Branston had whole-heartedly agreed with the view (not that he was a knob-end, which he was) that the referral was inappropriate, especially since his team were looking after two whole patients… sorry, *one* whole patient post-bunion surgery, ever since the death of Mrs Granger and the fact that their routine admissions were all cancelled as there were literally no beds to put them in.

"Branston here!" he'd aggressively announced as soon as switchboard had put me through to the outside line.

Here we go, he's going to try and put the brakes on my patient turf to orthopaedics.

"Dr Mans…" I began.

"What's this utter nonsense and tish-tosh I hear from my *registrar*?" He inadvertently promoted Dr Winston-Waring which worked for dramatic effect.

He continued. I held the receiver further from my ear to reduce the volume of 'Branston'.

"I'm sorry but we're *NOT* taking that lady. We'll come and review her on our rounds tomorrow, if we have time. Perhaps you'd order a pelvic x-ray and some dedicated lateral views of the hip. Perhaps arrange an MRI scan if there's any doubt about a fracture, but of course it's unlikely we'll be operating on her. Too old."

The orthopods would also create some other fantastical, fabricated excuses to not take over the care of a patient (whilst usually sat watching telly or playing *Sony Playstation* in the mess) that might have fallen because they could have had a mini-stroke, a fit, or a dizzy spell because of a sudden missed heart beat or an unexplained drop in blood pressure.

"Well, it could be a transient ischaemic attack, an atypical seizure, a paroxysmal bradycardia or unexplained vasovagal syncope."

They hadn't a clue what any of that meant but they had learned some buzz words that 'allowed' them to chuck patients back our way under the care of the medics. You then couldn't argue with that.

We'd keep the patient for investigation, rehabilitation and the longest human MOT.

"But, Mr Branston?"

"Yes?"

That simple three-lettered word was generously laced with anger and irritation.

"She fell over… in *Waitrose*[19]."

"Ahhh… indeed."

The sound of the penny, or should I say pounds, dropped in Mr Branston's ever-expanding offshore Cayman Island bank account.

"Well, I might just have an opportunity for a full assessment up the road at The Tower. I believe that there *is* a free theatre slot in the morning. Does she have private insurance or will she be self-funding?"

To be honest though, as you've already heard, the patients were probably best off under the medics rather than the orthopods if they had other medical problems besides a broken bone.

---

[19] Waitrose has a reputation for being an upmarket grocer and won supermarket of the year in 2017.

Now, what you absolutely did *not* need during your incredibly busy on-call was some 'funny guy' who had managed to get out of this godforsaken place at five o'clock, gone down to the pub, got pissed and decided he was going to fake a few GP admissions for you by pretending to be one of, for now we'll call them, the shite ones.

BLEEEEP BLEEEEP

Switchboard.

"Hi, Switch, Dr Manson here."

"Hello, Doctor, we haven't heard your voice for a couple of days. We have a Dr Podgorny from Chigwell Green Surgery for you. Can I put him through?"

"Pppffft!" I hissed. "Okay, sure."

Dr Podgornay, from Chigwell Green, was one of those GPs with the reputation I have been alluding to. But he also made for the prime candidate to impersonate if ever you were going to pull a gag on one of your mates whilst on-take.

Honestly, drunken doctors off duty can think they're real jokers.

"Hello, Dr Manson speaking?"

"Hulllooo, Doe-cter," came the very stark and thick Scottish accent. "It's Doe-cter Podgornaaay frum Chigwayl hee-arr."

The first signs of suspicion were internally ignited.

"Hello, Doctor Podgorny, how may I help you?" I thought I'd entertain my attacker by feigning a degree of professional sincerity.

"Waayl, Doe-cter. Ay wunder uff yoood be kaynd enuff to admut my patient pleez?"

He swallowed a few syllables in his particular north-of-the-border style.

"Mm kay…?"

The flame of suspicion began burning a little more strongly, perhaps with the odd crackle as the early irritable tinder caught alight.

"Wayl, I've gote a fuffty year old hydrocephalic dwarf hee-arr with a haematemesis… or is it an epistaaaarxis…?"

He sounded like he'd stopped to re-examine the patient.

"Yes, no, it's derr-fin-itly a nose bleed."

The dry logs of suspicion suddenly caught fire into a dramatic, blazing inferno of heat and ferocity. I'm sure I heard an Australian undertone in those Scottish tones or had Dr Podgorny spent some time down under?

Did I also hear laughter in the background, did I?! Did I hear pub music? Was it Dr Podgorny's radio in the background?

Matt Dundee?!

"Oh, just *FUCK OFF*!!"

For avoidance of any doubt, I elected to go for good old-fashioned four-letter clarity.

I slammed down the phone. I did not need this right now.

BLEEEEPPP BLEEEEPPP

Ward bloody 16, again?!

"Dr Manson."

Anger exuded from my voice with no regret.

"Oh, sorry to disturb, but…" rolled the 'r's of the male Italian voice.

"Yes I know, the death certification!"

"Well, yayce," came the slightly effeminate but kind of musical Italian accent. "But I also ringing about wan of our adder patients. Ee ees een urin-ary retention and ee need catheterising urgently."

"Heyyy, Val? Is that you?" I sounded like the *Fonz* from *Happy Days* laced with a little *Marlon Brando,* when he played the *Godfather,* whenever I spoke to Val. I just couldn't help it.

"Heyyy, Jayce? Yayce eet eez."

I sensed the smile on his face at the other end of the phone.

Valentino Balboa was an Italian male nurse and he was very proud of his roots. He always came across as a bit of a charmer to the ladies (or the lie- deez), but I presumed that one day he'd finally come 'out of the closet'.

Unlike his boxing movie namesake, *Rocky Balboa*, Valentino was not the picture of meathead muscularity or indeed any form of athleticism or dead animal. He was about five feet five tall, thinning black hair and a layer of greying, fluffy, patchy stubble. He was a sensible, conscientious nurse although he always loved a bit of cheeky banter.

"Heyyy, Valentino, how you doin'? Sure, I'll be up there soon. I'll bring Don Davinder with me too."

Dave stood next to me now and nodded at this suggestion. He hadn't seen me much all day and I think was beginning to miss me.

I was not beginning to miss him.

I did however jut out my chin, puff out my lower cheeks a little recreating my best *Brando* face, and firmly patted him a couple of times on his chubby, brown cheek with as much mafioso spirit as I could muster.

His cheek wobbled in protest.

"You up for that, Dave? Because... if yer not... I kill you... and all yer family."

I patted his face again.

Dave swatted my hand away.

"Getting off me!"

"It's the only getting off you'll be doing, Dave. Come on let's go."

It was rather late now and we hadn't really eaten or drunk much, aside from grabbing a few random chocolates on the wards or some leftover sandwiches outside of seminar room doors from the variety of lunchtime meetings.

My stomach grumbled with dissatisfaction at this state of affairs.

"Oi, you two!" Fi called over. "Let's go and chill in the mess for a bit and have a cuppa and some toast. You both can go up to the wards and sort the other crap out in a bit and I'll see any more of the admissions. I'll let switch know and they can bleep me with any GP calls."

Fiona Feelwell was truly a total darling. She also seemed to know when we needed support the most. Whilst we had all adopted a healthy piss-taking of each other, she had been through it all, like we were doing now, but was just that bit more resilient.

"Oh, by the way, Matt Dundee rang up from the pub with some shite fake admission."

"He's so up himself sometimes." Fi confirmed my very own impression of Matt.

Just because he had that Antipodean accent, he thought he could do what he wanted and pull any woman he wanted.

We all pottered back to the doctors' mess together for a sit down... and hopefully a good 'sit down' on the ceramic as well.

As we wandered in, the smell of stuffy man sweat greeted us and sure enough, true to exact form, the *A-Team* was playing on *Sky* TV and Isaac was lying on his back on the sofa, glued to both.

"AAAAAhahahahaha! I luv Meesta Tee. Ai peety dee fool! Hahaha!"

He was mid conversation with himself, oblivious to his surroundings. His socks were off and his shirt was untucked. There was a layer of scattered biscuit crumbs and broken *Pringles* all over him and a few empty cans of non-alcoholic beer on the coffee table that he'd brought in, clearly knowing how busy he wouldn't be.

"Hey, Isaac, you do know that Mr T is not Nigerian right?"

"Ah, you two! I haff only just gat back to dee mess myself."

Really.

"You are lookings quite relaxed to me," said Dave, admiring Isaac with a glint in his eye.

"Hey, Dev, com an sit wid me and watch teevee." He moved up a bit but just enough for Dave to squeeze in by Isaac's now slightly bent knees as he lay down.

Fi and I went to make some tea.

Isaac's pager went off, probably for the first time since we saw him at breakfast.

"Oh my god, dees ting has been goin off arl day, I have nat eeeven had time to tink."

Not even had time to get off your big arse, I thought.

"Hey, Dev, pass me dee phone pleez?"

Dave got up and went to the other side of the room to pass Isaac the cordless mess phone. Just a flirt.

Isaac dialled the ward number... it was Ward 11.

"Dr Ali hee-a, what doo yoo want?"

"Dr Ali, could you please come up to the ward to see Miss Anderson?"

I sat down with my tea next to Fi on the other sofa and thought I'd heard the dulcet Dudley dialect of Nurse Totten on the other line.

"Com too dee ward? But I am veeeree bee-zee at dee mow-ment."

Just as he said it, there was loud machine gun fire on the TV followed by:

"*I ain't gettin' on no plane, sucka!*" said Mr T as *BA Baracus* from the *A-Team*.

"Sounds like you are very busy, Dr Ali. One of our patients who's going home tomorrow has got a gynae problem."

It looked like the *A-Team* was in the final ten minutes or so of that episode.

"Can it nat wait unteel tomorrow? What eez dee matta?!"

More machine gun fire and a huge explosion.

"Miss Anderson has got an itchy vulva."

"An itchy vulva... Miss Anderson has an ITCHY VULVA?" He suddenly became particularly loud and shared this somewhat personal patient problem with all of the on-call doctors in the mess and probably all the lucky ones now asleep given how thin all the walls were.

Miss Anderson? Well that was unsurprising. She was one of *our* patients and I was kind of relieved that Jessica thought to call gynae on-call rather than us first.

Fungal infections thrive in unhygienic and moist environments becoming malodorous, erythematous, sticky and itchy.

Just think tinea pedis and tinea cruris - athletes foot and scrot rot!

I'm sure that Miss Anderson's nether regions were extremely warm and welcoming to their fun, fungal friends.

"*AN ITCHY VULVA*?!" He was getting rather overexcited now.

"What shall we do, Dr Ali? Could you come up and prescribe some cream perhaps?"

Nurse Totten, I'm sure, would have been becoming increasingly infuriated with Isaac who looked up to the ceiling in fake ponderous thought.

"Well... why don't *yoo* go over der... and *SCRATCH EET*! AHHHHHHHAHAHAHAHAHAHAHAHA!"

He flung his head violently backwards and absolutely fell about in some of his most incredible hysterics to date, beating his hands on the leather sofa and now also all over Dave, who tried to cover his head for protection, given Isaac's now flailing big, bare, sweaty feet.

"*I love it when a plan comes together!*"

John 'Hannibal' Smith, leader of the *A-Team*, smiled a broad, perfectly toothy grin and sucked on a giant Cuban cigar.

Chapter Fourteen

Rockets and Apple Pie

Is that who I think it is?

"Fkssssake, come on Dave! Let's go and finish the crap on the wards and get that catheter in... oh *and* that dead body," I remembered.

Isaac was lying on top of Dave on the sofa, still laughing and Dave was having trouble maintaining oxygenation and to a certain degree, consciousness.

I pushed big Isaac off little Dave and grabbed him by the white coat.

Fi just sat cross-legged reading a copy of *Hello*, the celebrity gossip magazine and, as usual, she just shook her head and blew another shaggy lock of hair off her forehead. She took a sip of her tea without wasting any energy looking up.

"We need to... do drainings of Mr Clementine's ascites as well," Dave reminded us, trying to get his breath back and tucking his shirt back in.

We wandered up to Ward 16, the bane of my life today.

The ward was surprisingly tranquil in contrast to the rest of the day and we were quickly greeted by Nurse Val Balboa.

"Heyyy! Welcome to my home Jayce... and Don Davinder!"

"Heyyy! Valenteeeenooo, how you doooo-in'?"

We both flung our arms open and gave each other a hug. I tapped Val on the left cheek with just enough force to rotate his head a few extra degrees to the right.

Perhaps a bit hard.

"Ayy, come on then!"

He put up his fists, lowered his head behind his gloveless boxing guard and peered upwards through it in a much smaller version of *Rocky Balboa* going into the first round of one of his fights towards the end of each movie.

"Okay, Val, where's this catheter-man? Or d'you want me to see the dead body first?"

"I think the body can wait," he sensibly prioritised.

Val showed us across the ward and, given that there was a peaceful atmosphere in the ward that night, he kind of floated with little steps and purpose, wearing his black work *Hush Puppies,* towards retired national politician, Mr Jack Hunter MP.

Unfortunately, Mr Hunter's urinary retention had reached critical levels. His prostate gland had enlarged to the size of a tennis ball which was blocking the exit to his bladder causing it to enlarge to the size of a basketball and probably under a great deal of pressure.

Comparing bodily structures to various ball sports was always a fair method to get your message across.

He was being investigated for prostate cancer but was on Ward 16 with a urinary tract infection as well that had caused him to become septic.

His kidneys were having great trouble filtering blood and excreting urine due to the massive pressure of the outflow obstruction and they were beginning to give up allowing Mr Hunter's toxins and waste chemicals to accumulate in his bloodstream instead, not to mention the infected urine causing his fever.

He was lying flat in his bed in a massive amount of discomfort. He was sweating profusely, pale and intermittently rolling left to right and groaning.

"Help me, help... me," he whispered softly, his voice gradually expiring.

The curtains were drawn around him and his small bedside table light was pointed a little upwards, illuminating him in an orangey hue. He held a plastic urine bottle between his thighs and into a small gap in his pyjama bottoms.

It was empty. His retracted and probably petrified penis was determined not to take centre stage in this particular show.

"I can't… I can't… *please*… Doctor…"

Our little interval mess visit to have a cup of tea and a 'sit down' had probably not helped his situation and I think Mr Hunter was beginning to hallucinate with the agony he was clearly in, probably desperately wishing he'd done more to support his local NHS Trust when he *was* politically active.

"Eeez creatinine level is nearly 400," said Val handing me the latest blood results.

"M'kay, Val. Get the catheter trolley and we need one of those slightly more rigid prostate catheters please?"

I reverted back to normal speak, although I think 'Don' Dewani would have rather just put a horse's head in the bed with Mr Hunter and gone back to the mess.

Dave hated politics and the games politicians played with the public's lives and emotions, and *our* lives and sanity. You just can't run a public service like a normal business.

Val returned with the trolley and we began preparing Mr Hunter. His heart rate on the monitors had increased to 140 beats per minute; most of this was probably from pain rather than purely because of his infection.

I stood opposite Dave and let him do the catheterisation under my supervision. This might be a difficult one but he was a pretty fast learner and I could trust him with most, relatively basic, procedures now. Plus, I don't think he was planning to try and masturbate Mr Hunter in the same way that Nurse Totten had inadvertently demonstrated. I hoped.

Val stood at the foot of the bed and tried to reassure Mr Hunter with his confident explanatory narrative at every step of the procedure, like a good and caring nursing assistant.

Good communication. Keep the patient informed.

I don't think Mr Hunter really appreciated the running commentary though.

"Don'ta worry, Meester Hunter. The doctor is just looking for your penis now... to put some anaesthetic jelly in it."

That was perhaps a little loud given that some of the other ward patients had not yet got to sleep.

"Ohhhhhhharrrgghhhh!" Mr Hunter replied, as if now trying to haunt the ward in the style of a poor quality pantomime or an episode of *Scooby-Doo*.

"I am not findings it, Jace."

Dave had is face about two inches from where the gap in Mr Hunter's pyjama bottoms had been before we pulled them down. He had his pen torch out and was shining it one way then the other like a search light where he thought he'd find Mr Hunter's little man.

We'd normally use our pen torches to test pupillary reflexes during a neurological examination but they obviously had other uses.

"Dave, just get your hands in there... *gloves,* Dave!"

"We're just 'aving a bit of trouble finding your penis, Mr Hunter, but don'ta worry, I'm sure eet eez een there somewhere."

Probably not what he wanted to hear whilst agony enveloped him like an old friend.

"Dave, dry the jelly off a bit so you can get some proper grip and then try and pinch it at the base."

After more of a fiddle, Dave managed to get a good grip on what little tissue he could and proceeded to slide in the tube.

"We're a justa sliding the tuba in now, Meester Hunter."

Honestly, as if he hadn't realised by now...

"It's prretty tight in here," Dave rolled a concerned 'r' and clicked his 't's on the roof of his mouth.

He felt the resistance of the enlarged prostate gland in his way like a bouncer at a nightclub. Normally, Dave would have turned around and gone to another club but, on this occasion, his persistence proved successful.

A sudden loss of resistance as the tube advanced just enough for the tip to enter the bladder.

Before we had even a fraction of a second to direct the other end of the tube into the disposable cardboard kidney dish and attach the drainage bag, the catheter tube went rigid and erect, then angled itself upwards and towards Val, who stood in it's line of fire.

WWWHHHOOOOOSSHHHHH!

The release was truly incredible, like the waltzing fountain waters in front of the *Bellagio* hotel in Las Vegas...

... but at NASA.

Val ducked just in time but felt the air displacement of the rocket of steamy, infected, yellow urine just miss the top of his head and pass through a gap between the top of the curtain, the hanging rail and the curtain rings.

"OOOOOHHHHHHH, YEEEEESSSSSSSS! OHHH HHH, AHHHHHHHH!"

The relief and joy in Mr Hunter's scream was unbridled.

"Ohhhh, thank you, thank you, *thank you*, I love you, Doctor, I... *LOVE YOU*."

Call it a rescue romance or hero worship but it was a perfectly understandable human response to his near 'death' experience.

"Oiiii!"

A voice from the opposite bed hollered, where Mr Albert Skinner was reading a newspaper whilst waiting for his sleeping pills to kick in. He'd recently had a pacemaker inserted; good job it was working.

I nipped out from behind the curtains to see Mr Skinner sat up in bed. His hair, face and, more importantly, his *Daily Mail* were soaked in urine.

He spat out a few drops and glared at me.

"I'll just get a nurse," I reassured him and popped back behind the curtains like the *Wizard of Oz*, the great and powerful.

Nothing to see here.

"Dave, you wanna write in the notes and I'll go and certify that body."

"Okay."

Dave gave me a thumbs-up feeling very proud of himself that he'd earned the actual love of a retired politician.

"Where's this body then, Val?"

"In side room two. The morning shift dealt with it I think. There's been a bit of patient shuffling around the wards today by the bed manager and they weren't expecting side room two to get filled so soon."

It was no wonder that we lost our patients. The beds aren't a bloody pack of cards.

Val helped Dave to clear up and attach Mr Hunter's drainage bag which cordially obliged by filling up very quickly.

One of the other night nurses went over to dry off Mr Skinner and fetch him a clean pyjama top. He was still glaring at me out of the corners of his dripping eyes.

It wasn't my fault, it was Dave's. I kept my thoughts internal.

I opened the door to side room 2. It was in the corner of the ward and in view of the nursing station.

Side rooms were often used for patients who had to be barrier-nursed due to infections such as tuberculosis or nasty forms of diarrhoea. They were also used for patients who needed to be protected from infection including those on chemotherapy whose immune systems were suppressed. But commonly, they were used for people who were terminally ill and required palliative care and privacy.

The room was dimly lit, the blinds were closed and a subtly sweet yet musty smell could be appreciated. It was actually very quiet, very peaceful and very tidy in there.

On the bed lay a rather rotund body, the body that I'd been asked to come and see for hours but just had no real time to do so.

Priorities: Living first, Dead later.

It had been totally wrapped up perfectly neatly in white, plasticky fabric or tarpaulin so you couldn't even see the identity of the person within. A small, pretty orange flower had been placed considerately on the centre of the chest.

"Oh, for fucksake... Val! Val?"

Val trotted over.

"Wassup, man?"

"Look… well if they weren't bloody dead before… they bloody well *are* now!"

"Hmm… by suffocation?"

"Exactly! I suppose we'd better go through the motions anyway, now that I'm finally here. Can we take that tarp off?"

The pack had been shuffled and here was the Joker.

It was like uncovering an old car in storage.

We walked back into the room knowing what a totally pointless exercise this was going to be and slowly peeled off the sheeting from the top.

I heard myself gasp momentarily and I was unable to exhale again. I suddenly felt my eyes swelling and filling with painful tears.

Purple-rinsed hair.

My chest felt heavy.

Mollie 'almost' Sugden… Sweet… as Apple Pie…

Chapter Fifteen

Relations and Revelations

Some Good Advice

I cried for the first time in a long time. I just couldn't control it.

Walking back to the mess by myself, I began to really understand why we have to care for our patients but not *actually* care. If you share too much with them, if they become your 'favourites', if you liken them to a close relative or friend, if they end up becoming a friend, you will set yourself up for inevitable deep and real sadness. You can't keep doing that to yourself as a medical professional.

I went back to my on-call room.

Dave told Fi what had happened and they went to finish up and also drain Mr Clementine's belly.

I rang Ward 11 from my bedside phone. I just had to make that call.

Twenty minutes passed and there was a knock on my door.

Nurse Jessica Totten stood there, lips still glossy and thick, dark hair in a sheeny ponytail.

"I'm on me brayke now." She stepped in, closed the door, unpopped the poppers on her uniform with a single swift pull letting it fall to the floor in a small heap.

Stepping out of it, she pushed me onto the bed.

"You can leave that white coat on now," she whispered.

The relief was required, there was no conversation exchanged.

Jess slipped her shiny, black tights back on, clipped up her bra, slid her uniform back on and left as quickly as she'd arrived.

I showered to refresh myself but I just stood under the lukewarm water and let the sensation flow over me whilst I tried to recalibrate my thoughts.

Sexual therapy seemed to be the easiest kind, but probably the most short-lived.

Yet another day had been a bit of an ordeal, to say the least.

As usual, I grabbed a set of scrubs and positioned them in their familiar concertina'd way on my trainers in readiness for any further unwanted (medical) action in the night.

I turned off the lights and lay back in bed wearing just my underwear.

I felt something under the sheets at the end of the bed with my toes. I gripped on and bent my leg up to see what it was.

A tiny, black thong. I slid it under the pillow for safekeeping.

Knock Knock

There was a very tentative tap on my door. It must be bloody Dave.

I got up and went to answer it, leaving my light off. Little git, what did he want now? I opened the door and squinted in the light of the corridor outside.

"Shift is over, Doctor."

Kate Ellis stood outside my on-call room door and looked me up and down.

"Oh, hello! I'd forgotten how fit you were." She looked slightly surprised, relaxed one hip and placed a hand on it; a familiar pose.

She let down her blonde pony tail and allowed her hair to cascade over her shoulders which covered her Ward Sister lapels.

"Aren't you going to invite me in?" She smiled again, coyly.

Our time in cubicle 7 was clearly unfinished.

"Of course I am."

Well... I *did* say that sexual therapy was short-lived!

Thankfully, my cardiac arrest bleep didn't go off. Maybe the battery was finally flat.

My alarm went off at 7.00am. Wow, I must have had a few hours' sleep after we'd finally crashed out.

Kate was tucked up along side me in the single bed, her legs intertwined with mine and her naked bottom pressed against the wall. I'm glad the bed was up against one wall or one of us would have surely fallen out in the night.

Her beautiful eyes opened. "Oh, good morning, Doctor!"

She placed a soft hand where my 'morning' had suddenly become quite glorious.

"Good morning, Nurse." I kissed her on the forehead. "I'd better get up, we've got Dr Bodman's ward round in a bit."

"Seems like you've done that already!" She squeezed me gently. "I've got a day off today."

She stroked circles on my chest with the other hand.

"Lucky you!"

I really didn't want to get out of bed now.

"Well, *I'd* better leave before the on-call doctors get up and the other ones arrive."

"Okay, " I conceded.

She slipped out of bed and I watched the silhouette of her naked body quietly slide back into her uniform.

She came over and kissed me again. "Have a good day, you. Here... something to remember me by..."

She threw a pair of white, lacy French knickers at me which landed on my forehead.

As she stepped out of the door, she bumped right into Isaac, naked and clutching a bundle of clothes in his arms which dangled down just enough to cover his Prince of Nigeria...

... whilst slipping out of Davinder's on-call room next door.

Not a word was spoken, just a sudden brief look of surprise was exchanged. They both knew that they were where they shouldn't have been.

The unspoken but recognisable conversation clearly said, "I won't tell, if you won't tell!"

I grasped the black thong from under my pillow and held both pairs of memorabilia up in front of me, one in each hand.

I had to shake my head slightly and smile... on the inside.

Uncomplicated mutual comforting at it's finest.

The day continued as if nothing untoward had happened.

I got dressed after a slightly sleepless night and although I harboured significant sadness for Mollie 'almost' Sugden, I had to find some way to quickly dissipate those feelings entirely; certainly the night's activity went some way to initiating that therapy.

As I closed the on-call room door to grab a bite of breakfast before going to meet Dr Bodman, Dave also left his room.

"Alright, Dave?"

"Alright, Jace?"

A nod was exchanged. Did either of us know?

Did he know that I knew? If he did know that I knew, he looked like he was pretending that he didn't know that I knew, but I knew he was pretending not to know.

I smiled at him, he said nothing else but walked off to prepare for the ward round like he usually did... he *was* walking a bit funny though.

When I arrived on the ward, happy to have eaten something, Fi greeted us looking quite refreshed. I wished I could power nap like her.

"How are you doing? I heard about Mollie... I didn't get a chance to see her after they shuffled our patients around."

"It happens." I tried to disguise my true feelings and harden up inside just a little more.

The fact is, having bad heart failure is almost like having a cancer diagnosis[20].

Dave was pottering about getting the blood results finalised and all his paperwork in order in preparation for any questions Dr Bodman might ask.

"Isn't he here yet?" I checked my watch. Dr Bodman was always on time despite his extracurricular activities.

"Ahhhh, Dr Manson! Good morning to you my good man!"

Dr Bodman appeared from behind a closed curtain with his white coat fully buttoned up and stretched over his expanded midriff.

Dave's old stethoscope was around Dr Bodman's neck and his brown pen, fully locked, loaded and ready for action, was in his top pocket.

---

[20] Although there have been recent improvements in congestive heart failure treatment, researchers say the prognosis for people with the disease is still bleak, with about 50% having an average life expectancy of less than five years. For those with advanced forms of heart failure, nearly 90% die within one year.

He had a beaming smile on his face and a glint in his eye. He even gave me a special wink with his right eye whilst looking slightly off to the left with the other.

"Good morning, sir."

I smiled suspiciously but, on balance, I was almost happy that his smile was genuine and there was no reason for even the slightest of suspicions at all.

Having said that, Dr Bodman had extra specially singled out a particularly jolly and very exceptional 'good morning' greeting in my general direction, as if he really and truly sarcastically meant it.

I say 'in my general direction' given that it *was* a bit off to the left.

The faintest smell of a rat wafted gently under my nose and nibbled at a stray nasal hair.

He came right up to me, still grinning, stooped a little and put his head and a podgy cheek next to mine to talk softly and subtly in my ear.

He smelt of *Old Spice*.

"I hear you told Dr Podgornay... to fuck off."

GASP!

I felt my heart sink, whatever that expression was anatomically supposed to actually mean. I felt my chest tighten with a central heaviness, my usual brownish complexion took a turn for the paler and several beads of sweat abruptly appeared on my brow as if to say, 'You're busted, here we come, ready or not!'

"*Whaaaaaattt?!*"

The words split my brain with sheer terror. Dr Bodman was a close personal friend of Dr Podgornay, as it came to pass. They both played golf together, as I *now* know.

Dr Bodman placed a large, warm, chubby hand on my shoulder and guided me into the cubicle with a firm but friendly arm and a little chuckle.

As we entered a small gap in the curtains, to my absolute horror, there sat upright in the bed...

... a man of very short stature, a somewhat disproportionately large head and a chunky, blood-stained nasal pack up each nostril[21].

"*Fuck!*"

The little man mouth-breathed a bit to prepare himself for a sentence, then said, "Hello..." he inhaled again, "... Doctor."

He gasped once more and coughed a bit, spitting up a small, purple clot into a cardboard kidney dish.

Dr Bodman had been called by Dr Podgornay in the middle of the night after he'd tried and failed to admit one of his long-term patients. I had hung up on him with nothing short of a huge, unadulterated mistake.

"But... but..."

"It's okay. I spoke with Fiona and she told me that you'd received a call. We've seen Mr Bignall and he's all sorted out now. We thought it best not to worry you as you've been rather busy."

He winked at me again.

Mr Aloysius 'ironically' Bignall snorted some more thick blood clot and waved a little hand at me.

---

[21] Patients with dwarfism or achondroplasia can have growth problems at the base of the skull which can prevent the cerebrospinal fluid from flowing freely in and out of the skull resulting in hydrocephalus. In babies, the most evident symptom of hydrocephalus is a quickly enlarging head.

I had to shake my head again and blink, wondering if I was in some form of Wonderland. Maybe the *Mad Hatter* would be in the next bed with a migraine followed by the *Queen of Hearts* with angina.

I hoped that he didn't know about the particulars of my rather specific and directionally precise 'specialist' advice I had given to Dr Podgornay.

"Good morning, Mr Bignall... a pleasure to meet you." I smiled at him with my mouth but I'm sure my eyes said that he indeed was but a figment of my imagination.

Fiona slipped in behind the curtains with us, stood next to me, pushed up her glasses on her freckled nose and gave me a very subtle but absolutely noticeable knowing nudge with her elbow right into my ribs.

My jaw remained tightly clenched.

We plodded though several of our long-stayer patients.

Honestly, we should be charging them like an airport car park.

Dave continued to write plenty of 'awaiting nursing home, awaiting stairlift, ISQ/continue, await physio, await occupational therapy assessment...' and we soon reached Mrs Blaise Laflamme.

[*Now, fluid restriction is used as a way to avoid overloading your heart if you have heart failure, because more fluid in your bloodstream makes it harder for your heart to pump. It is also important to restrict salt, which makes your body hold extra fluid. Easy.*]

I'd given explicit instructions to fluid and salt restrict Mrs Laflamme and started her on industrial doses of diuretics for her massive fluid retention, even the legendary Metolazone[22], which sounds like something from a *Superman* comic book.

One of the ways to monitor this, aside from accurate fluid balance charting, was for the nurses to record serial weigh-ins. The lighter you became, the more fluid we were taking off.

Despite this clever cocktail based on exceptional physiological, biochemical and pharmacological knowledge, our very own comic book, fiery-haired, red-lipsticked, green-eye shadowed and now generally *Joker*-esque Blaise Laflamme continued to swell like the *Michelin* man in the vacuum of space.

She had put on more weight, which was being beautifully, accurately and obliviously charted by the nurses, and her breathlessness continued to worsen due to the fluid accumulating on her lungs.

"Hand me the fluid chart, Dr Dewani, please?"

Dave handed it over like his future job reference depended on it. It did, of course.

Dr Bodman, in his usual style of bedside manner, sat on the right-hand edge of Mrs Laflamme's bed and took her by her right hand. Well, more accurately, he practically lay next to her and shifted her over to the left. He'd probably try and steal her duvet if he could... if patients were provided with proper duvets rather than

---

[22] Metolazone is a thiazide-like diuretic which is primarily used to treat congestive cardiac failure and high blood pressure. It indirectly decreases the amount of water reabsorbed into the bloodstream by the kidney, so that the blood volume decreases and urine volume increases. This prevents excess fluid accumulation in heart failure. It is sometimes used together with other diuretics but these combinations can lead to dehydration and electrolyte disturbances.

a flimsy, pseudo-woollen blanket or two with a few holes in it.

She smiled a toothless, red lipstick-framed grin.

"How are you today?" He enjoyed slightly flirting with the older clientele and they actually quite liked it.

"Oh, Doctor... I'ms not good," she pluralised.

She tried to tidy her Toy Troll hair a little by lightly patting and moulding it with the palm of her hand.

At the bottom of the bed was a specially made nurses' sign to let everyone know... clearly... that Blaise was on a 1000 millilitre *fluid restriction*; that's about one hospital jug full.

If I had a chance to drink half of that on a working day, I'd be lucky. Honestly, most of us were running on water vapour most of the time. I want a sign on my back saying, 'Please do NOT fluid restrict'.

"Well, looking at this fluid chart, you've drunk six and a half litres of water!"

"What?! Six and a half litres?!" I couldn't help but blurt out.

You could fill a frickin' water bed with that.

So, one of the nursing auxiliaries had been faithfully recording Mrs Laflamme's blissful and steady consumption of the Dead Sea without so much as a question?

"*Shit!*"

"Oh! But, Doctor, I feels so thirsty all the time," she pleaded.

"Really? *That* thirsty?" Dr Bodman raised his eyebrows in surprise, turned around and looked at me... or maybe Dave... but it could equally have been Fiona.

A moment of confusion passed between us all, paused, frowned a little, then floated away still looking somewhat perplexed.

"By the way, Doctor... is it okay to eat these?"

Mrs Laflamme reached into her bedside cabinet and pulled out an *OXO* cube. She held it out in front of her, balanced like a small, silver-packaged trophy on the tips of her thumb, index and middle fingers that were brought closely together like a little, swollen tripod.

An OXO cube??

Now, whilst 'transforming your meals with rich and versatile little magic cubes packed with big flavours' such as beef and chicken, might be a quick, easy and tasty option for some, each cube contains one hell of a lot of salt; it's origins likely came from the word 'Ox' given that the first cubes were made from beef stock.

Realising the biochemical and renal implications of this, I slowly began to put my head in my hands.

"So, *who* is making this drink for you then?"

One would usually dissolve these little packets of cardiotoxicity in boiling water.

Dr Bodman enquired with the tone of voice that implied that whoever it was, was likely to be fired, or at the absolute very least, shot slowly and painfully at dawn... once we'd had coffee, obviously.

"Oh, no, Doctor, I's just eats them raw."

She smiled another cartoon smile.

Urghh!

"So... erm... how many are you eating a day, might I ask?"

"Oh, just a couple of boxes."

"You mean a couple of *cubes*? Because that is quite a lot of salt, Blaise."

"Ooo! No, Doctor, a couple of boxes."

She pulled out a box of twelve!

"Twenty-four *OXO* cubes... a *day*?!"

"Oh, I'ms addicted to them I am. Can't get enough, although I really do get very thirsty."

She took a slurp of water through a pink, curly, crazy straw given to her by one of the auxiliary nurses.

TWENTY-FOUR?!

She really *was* drinking the Dead Sea... the deepest hypersaline lake in the world with a salinity of just over 34%. There is 30.7g of salt per 100g of OXO cubes, so we are certainly getting there.

Inadvertent suicide... by OXO cubes.

"I'll be taking these away I'm afraid, Mrs Laflamme. You have found a way to work against us. One jug of water now and zero OXO cubes."

Kidneys... brace yourself because those drugs are about to give you a good hiding.

"Nurse, please take these away and throw them out."

Nurse Becky 'Nightshade' came over, chewing her bottom lip where there was also a body piercing lip ring in the centre. She looked somewhat sheepish. It was almost as if she somehow knew about the secret stash of OXO cubes and perhaps had ill-advised Blaise that she was sure they'd be fine, or some other pseudo-confident reassurance when someone has literally no idea what they're talking about, but if you say it confidently enough, it becomes a true and unchallengeable fact.

I won't bother with the seatbelt... I'm sure it'll be fine.

I think this parachute isn't packed correctly... I'm sure it'll be fine.

I'm going to stick my head out of the train window at 110mph... I'm sure it'll be fine.

You get the picture.

Well, Nurse 'Nightshade' was living up to the name that she had no idea we gave her.

BLEEEEP BLEEEEP

"Sorry Dr 'B', just gotta get this… outside line."

I called good ol' switchboard.

"Dr Manson here."

"Ah, Dr Manson, you've got such a lovely telephone voice, so smooth and seductive… you should be on the telly with that."

Just bloody put me through to the caller instead of flirting, you're old enough to be my Gran.

"You're too kind 'switch', perhaps we can continue this over dinner?"

"Ooohh, Mavis, that's an offer you can't refuse! Oooo, hoo-hoo-hoooo!" came the howling background banter. "I'll just put you through… oooh, I've come over all of a quiver!"

Her voice faded. I could almost sense the actual menopause over the phone line.

"Hello," came a soft, breathy and beautiful voice. It was Karen.

"Hi!"

Guilt rappetty-tapped upon my shoulder yet again and as I turned to see who it was, I also received a firm clip around the ear by Selfishness and a smacked bottom by Insensitivity.

All three of them were far from happy with me.

"I haven't heard from you for ages. I thought we were going to meet up?"

"I know, I'm sorry. I just haven't had the chance."

I heard her sigh with disappointment and I felt terrible. I did miss her so much, if I could clearly remember the feeling of what it was like to miss someone.

It was almost as if she was living in a parallel universe or another dimension and at some point I'd break out of this bubble where time stood still and escape back to 'normal' life where I'd have a normal relationship, have normal feelings, have normal sensitivity and normal compassion.

I wouldn't be a self-absorbed arsehole, scrabbling around for consolation and mutual comfort through a series of meaningless sexual encounters in the workplace.

"It's okay. I understand."

She, of course, couldn't possibly understand what it was like... nobody could.

Only me.

"Thanks, I really will try and come and see you very soon. How's your mum doing?"

"She's not very well. They're trying to make her as comfortable as they can but she's lost so much weight."

I heard her begin to cry over the phone.

"Look, I'm so sorry, I've got to go, I'm on the consultant ward round."

I couldn't deal with this right now. The patients needed us.

The right thing to do would have been to hand over my bleeps, turn in the stethoscope, pen torch, tendon hammer, badge and gun to Captain Bodman of the *Bay City PD* and get of there!

"Get back here, Detective Sergeant *Starsky*!"

He'd shout at me spitting out a shower of his morning doughnut whilst slamming his clenched fist down on his old, brown, wooden desk, the vibrations knocking over a cardboard cup of coffee all over a mass of strewn paperwork containing unsolved murder cases.

Isaac really had far too many seventies cop shows on TV in the mess.

Chapter Sixteen

Planning a Night Out

Peace and Safari

Having an evening off, actually having the volition to go out and not just partake in mandatory catch-up sleep, was a relative rarity.

But if you did live in hospital accommodation of some description or just couldn't be arsed going straight home from work, it was very easy to get swept away in the tide of hospital staff going down to the pub or a local seedy, yet traditional, nightclub. Although, the 'pay day party' was probably the best day of the month to do it.

Going out to have a few drinks with the team was generally fun and whilst we had to try and avoid talking 'shop' with various drinking game forfeits if you did utter a word of work-talk or if you found the need to bitch about something work-related, this came with the appropriate alcoholic penalty.

Honestly, now even Dave was up for a bit of drinking. That shot of rum and ginger beer had whet his taste buds. Plus, I think the stress of not only work, but also his 'secret' liaison with Isaac was beginning to exert a small weight on his mind.

I needed to dilute the embarrassment of the day and try to forget about the fact that *Tweedledee* was actually very short and very real and currently sat on the ward with his nose packed. I needed to drown my sorrows of Mollie's demise and my guilt of not seeing her sooner.

I also needed to see Karen but Guilt would be disobeyed yet again tonight.

Fi couldn't be arsed revising for her exams and she wasn't bothered about sleep right now either given her pattern of 'little and often'.

Perhaps I could learn from that.

She also had a certain anaesthetic registrar, with a penchant for *Donald Duck*, on her mind and was grappling with whether or not to ignore her basic rule of not dating whilst studying for an important professional exam; too distracting.

I wondered whether Jessica would be out tonight, or Kate or Alice for that matter.

"Hey, Dave!"

"You called, my Master!" He faked a subservient tone with a certain elevated level of self-confidence.

"Alright, Dave, don't start getting cocky just coz you've been getting some... err... anyway..."

"Shuttings up!" he grammatically crucified.

"Hey, Dave, you wanna get pissed but avoid a hangover in the morning?"

"Yeah, what you havings in mind?"

I didn't bother to police his continued word crimes.

"Well, if we cannulate each other's veins with a nice green *Venflon*..."

"What?! I don't like needles!" Dave almost shrieked like a little girl.

"Just hear me out, Dave... I'll even spray on some of that kiddies local anaesthetic cold spray for you, you big girl's blouse. We each get a bag of *Hartmann's* solution[23] and a fluid giving set, hang up the bags of fluid on the back of a door for when you get back from the pub and just connect up our little intravenous magic hangover cure! Bob is, quite frankly, your proverbial uncle, Dave."

---

[23] Ringer's lactate solution, also known as sodium lactate solution and Hartmann's solution, is a mixture of sodium chloride, sodium lactate, potassium chloride, and calcium chloride in water. It is used for replacing fluids and electrolytes in those who have low blood volume or low blood pressure... or a hangover.

"I am not knowing Bob. I'm having Babu-uncle though…"

"No, Dave, it's a saying… look never mind, let's just get a couple of cannulas and get ready."

We 'half-inched' a couple of *Venflon* intravenous cannulas from our main ward. No-one asked any questions as it really isn't unusual for doctors to need bits and pieces of minor cheap medical equipment. We'd often just shove a few spares in our white coat pockets, just in case. It saved fumbling around on some wards that had a less than organised clinical equipment room.

Tourniquet tightly on the upper arm, pat down the veins as if they were criminal suspects, open and close your hands to pump more blood down the arteries but stop it leaving via the veins like a road block, which cordially begin to swell like little green snakes filled with blood ready to puncture.

I didn't bother with Dave's girlie magic spray as I couldn't find any and also couldn't be bothered looking properly.

"You'll just feel a little *pri*…"

"Arrgh!" He winced like he were trying Brussels sprouts for the first time.

"Shut up, you big nonce."

"It's hurtings…"

"Well, now you know how the patients feel, Doctor Dewani! There, all done."

I took out the central needle, left in the small plastic tube section, flushed the residual blood through the little tube with five millilitres of sterile saline solution, dressed it neatly with the special moulded fixing tape and put a nice bandage on for Dave to safeguard our great feat of medical ingenuity.

Dave returned the favour, taking extra special care to have two distinctly separate shots at my juicy, large calibre vein on the back of my hand that anyone could've hit with a hosepipe from the other side of the room... blindfolded... *bastard*.

"Argh! Dave! Just coz you're getting it now."

He smirked, again drawing upon his new found, no-longer-a-virgin confidence.

He put on my bandage and we set up the drip bags in one of the unused on-call rooms and were ready to go out.

The Carpenter's Arms was always a decent place to start and often also finish... with all the rest in between.

Me and Davinder wandered in (I'd like to say, "Dave and I," but he isn't yet important enough!). Dave, armed with his modicum of self-confidence, strolled nonchalantly to the bar to order some actual alcohol.

He tripped on some loose tiling, skidded slightly on a puddle of spilt beer, tweaked a hamstring and then stumbled forwards, almost careering into Fi and Rob who were already there standing by the bar having a cocktail... *together*.

He just managed to stop himself from taking out Rob completely, whilst he was in full flirtatious flow, by grabbing onto an empty chair.

He came to a halt whilst only just nudging Rob's drinking arm. Rob's cocktail umbrella wobbled slightly, fell out of the glass while floating and spinning like a tiny version of *Mary Poppins*, all the way to the floor.

"Alright, Dave!" said Rob, picking his pink paper brolly up off the floor, closing it gently and casually putting it in the top pocket of Dave's shirt. "What are you having?"

"Rum and ginger beer… doubling it please!" He thumped the bar with his pudgy fist.

"A 'double', Dave." Fi corrected him. "You hurt your hand, Dave?"

Fi took hold of Dave's bandaged left hand.

"Oh, just a little cuttings on a glass vial."

Dave tried to cleverly disguise our cunning plan by using the excuse of a commonly experienced accident; opening glass vials of drugs often resulted in shattering shards of glass into your fingers, thumb or palm by crushing it within tired and irritable grasps.

I scanned the pub for potential problems.

No Kate. No Nurse Totten. Alice sat in the corner with some other young, presumably innocent and impressionable student nurses, all oblivious to the war into which they were about to be drafted.

I caught her staring over at me with doe-eyes and she suddenly looked away, again achieving full geographical crimson. On this occasion, she was too far away for me to effectively utilise my cartographical skills.

Karen called again… I had to ignore the call.

A small wave of disappointment washed over me, then quickly crashed against a small cluster of rocks on the coastline of my increasingly and inappropriately perverted mind when I saw another very attractive group of girls.

Blondes, fake blondes, brunettes, a red head, vivid lipstick, make-up, cleavage, jewellery, bare and tanned athletic legs, high heels and fake designer handbags probably to dance around later that evening in some sort of ritual.

Physiotherapists were arguably the most desirable of all the staff groups in the hospital, not that I am necessarily saying that they should be 'desired' as an entity in any shape or form. They were usually female, with the occasional very lucky male who was often surrounded by his laughing and obliging female compatriots; he had probably already had relations of some description with most of them who were generally fairly attractive and almost always very sporty from playing in local netball or hockey teams, therefore having very fit physiques, slim muscularly defined legs and toned, pert glutei.

They usually hunted in packs of at least six, generally working closely together as a team, a bit like hyenas or cheetahs. But by and large they'd all stand around together making a lot of noise and chatter, wearing brightly coloured and revealing attire, usually attempting to attract attention by way of a mate... like a flock of flamingos.

It was tough to penetrate this phlock of physio phlamingos though, without feeling a certain level of intimidation.

What if you were rejected?

It'd be like the whole phlock rejecting you and then you'd get a reputation which would prevent you from trying again with another phlamingo... ever!

The best course of action would be to try and get one to notice you and perhaps it would break off from the rest of the phlock and come over for a separate, yet risky, encounter without it's usual support network.

They'd often be seen interspersed with the odd orthopod either for show, grooming or some sort of

MAXIMILIAN VAN DEN BOSS

security to protect them from unwanted predators such as non-orthopod junior doctors or random members of the actual public.

The orthopods could be quite powerful creatures especially given that they had to use big hammers and saws and grapple with metal joint replacements and things. Many of them had quite roughened knuckles where they dragged them around on the floor, like the primitive ape; although I do the ape an injustice by making this comparison.

Contrary to this notion, tonight the phlamingos surrounded Dr Johnny Winterson-Waring. Aside from being of an extremely pale complexion with almost white blonde hair, Johnny was short, about five feet four inches tall, with a sort of rodent-like facial composition. His posh, high-toned and slightly blocked nasally voice chatted and laughed with orthopaedic surgeon-like confidence as the phlock safely phlirted with him.

Johnny hadn't actually even operated on anyone yet, aside from holding a few retractors[24] for the consultant or handing over some screws or the drill in theatre. He also had to stand on a box, whilst assisting, in order to see what was going on, especially as Mr Branston, his boss, towered over Johnny at nearly six feet five.

The phlamingos, like everyone else, were convinced that Johnny was gay except for Johnny himself who naively thought he was totally 'in' with the physiophlamingos; they never actually revealed to him that they

---

[24] A retractor is a surgical instrument used to separate the edges of a surgical incision. It is also used to hold back organs and tissues so that other structures may be accessed.

thought he was gay so that made his ridiculous demeanour even funnier.

How they chortled and guffawed at his non-jokes and his mock stories of theatre life, saving lives and limbs... well a few joints and bunions anyway, probably not even that - he'd apparently dropped a new sterile knee joint replacement once, and they're not cheap.

But the phlamingos seemed to behave like this because they didn't feel threatened by Johnny and they could utilise this pseudo-mating ritual to attract other prey for either consumption, mating practice or for a genuine, full-on lifetime partner.

Many phlamingos wanted to be stalked by the prized rugby player; whether he was good looking or not, the rugby player was the ultimate goal. They frequently overlooked the fact that, like certain other animals for various reasons, the rugby player was autocoprophagic[25] as part of it's competitive nature and eagerness to impress. Occasionally, it could be seen consuming large receptacles of urine and other excreta donated by many of it's own species.

Their laughter at Johnny was all an integral part of this veil of game-playing and pseudo-enjoyment. It was like something out of a reality TV series[26] full of fake attractiveness.

---

[25] Coprophagia is the consumption of faeces with autocoprophagia being the consumption of one's own faeces. However, outside of varying degrees of perversity and mental illness, the practice of coprophagy amongst humans is considered to be completely repulsive.

[26] We didn't really have reality TV in the 90's, but if we had... The Only Way Is Physio?

Lights, Camera... ACTION!

"*Who are those gorgeous girls having so much fun over there with their laughing and their joking and standing intermittently on one high-heeled leg whilst rubbing the other toned calf upon the other?*"

The onlookers and potential mates would surely be asking themselves this.

Winterson-Waring?

"*Wanker*" is what *I* thought.

Perhaps I'd just join Dave and the team for now. Besides, none of the phlamingos looked like it was going to separate from the phlock at the moment; the time wasn't quite right as the mating season truly began in the Summer.

Plus, Winterson-Wanker was in the way, well, in the centre of the phlock, like an unhatched and rather annoying egg.

I walked over to the bar and joined the team plus... Rob Banks.

"CoQuack-sch, CoQuack-sch!"

I contorted the side of my tongue in my mouth and produced my best *Donald Duck* voice.

"Twat," said Rob dryly, "can I get you a drink, matey?"

"Cheers, man. I'll have a vodka and *Red Bull*. Better make it a double." I reverted back to normal speak.

Rob bought the drink for me without a thought.

"Jeez, you two are going for it today!"

Fi smiled. She was wearing contact lenses *and* make-up. Whilst her hair was still bedraggled, she'd otherwise made quite the effort for Rob.

Rob was a lucky boy and I think he was fully aware of this.

"Ah, well, we've had a shitty time recently and I'm helping Dave celebrate losing his... *urrrghh...*"

Dave elbowed me hard (for him) in the side, during a fake accidental swivelling 180 degree turnaround as if he'd notice something on the other side of the bar.

"... losing his... err... old stethoscope to Dr Bodman and buying a marvellous new and expensive 'cardiology' stethoscope."

"So, I see you've hurt your hand too, like Dave?"

"Oh, yeah, erm..."

RRRIIIINNGGGG

My phone rang... switchboard?! What do they want? I'm off duty.

"Hang on..." I stepped outside of the pub for a minute without having to invent an instant excuse for the bandaged up and hidden intravenous cannula.

"Hello, Dr Manson?"

"Nurse on sixteen, I'll put her through..."

"Yeah, but, I'm not on-..."

Switchboard, switched... board before I could remind them that I was not on-call.

"Hello, Dr Manson, this is Nurse on Ward sixteen... it's about Mrs Migginski."

"Look, I'm not on-call."

I took a large sip of my double vodka and *Red Bull* mentally and physically confirming that even if I had wanted to, I would not be going into work as my blood alcohol levels would be too high.

I'm not going back to work.

"Yes, I know but she's your patient."

"Look, I am *not* on-call! Call the on-call medical team."

"Oh, I didn't want to bother them as she's *your* patient."

I wondered why she hadn't called Dave or Fi either.

"For crying out loud!" I started to get a little annoyed, obviously.

"But she's your patient isn't she?"

"Yes, but…"

"So, I need to let you know that…"

I interjected quickly this time.

"Look, Nurse…?" I inflected, expecting an answer to my implied enquiry as to her name and rank.

"Becky, Staff Nurse Becky Branksome."

That's Nurse bloody Nightshade!

"You *do* understand how *on-call* works don't you Nurse Branksome?! Anything out of hours goes to on-call and we will pick up any issues *tomorrow*. I am *not* in the hospital, I have a night off and I am at the pub, so stop disturbing me when I am not at work!"

"Oh… but I just thought I'd let you know that Mrs Migginski has had a bowel movement."

I took a very large swig of vodka-laced *Red Bull*, blew my cheeks out and sighed. Whilst leaning against the wall of the pub outside, I mouthed the word 'muthafu*£er' and I shook my head. Then I turned around to face away from the onlooking world of idiots, lightly banged my forehead against the unsuspecting brickwork and pleaded for common sense to give birth on her face.

Now, we were indeed hoping that Mrs Migginski's rectum and it's granite-like contents would eventually respond to her personalised cocktail of enemas and other laxatives, by either passing a little flatus, or perhaps even a small, and probably reluctant, stool. I certainly was totally uninterested in the contraction of her colon and relaxation of her anal sphincter whilst I was down the pub getting pissed on my night off.

"Goodbye... Nurse *Nightshade*."

I hung up, accidentally on purposely revealing that I knew her true identity.

She *will* regret that call.

Speaking of cocktails, Dave was on his third *Mojito*.

Jesus, I'd only been outside on the phone for a few minutes and he was necking them like there was no tomorrow.

Speaking of necking...

And Rob and Fi are snogging... what?!

Have I just been in a fourth dimension whilst all this has been going on? Well, Nurse Nightshade should be in one, as it might just be safer for the whole of humanity.

"Fi, you dirty slut." I lightly pinched her bottom.

Rob took his face out of her mouth for a second.

"Honestly, get an on-call room you two! Anyway Fi, I thought you were doing exams and a *relationship* was too distracting?"

"Piss off, Jace!" She smiled, stuck two fingers up at me, flushed and carried on the consumption of Rob's very, very lucky face with her arm around his waist and her *Slow Comfortable Screw* in the other hand.

Rob could be a persuasive gentleman and, on this occasion, probably offered her a trip to his own *Magic Kingdom*.

"Bloody hell, Dave, you're going for it tonight!"

He staggered up towards me.

"After that double rum," he rolled his 'r's like an old Royal Enfield motorbike[27], "I thought I'd be startings on something a little more... strongerer."

His 'r's rolled with ever more ridiculous revolutions.

"Slow down man or we're gonna have to attach you to that drip a lot sooner!"

"Hey, there's Isaac!"

"I'm *not carrying* you back, Dave! Remember that!"

My words scattered on the sticky, beer-soaked vinyl floor like seed on stony ground.

He trotted off in a small, light-headed zigzag to the other side of the bar where Isaac stood, he spilled a little of his *Mojito* but was armed with drunken excitement and he wasn't remotely bothered.

Isaac was ordering drinks for a couple of other gynaecology colleagues discussing how many 'faginas' they had examined in clinic today and which type represented the gold standard in faginal grooming, odour and overall optimal anatomical structure and proportion... well, that's what Isaac was discussing anyway.

The others listened with embarrassed and uncomfortably fake interested smiles desperately hoping that no-one else could hear their conversation... or more accurately Isaac's 'fagina monologue', interspersed with his excitable cackling and inevitable whiplash.

He had an unbuttoned, untucked floral shirt on and three gold chains around his neck, one of which had a moderate-sized medallion dangling off it.

---

[27] The Royal Enfield is regarded as the oldest global motorcycle brand still in production and manufactured in India.

"Christ, he actually looks like Mr T out of work too!"

He wore baggy, black trousers and golden-coloured leather Nigerian sandals with his big toes projecting too far out of the front.

I noticed Dave giving Isaac a big hug and watched as his partially unbuttoned shirt had popped out of his trousers again as he stood on tiptoes. His fuzzy navel[28] clearly fancied a drink too. I wonder what it'll have?

"Dev! How a-yoo ma leetl fraynd? An-udda moheetoe?"

In their own carefree manner, traversing intercontinental obstacles, their eyes met and it really was a one hundred percent probable match made in someone's heaven, possibly... with the eye of faith.

I was really pleased for Dave though, he had a good heart and deserved a break.

I liked him.

He seemed to be getting *really* very drunk though.

---

[28] A fuzzy navel is a mixed drink made from peach schnapps and orange juice. It can also be made with lemonade or a splash of vodka.

Chapter Seventeen

Dehydration

It's a Mug's Game

Dave had got utterly shit-faced. I'd had a fair skin-full myself and only just managed to avoid the youthful advances of Alice's roaming eyes.

I hated temptation. Sort of.

Isaac wasn't about to abuse Dave in that state either, I'd made sure of that.

Poor lad. (Poor Dave, not poor Isaac.)

I carried Dave back to the unused on-call room where we'd both set up our drip bags and I sat him down on another of those 1970's, slightly knackered, brown chairs.

He seemed to perk up a bit when he realised I was struggling to get him comfortable.

"What are you doings? Leaving it to me, I'll do it..."

"Hey, alright, man!"

My head was spinning and I began to really feel like I was about to throw up, so letting Dave sort himself out was fine by me.

Anyway, I'd done my bit by getting him back safely and away from the 'Prince of the Nigerian Nightshift'. At least for now.

I slid my bed over to the closed door and hung the bag of Hartmann's solution on the hook at the back. Using the small wheel-clamp control, I ran the fluid through the clear plastic tubing of the giving set.

When all the air was expelled and the dribbles of fluid flowed out of the end, I connected it up to the end of my cannula that I'd partially exposed beneath the bandage on the back of my hand. I set the small control so that the one litre of elixir would slowly drip into my veins over the next four hours or so.

This, of course, was my best estimate given that my current blood levels of alcohol would be affecting my usual fine judgement.

Dehydration causes many of the symptoms of a hangover and the best time to start rehydration is before you go off to sleep.

Even more ideal, is to do it whilst you're actually sleeping and water needn't bother sitting around in your stomach twiddling its thumbs waiting for its journey of intestinal absorption and hoping desperately that it wouldn't be vomited back up in the dead of night.

Dave fell asleep very quickly on the old chair.

His body commenced its own overnight magical mystery tour of biochemical delight and his upper airways attempted an orchestral brass symphony in B flat with Dave starring on the tuba with additional cameo on the timpani.

He let out a slow, wet, yet oddly musical fart and his body twitched.

A myoclonic jerk; when they occur whilst nodding off to sleep, they are called hypnic jerks.

I threw my shoes on the floor, left my clothes on, lay back on the bed and closed my eyes. My head started spinning and my body felt like it was sinking heavily, being pushed down by the intensely strong arm of nausea. I wretched momentarily then fell asleep too.

There was a bang on the door.

"Cleaners!" a gravelly, female voice informed.

What the hell is the time? My watch said nearly 10.30am. At least it was Saturday. No ward rounds.

"OKAAAY!" I shouted, hoping she wouldn't just walk in.

"Oh, sorry, Doctor." I heard her trolley trundle to the next room.

I took a deep breath in and realised that I felt... GREAT! Not even the slightest essence of a headache and my nausea was no more.

I looked up at the drip bag. Empty.

Awesome! It worked.

"Dave?" I croakily enquired.

"Urrgggghhhhhhnnnnggg," came the less than intelligible response.

Well, at least it was a response to my question, which also gave him at least 2 points on the Glasgow Coma Score in the 'verbal' section.

2 out of 5... for sounds... not great.

I sat up on the side of my bed and detached the drip, pulled out the *Venflon* and applied some mild pressure using the bandage to stop the minor venous bleeding.

I glanced over at Dave. He'd slumped to the floor from his chair.

His drip bag was also lying on the floor beside him; it had expanded in volume with not only the original volume of clear fluid but it had been gleefully joined by about two units of, the now clotted, Dewani blood and the tubing had also clotted right up.

"*Fuck!*"

"Dave!" I shook him by the shoulders. He opened his eyes.

3 out of 4... opens eyes to sounds... okay.

I detached the drip tubing.

"Jce? zat-you?"

His mouth was dry, his tongue was purple, dry and a little shrivelled, his lips were a bit flaky and his eyeballs had relaxed backwards a few notches into his skull. His face was also more of a coffee-stained magnolia colour now.

"Yes, Dave it is me!" I lay him down flat. "I'm gonna put your feet up on the chair to get some blood volume to your Humpty Numpty head!"

"nnn'kay," he groaned.

"Here, lift your legs a bit?" He tried to oblige. His socks were falling off and a bit damp.

6… obeys commands on the 'motor' section… great. GCS = 11/15 and hopefully rising.

I poured out some water from the tap into a mug that had been left by the sink.

"Here, start drinking this."

I held up the mug to help him sip.

"Head… hurtings…"

"It's called a fuck-off hangover, Dave, laced with you accidentally venesecting[29] about two units of blood off yourself, you idiot. What did you do?!"

Dave took another sip of water and put his hands on the sides of his temples.

He turned to look at the drip bag on the floor which was full of burgundy clotted blood.

Dave's blood. Dave's life force. Dave's iron carrying workhorse. Dave's plasma.

"Jeez, man, not only did you get shit-faced but you go and do this?"

"I remember puttings drip bag on nail in wall after I took picture off it."

---

[29] Venesection (Phlebotomy) is the act of removing blood from the circulatory system through an incision or puncture for the purpose of analysis, blood donations or treatment of certain blood disorders. When performed as part of a patient's treatment, the aim is to decrease the iron content in the blood or decrease red blood cells.

Dave's grammatical articles were clearly still drifting in and out of a coma.

The picture was indeed on the floor, placed safely against the 'afterthought-of-a-shower cubicle' door. The nail was no longer in the old wall though. Just a small hole and a missing chunk of plaster.

"Looks like the nail you hung it on, Dave, fell out of the wall... with some actual wall."

"Ohhhh," he groaned.

"And how much did you fucking drink last night, man? You were chucking down those mojitos like they were sodding fruit juice!"

Dave was, of course, new to alcohol and had started the evening with a double.

"Don't know..." he took a slow and deep sigh. "Had about eight *Virgin Mojitos*."

"Say what, Dave?" I sat back on the side of the bed, blinked and frowned. Disbelief shrugged it's shoulders and tapped *me* on the shoulder to echo my own surprise.

"I had about eight Virgin..." he repeated.

"Yeah, man, that's what I thought you said! You total Dick-inson! So let me get this straight, you had a double rum... followed by *EIGHT Virgin* Mojitos?!"

"yeah..." he croaked, whilst having only just boarded the slow train to rehydration.

I shook my head and looked up at the crappy polystyrene ceiling tiles, wondering how I had surrounded myself with such intellectual talent.

Is that asbestos up there?

"There's *NO* bloody alcohol in a *Virgin* Mojito, Dave... that's why they call it that! It's *not* a mojito for virgins!"

My exasperated, and indeed non-hungover, voice raised an octave as Dave received his well-earned reprimand.

"Uhhh?" he intelligently retorted, struggling to provide a coherent defence.

"So here *you* are, lying on the floor with a 'hangover', utterly dehydrated and you got battered on what can only be classified as... *fruit juice?*!"

Chapter Eighteen

Home 'Sweet' Home

Death is a Bridge Too Far

Dave and I left the on-call room and disposed of our 'evidence' in a yellow clinical waste dumpster.

Whilst he was probably a bit anaemic and hypotensive now, there was nothing a good cup of tea, about two litres of water and a *Lucozade Sport* couldn't solve.

And maybe some iron tablets... and a blood transfusion.

I decided that I needed to go and see Karen. It'd been far too long and my conscience was having a right go at me.

I went back to my flat which was only about ten minutes walk from the hospital. I'd almost forgotten what it was like. I lived in a two-bedroom basement flat of an old Victorian building; well, it was sort of one small double and one single room that you could squeeze a small double bed into if you didn't want to get out of bed at the sides, then you could call it two doubles.

I walked through the front door and heard the steady dripping of water. As I looked up, I could see a large damp patch on the ceiling and little beads of water were still forming as I watched... drip, onto my face.

"*Bloody hell!*"

Wait... and it smells absolutely...

Lovely!

The water was a very pleasantly sweet, peachy, fruity and slightly herbalescent odour and just a tad... bubbly.

I could hear the sound of running water and realised that the girl who lived in the flat above was clearly having a blissful time, singing, probably shaving her lovely, long legs and sticking cucumber slices to her eye sockets or whatever else women do in the bath (my mind did wander elsewhere momentarily), whilst her bath selfishly overflowed and found it's way through the floorboards to my flat.

"*For fuck's sake!*"

When I had moved in a few years earlier and not long before finishing medical school, there were other overhydrational issues; the estate agent had called me on the day of exchange to joyfully bleat that he'd got good news and bad news... I hated that shit, although we did on occasion, use it on patients.

But not all that "you've got twenty-four hours to live but I should have told you yesterday" nonsense.

The bad news was that there had been a flood because of some washing machine plumbing malfunction and my ceiling was bowing downwards. The good news was that he'd managed to poke it with a broom handle and let all the water out.

Idiot.

The smaller of my two bedrooms also had a real damp problem when I'd moved in and during the work, the builders had discovered a bricked up doorway which led to another hidden room that apparently used to be the old coal cellar.

The room was filled with large rocks and rubble. We'd discovered it at the same time as the Fred and Rosemary West[30] murders were being gradually uncovered which of course led to the 'hilarious' mockery by

---

[30] Fred West (29 September 1941 – 1 January 1995) was an English serial killer who committed at least 12 murders between 1967 and 1987, the majority with his second wife, Rosemary West. The victims dismembered bodies were buried in the cellar or garden of the Wests' Cromwell Street home in Gloucester which became known as the "House of Horrors".

the builders that they'd started to uncover skeletons and rotting corpses.

In fact, the cellar led to yet another bricked up underground doorway but enough was enough.

Anyway, I hadn't got the money to keep going with that or pay for the legal fees should I uncover any actual bodies. I'd had enough of corpses at work, so was not really in the mood for that kind of additional entertainment.

I eventually converted the old cellar and whilst it was never on the original plans, it made for a great secret room if ever I had the need to dispose of anything... or anyone!

I checked my fridge for food. The ice box flap was being forced open by the small glacier within, and you could just make out a bag of frozen peas; I don't even like peas. I must've bought them for soothing one of my regular gym injuries.

Out-of-date milk, soggy salad, mouldy cheddar cheese, an empty jar of marmalade and a slice of pizza which was also gradually evolving a new civilisation.

I closed the door. What's in the cupboards?

Cereal, cereal and more cereal.

That's what happens after an on-call shift or whenever you wake up, you just reach for the cereal. Sometimes an entire week would go by and I'd have lived off cereal.

So much for a balanced diet.

It was cold and dark, even though it was late morning, because the front of the flat was below pavement level and you had to turn the lights on in the daytime. The place was also a bit dusty as I never really had time to vacuum. Plus, when I did have time off,

I was always too knackered and therefore couldn't be arsed.

To be honest, the place was feeling less and less like home and not very private given that you could always hear conversation, heated arguments, foot steps and the inevitable end-results of make-up sex upstairs.

I got showered and changed and began to feel more normal. I tried to dress a little more smartly as I was planning to go and visit Karen's mum.

At least I didn't have a hangover.

I spared a thought for Dave… just a fleeting element of a thought! Well, my mind contemplated whether or not to formulate a thought for Dave but then decided very much against it.

Let's not go overboard.

I gave Karen a quick call to let her know I was setting off.

"Oh, I'm so pleased you're coming over." Her blissfully, beautiful, breathy voice was a genuine tonic to my increasingly stale mind.

I yawned. I wasn't really in the mood for anything except to sit and watch some TV or maybe go to the gym.

I got into my old 'one litre *Peugeot 205*' that fired up with the usual vibrational rattle and hum, the exhaust sounding like an old scooter. It always felt a bit tinny and the crumple zone was probably a full car length.

But it was my own car. One day, I would upgrade when I could afford it.

I sat driving down a dual carriageway feeling generally quite vacant but was also fairly apprehensive about seeing Karen's mum. She really didn't sound well and seeing someone that you know very well, close to death, I guessed, would be a little different to what we were accustomed to at work.

Or were we in some form of bizarre Death Desensitisation Training Camp?

Maybe I would gradually become so desensitised or utterly numb to death, that it would eventually have absolutely no effect on my reactions or my emotions.

Maybe I would no longer fear death.

I was already beginning to recognise the subtle scent of death before it had even struck. I'd witnessed death in a variety of guises and I'd also learned that Death had innumerable tools at his or her disposal to inflict death upon those who were aboard the Death Express.

Most of us were on the slow train with several stops left and quite a few changes. But there were plenty of people and patients who were hell bent on getting to their destinations as quickly as humanly possible.

The scene of Mollie 'almost' Sugden in that white death-wrap on the wards appeared in my mind as I drove.

There wasn't a lot of traffic that Saturday afternoon which allowed for excessive daydreaming and lapses in focus and concentration.

"*Wait...what the...?!*"

About two hundred metres up ahead, there was a public footbridge and what looked like a young lad in the middle of it looking down towards the road beneath.

I hope he isn't planning to throw rocks or something at me as I drove underneath.

I slowed a little.

"*Fuck! He's jumped off!*"

He hit the road like a sack of potatoes or part of a humanitarian airdrop operation. No bounce though.

I slammed on my brakes and screached onto the hard shoulder leaving two long tyre tracks behind me.

I checked my wing mirrors and leapt out of the car. Nothing coming.

I sprinted out into the middle of the dual carriageway to see this young, skinny, scruffy and crumpled heap.

"*Quick... shit!*"

I had no time to even think and just grabbed any part of his clothes that I could and hauled him onto the hard shoulder in front of my slightly skewed car before anything else drove passed and squashed us both.

I laid him flat and shook him a little. He groaned.

I knelt bedside him trying to avoid the bits of broken glass, tyre rubber, fag butts and old chewing gum on the side of the road.

"Hey, buddy, you there?"

He groaned again.

He was breathing and had a pulse.

Both of his femurs and ankles were clearly broken where he had landed. I guessed he might have had a spinal injury as well. He moved his head a little to the side and it didn't seem to cause him pain.

Cervical spine probably okay. No blood I could immediately see.

"*Shit, I don't have a mobile phone... or a stethoscope, or an intravenous line, fluids, chest drain kit, defibrillator, bag and mask, oxygen... any tools of the trade AT ALL!*"

"*I'll be useless, I'm a doctor but I'll be bloody useless!*"

I got up and ran to the back of my car and started waving frantically to flag someone down. To my amazement, given that no one ever seems to stop for hitchhikers or people in distress for fear of their own safety, the first car to drive towards me indicated left and pulled over behind my car immediately putting on his hazard lights.

A slim, middle aged man got out and came towards us.

"Please, sir, do you have a mobile phone?" I panted.

"Sure, what is it?"

I jogged quickly back to my young companion on the floor. The man followed and then the colour drained from his face.

"Oh, shit! I'll call an ambulance!" He frantically dialled 999 and stumbling over his words, relayed all the necessary details.

"Thanks, mate. I'm a doctor. Jacen."

I crouched down by the young lad who wasn't especially talkative, so I had no idea of his name. But, he *was* breathing and I kept a hand on his carotid artery just in case his rapid pulse decided to fade away entirely and then *The Bee Gees* would be summoned, again.

He was getting paler and clearly bleeding; his fractured femurs might have lacerated his superficial femoral arteries and he'd be losing blood volume quickly into this thighs.

I took off my utility *Bat-belt* and my heroic-member-of-the-public sidekick, we'll call him *Robin*, also offered up his own belt and I placed tourniquets on both of our patient's upper thighs that were now actually looking rather swollen and purple.

His ankles looked a mess and really weren't supposed to be facing in the directions that they had currently decided upon.

Blue lights and wailing sirens blazed…

At last, although that didn't take long!

The happy face of Freya eagerly jumped out of the ambulance landing athletically with the balance and poise of a leopard, her golden hair billowing in the breeze, followed by the ambling, slightly overweight Phil with the poise of a hippopotamus, her faithful paramedic partner and certainly less athletic counterpart.

He didn't have much hair to billow in a hurricane.

It was like the arrival of *Wonder Woman*. In my head, she'd also arrived in a bizarre, soft focus, slow motion.

There weren't any superheroes that could describe Phil's arrival. Perhaps 'like the arrival of *Phil*' was enough.

"Jacen! I should've known! You're always finding trouble." She smiled and put down her rucksack full of kit next to us.

Phil brought over the stretcher especially designed to cleverly scoop up patients with suspected spinal injuries.

I told her what had happened, basically recounting how *Superman* here seemed to have had kryptonite for breakfast.

An oxygen mask was put on, an intravenous line was put in, fluids were started and analgesia administered in the blink of an eye.

His pulse was fast, his blood pressure low but *Superman* was still alive.

Freya and Phil scooped up the young *Kal-El* and faster than a speeding bullet, they were gone!

True heroes.

I really must get a mobile phone… and a new utility belt.

Chapter Nineteen

How Did I Even Get Here?

It's not all Fairies and Magic

Yet again, I postponed seeing Karen and was really feeling that external forces were not in my favour. I was in no fit and clear state of mind to deal with the inevitable personal distress, especially with my recent human salvage efforts.

Some time to myself would also be most welcomed at this point. I didn't know what I was becoming.

Why am I doing what I'm doing? How did I get into all of this in the first place? Am I just here to help others at the expense of myself and my own life? Is this job going to continue to dominate everything about me? Will my job define me? Will it ultimately dictate my fate?

Am I playing a complex game of cat and mouse with Death him, her or itself? Death is present around every corner, fuelling every disease process, every cigarette, every alcoholic drink, every narcotic... every truck, every car, every motorcycle and every bridge.

It was merely a matter of time.

Am I the hero or the villain of this piece?

Why am *I* here?

My family's background was something of a story of resilience and courage.

Nana and Grandad had met during World War II, like many of our grandparents. Grandad was lucky to be alive after he managed to blag his way onto a Polish battleship from Belgium and then survive being torpedoed by a German U-boat whilst onboard.

Nana survived many an attack whilst driving Jeeps with supplies for the British Army, often in horrific weather conditions. She faked her age and indeed her height in order to enlist in the first place; she was only five feet two inches tall... and sweet as apple pie, I might also add.

Dad was never meant to stay in England either. He was practically in transit from foreign lands and on his way to America but he met my mum en route at some 'International Enchantment Under the Sea Dance' or something.

Mum always played hard to get because she knew that she'd end up marrying him... what a tease!

I mean seriously, it *is* a wonder I am even here!

I also discovered after very many years that I was born in the early hours of the morning, 1.15am to be precise. I weighed eight pounds and ten ounces and had to be levered out by forceps delivery.

It is also a wonder, therefore, that my skull looks so good. I mean, if you've ever seen the carnage that a forceps delivery can cause, it can be positively brutal. I believe that some babies' heads have been pulled clean off. Perhaps that was just in the nineteen seventies?

Sorry! I acknowledge that you probably had no idea that could happen and need a moment to breathe or actually throw up.

I don't. I can happily move from one macabre thought to another totally different and jolly thought without a flicker. Clearly, the hospital is training me well.

I am pleased that I still have my head... physically anyway.

When I was revising for my fourth year final medical exams, my mum noticed that I was reading about 'foetal distress'.

"Oh! That's what *you* had."

She always told me that I had nearly died during childbirth but I never knew why or how until then.

For a start, Mum never believed she'd become pregnant at all. She subsequently had me and, four years later, my brother.

We were her 'little soldiers'!

"I knew which one was you in the maternity ward because you were like a little foghorn!"

I don't think that I've become that much quieter with age, to be honest.

"You both are my little miracles," she'd remind us.

But most importantly, she'd always tell my brother and I from a young age, which has never left me, "*you are here for a reason.*"

I have never really fully established what that reason is, but if I reflect on my career to date, there must be a thousand reasons right there... perhaps... and maybe a thousand more to come, who knows?

Mum was diagnosed with a condition which causes muscular weakness in all muscle groups; most vitally, it can cause profound weakness in the respiratory muscles. She eventually had to give up being a nurse.

At first we thought it was due to work fatigue but then she began to fall and one day sustained a bad head injury. CO_2 narcosis... Type II respiratory failure: low oxygen levels, high carbon dioxide levels.

Potentially fatal if you fall asleep. Crash out and you might crash out for good.

She has to live with the use of a ventilator at night when she goes to sleep.

This reminds me of another curious condition that does a similar thing, which has the fantastical name of Ondine's Curse![31]

---

[31] Central hypoventilation syndrome (CHS) is a respiratory disorder that results in respiratory arrest during sleep; it can either be congenital or acquired later in life. It is fatal if untreated. It is also known as Ondine's curse.

It is worthy of a short interlude...

Ondine was a nymph, a water goddess and breath-takingly beautiful (in a French folk tale written by *Friedrich de la Motte Fouqué*). The tragic and tender love story kind of goes like most tragic relationships of modern times when a man decides to trade-in for a younger and fitter model, only the women don't usually have the same level of magical powers as Ondine; some may think that they do.

Isaac has certainly tried to describe the occasional enchanted one to me.

So anyway, Ondine lost her immortality and ever-lasting youth once she fell in love with Palermon and began to age as a normal mortal woman. He declared that "every waking breath shall be my pledge of love and faithfulness to you."

After she had a son, she began to lose that youthful beauty and when Ondine later discovered that Palermon had gone back to his ex, Berta, she cursed him such that so long as he was awake he could breathe, but if he ever fell asleep, he would stop breathing and die.

Moral of the story... don't mess with water nymphs or... nymphomaniacs or something.

So Mum, whilst she was weak physically, mentally she became an incredibly strong person. If ever I needed someone to bring me back to Earth when I felt like life was getting to me or I felt like I'd had enough, I just had to think of Mum.

"You are here for a reason, son."

But why did I choose medicine in the first place?

Well, to begin with, my dad would tell me that the only jobs to choose from were a doctor, a lawyer or an engineer. He was a pretty pushy parent but his mantra was always, "once you have your education, no one can take it away from you."

Apart from possibly Dementia herself.

I now know that he did have a fair point.

He'd also tell us that, "if you aim for the stars, you may hit the trees, but if you aim for the trees you may hit the ground."

I liked that one too.

I hated maths and I didn't fancy being a lawyer, so that left one whole career choice! Fortunately for me, I quite enjoyed biology, and in particular human biology, zoology… and dissecting rats! The stage was inevitably set.

I managed to get a small variety of jobs in the hospital as an A-level student just to get some vague experience of what it might be like. I mean, if I hated the general smell of the place then that would not be the best of starts.

Having said that, I can't really see *Tom Ford, Giorgio Armani* or *Paco Rabane* developing any associated Health Service sponsored fragrances in a hurry.

Imagine, '*Flatulence*' by *Calvin Klein*, '*Odour Colon*' by *Givenchy* or '*Stinksofpiss*' *by Aramis*

I can't see it myself.

So I've worked in the Hospital Episodes and Statistics Department which gave me several weeks of experience with hours of filing and coding patients' case notes. Imagine how I would have felt if a clumsy medical student decided to chuck them all over the floor?

I have worked as a hospital cleaner and now have an excellent insight into that world. It is, of course, a vital job keeping everything dust-free; there's a lot of flaky skin in hospital. There's a lot of floor space to mop and several flights of stairs to keep clean, making sure they aren't too slippery and wet so as to cause an unwitting member of the public to become another inadvertent Casualty admission.

There are many bins to empty, many toilets, sinks and baths to keep clean. The army of hospital cleaners, like unsung Oompa Loompas[32], have an unenviable task.

I worked with a private cleaning firm subcontracted by the local hospital which largely employed foreign workers mostly from the African subcontinent. I enjoyed working with them all as they were all always very upbeat. I'd always partner with my experienced friend, Herbert (or Her-bet, as he would pronounce it and what we shall call him), Herbet was also from Nigeria, like Isaac.

I learned an important and insightful lesson from Herbet one morning though. We'd been called up to the wards for Herbet's preferred job, to clean the floors and under the patients' beds on the ward itself. I had been cordially designated the special mission of cleaning all the toilets and bathrooms, obviously, as I was the new boy.

An hour passed. I'd finished.

"Herbet, I'm finished, man. What next?"

"What?! Yoo av feeneeshed arlraydee?"

His succulent, deep voice inflected in astonishment.

---

[32] They come from Loompaland, which is a region of Loompa, a small isolated island in the Hangdoodles. In the Roald Dahl book, they are the only people Willy Wonka will allow to work in his factory because of the risk of industrial espionage being committed by his candy-making rivals.

"Yep, where now?"

I was raring to go, absolutely delighted with my work and my overall efficiency. Everyone would be delighted with my work.

Spotless and beautifully clean.

"Reeelee? Yoo av dun evreetheeng? No-no, nooooo! Jay-san, Jay-san, leesen tu me. You muss tek yor tam... tek yor tam!"

"Hmm, 'kay? Why?"

I was disappointed that my excellent work was seen as somewhat of a failure. Herbet, wasn't best pleased.

He put his arm on my shoulder.

"Jay-san, Jay-san... yoo get ped nat far wat yoo do... but dee tam dat yoo tek to do eet!"

Hmm, okay. I pondered.

"Tek yor tam... tek yor tam!"

You can also work as many hours as a cleaner that you like with loads of ova-tam... err... overtime.

Now, in retrospect, this mantra is fabulously revealing with respect to what happens in hospital these days!

I have also worked as a nursing auxiliary, so I know what it is like to do the general chores of feeding patients, bathing patients, doing the observations round (measuring the blood pressures, pulse rates, temperatures and fluid balance charts), emptying catheter bags and commodes, making beds with perfect hospital corners and doing some nursing night shifts.

So contrary to what you might now think of me, I do have the utmost respect for my nursing colleagues.

On that note, it is interesting to observe that the body habitus of nurses doing night shift is rather more different to that of the day shift. There is a lot more sitting around the nurse's station at night which is quite peaceful, as most people are asleep of course. There's a lot of reading of gossip in women's magazines, although I did find myself reading anatomy textbooks just to make it known that I was no regular nursing auxiliary... in between the gossip mags, clearly.

The night shift nurses had the luxury of being able to consume all the gifts of chocolates and biscuits given to the day staff by the discharged patients' relatives, because the day shift nurses never really had the time to eat them.

Night shift also has a better pay bracket being 'unsociable hours', but if you were antisocial anyway, you were also quids in!

So, as you can imagine, the body mass index of night shift staff was generally much higher than day shift... especially if you were a more permanent night shift fan, which also probably meant you weren't much of a fan of people when they were awake either... and probably, single or divorced... or wanted to be divorced.

So, I knew I could handle the wards. The respect I had gained for the nursing staff was a vital thing to appreciate as a junior doctor; it's kind of like being a motorist and also having passed your motorcycle test where you ought to have an added, vital and more considerate perspective.

During this job, I was also given the opportunity to attend the operating theatre for the first time. The surgeon, who knew my mum was a nurse at that hospital and that I wanted to attend medical school, kindly allowed me some observer experience. I remember that very well.

The first operation was a thyroidectomy. Now, the thyroid gland is in the neck and if it enlarges it can be over- or indeed underactive and it can cause a swelling or 'goitre' which can, in turn, cause airway compression and shortness of breath.

So, my first patient was being prepared, I had scrubbed up in baggy blues, had my white theatre clogs on, which were a bit hard underfoot (we wear soft rubber *Crocs* nowadays) and I wore my nice blue theatre cap.

The patient had their head and body covered, aside from a rectangular window over the neck which had been prepared by brown, liquid iodine to sterilise the skin.

The theatre felt warm, the lights were dimmed aside from the ceiling mobile spotlights that brightly focused on the surgeon's operative field.

The scalpel was handed over by the scrub nurse to the surgeon. The blade glinted in the light and a silver, metallic flash briefly struck my retina.

I blinked. I felt a little sweaty. My throat was a little dry.

Could I do this?

The patient's throat was cut from left to right, the underlying yellow fat cells revealed themselves by rolling outwards at the edge of the incision in a collective, synchronised display and blood oozed and trickled out of the wound.

I rubbed my own neck in empathy.

The surgeon used the diathermy forceps to coagulate the multiple tiny capillaries to stop them from bleeding. The smell of burning, cooking flesh drifted pungently towards me. I unavoidably inhaled it.

The lights got brighter. I became sweatier. A wave of nausea enveloped me.

The lights got suddenly darker.

Now the back of my head hurt and felt a little sticky. I leaned against the cold wall at the back of the theatre and felt heavy. Two pretty faces were in front of me.

"Is he okay?" a male voice enquired, a few feet away. Sounded like the surgeon.

"His eyes are open now and he's a bit pale but we'd better clean up the blood," came the reply from the woman before me.

The cold wall was known by everyone else in the room, as the *floor*. The blood was mine. The pretty faces had come to welcome me back to the conscious world.

Is that a spot of blood on the ceiling?

Chapter Twenty

Fire!

Mondays, Goosebumps and Prunes

I sat at the nurse's station having a cup of tea and tucking into the *Quality Street* on the desk; the particularly popular chocolate-covered hazelnut ones in the shiny, purple wrappers had all gone. The box was full of scrunched up, used wrappers and there were only the solid caramel ones left; they were getting really stuck in my teeth.

It felt kind of weird having had a weekend off and I also wondered what mischief our patients had got up to whilst we were away and if we'd acquired any new ones - sometimes that happened if the bed managers wanted to play 'musical beds' or 'hunt your patient' again.

You also had to trust the other teams and the nurses to carry out our clinical management plans. That meant they'd have to read our carefully structured scribbles in the notes and for the nurses' handover not to become a game of Chinese Whispers.

It really is horrifically amazing how many times a patient can develop a new diagnosis just because somebody didn't listen or read properly.

Davinder rocked up on to the ward, not only still looking decidedly pale, for him, after our night out but he was walking funny again. Dirty boy. I put two and two together... and got Isaac.

"Good weekend, Dave?"

Despite his pallor, he still had a little glint in his eyes.

"I spent most of it trying to sleepings off the hangover..."

"The exsanguination, you mean?"

"Your fault, not mine," he reminded me.

He pottered about getting the usual blood results, microbiology culture results and x-ray reports from the weekend.

Fair shout, it was my idea to cannulate ourselves and perhaps I should have at least made sure his drip bag was hung up properly, but then again, I'd hardly been fully compos mentis myself.

BLEEEP BLEEEP

Outside Line.

"Jace, it's Fi. I'm not coming in this morning... gastroenteritis, really bad, really, err... liquidy... haven't been off the loo all night."

Haven't been off the Rob all night, you mean.

"Duvet day then, Fi? Well, it's really lucky that it's Monday. Who likes Mondays?"

The Boomtown Rats don't, for starters. Plus, Monday is the most common day of the week for sickness to strike like a bolt of lightning from the blue. How selfish it is of bacteria, viruses and migraine to pick on a Monday morning to strike down the workforce of Great Britain straight after a weekend of drunken debauchery and shenanigans. Honestly, illness on top of a hangover was too much for anyone to take.

"Yeah, sorry, I'm sure you guys will cope. I can't come in for another two days either, even after I feel better with a fully formed stool, according to 'micro'."

Microbiology had its rules and regulations to avoid transmission of fatal infectious disease. After all, what might knock some of us down for a few days might kill some of our more brittle and vulnerable punters.

"Okay, enough information. Just make sure that the *Disney* Princess takes good care of you!"

"Piss off, Jace... *shhh... Rob, get off me, I'm on the phone to the hospital,*" came a muffled voice. Fi hadn't quite managed to cover her hand over the receiver and her current and obvious nakedness exuded down the phone line, I imagined.

She deserved a duvet day. Dave and I would be fine. Dr Bodman would be up at the Tower today as well.

Nurse Becky 'Nightshade' joined us for our round. She was chewing some pink gum, squinted in my direction and blew out a bubble which popped before it could reach a size whereby it'd be noted as blatantly unprofessional behaviour.

I focused on her with knowing, irritated eyes as my irises momentarily constricted and turned from brown to a shade of red and my stare bore a clean, imaginary split right through her cranium.

Our last exchange revealed how little she knew about the on-call rules and etiquette. *Mrs Migginski has passed a stool...* indeed she may have done... Nurse Nightshade would regret that.

"On night shade... er... shift last night, Nurse?"

She suppressed a yawn, knowing she'd be off duty soon and then off to bed.

"Yes, Doctor Manson. Why?"

"Oh, I don't know, you just look pretty *rough* this morning, Nurse... like you could really do with some undisturbed sleep?"

I wasn't about to waltz around a polite insult. I cogitated upon the copulation of cunning and catharsis culminating in the creation of the foetus of revenge.

Maybe I wouldn't get her back today or indeed tomorrow, but I would get her back and from this day forward I'd be ready for my revenge, stalking and plotting, waiting to get her back and whenever she looked behind her, she'd see me there, waiting... to get her back.

"Oh, thanks," she said, clearly insulted by my compliment.

"Come on, Dave," I beckoned.

"Comings." He bobbled over with the notes trolley.

"So, Mrs Laflamme…" I flicked through her weekend cases notes and observations chart.

I looked up.

"Where's Mrs Laflamme? It says Blaise Laflamme on the headboard."

"That *is* Mrs Laflamme, Doctor," Nurse Nightshade confirmed and flashed me a sarcastic, brief smile, her bottom lip stretched pulling her lip ring taught. She obviously still had 'the hump'.

Oh, that's just the beginning, Nurse.

Mrs Laflamme had no make up on, her red hair had been combed to the side and she was as thin as a stick and rather shrivelled.

"Bloody hell! How much weight has she lost?"

Shit, no one has reduced her diuretics over the weekend. Industrial dehydrating agents and we'd banned the OXO cubes and the water.

"She hasn't been weighings today," said Dave, "but she has passings lots of urine."

We need to stop these water tablets.

"Why didn't you call anyone, Nurse? She's turned into a prune! In fact, prunes themselves would be accusing her of having an eating disorder."

"I'm a bit dizzy, Doctor," Mrs Laflamme tried to unstick her tongue from the dry roof of her mouth to lick her brittle lips.

"Don't worry, Blaise, we'll get you sorted."

She took a sip of water through a pink crazy straw and let out a small eructation.

Burp!

"Oh, excuse me." She placed an apologetic, shrivelled hand on her chest as if trying to block more wind from escaping.

I crossed off some 'poison' from her drug chart and we moved on.

You can't trust anyone.

Sat upright in the next bed was a rare vision reading a copy of *OK! Magazine*.

Dark-blonde, shoulder-length hair, with a slight natural curl and green eyes. She clearly kept herself in great shape. She was deeply tanned and she made the hospital gown look like it had been designed by *Versace*. It hung off one smooth and blemish-free shoulder and a couple of centimetres of cleavage took a slow, succulent, deep breath, stretched seductively and wished Dave and I, well just me, a very "Good Morning!"

What on Earth was she doing on our ward?

"Sarah Henderson… twenty-eight, moved by the bed manager, flown back from Australia, presented with a swollen left calf, probable DVT[33]," Nurse Nightshade officiously informed us without insinuating in any way that our next patient might very well be insanely attractive.

Miss Henderson looked up at me from her magazine, fluttered her emerald eyes and smiled a xylophone of straight and very white teeth… perfect… dammit.

Doctor-patient personal relationships were very much frowned upon, so special care, caution and subtlety would be required here.

---

[33] Deep Venous Thrombosis - clot formation, commonly in the deep calf veins of the legs but they can occur elsewhere.

"Dave, move on to the next patient with Becky and I'll just pull these curtains round and assess our new patient here."

Dave looked at me, fake-gasped whilst putting his hand in front of his mouth and awkwardly winked at me.

Dave and Becky moved on as requested, I sat on the chair beside Sarah's bed and thumbed through her sparse set of admission notes.

"So, Sarah, a long haul flight... I see you are... on the pill..."

"Yes but it's not because of sex," she quickly blurted. "I'm just on it for period stuff... you know, just so you... err... know... *Doctor*."

It seemed like her reaction was some sort of hint which I would need to acknowledge with the utmost professionalism and not see it as an overt come-on.

"I see," I continued, seriously furrowing my brow and trying to feign some concentration and a consultoid-tone, whilst annoyingly feeling a wave of attraction towards her, "and... I also see that you smoke about ten cigarettes per day?"

She noticed my disapproving tone and subtle shake of the head.

"But I'm giving up of course," she followed up, again wanting to impress me.

"I'm sure you are, Miss Henderson. Well we need to run a few tests, check your clotting profile results and make sure you haven't got a type of thrombophilia[34] which can make it more likely for your blood to clot."

---

[34] Thrombophilia - a hypercoagulability or prothrombotic state, is an abnormality of blood coagulation that increases the risk of blood vessel thrombosis.

This was unlikely given the long-haul flight and her smoking and contraceptive pill history, but we could certainly hang onto her for a couple more days. Not the end of the world.

"I just need to examine your leg, Sarah, if you could just come and stand up here."

I turned around, squatted down, placed the notes on the chair and started to put on a pair of gloves. As I did so...

"Oh, good, so you'll need me to take my clothes off to have a proper look..."

Before I could say anything further, I spun around still on my haunches to be greeted by Sarah, at about five feet four inches tall, standing facing away from me, her peachy, pert, tanned and lightly goose-bumped bottom merely centimetres from my face. Her perfect buttocks were fabulously divided within her natal cleft by an extremely small, lacy, purple thong.

The missing Quality Streets.

She had a small heart-shaped tattoo just beneath her left gluteal fold at the top of her smooth hamstring, I couldn't help but notice.

Her thighs and calves were clearly very athletic, except for the left one which was indeed ever so slightly more swollen than the right. Her feet and toes were well cared for and her toenails were a lightly, glossy purple to match her underwear.

Sarah had slipped off her *Versace* hospital gown, allowing it to fall to the floor beside me and she had not been wearing her bra. The absence of tan lines on her back sent my heart racing a little faster.

A full examination would of course be required... she could 'easily' have a pulmonary embolism and I'd *need* to fully examine her cardiovascular system which would mean a stethoscope to the chest, palpating her... apex beat beneath the left breast, pressing a palm to her sternum and feeling for a right ventricular... heave...

I felt my brow sweating and a sudden vague but very real disturbance in my *Calvin Kleins*.

Okay, stop. No, No, NO!

"*NURSE*... Chaperone *please*!"

I grabbed Sarah's hospital gown and covered her up just as Nurse Nightshade popped her head through the curtains.

"Nurse, I'd just like you to get Miss Henderson comfortable on the bed so that I might examine her properly?"

I held my breath for a few seconds and exhaled a sigh of relief whilst also allowing the increased blood supply to my own 'swelling attention' to be otherwise re-diverted.

Sarah lay down in a more conventional position on the bed for her clinical examination.

Right move. This could have been worse.

Nurse Nightshade watched me like a necessary hawk whilst I confirmed that Sarah's physical examination did not reveal anything unexpected.

Her skin was like velvet.

"Okay, Sarah, we just need to get some test results and get you stabilised on the blood thinning medication and then we'll let you go home."

The beads of sweat on my brow were still engaged in a sociable gathering.

"You're the doctor, Doctor," she sighed, smiled and winked at me out of Nurse Nightshade's field of view.

"Err... yes... absolutely," I stumbled over the few words that had decided to make the short trip from my mouth and into her general direction, "and we'll have to review you again back in clinic in about four to six weeks after we send you home... erm... just in case."

Of... what... exactly??

"Oh, yes, I really *mustn't* miss my clinic appointment with *you*, Doctor. Best to make sure... and get all the test results, of course."

Ah, yes, the test results!

"err... yes... of course... the test results... yes, good. So erm, yes, well I'd better finish the ward round, so I'll check on you later."

"Don't forget, Doctor... Manson." She read my hospital identification name badge which was clipped to my trouser belt, the photo ID card hanging over my trouser zip. She look at my groin and slowly licked her lips.

WAAAAILLLLL WAAAAILLLLL

I jumped out of my trance. The ward sirens and lights flashed.

A very well-spoken and unruffled female voice proclaimed:

"*An incident has occurred in the building, please proceed to the nearest emergency exit. An incident has occurred in the building, please proceed to the nearest emergency exit.*"

The noise grated loudly and the red flashing lights threatened to induce an epileptic seizure.

Fkkssake, the bloody fire alarm.

I bet Isaac was making toast for breakfast in the mess again. It *was* just after midday after all.

So, for each fire engine, the hospital would be charged in the order of four thousand pounds and the fire brigade were usually kind and generous enough to send at least two, big, shiny red ones and at least a dozen strapping firemen.

All the nurses quite enjoyed the break of a fire alarm, not just because of the break from ward life but because some used the experience to try and attract the attentions of one of the firemen; it is a wonder we didn't have even more false alarms and eat more burnt toast.

You were obliged to drop everything, except a patient dangling naked on a hoist hammock, mid-transfer, onto their bed or into a nice hot bath. Ward Sisters usually left skeleton staff on the wards to look after the remaining patients whilst everyone else dashed for safety.

Many of us just put our fingers in our ears to mute the alarms and got on with our lists of essential tasks. But seriously, if I was truly involved in the remake of the *Towering Inferno*, if I could smell smoke, feel the heat and see actual flames of fiery fireness, I *would* be out of there. Of course, if there *really* was a fire, then everyone would be evacuated in a quick, slick, panic-free and well-rehearsed fashion.

Yes, I do recall a total of… mmm… *zero* hospital evacuation drills to practice this.

It was, however, an interesting experience milling around outside of the hospital in whatever zone you had gathered in. There were staff, members of the public and of course the ambulatory patients.

Many of the patients seemed clearly fit for discharge; they adopted the 'sick role', they had lost their power and their identities whilst wearing their hospital issue gowns and pyjamas. Some were also garnished with a cigarette and copy of the *Daily Mirror* tabloid newspaper in one hand, a coffee in the other, whilst dragging an intravenous drip stand on wheels.

On this occasion, I couldn't be arsed staying on the ward and I probably needed to mentally and pudendally[35] cool off after my experience with Miss Sarah Henderson.

I wandered off leaving Dave to fend for himself and queued up to grab a quick life-saving coffee and a small, homemade *Bakewell* slice on the way out, just before the elderly voluntary workers of the WRVS[36] had to leave their posts to also urgently save themselves from the raging, burning, smoking, melting building.

A darkly bearded, emaciated, pale man sat on his wheelchair outside the hospital main entrance wearing a hospital gown and open-toed slippers. His legs were flung apart and his orangey-pink and hairy testicles hung unceremoniously on display for their 'one afternoon only' exhibition for everyone outside to appreciate, whether they wished to catch a glimpse of them… or indeed not. He had a half-burned cigarette in his stiff, bony, nicotine-stained fingers.

The lifetime barrage of cigarettes had gradually and completely blocked the arterial supply to his lower legs and, in particular, his tootsies; well his legs were kind of patchy, purply, puce and he had ten shrunken, shrivelled, black toes.

Ten flame raisins all in a row.

It looked like dry gangrene and at some stage they would all break off in turn. This often happened whilst

---

[35] The pudendal nerve is the main nerve of the perineum that carries sensation from the external genitalia of both sexes and the skin around the anus and perineum.

[36] Women's Royal Voluntary Service - or the 'Doris Shop' as I'd like to call it. They were usually called Doris you see.

patients slept, snapped off by a stiff, starched hospital sheet.

Another day, another toe would be lost only to be discovered by an unwitting student nurse whilst changing the bedsheets.

Several other visiting members of the public stood around 'gassing' to each other, sporting varying degrees of obesity and smoking because of the stress of 'it all'. They'd be simultaneously stuffing their faces with pasties or doughnuts in front of a hospital sign saying 'NO SMOKING AREA' and stubbing out cigarette butts on an ever expanding orange and white pile of other used death sticks.

What a fabulous advert for our wonderful National Health Service.

What really pissed me off though, was seeing members of staff smoking too and I couldn't help but notice one of the senior consultant *cardiologists* sucking in a gratifying drag, whilst the firemen wandered past with their big, yellow helmets and black boots.

Self-proclaimed Professor James McTavish was a tall, greying, Scottish cardiologist who always stunk of stale tobacco on his ward rounds. I mean, Jeez, you're a cardiologist dealing with coronary artery disease caused by excessive smoking and you have the gall to do ward rounds reeking of fags whilst preaching the benefits of not smoking?

Cunning? After all, smoking keeps us all in business. The more the public smoked, the sicker they got, the more smoking-related diseases they were awarded, the longer they waited on the ever increasing waiting lists and the more likely it was that they... *would go Private*!

Ker-ching. £££.

Ban smoking then. I hate it. Oh, but why?

Yes, the government reaps the benefits of taxes on cigarettes and then has to re-plough it back into the NHS to treat the very diseases they could have prevented in the first place had they bothered to ban cigarettes, at least in public places.

But, this is offset by the fact that these tar and toxin-poisoned humans will die early from heart disease, emphysema and cancer; cigarettes accelerate the ageing process, unravel your genes and damage their reparative capability.

These people will no longer draw their pensions when they are dead and no longer be a burden on the NHS; some might posthumously try via relatives who'd prefer to illegally keep their financial memory alive.

Ker-ching. Everyone's a winner.

I mean, what's the point of curing everything with common sense or a magic bullet? We'd be out of a job!

Why even find a cure for cancer? The drug companies make billions of pounds from drug therapy that may or may not give you a few extra days or weeks of miserable, painful, nausea-ridden and opportunistically-infected life.

What if I told you that you could cheaply consume, for example, high doses of vitamins, an aspirin or a turmeric capsule per day and you would no longer need expensive drugs? The drug companies would not take long to silence me. They'd stand to lose one massive income stream.

As I've already said, there's money to be made off other people's misery.

Same goes for the obese and the alcoholics. Everything in moderation. But if you can eat yourself to death with sugar, fast food and processed food whilst washing your misery down with a copious amount of fizzy drink and cheap alcohol, go for it!

Once you're dead, you're dead.

Start them young too... make fizzy, alcoholic, sugary addictive drinks for the young punter. *Alcopops*, easy to drink, taste great, get battered, fall over in the street with your short skirt over your face or your piss-soaked trousers around your ankles, have a fight, smash yourself up, drive your car whilst you're pissed or high as a kite. Crash your car, kill yourself horrifically and instantly or perhaps try stretching the experience out a little more and get young-onset liver cirrhosis. Suffer *that* way instead whilst your liver packs up and you bleed to death in a sea of jaundiced soup.

Let me tell you, it's not great viewing, whilst trying to stop a young person drowning in their own blood and bilirubin.

It *will* be an epidemic and there aren't enough transplants to go around. Well, unless you give the livers of the accident victims to all the other kids.

What a bloody mess. But don't worry, the NHS is here to save the day.

Don't even get me started on recreational drugs... yet! Anyway, I digress... again.

At least Fi was at home avoiding all this excitement.

I noticed Isaac ambling out of the front of the hospital. At least it wasn't raining either, or his feet would get wet.

"Isaac!" I waved him over.

He wandered over, his shirt untucked and his golden leather sandals were on the wrong way around.

"Dee faya men told me to leev dee mess."

"Oh no, Isaac, the firemen told you to leave the mess? How could they interrupt your busy day like that? What was on TV?"

My monotoned sarcasm oozed gloriously from every syllable.

"Yes, I know! I was get-een ray-dee fa fagina cleeneec. I had jus med tost an was watchin Staskee an Hoach an dee teevee."

"Yes?" I waited expectantly for the impending admission of arson.

It wasn't the only arson he was getting.

Whilst I did love *Starsky and Hutch's* adventures in *Bay City* with *Huggy Bear*, I didn't usually have the same amount of time in the doctors' mess as Isaac to sit and watch an entire episode without interruption.

"Eet was nat ma folt dat dee tost cat fayar!"

Fkksake!

Chapter Twenty-One

April Fools

Trying to get Ahead of the Game

I must have been in REM sleep[37] about to wake up and I was feeling a delightful, warm, soft sensation below my waist as if I was wading through warm, tropical waters. I was really enjoying this dream.

A sudden surge of excitement overwhelmed me and I awoke with a gasp and a spectacular display of blue and green flashing spots sparked and showered before my eyes.

"Mmm, good morning," whispered Jessica, licking her lips and swallowing slightly.

Her dark hair fell shaggily over her face and as I looked down, she revealed herself from under the duvet, lightly brushing her ample assets across my lower abdomen and she settled her head on my chest.

A very good morning indeed.

I took a very deep breath in and turned to check the clock on Nurse Totten's bedside table.

7.52am. I had about half an hour to get ready. At least she didn't live far away from the hospital.

"I'd better get up."

"So soon? I *am* impressed," she teased.

"Funny. Hey, you got Becky's home number? I need to let her know about one of her patients," I innocently enquired, remembering my vow.

"Sure, it's in my phone by the clock. She's on nights though I think."

Good. I chuckled internally.

"I'm going to run a bath. My shift isn't till this afternoon and I fancy a soak."

---

[37] The sleep that occurs at intervals during the night characterised by Rapid Eye Movements and often dreaming; it occurs in cycles of 90-120 minutes.

She pulled back the duvet, planted a juicy kiss on my lips and got out of bed. She lit up a cigarette, dipped her little finger in a small packet of white powder by the bed and rubbed it around her gums.

"See you around."

For now, it was best just to ignore all that shit if I could wake up in the manner that I'd done this morning. Right now our 'relationship', if you can call it that, was just a drop-in service but it suited both of us with our busy jobs and shift work. We didn't need the hassle of commitment.

I wasn't sure, but I might have been starting to feel some real emotion for Jessica.

Although, I did recall that I was actually supposed to be in a committed relationship already but I couldn't really commit to it right now. Karen might as well have been resident in the parallel universe that I should have been inhabiting.

I checked Jess' mobile phone, found Becky's number and put it in my own new mobile phone.

Good. I am now armed and dangerous.

I left Jess' place wandering past the various members and non-members of the house in their varied states of inebriation and states of reality.

Some of them I recognised as residents and some I didn't. It was hard to tell who was actually living there and it felt more like a kind of hostel rather than a house of flatmates. People would just come and go freely, some would sleep over and some would have lost consciousness due to pharmaceutical intoxication in the large top floor lounge.

There was a general respect for the house though and you knew that there was a sort of controlled chaos about the place.

I slipped out of the front door with an acknowledging nod to another semi-conscious male stranger as they wandered in fresh from late night, early morning clubbing. I noticed, as he passed me, that his pupils were paradoxically rather dilated as it was actually quite bright outside this morning.

I took a short cut into the main hospital by slipping in through the Casualty entrance. A nurse was sat on a chair on the inside of the automatic sliding door, greeting people as they entered.

"Hello, good morning, welcome to Accident and Emergency. Please check in at reception, take a seat and you'll be seen as soon as we can."

With her clipboard and pen in her hands, she smiled broadly. Whether she was doing an audit of patient attendance or something, I didn't know but she *was* a fully trained staff nurse, maybe newly trained, but trained nonetheless.

It was like going shopping at the *Disney Store.*

"Well, hello there! Welcome to the Disney Store!" the bouncy, musical voice would sing. *"Let me know if I can help you in any way. Just to let you know, we have offers on Mickey Mouse rucksacks, Donald Duck talking toys and you can even stuff your very own cuddly Disney Princess. Have a magical day now!"*

You might even get a cartoon sticker slapped on your chest and a fake, cheesy grin to painfully scrape out of your consciousness when you left.

So... very clever. The hospital could statistically report back to the government that *all* patients are seen by a trained nurse almost immediately upon arrival in Casualty. The fact that the less urgent ones would have to wait six hours to see a doctor for actual treatment didn't really matter.

It's now a numbers game. And not an especially *magical* one at that.

Isn't it April Fool's Day? Maybe this was a prank.

Nope… it wasn't.

I wandered up to the mess to meet up with the team.

"Mornings, Jace. You get luckings last night?"

"Morning, Dave. No. But I did this morning."

Fi was cozied up to Rob on one of the sofas like a sickeningly happy couple in Annoyingly Nauseous Land.

"Alright bar-stard. We're on-call again today," sang her familiar and irritatingly joyous voice, "we've also got a final year med student, Helena, joining us on-call today. So be nice to her, Jace."

"Is that an April Fool, bitch?" I casually gave her the middle finger but I knew that she wasn't lying.

"Cuppa Mrs Brown[38] before we start?" I generously offered.

Rob and Fiona, or *Robona,* as they were now known, both nodded. A refill was totally required.

"*Dave*, stick the kettle on again matey?" I slumped down on the other sofa next to Matt Dundee who was just finishing his shift on Intensive Care.

"I'll have a cup too, please!" I hollered.

"Basta*rrr*d!" Davinder gave me an extra special release of a rollocking, rolling 'r' before buggering off to the kitchen.

---

[38] 'Mrs Brown' was code for a cup of tea. So in the middle of a ward round, we could peel away from any situation for a break by uttering those all important words, "we need to urgently review Mrs Brown next."

"And some toast pleaaaaase... with jaaaaam! Thank yooooouuu!" I tried to sound all grateful but this was probably now defined as bullying and abuse in the workplace.

"G'day mate! Howzit hanging?"

Idiot.

"You gonna play any jokes on the nurses today?" he upwardly inflected in his probably fake nasally twang.

"Hmm, yeah might do. I got a couple of tricks up my sleeve."

"You tried getting one of the student nurses to catch a flatus sample for microbiology? I tried that back in Oz. I hid behind a curtain and watched her trying to shove the sample bottle up the patient's arse... brilliant!"

I fell about laughing imagining Alice trying to get someone like Mrs Migginski to fart into a sterile sample tube and screw on the cap before all the gas escaped.

I might try that one myself.

"Well, last year I sent a full blood count bottle to the haematology lab filled with sterile water for injection with the clinical details 'query anaemia' on the form."

"Yeah, good one mate, I like that."

We chuckled again at our childish, superficial banter.

"Anyway, I gotta shoot mate. I'm off shift now. Couple of days off. Might go for a surf."

Bloody anaesthetists.

I don't know. Anaesthetists and radiologists (I imagined) had it very easy. Well certainly Isaac's style of gynaecology also seemed like an easy life.

It was, after all, about work-life balance... that Mecca, that Utopia, that Heaven on Earth.

Waitress Davinder delivered our final tea and toast before hitting the frontline.

We got up to go to the ward where we needed to review Peter Clementine. He'd been with us for ages. His liver really wasn't playing ball and we were having to keep draining fluid out of his abdominal cavity, give him intravenous vitamins, antibiotics, protein and clotting factors. I wasn't sure if he was really going to get home, although he remained as cheery and as yellow as always.

He also continued to get rather skinny aside from his fluid-inflated belly.

Peter was sat up in bed with his black glasses over the tip of his nose reading a crossword puzzle book to help pass the time.

"Alright, Doc! What do doctors do when us patients die?"

"I don't know, Peter, what do we do?"

"Barium."

"Okay. Nice one, Peter, and surprisingly clean for you!"

Student Nurse Alice Sharples joined us today. No trained staff again but she would absolutely do nicely.

"Good morning, Dr Manson."

Alice tried hard to sound like the increasingly confident and more experienced nurse she was becoming but succeeded in going deep red and blotchy with embarrassment... again.

I clearly noticed but didn't want to draw attention to it. I liked Alice, she was very good at her work, very professional and always extremely eager to help in any way she could.

"Oh, look! She really fancies *you*, Doc! Look at that lovely blush! Ain't she cute!"

Peter wasn't about to ignore Alice's unfortunate gift of patchwork colour and sat with his arms folded and a broad grin across his yellow face.

Alice's shade hit another level of red. We could almost make out a red Martian landscape on her neck and I was desperate to make Peter stop.

"Come on, Peter, leave her alone."

"Sorry, Nurse." He looked apologetically at Alice who smiled at him through gritted teeth.

"That's okay, Peter." Her lovely Irish tones were a tonic and Peter calmed right down.

"Peter needs his cannula re-siting, Doctor," Alice said, passing on vital information from morning handover.

"Thank you, Alice, Dr Dewani will be around later."

Fi arrived with Helena to join us wearing her short, white 'student doctor' coat.

Helena was of Greek-Cypriot origin with olive skin and shoulder-length, dark hair. She had a reputation for being a keen and excellent distinction student.

Honestly, can I please start working with far less attractive people? It is messing with my deranged brain. Can I also please stop thinking like this?

It's quite okay, I am indeed working with less attractive people. I was stood next to Dave.

"Team, this is Helena."

We all nodded our greetings and before Peter could spout out anymore embarrassing comments, I rapidly pointed a stern finger straight at him like a quick-fire draw in a Wild West shootout and then waggled it from side to side.

No, no!

He formed an imaginary zip at the corner of his mouth and slowly pretended to zip up his lips whilst raising an eyebrow over one of his deepeningly jaundiced eyes.

I had an idea.

"Fi? You, Dave and Helena carry on and I'll re-site this IV cannula on Peter."

Dave momentarily looked shocked that I'd volunteered for such a mundane task that was surely well beneath my high level of clinical skills.

He should be... and it was.

"Okay, see you in a bit." Fi took the team onwards.

I went and sat next to Peter.

"Hey, Peter, you know it's April Fool's Day today right?"

"Is it? I'd lost all track of time, why?"

"Well, I've got an idea to get Alice."

"I am all ears, Doc!"

He put down his crossword book again and pushed himself up a little further in bed.

"Now, I was going to try and get her to catch one of your farts to send to microbiology, but a) I think she's too smart and would see right through that one and b) it's probably not that fair on you to get your bare bottom out for her."

"Oh, I don't know about that, Doc! I think she's seen it before though."

"Really?!"

"No, you're right, Doc. She'd fall in love with me straight off at another eyeful!"

We sniggered like two naughty schoolchildren.

"Well, I've got another idea. If you roll up your pyjama sleeve, I'll put the new cannula in there for your IV fluids 'n' stuff. That'll be your real, working one. We'll then roll down your sleeve to cover it."

"Okay, Doc... where's the fun in that?"

The best places for intravenous cannulas were in the back of the hand, the wrist or the elbow creases. If you were desperate, you could try a foot vein and if you were more adventurous, you could just stick a decent line in the internal jugular vein in the neck or the common femoral vein at the top of the thigh.

"That's not all."

I leaned in a little closer and looked around me like an overacting, fake secret service encounter with a Russian spy whilst checking for enemy snipers. I then lowered my voice a little more to the level of an audible whisper.

"Then, Mr Clementine, my good man... I will stick a *fake* cannula to the middle of your forehead[39]. But don't worry. I won't put a tourniquet around your neck to get a vein to come up as that would risk shutting the blood supply off to your brain and probably cause your face to swell like a balloon."

"Oh, good, thanks for that, Doc." He nodded approvingly.

An iatrogenic hanging on the ward, even on April Fool's Day, would be frowned upon by Sister Sledge.

"I'll first remove the central needle and just stick down the plastic tube on top of the skin with the special dressing for it, so that it looks good and authentic."

We proceeded with our plan and I joined back up with the others.

---

[39] The supratrochlear vein begins on the forehead in a venous plexus which communicates with the frontal branches of the superficial temporal vein; these veins converge to form a single trunk, which runs downwards near the midline of the forehead. An ideal candidate for an intravenous cannula!

"Hey, Alice, the cannula is done for Mr Clementine. He's got difficult veins but it's okay, I found one."

"Okay, thank you, Jacen," came the grateful Irish, elvish response.

Alice was so lovely and sweet that I almost began to feel guilty... but not *that* guilty. In fact, Guilt on this occasion, had it's feet up in the corner with a coffee whilst reading a book called *Guilt is but an Illusion*.

She excused herself and went to set up Peter's next intravenous drugs.

He was still sat in bed doing his crosswords with a nice, neat bandage around his head.

Alice expressed a little surprise but given that Peter wasn't complaining, she uncovered the end of the cannula and set up the intravenous line, unconventionally sticking the tubing with great care to the side of his head and cheek and switching it on.

Peter looked totally ridiculous, the cannula was of course not in a vein and the fluid began to flow down the side of his nose, across his face and drip rapidly on to his pyjamas.

"Oh, no! I'm sorry, Mr Clementine, I don't know what has happened here. It must have tissued out of the vein." She panicked.

Peter started chortling, clearly not minding in the slightest.

Sister Sledge walked over, suspicious of all the commotion. She just stood behind Alice, folded her solid arms like a Sergeant Major and stared at Mr Clementine, who was soaked.

"Alice! What in the name of Florence Nightingale are you up to? Who put that cannula in Mr Clementine's head?! I'll be filing an incident report about this Boo-ha-ha, Hullabaloo and Tom Foolery!"

As she pompously exaggerated her displeasure, it dawned on her today's date.

"Oh, Alice, you silly girl! Turn off the drip please. Mr Clementine, *you* should know better!"

Peter felt like a naughty school boy being reprimanded by headmistress but it was the most fun he'd had during his rather protracted hospital stay.

Sister Sledge softened a little and the suggestion of a smile began to migrate across her pinkish face.

"I'm going to give that mischief-maker, Dr Manson, a piece of my mind!"

Of course, I'd talk my way out of it with just a dash of flirtation, some *Jaffa Cakes* and all would be well again with Ward Sister.

We finished the round in good time today and managed to discharge a decent bunch of our long stay patients.

Social care had finally come up trumps, stairlifts had been installed, Occupational Therapy assessments had been done, Warfarin anticoagulation levels had stabilised, antibiotics were working, some of our patients had actually begun to feel a whole lot better and were ready to get out of this place.

Were we being pranked by Social Services today? I really hoped not.

Just as well, as we really needed the beds. The GP calls were already starting and I was sure that we were going to get busy... but then again, when weren't we?

One could always hope.

The team began its usual penance back to the Medical Admissions Unit and Casualty.

I took the opportunity to liaise with the others after taking a well-earned 'natural break'. After all, these breaks were apparently allowed as paid NHS time, not unpaid leave, overtime or study leave… although, you could actually get a fair bit of revision done whilst sat on the toilet and sometimes it was the only time you got whilst at work. Always a good place to do a few multiple choice questions for the College Membership exams, which I had now started to revise for.

Whilst I was on the loo, I thought I'd give my great friend and colleague, Nurse Nightshade, a call using my shiny, new mobile phone. She'd be fast asleep in the Land of Nod on this mid-afternoon and her deep and blissful sleep would be preparing her for the trials of her third nightshift in a row. She'd need all the uninterrupted sleeping REM[40] pixies she could get.

The voice on the line croaked and yawned with barely an intelligible word heard.

"Mmm? Nse Brnksm here," came the knackered and squeaky voice of Nurse Becky Branksome alias… Nurse Nightshade of the Order of Witches and Purveyor of False Alchemy.

"Hi, Nurse. Just wanted to let you know that I've just had a good *shit*."

Revenge is sweet. Judge me if you will!

And once I'd flushed, Revenge should also probably give it five minutes…

---

[40] Rapid eye movement (REM) is also the stage of sleep where the activity of the brain is similar to that when we are awake; most of our vividly recalled dreams occur during REM sleep.

Chapter Twenty-Two

Do you work in PR?

Camping it Up

Down in Casualty, things were fairly under control for a change which was actually quite good for Helena, who was just being gently introduced to our chaotic world and there was little point in crucifying her quite yet.

She'd soon experience extreme sleep deprivation, death and destruction.

For now though, she was behind the curtain in cubicle two clerking in a new admission with vague abdominal pain and a history of acute intermittent porphyria.

The surgeons had no idea what this was, so she was referred to us medics.

Sister Kate, in all her blonde and attractively flustered glory, popped her head outside the curtains where she was chaperoning Helena who was with a male patient.

"Ah, Dr Manson, good!"

I clearly recalled the lacy souvenir that she had left me which now had pride of place hanging off a bed post back at my flat, with four or five other pairs. We hadn't yet had another encounter since then.

She came over to me.

"Your student is having a bit of trouble with this loser behind the curtain. She's trying to do a rectal examination but he's being difficult and sexually... provocative."

Great. Sexual harassment. A perfect, gentle introduction to on-call.

Kate gently and syllabically-divided a whispered repeat rendition of 'pro-voc-a-tive' in my right ear and then blew gently into my ear canal sending a brief shiver up my spine causing an army of goosebumps to obediently stand to attention.

"Err, right, okay… erm, I know, let me get Dave."

"Why *Dave*?" She looked surprised expecting me to gallantly enter the cubicle and assist the now fumbling Helena.

Helena's attractive Greek goddess looks had not gone unnoticed by our middle-aged, tattooed patient.

Davinder wandered into Casualty as I said this, looking a little bit forlorn.

"And the devil himself shall arrive! Alright, Dave? Wassup, man?"

"Telling you later, Jace."

"Okay, mate. Hey, can you help me? We need to do a stealth rectal examination on a patient whose being a right pain in the arse, so to speak."

"Sure things, what are we doing?"

"Teaching him a lesson, Dave. Can you put on your best camp voice and do you think you can do some excessive mincing?"

"Shhhure, Jathe, I can jutht be mythelf!" He lisped and upgraded the camp tone in his voice a couple of notches, let his hip fall a little, placed a pudgy palm on it and with the other hand he exaggerated a very limp wrist saying, "no problem."

"Great! Just do that. Now, we'll get Helena out of there. You go in and tell the patient that *you* are going to do the rectal examination. Let me do the rest."

"Oooo-kaaay! You're the bo-th!" He maintained his lisp-filled charade.

"Yes, Dave, I *am* the boss."

I went behind the curtains to see Helena wearing a rubber glove and holding up a generous blob of KY jelly on the end of her index finger whilst trying to negotiate doing the PR[41] and overheard the patient saying in his best, crude, laddish North London football supporters manner, "...only if I can *do you* next, babe! I'd love to pop a finger *in you*, love!"

"Right, sir, that is enough, we don't take too kindly to that kind of crudity and if you don't pipe down, you can leave. Helena, come with me please. Dr Dewani will be doing the rectal examination."

Enter Davinder, stage left... like the sugar plum fairy.

"Hiya, thirrrr! Mithter Miller ith it?" His voice sung with optimal musicality.

He virtually skipped in with as much anti-gravity floatiness as his plump frame would allow. Dave had developed a sudden ability to overact... or had he been let off his homosexual mental leash?

"Mkay, thir, pleathe can you roll onto your left thide bicoth, I jutht need to pop my finger in your... back... pathage."

"Oh, *no*... not you, mate! Get that sexy bitch back in here, *she* can stick her finger up my arse now. I'm not having you do it, you camp bar-stard."

"I'm afraid, thir, that you've had your chanth and if you don't comply, I'm afraid we can't treat you and we'll probably have to report you for thexual harrathment."

He lightly tapped Mr Miller on his right thigh to offer some feigned encouragement.

---

[41] PR - Per Rectum; by or through the rectum, denoting a method of examination or treatment. Contrary to those that define their professions by telling a medic that they're in PR, when they mean Public Relations. I always find that hilarious! "I'm in PR." "Really?! Enjoy it do you?"

"Roll over onto your left thide to fayth away from me and I'm jutht going to pop your troutherth and underpanth down a bit. Pleath bend your kneeth up to your chetht?"

Dave took his lisps to a new high.

Mr Miller had relatively little choice and reluctantly complied.

Whilst he rolled over, Helena and I quietly popped in behind the curtains.

Dave loudly snapped on a rubber glove for dramatic effect.

SCHWAKK!

"Jutht a bit of jelly on my finger, thir," Dave informed Mr Miller. "Jutht... relakth your bottom for me."

Dave slipped his jellied index finger in Mr Miller's anus and pushed deeply to get it in as far as his stumpy digit could muster and began to swivel his finger around palpating for unexpected masses, the prostate gland or for internal haemorrhoids.

"Urrghhh... hurry up you little, fucking queer!"

As he did this, I put two 'additional' hands on Mr Miller's shoulders as Dave kept his finger deep inside and he enquired, "Are you alright, thir, shall I go a bit deeper?"

"Aaaarrghhh... ooooohhh! *What* are you *doing*?"

Mr Miller shrieked.

Helena and I could hardly contain our silent laughter. Tears of hilarity were beginning to roll down our cheeks as we crouched down by the bed and snuck back out of the cubicle.

"Well... all theems to be fine, Mithter Miller."

Dave extravagantly snapped off his glove as Mr Miller grabbed his pants and underpants and aggressively pulled them up.

As he turned back around, Dave briefly fiddled with his trouser zipper for full effect.

"Good, no blood in there either."

And… exit Dr Dewani stage right with resounding audience applause… but falling just short of a standing ovation.

"Is everything okay in there?" Kate looked at us wide-eyed.

"Justice has been served I would say, Sister."

"That was *so* funny, Dr Manson!" Helena giggled. "Is it like this every week?"

"Well, just keep that to yourself, Helena. He did deserve it though!"

Dave came over, a little flushed but with a broad grin across his face. He pushed his glasses up a bit and exhaled, "I enjoyed that!"

BLEEEP BLEEEP

Outside line again.

"Hullo, Dr Podgornay, Gee-Pee, Chigway-ll, he-ah." He swallowed some Scottish Highland syllables.

Jockstrap.

"Ah, Dr Podgornay! How are you, sir? It's Dr Jacen Manson here. I'm SHO on-call for medicine today. How may I help you?"

"Ach, well, I've got a young girl, Miss Catherine Bradley, nineteen, here with an SVT. She's rather short of breath and tight-chested. She might have taken some drugs last night too, she says. 'Ecstatically' or something I think the young ones call it. She probably needs cardioverting and possibly loading with some Amiodarone."

I will be the judge of that, Dr Podgornay, you useless c… aber tosser.

"Absolutely, sir. What sort of heart rate is she running at? Blood pressure?"

"About one hundred and fifty beats per minute, BP ninety systolic."

"Hmm, supraventricular tachycardia possibly atrial flutter, maybe decompensating. Send her in straight away, sir. It would be my absolute delight to see her, of course. Please send my regards to Dr Bodman if you see him on the golf course. I think he might be on leave this week."

"Hmm... yes I certainly will... hey, you're not the one who told me to..."

"So, we'll look forward to seeing her shortly then," I interrupted, "send her straight to Casualty."

I hung up on *him* before he could finish his unwelcome line of enquiry.

Well handled, I thought.

BLEEEP BLEEEP

"Fksakke!"

Outside line again.

"A *young* girl for you, Dr Manson." Post-menopausal switchboard sounded especially jealous.

"Hi, Jacen?" Karen sobbed. "Mum just died."

"Oh shhhit!" My heart sank as if it were strapped to a lead weight and tears welled up in my suddenly painful eyes, only this time the joyous ones were forced to politely step aside for the ones of intense sorrow.

"Hey, sweetheart, I'm so sorry. I'm sorry I couldn't be there with you when it happened."

"I told you she was sick. Can you come *now*, please?" She asked, knowing what the answer was highly likely to be.

"Oh, god, I just can't. I want to but I really can't. I'm on-call again and there isn't anyone to cover. I'm sorry, Karen, *really* I am."

"Okay, well… I guess that's it isn't it. You're *never* here for me when I need you."

I could almost feel her tears falling over her beautiful face. I honestly was an utterly shite boyfriend.

"But, I'll really try and come and see you tomorr…"

She hung up on *me*.

I clenched my teeth, took a very deep breath and held it in. I squeezed both hands into fists. I felt my arms and shoulders stiffen and I looked up at the bright lights of the Casualty ceiling, subconsciously searching for some sort of sign or heavenly body to advise me on what to do now.

There were dead moths in the light fittings.

Shit.

Chapter Twenty-Three

A Day to Remember

Or to Forget

I needed a change of career, or at least a re-evaluation of my choice of specialty. I'd overheard Fi contemplating training in radiology.

Once she'd finished her Membership of the Royal College of Physicians exams, which were taking a massive amount of time to revise for whilst she was working a hugely busy clinical job and now trying to have a relationship, she'd then have to study for another five years for her Fellowship of the Royal College of Radiologists; this was also in multiple parts and well-renowned for being a very difficult and life-consuming examination.

You had to know everything, relearn about all diseases in all specialities, you had to know your anatomy inside out, upside down, back to front and in multiple cross-sections and even learn about the medical physics of ultrasound, ionising radiation and the effect of magnetism and radio frequency waves on the protons in the human body.

Radiology?! What? X-rays, barium enemas and defaecating proctograms? Boring. Sod that! I'm not sticking pipes up people's arses all day.

At that stage I could not have foreseen the current explosion in the use of medical imaging and scanning technology. As computers became more powerful and software more advanced, so did medical diagnostic imaging.

Just look at what's happened to computer gaming; imagery is so advanced that we can't even tell fantasy from reality... in fact, fantasy augments our reality.

There is ultrasound, Computed Tomography (the CT or 'CAT' scan), Magnetic Resonance Imaging (MRI), Interventional Radiology - 'pinhole' surgery manipulating small tools and devices using real-time image guidance, functional molecular metabolic imaging in the form of nuclear imaging such as Positron Emission Tomography (PET) with various forms of fusion imaging of any of these modalities put together.

It was all due to become rather complex such that the field of radiology is now a key orchestrator of medical and surgical management, and a vital specialty without which the NHS would surely crumble.

Exposure to radiology as a medical student was effectively non-existent. Back then, things were more primitive. Even the CT scanners of the time were alright for brain imaging if you had five minutes to wait to acquire the pictures and another twenty minutes to wait for the images to reconstruct on the old computer. Then you could squint at the pictures, throw up a piece of fluff in the air, rub your tummy, pat your head, scratch your chin, then make something up which resembled the vagueness of a diagnosis.

Ultrasound was originally done in a big water bath and the images were like nothing short of seeing TV static in a snowstorm. X-ray radiation doses were high for the patient and high for the operator, with the associated increased lifetime cancer risks.

Nowadays, there is three-dimensional ultrasound and portable ultrasound using handheld probes that you can plug into your mobile phone to see the images, whole body CT scans are done in a matter of seconds and with very minimal ionising radiation exposure. Cross-sectional MRI and CT images of the moving, beating heart and the coronary arteries can be acquired with the most beautiful detail.

Radiology is currently an incredible specialty and increasingly popular. Medical imaging is currently where it's at. Make no mistake.

But what did *I* know back then?

Radiology?! That's shite, there's no way I'm doing that.

"So, what's the matter then, Dave? You were all grumpy and downhearted when I saw you earlier."

"I'm stressings. My parents are trying to arranging marriage for me."

"Oh, yeah? I wouldn't want that. I wouldn't trust my dad!"

"But I haven't telling them about my feelings for Isaac. It will bring shame upon my family. *And* Isaac is black."

"Man, that *is* a tricky one for the old folks to take."

"It's hard enough workings in this place without worrying about telling my parents that I'm different. I was being happy earlier when we did that joke."

"Yeah, man, you looked like you enjoyed that." I tapped him on his shoulder.

He smiled, "I was able to be more myself."

"I thought you were indeed an absolute natural, Dave."

The Casualty automatic doors opened and the paramedic team duo of Freya Williams and Phil walked in with our young girl, Miss Catherine Bradley, on a trolley with an oxygen mask on and an intravenous line already in.

Freya was looking decidedly pale and her blue eyes were reddened where she must have been crying. She wasn't her usual bubbly, *Wonder Woman* self.

"Hey, Freya! This our girl from Baron Podgornay of Chigwell?"

"Yes."

"Is that it? Any referral letters?"

"Oh, yeah, of course, here... and the 'obs' chart."

She was very flat indeed for her. I gave the letter to Dave.

"Here, Dave, go with Phil and Sister Ellis and get Miss Bradley on a monitor, full obs and see what's going on. She looks rather short of breath, grey and sweaty to me. Get a full biochemistry and toxicology profile please."

"You're the bo-th!" He lisped, smiled and tried to fake a little cheer.

"Can I go?" Helena bounced.

"Of course, go and help Dr Dewani."

She clapped her enthusiastic hands together a couple of times and bounced up and down again flashing me a bright smile of youthful, medical naivety and idealism.

That was something I recognised from distant memory.

"What's the matter, Freya?" I put an arm around her shoulder.

"Awful morning, Jace. Just before this call, we went to an accident on the dual carriageway into the City. Decapitation."

"Fuuu... you okay? What happened?"

"I can hardly talk about it, but some woman parked on the hard shoulder with a flat tyre. She must've got out on the driver's side and was apparently sucked into the road by the airflow of a passing lorry. She was struck by the wing mirror of the next truck... took her head clean off."

"Jeeeez! Shiiiit!"

"Yeah, fucking mess!" She rarely swore. "The head was another half a mile down the road by the time we got there and the rest of the body was in a right state. Smashed around by the following traffic before the motorway came to a grinding halt."

"Shit, Freya, you need to go home."

"I know, but I can't. We're already really short-staffed and the calls keep coming. There's no time to sit and ponder over the dead... but I just can't get the image of that *head*... out of my... head. You could hardly tell it was still a head apart from the long, ginger hair in a plaided ponytail... and she was frickin' *pregnant*."

"Oh my good god... Freya!" I felt my blood run even colder than it had already become.

"Hey, hey, look, we'll just deal with this *Little Miss Muffet* who's actively trying to kill herself with 'Ecstatically', as Dr Podgornay puts it, and you go and get a strong coffee. We'll send Phil over to you when we're done. Don't respond to any more calls!"

I kissed her on the forehead.

She smiled just a little and gave me a tight hug and exhaled on my chest. It lasted the perfect amount of time... for a friend... and then just a little bit longer.

Her hair smelt of coconut... and blood.

I went into the resuscitation area.

"What's going on, Dave?" I looked at the cardiac monitor.

Dave looked somewhat panic-stricken and Helena had stopped bouncing. Phil looked like he needed to join Freya for a coffee.

Miss Bradley didn't look too hot either.

Relative inactivity had consumed them all.

"SVT, about three hundred beats per minute, BP seventy over forty, Jace... never seen it that fast before."

"Shit! She has been in atrial flutter and *now* with one to one atrioventricular conduction. She must have undiagnosed WPW... fuck, she could be in VF in a minute! Get her flat and get the defib."[42]

"Oh my god! What's WPW again, Dr Manson?" Helena's frozen and inexperienced, but otherwise very clever, medical student mind had prevented her ability to recall... facts.

As we got Catherine flat on the trolley, now beginning to groan and clutch her chest with the sensation of extreme pressure, I tried to educate our student.

"Wolff-Parkinson-White Syndrome, a form of ventricular pre-excitation syndrome... accessory electrical pathway bypassing your atrioventricular node... look, it's basically an electrical short circuit and her atria are whipping her ventricles into a frenzy!"

"I've bleeped the anaesthetist... we'll have to do cardiovertings."

"Agreed, Dave. I hope it's not that *Twat* Dundee though."

Fi wandered in to all the commotion and overheard us.

"Twat's off and Rob's on."

"Oh good!"

"What's going on, boys?"

---

[42] Atrial flutter with 1:1 atrioventricular conduction is an uncommon presentation of Wolff-Parkinson-White syndrome with potential degeneration into ventricular fibrillation... Death, uninvited, is usually queueing up to gatecrash the party, unless you can make him/her/it wait outside for a bit.

"Miss Catherine Bradley, nineteen, amphetamine abuse, gone into flutter, probable WPW, hypotensive."

"Shit! Draw up some Midazolam, we'll have to sedate and just shock her. I dunno exactly how long Rob's gonna be."

Sister Kate went to get the drugs for Dave.

"How do you know that you don't know *exactly* how long Rob's gonna be?"

"Err, nothing, no reason."

Despite, the seriousness of our current predicament, I couldn't help but notice that her blouse buttons were done up out of line... *two* buttons out of line at that... *and* there was a small, fresh, evolving capillary bruise on her neck just beneath her right ear.

"Oooo... key, dokey then! Better crack on." I resisted the urge to give her a knowing nod as it wasn't really the most appropriate forum.

'Distracting' the emergency anaesthetist on-call would naturally introduce an element of delay, should you require said anaesthetist in a hurry.

Post-coital fatigue, a snooze, in the shower, lost his underpants or any combination of those could play a vital part here.

"BP forty systolic!" Phil still hadn't gone for coffee but this was clearly an important observation.

"Fuck, she's *CRASHING*!"

I snatched the Midazolam vial off Dave, who was slowly fiddling about with a swab trying to snap off the glass top in the correct direction and in a safe way without cutting his fingers open.

Knobhead... hurry up!

SNAP!

"Arrggh, fuuu…" I cut the end of my thumb on little shards of glass.

"Fuck it!" I drew up the drug anyway as quickly as I could whilst blood flowed in a gentle sticky dribble down my wrist and into my palm.

"Another five mill vial, Dave, please."

Sister Kate Ellis handed it to Dave who immediately handed it to me. Just cut out the middle man, why don't we?

Fi was getting the defibrillator ready to charge up and laying the gel pads on Catherine.

I opened the second vial, with a swab for protection that Dave was about to use before I snatched the first one off him, with success and whilst simultaneously absorbing some of the blood that was already all over my fingers and hands.

"Okay, oxygen on full, just hammer in all ten milligrams," Fi commanded.

I did. We took the edge entirely off Miss Bradley's already fading consciousness and into full and rapid unconsciousness with the added benefit of some hopeful post-shock amnesia… a welcome side effect again.

"Phil, get ready for chest compressions if we need you." Phil sucked in his belly and let his shoulders posture a little as if preparing for imminent battle.

Fi laid on the paddles.

"Dave, charge it up!"

"Chargings!"

I resigned to just rolling my eyes at him again and shook my head a little.

I had a vial of Flumazenil, the benzodiazepine antidote, next to me to reverse the effect of the Midazolam quickly if I needed to.

"Stand clear!" Fi commanded us again.

There was certainly something about her when she took control.

"It's not chargings up properly, Fi!"

The machine was squealing at us but the charge wasn't completing.

Helena's olive skin had lost it's freshness and she looked as if she was holding her breath.

"Try again!"

"Chargings!"

CRESCENDO SQUEAL... constant and monotone midtone squeal...

I hit the top of the machine with my hand... hard. *The Fonz* would be proud.[43]

CRESCENDO SQUEAL to high pitched squeal.

"Fully charged!" Dave shouted.

"Stand clear!"

THUD

Catherine jolted.

Must have been a loose connection or something.

"Aw shit, no, now she's definitely in VF! No carotid pulse, Phil, you're up!"

Phil positioned himself over Miss Bradley's chest and interlocked his knuckles, straight arms, positioning the heel of his wrist in the lower third of her sternum.

"Well.. you-can tell ba the way a use ma-walk, a-ma wo-man's man, no time to talk... music wald and

---

[43] Arthur Fonzarelli (Fonzie) of *Happy Days*, typified the essence of 'cool'. He would demonstrate an almost magical ability to manipulate technology with just a nudge or a snap of his fingers; he could start a car, turn on lights, get free soda from a vending machine, make girls respond to his advances or change the song selection on a jukebox. Cool!

*women warm, av-bin kicked arand since a was bawn...
well it's al-rat, it's okay, you-can look the uther waay...
we-can-tra ter anderstand, that New York tams affects a
man. Staying Alive, Staying Alive, ah, ah, ah, ahhh...
Staying Alive, Staying Alive..."*

I felt my foot tap and my head nod to the life-saving
rhythm. Dave was doing it too.

"Shit, Phil, you got quite the voice on you, even the
falsetto bit!" I couldn't help but appreciate.

"For fuck's sake, you two! Okay, charge up again,
Dave," ordered Fi.

"Chargings!"

Brief crescendo decrescendo squeal... nothing.

Rob entered.

"You bleeped me? I thought the number was resus...
oh shit!"

His anaesthetic sixth sense had immediately assessed
the entire scene and he knew that Death was probably
right outside discharging another patient.

"Defib's fucked babes... err... Dr Babes... B-Banks...
won't charge," stumbled Fi.

"Isn't there another one?"

Why hadn't we thought of that?!

"Yeah, but that's only just been plugged back in. It's
been playing up as well. Shocked a paramedic last
week... spontaneous discharge or something," said
Kate.

"... ah, ah, ah, ahhhh... Staying Alive, Staying Al..."

"Stop a sec, Phil?" Fi popped a hand on his arm.

Still ventricular fibrillation... oh... no... ASYSTOLE.

The monitor decided upon a decidedly different and
far less pretty pattern of fatal rhythm disturbance. A
rhythm that gently and constantly undulated along a

baseline of zero electrical cardiac activity, which one would really define as no rhythm at all.

Death cordially, and indeed uninvitedly, entered the *Resuscitation Room* wondering what all the sombreness was about, as he, she or it usually did.

"I'd change the name of this room, if I were you," Death thought, sarcastically.

Chapter Twenty-Four

Sex, Drugs and Rotten Rota

Keep it Clinical

Ecstasy is a hallucinogen with stimulant effects. It is made in illegal drug laboratories and the purity and quality are highly variable and unpredictable. Because of this, the effects and the harm it causes are equally difficult to predict.

If it's used in combination with other street drugs, this will increase the unpredictability and adverse effects even more.

Some people, like Miss Bradley, the 19 year old girl with her whole life ahead of her, are more susceptible to the toxic effects than they might realise.

As a young doctor, once you have witnessed the death of a young person on drugs, you think twice before considering using them yourself. Perhaps you needn't even have to think the once.

"Oh, but hardly anyone dies of using ecstasy!"

Well, maybe in *your* little naive world kids... but we have to deal with your shite when it hits the fan.

Sometimes the fan is spinning pretty goddamn fast. Sometimes the fan won't charge up.

Although having said that, very occasionally we actually prescribed amphetamines in the form of dextroamphetamine (or dexamphetamine) for severely depressed elderly folk; it's also used to treat attention deficit hyperactivity disorder and narcolepsy.

The euphoric and aphrodisiac qualities, and the encouragement of the little 'get up and go' that you first wanted, might turn depressed Doris into a raving octogenarian nymphomaniac overnight... or in fact, during the night!

The ward 'midnight madness' would become ever more interesting.

It was bad enough when elderly people were merely removed from their own blissful and automated domestic routines and re-planted on a hospital ward cordially embellished with a fever, infection and electrolyte disturbances with all the associated bizarre occurrences that went on during 'normal' ward life, like some antithesis of a *Centre Parcs*[44] holiday camp. Add drugs to that and you've got yourself a party... or an orgy.

But after that day to forget, we were all running very low on enthusiasm and any definition of morale you'd care to offer up. I could do with some 'dex' myself.

I was discovering that the more detached I became from real world problems and responsibilities, the more remote from real world relationships I wandered and the more absorbed in the freaky, surreal world of hospital life I became, the greater the aphrodisiac effect it was having.

But the brief encounters were not exactly meaningful for many of us. They became simple raw human necessities.

Care for people, cry for people, cure people, cremate people; emotions were one monster of a roller coaster.

Control your feelings, modifying your feelings, pretend to feel, build a wall around your true self if you know who that even is anymore.

I'm not even sure I know what real feelings and emotions are any longer. Have I stopped *feeling* altogether? I think I'm beginning to dislike what I am

---

[44] *Centre Parcs* offers hundreds of acres of natural landscape, beaches and both indoor and outdoor activities for all the family; you can't do any of that in hospital.

becoming… or have become. I'm hardening, I'm cynical, I'm crude, I can be rude, I can be inappropriate, I'm angrier and I'm judgemental. Do I really even *want* to help anymore?

How do you defend and protect yourself when your very being is subjected to such a perpetual emotional, physical and psychological onslaught?

I wondered if it was because we were still growing as people. We were still young and hadn't really worked ourselves out yet. We didn't really know who we were because we hadn't yet become who we were meant to be.

But was the job part of that natural development and was it to catalyse an inner strength by vital life-training or was it ruining us?

Was it ruining me?

I think so.

I was in my on-call room. My pager went off. It was about 8.30am.

I rolled over and leaned across a naked and softly sleeping Helena. Well, she *was* rather upset after the untimely death of Miss Bradley.

"Hello, Dr Manson here."

"Good morning, Doctor, you do know that you've got outpatients clinic this morning?"

"What?! But I was on-call *all* yesterday *and* last night. We've got to do the post-take ward round and…"

"Well… that isn't my problem," came the stern reply of Clinic Sister, "speak to the person that writes your rota. What do you want me to do? Cancel all the patients? Some of whom, Doctor, are already here and waiting for you. And I presume Dr Feelwell will also be here?"

"Okay, I'll be there as soon as I can."

I slammed the phone down.

Helena woke up with a start.

"Hey, sorry."

Spooning, she wriggled herself closer to me and pressed her very cold bottom against my stomach.

"That's okay. It was lovely of you to look after me last night. I really enjoyed the experience of my first ever on-call."

I exhaled and could see my breath in front of me. The central heating had failed in the doctors' quarters. Again. It was so cold that any thought of some morning frivolity was dismissed. Surely it should be warmer at this time of year.

The pleasure was all mine, naturally... well not *all* mine.

"Well, they're not *all* like that, Helena."

"Oh... that's a shame!" Her teasing, peachy bottom nudged me again. It still hadn't warmed up but was exceptionally firm and silky smooth. You win some, you lose some.

I'd learned that her 'clinical skills' were indeed very accomplished. She was certain to do well in her career.

"Gotta get up for bloody surprise clinic."

"Sure, I suppose I'd better go home then."

One of the few advantages of still being a student doctor... you got to go home when you wanted.

She got up out of bed, her entire naked olive-skinned body was instantly covered in goosebumps and accompanied by bilateral extreme areolar smooth muscle contraction, I couldn't help but notice; it really *was* chilly in that room.

"Can I join you on-call again sometime before I do my final exams?"

"It would be my absolute pleasure."

I mean, what else was I going to say with that vision of a Greek goddess before me? In my mind, I bowed before her royal Mediterranean majesty.

She came over and kissed me heavily on the lips.

"And mine," she whispered.

I arrived in clinic just after Fi had turned up. We were both a bit late.

Clinic Sister wasn't best pleased but it was better than her having to cancel the entire clinic, send people home or cancel hospital transport already in the middle of redeploying our respected war veterans who had planned to attend their appointments, with their own well-drilled military precision, several days in advance. She'd have to file endless incident reports and deal with the aftermath of the inevitable hospital complaints coming her way.

She ought to be thankful for small mercies. At least we turned up at all.

We'd blame it on 'the system' and all would be fine.

Dave was instructed to do the ward round with Dr Simon Everage. He was the consultant covering for Dr Bodman who was definitely on leave, although I'm sure he hadn't mentioned it to any of us.

Dr Everage was funny. We'd call him Dr Everett due to his striking resemblance to *Kenny Everett*, the bisexual, controversial comedian, radio DJ and TV entertainer who died in 1995 of AIDS. I think he was mates with *Freddy Mercury* too.

Dr Everage was also skinny and pale, had dark, shaggy hair and an unkempt beard. He was not your typical consultant-type but he was very clever and also great with patients, if a bit camp... he was a *Queen* fan too. He'd wear mismatching brown suits usually half-corduroy with patches on the elbows; this was sometimes referred to as 'GP-attire'.

He and Davinder would get on like a house on fire, as long as...

"It's all done in the best *possible* taste!"[45]

"How was your night Fi?" I enquired probingly.

"How was yours?" she Socratically retorted.

I think we both knew exactly how each other's nights had unfolded.

"Here's the clinic list for today." Clinic Sister handed us each a copy.

"Wait, what's this? The ten minute slots are treble booked!"

"Treble booked?!" Fi echoed... just rather more loudly than me.

Forlorn hope washed over us.

I mean double-booking a ten minute slot is one thing, well, seeing *one* person in ten minutes was impossible. You couldn't even say 'hello', get a history, get your

---

[45] One of Kenny's characters called Cupid Stunt was a blonde American B-film actress with pneumatic fake breasts with no attempt made to disguise Everett's dark beard; her final action in each comedy sketch was to uncross her legs then swing them wildly to recross them (brazenly giving viewers an eyeful of her red lingerie) as she uttered the catchphrase, "It's all done in the best *possible* taste!"

patient's clothes off to examine them, write out a prescription, order some investigations, take some blood, get them dressed, chat about the pets, get them up off their chair or the couch, and indeed onto the couch in the first place, help them to the door using a walking stick, frame or other walking aid, say goodbye, get delayed a bit by learning how little Johnny was growing up so fast... never mind two or THREE patients!

"Jesus Christ, Sister!"

"*Language*, please, Dr Manson! You're in earshot of a waiting room *full* of patients."

"Sorry."

"Fuck!" said Fi and walked off to her clinic office.

"Well, you don't know who's going to 'DNA'[46] and there are so many on the waiting list, we have to give them all an appointment."

"Sister, we're going to be here all day, we have to do the ward round as well."

"Well, you'd better get started then, Doctor! I think most of them will be ward follow-ups with only a few new patients I think. Tea?"

"Yes please. Biscuits?"

"Don't push it!"

I sat reading the notes of the first patient, half concentrating and half trying to decide what branch of medicine I'd rather do my specialist training in.

I like dealing with cardiovascular diseases but I also liked the gastrointestinal (GI) stuff.

Hmm, Blood... or Guts?

---

[46] DNA - yes commonly known as deoxyribonucleic acid in genetic circles but right now, plain old... Did Not Arrive!

Who's this, Claire Longoria, 37, ginger hair but dyes it blonde hoping to be seen more quickly. We admitted her with abdominal pain and GI bleeding a few weeks ago. Turns out she'd swallowed about thirty razor blades. That came as a shock when we reviewed her abdominal x-ray... lots of tiny rectangular blades of metal in variable stages of gastrointestinal transit.

Couldn't really do much about that. You can try and fish them out with an endoscope or excise them surgically but mostly the 'conservative' management strategy was best. Just eat lots of fibre and bulking agents and hope that all the blades get enveloped by a decent protective stool. With any luck and a following wind, so to speak, you'd uneventfully pop them all out!

"Miss Longoria, please?" I called out her name in the waiting room.

I was, of course, greeted by the usual looks of 'why didn't you call *my* name out', 'I was here before her', 'they're taking such a long time in there', 'I've been waiting for ages', 'my appointment time was twenty minutes ago' and 'I'm going to complain about this'.

You get seen when you get seen. It'll take as long it's going to take and I'll get to you when I do. That's it. If you get seen at all, be bloody thankful.

"Ah, Miss Longoria, how are you?" I lightly put a hand on the back of her shoulder as we walked, mainly to subliminally hurry her along to my clinic room.

"Oh, I'm fine, Doctor, I've been getting a few mild tummy pains but I think all the blades must have gone now. I've been getting some help from a counsellor and I feel much better."

"Ah, good."

She sat down on the patients' chair strategically positioned by my desk and I sat down on my very special doctors' chair... that really had nothing special about it at all, apart from the fact that it kept squeaking if you moved even slightly. The sounds were making my teeth tingle.

"Well, I think we can discharge you then. Good luck with the counselling."

I stood up again, re-opened the door and held it for Miss Longoria who'd only just put down her large and clearly fake '*Eves Saint Laurence*' handbag, removed her naturally fake fur coat (I was certain that there were no real pink zebras in the wilds of Africa) and hung it on the back of our clearly very cheap and very nasty NHS chair.

People did tend to dress up for the 'occasion' which in this case... never happened.

"Oh, is that it?"

"Absolutely. I'm so pleased you're on the mend."

"Well, that was a bit of a waste of time. I'm complaining about this."

"There is a poster on the wall outside about how to make a hospital complaint. I'd fully support you on that if you feel that you've been mistreated in any way."

She got up and left.

Two minutes, one down... *Shoot and Scoot!*

Ah, Mrs Laflamme next! I know her well.

"Mrs Laflamme, please!"

A very svelte, red haired, Blaise Laflamme walked over cheerfully and just a little breathless from her chronic emphysema. Her green and white make-up and purple dress drastically fortified that *Joker*-esque look we had first encountered.

I think she suffered from mild mania but why suppress such a flamboyant personality?

"Hellos, Doctor! How's yous?"

Her pointless pluralisation regrettably persisted. But I employed a similar encouraging tactic of an arm around the shoulder.

"I am very well, Mrs Laflamme, albeit a little tired. But more to the point, how are *you* doing?"

"Oh, you doctors work so hard... I'ms okay. I'ves stopped taking those blasted *OXO* cubes like you said and I'ms taking the water tablets."

"That's excellent, Mrs Laflamme. Let's just pop you up on the couch and have a little listen to your back..."

"Oh, should I take my things off? I'll just pop my bag down here."

I wondered whether it'd be boobytrapped, then I'd have to bleep...

The Batman.

"Oh, no, that's okay. I'll just pop the stethoscope up the back here, there, deep breaths in and out, very good nice and clear. Oh, let's see your ankles... oh, look at that, Mrs Laflamme, you have ankles today! Not a bit of swelling in sight. Your breathing seemed reasonably okay walking from the waiting room to here as well."

"Oh... that's erm, lovely, Doctor, so do I needs to see you again?"

"I think we'll make an appointment again in six months just for a quick check over, but your GP should be able to take care of things, probably just a blood test to check your kidney function."

I put a hand on the door handle and Mrs Laflamme took the hint and picked up her boobytrap.

"Bye for now, then."

"Byes, doctor!"

6 minutes, two down… Boom! *Guerilla tactics.*

Mr Aloysius 'ironically' Bignall was up next on my list.

I'd need to be extra careful here. I still didn't know exactly how much he knew about my exchange with Dr Podgornay. Dr Podgornay also wasn't especially happy to receive the news of Catherine Bradley's untimely demise either.

Back to the large waiting area.

"Mr Bignall, please?" I looked around.

"Mr Bignall, please?" I called louder and looked around again.

No Mr Bignall. Must've DNA'd, I thought.

There was a firm yank on my trouser leg. It pinched a bit of skin and plucked out some leg hair too.

Ambushed.

"Ow!" I looked down.

"Ah! Mr Bignall. Hello, sir!"

Mr Aloysius Bignall was stood next to me the whole time with his arms folded, looking somewhat disgruntled.

He could've said something. He was probably making a point that he never gets noticed by anyone taller than him, which was virtually everyone.

Think… Bike!

Think… Midget.

Yes, I know. How pejorative of me! Well I am in a rush.

"Come through, sir, it's a pleasure to see you again."

We walked through to my office. He was looking very smart in a little, I guessed, specially tailored suit and a small tie.

"How have you been?"

"Fine, I don't really know why I'm here and I thought I was seeing the consultant anyway," he complained.

He was a little *Grumpy*.

"Well, I'm sorry about that, sir, but Dr Bodman is on holiday."

He folded his short arms together again and frowned, lightly crumpling his prominent brow. He certainly wasn't *Happy*.

"Perhaps we'll do a quick examination and I'll just check your blood clotting results. It was a big nose bleed wasn't it. Headaches?"

"Just the usual."

His head was still on the large size.

"Just hop up on the couch while I check the computer."

I tapped a few keys and tried to access the lab results. The computers were extremely slow.

"Okay... the clotting results are... all... fine, full blood count... normal. Good."

I turned around to see Mr Bignall still standing next to the couch.

"Oh, I'm so sorry, sir, where's that step?"

Dopey.

Shit, where's Sister? Time is ticking. Fuck it!

I squatted a bit to get some assisted leg power and picked up Mr Bignall under his arms and planted him on the side of the couch. Gym training was useful for some things, although I didn't make a habit of squatting people of short stature.

Better?!

"Oof!" Mr Bignall let out a splurt.

"Sorry, no step. I just need to listen to your heart... and lungs... quick feel of your tummy, where's my pen torch... pupillary reflexes... okay... moving all limbs, quick up the nose... no blood. Good!"

"Is that it?"

"Yes, sir, all good. I'll write to your GP with the results too. Please send him my very best and warmest regards when you see him next? Such a good GP is *Doc* Podgornay, Chigwell Surgery isn't it? You're in excellent hands with him."

I plucked my shallow compliments out of Dr Podgornay's proverbial backside and helped Mr Bignall down off the couch in as dignified a way as possible without dropping him.

He walked out, shaking his head.

Eleven minutes... three down... a *Counterattack*. Cutting it fine now.

"Who's next, Sister?"

"Here's your tea... and biscuits... they're from the nurses' biscuit barrel, so don't you be saying anything to anyone!"

She smiled and winked.

"If you keep this pace up, we'll be done on time."

"Yes, if we aren't bleeped by the ward and some patients don't bother to show up."

"Well, your registrar, Dr Feelwell, is seeing the new patients which takes a bit longer and she's probably quicker than you..."

Not strictly true but okay. I'll let that one go... for now.

"Miss Sarah Henderson, next?"

"Ah... Miss Henderson, lovely."

Tea, biscuits and Sarah Henderson. A very good morning indeed.

"Go to your office and have a sip on your tea and eat a biccie. I'll bring her through in a couple of minutes."

"Cool, thanks, Sister."

The nurses will look after you if you're good and don't piss them off... and aren't rude.

I straightened my tie, tucked my shirt in a bit and straightened my white coat. I checked my hair in the mirror in the office and my breath against my hand.

Mint... pocket... fresh.

"Miss Henderson for you, Doctor."

Indeed.

"Doctor Manson... how are *you*?" Sarah fluttered her eyes at me and smiled.

Her tan had faded. She had unbuttoned her blouse a little to reveal sufficient cleavage for me to quite easily and obviously notice.

I looked up again at her face.

"Erm, I am very well, thank you, Sarah, erm, so... oh, your leg yes... come over and lie on the couch for me."

"Oh, Doctor, no foreplay today? I wore a short skirt too, so it'd be easier for you to examine me."

How considerate.

She lay down and slipped it up a little higher revealing the edge of her 'lack of underwear'.

Shit. A Flanking Manoeuvre.

"Erm... any chest pain, erm... shortness of breath... more... err... swelling?"

My heart decided to do me the honour of noticeably speeding up.

"No, Doctor, but it seems like you do..." she playfully poked my groin, which also seemed suddenly slightly more keen to examine her.

Surprise Frontal Assault!

"Nurse! Chaperone, please?!"

Sarah pulled her skirt back down a little as Clinic Sister's head poked around the door.

"Did I hear something?"

"Err, oh nothing, err, could you just pop in for a minute, I need to, erm, examine Miss Henderson."

"Of course, Doctor, I'll be right in."

I pulled my white coat edges together. *Artillery Retreat.*

Sarah smiled at me knowing absolutely full well what she was doing and clearly enjoyed me fumbling nervously, caught between whether to act on my obvious reciprocated desires whilst simultaneously knowing that it would get me in a whole heap of professional trouble if I did.

Needless to say, I did *not*.

I finished the examination as platonically as possible, with a small dignity blanket over Sarah's young floral surprise.

Clinic Sister left the room.

"Come and sit down over here and let's check your blood results."

I helped her down off the couch and she made a special effort to brush firmly against me as she stepped by to sit down on the patients' chair by my desk. She deliberately and slowly crossed her legs.

She waved her high-heeled bare foot and ankle up and down pointing it in my direction, whilst allowing the shoe to swing subtly on her toes.

"So... the, erm, thrombophilia screen hasn't revealed anything unexpected. So, if you've stopped smoking..."

"I've stopped."

"Excellent! And erm… perhaps I can suggest an alternative form of… erm… contraception?"

"I'll have some by the bed for you."

She uncrossed and recrossed her legs doing her level best to impersonate the actress *Sharon Stone* in the 1992 erotic thriller, *Basic Instinct*.

Shitty shit festival.

"Right, well… erm… we probably don't *need* to see you again in clinic. Although, to be on the safe side…"

"Yes, Doctor?" Her expectant response was rather soft and breathy.

"No… *actually*, we don't. All is fine. Discharged from clinic."

I closed her small set of case notes.

"Oh, that's a shame. Ah!… but does that mean you're no longer my doctor?"

Shitsville.

Twenty-nine minutes… four down… *Hors de Combat*. Bugger!

Quick slurp of tea and shove a whole biscuit in. Nice… chocolate digestives. I love them.

Who's next? Case notes of… Mrs Magorzata Migginski, of second generation Polish decent.

Jeez, did we actually send her home in the end? I guess Fi or Dr Bodman must have discharged her after she'd had a really good poop.

Running behind by miles now… need to speed up.

"Mrs Migginski, please?"

There was a kerfuffle at the other end of the waiting room. Hospital transport had just dumped Mrs Migginski as far away as possible from the clinic offices and she was hardly the most spritely octogenarian.

This was going to take a little time.

"Sister, can you help me?"

We both directed Mrs Migginski each with one arm in our grip and shuffled along with her slowly and unsteadily across the waiting room.

"So, how are you, Mrs Migginski?"

I needed to start getting some history from the patient to save valuable clinic time.

"Oh, not good, Doctor. I can't go to the toilet again."

Not again.

"Oh dear. Anything else you've noticed?"

"I can't eat. I have no appetite at all."

She was looking a bit more frail from what I could remember.

"And the blood... oh, the *blood*, Doctor!"

"The blood?"

"Yes, in my pants... everyday."

The whole waiting room now knew all about this. So much for privacy and patient confidentiality.

"Nurse, can you get the scope trolley once we get her up on the couch, I'm going to have to have a look."

This was going to take longer but there were still efficiencies to be made.

Clinic Sister and I made Mrs Migginski comfortable on the couch and rolled her onto her left side and placed a warm blanket on her whilst we got the trolley ready.

The rigid sigmoidoscope was pretty much as it says on the tin. It's rigid, it's a metal tube and it goes up your bum. It has a little round window at the end, a light and a valve to pump some air in to inflate the rectum and sigmoid colon as you advanced it.

You could unscrew a little lock on the hinged window at the end which opened and allowed you to insert a swab-on-a-stick to take a sample for infection or perform a small biopsy of tissue such as a polyp or a piece of inflamed bowel wall.

"A bit of jelly on your bottom, Mrs Migginski, just popping the tube in. A bit cold and a bit of pushing."

The octogenarian anal sphincter is somewhat easier to negotiate, being more lax with age.

"Oh, Doctor... I haven't felt that since..."

Since when? I didn't need to visualise that.

I pumped some air in and peered through the little window.

Clinic Sister interrupted Magorzata's sudden reminiscence and gave her hand a squeeze for comfort.

What I was doing to her was not exactly comfortable or pleasant... I presumed anyway.

"You see anything, Doctor?" Sister enquired, trying to peer through the scope via the obvious back of my head.

"Hmm... I think there's a polyp up there... hang-on, there's a bigger cauliflowery thing up there too... and some blood."

"Biopsy forceps?"

"Yes please, Sister..."

I pumped a little more air in for better visibility. I had my left eye up against the little scope window, my right eye closed and I was holding my breath a little in concentration. The tube was now almost at the hilt which meant that my face was merely centimetres from Mrs Migginski's slightly blood-stained buttocks.

Sister handed me the forceps to try and grab a small bite of tissue... looks like cancer though.

I opened the little window to insert the forceps down the scope tube.

As I did, whilst running short of oxygen, I happened to inhale again, deeply, just as a gush of particulate air left the tube from the prior safety of Mrs Migginski's colon and was insensitively directed straight into my throat, down my central airways, only to be dissipated within each alveolus of every segment of every lobe of both lungs.

Gaaarrrghhh!! Chemical Warfare.

I coughed, choked and wretched whilst letting go of the forceps, which Sister grabbed off me just in time.

Shit.

Blood or Guts?!
BLOOD... EVERY TIME!

Chapter Twenty-Five

Hearts and Minds

A Cycle of Words

I had to plot a course towards a career in cardiology; it was clean, seemed fairly logical to me and heart diseases were interesting and varied. Heart disease was common, so the demand for a career in it would always be there.

There was the plumbing, the electricity, the engineering and the physics. I appreciated the complex, yet clever simplicity of the heart, it's beautiful architecture and fabulous physiology, I enjoyed the pharmacology of heart disease and how small biochemical manipulations could have a wonderfully curative effect.

Cardiology could be viewed as a life-saving specialty... whilst I don't like to compare surgeons to physicians, it was kind of the 'surgery' of medicine.

The heart is what made people 'tick'. The heart could be broken and we could fix it.

The heart of the human body is the pump, the boiler, the furnace, the central energy source, the emotion, the feeling and the love.

It's what keeps us alive.

I wanted to make an appointment to see the self-proclaimed Professor, John McTavish, for some career advice and ideally with the over-riding mantra of 'gizzajobmate'.

Ironically, yet predictably, he'd dropped down dead at home from a massive myocardial infarction the other week; a sudden rupture of an atherosclerotic plaque in a main coronary artery; the 'furring up' of his arteries, caused by his chain smoking, had cracked.

The body, when it deals with any damage or cut, will rush to try and heal itself by forming a blood clot. But if the damage is on the inside of a blood vessel only three to four millimetres in diameter, this life-saving process performed by the army of repair cells and chemicals is the very process that blocks the artery completely, thus stopping blood flow and oxygen perfusion to a chunk of heart muscle - the better known, Heart Attack.

Most people who drop down dead of a heart attack don't have any previous symptoms of angina. If you're lucky, you make it to hospital for urgent treatment.

Heart attacks are actually a great example of how the NHS has evolved in it's treatment strategies and use of ever more costly drugs, imaging investigations and clever therapies without necessarily requiring open heart surgery.

Back in the days of *Carry on Doctor*, if *Sydney James* had a heart attack and was lucky enough to get to the ward where all the inappropriately clad nurses worked, including a young and voluptuous Nurse *Barbara Windsor*, any previous risk factor history of high blood pressure remained rather more difficult to treat.

If Syd was lucky, he'd have been given an Aspirin but he'd certainly get at least six weeks bed rest to be waited on hand and foot and titillated by Nurse Babs. He'd probably also have to tolerate the consultant cardiologist actually smoking on the ward round, never mind just smelling of it. His consultant might well be recommending the very stuff that was killing him, so the adverts of the time went:

"More Doctors Smoke *CAMELS* than any other cigarette."

"Give your throat a vacation, smoke a *FRESH* cigarette."

"This is it, *L&M* filter cigarettes are just what the doctor ordered."

Sydney didn't really stand a chance.

We'd evolved to provide a greater variety of urgent drug therapies including the advent of intravenous thrombolysis or the 'clot buster' to unclog and restore blood flow to the heart. Then, if the patient was lucky, they would get some imaging of the coronary arteries within a few weeks of waiting around on the ward. Then maybe, if they weren't dead yet, they'd be referred for surgery or get a bucket of pills.

Nowadays, the quicker a patient can get to hospital and straight into the 'cath lab' for rapid catheter angiography to visualise the arteries and the blockages, the quicker they could be opened up with angioplasty and stenting and the faster the blood flow to the heart muscle could be restored.

Sydney would, of course, have needed far less time in hospital; he would have had tiny balloons inflated in the blockages and narrowings, little pieces of tubular scaffolding to hold them open and he would have had fabulous imaging of his heart to look at how well it was working and how much damage to the heart muscle had occurred.

The quicker you were treated, the less damage you got. 'Time is myocardium' as we say.

There are several disadvantages to these modern strategies; it costs a hell of a lot more than what would have been spent during *Carry on Doctor* and you don't get the same titillation from Nurse Babs like you used to.

But… there was a fairly decent chance that you'd get to live longer.

Self-professed Professor McTavish had been replaced by, debatably more genuine, Professor Kurt Klein from Germany. Professor Klein had brought with him an army of Germans to the cardiology department; it was rather akin to a take over or, some might have said, an all out ground assault on our hospital.

It's not uncommon to see when a football manager is sacked, or in this case dies, a whole new backroom staff being brought in to train and coach the team.

The Scotsman died, bring in the foreign manager.

And so it occurred. The Germans had arrived.

They'd better speak bloody English... in bloody Blighty.

Bad communication and misunderstanding was already all too common in the NHS and the source of many complaints and clinical errors.

Professor Klein came with a reputation for being a shrewd academic. Not only would he bring vital new-age clinical experience but he'd bring a research track record with him too. What a wonderful appointment this would be for our hospital.

The saviour of our time, the saviour of our hospital... the heart bit anyway.

Professor Klein liked a good cigar, the finest pipe tobacco and an expensive, aged, oaked, single malt whiskey or three.

Ah... the catch!

He also talked a good research game and promised much but again it was debated amongst the masses, the critics and the cynics whether, in fact, he would actually deliver on these promises.

Publish or Perish.

Right, I would now have to arrange a meeting with him by concocting some legitimate reason, research proposal or just good old-fashioned 'pandering to his immense ego' to be awarded an audience with Professor Klein, who would, of course, be a very, very busy man.

Shit.

BLEEEP BLEEEP

It was Jessica. She never paged me. I'd just usually rock-up to her house and we'd sleep together, then I'd leave. It worked for her and for me.

"Oyv meest a period."

She delivered the line with a factual Black Country venom.

Well, it wasn't *all* my fault. I mean, if you deliver the ingredients, you don't need to cook them all. But I'd keep my truculent attitude to myself on this occasion. This private versus professional conflict was unrelenting.

Scheisse (I had to start relearning my GCSE German at some point).

"Well, erm, is it mine?"

"Fuck off, Jace!"

She truly had a unique way with vocabulary.

"Well, is it?"

"Of course it *fucking* is!"

Out of all the present participles at her disposal, she picked the easy one at the top.

"Okay, well thank you for clarifying that."

"For fucks sayk, stop being a fucking arsehole."

I sensed that her thesaurus was firmly closed at this point. Maybe it was the hormones? Although it was also probably best, at this juncture, not to bring *that* up, given that it was likely her shock and fear of having to face the consequences of our carelessness.

I had worked out that Jess did have a very awkward combination of her usual menstrual cycle and her regular pattern of nursing night shifts; this did not lend itself to a, shall we say, stable personality.

Perhaps that's why she snorted so much cocaine.

So, in a nutshell, she had absolutely awful pre-menstrual tension and would turn into an absolute psycho with anger, irritability, painful and swollen boobs, intolerance to life in general and *me* obviously, interwoven with her already innate ability to exhaust anyone's library of profanities - magnified at least twofold.

So we had the PMT for a week, then the M for another week, along with its accompanying tearfulness, anger (again), irritability (for a second helping), some relief but generally heavy blood loss leading to more anger and fatigue.

There were a couple of days of what one might construe as 'normal' before the week of "fucking hell, I'm on nights *next* week!"

That was the best time to pop over, but you had to keep a really good diary.

Yes, I am very understanding aren't I? But, shit, try being on the receiving end!

This all inevitably and predictably ended with the actual week of nights where there was the "fucking hell, I'm on nights all *this* week!" This led to constant fatigue, irritability (for thirds; irritability was a greedy bastard), intolerance (for seconds) and hunger.

"Sorry, but I thought I'd better check."

"What do you think I am, some kind of slutty... slaggy... ssss-lapper?!"

At that point in time, no I didn't. But I did enjoy her turn of phrase.

"No, of course not, babes. Okay, well, what shall we do? I mean I've got a decent career, good prospects, we could keep it? It'll be tough but we could do it."

"I'm fucking getting rid of it."

Well, that's that decided then, I suppose. So much for adult conversation and rational discussion. Why she called me in the first place, I don't know. Obviously to inform me, in her indirect way, that I was a total wanker.

"Erm, okay, shouldn't we discuss it together though, maybe, and then decide? I mean it's a massive decision."

She hung up.

Ausgezeichnet! (my favourite word in German... *Excellent!*)

Chapter Twenty-Six

Sugar and Spice

And All Things Shite

I had at least a couple of research ideas and if I could meet Professor Klein armed with some vague suggestion that I was an enthusiastic and original thinker, that might just impress him enough.

I had to give him the impression that I was a doctor that could deliver, even if my original ideas included investigating serum rhubarb levels in African Tree Frogs[47] and their effects on amphibian cardiac function, that would be something... well, that probably wouldn't go down particularly well, but you get the point.

"Where's Dave today?" I enquired at no-one in particular.

I wandered into the mess to see Isaac lying on the sofa focusing more on the ceiling than on the repeat episode of *TJ Hooker* currently re-running on the TV.

"Shit, man, what's wrong? You'd rather be checking out the hospital's asbestos problems than focus on the sexy, hot blonde that is *Heather Locklear* in an inappropriately tight cop's uniform?"

I realised that Isaac would probably be more interested in *William Shatner* or *Officer Vince Romano* in a cop's uniform.

"A am theenkeen, Jayce... Dev is seein hees parents deesmarnin far brek-fast. Ee ees goin to tell dem bout us."

"Ah. So it's fairly serious between you two then?"

---

[47] The coronary arteries that supply oxygen to the heart muscle itself are clearly vital as the heart must never stop beating. Cardiac muscle needs oxygen until Death arrives and inevitably, Death does. In mammals this coronary blood supply branches from the aorta, the main vessel leaving the heart. Many lower vertebrates, including amphibians, have no specialised coronary arteries at all; the heart obtains its oxygen from the blood actually passing through it.

I have to say that, whilst Dave had been getting much more stressed at work with the pressure, the workload, the lack of any proper sleep, the increasing numbers of patients and not to mention the untimely deaths, his relationship with Isaac was keeping him happy-ish and putting a spring in his, otherwise weebly, step.

"Ai teenk so. Dev ees very worried hees farda won't be happy."

"No gynae clinic today then?"

"No. Ai go to dee wards een a meeneet."

"Blimey, you're not going to finish watching *TJ Hooker*? Hey, this is the one where rookie *Officer Stacy Sheridan* goes undercover as an exotic dancer!"

I sat down, looking forward to seeing *Heather Locklear*.

Isaac sucked some air through his teeth and glared at me.

"Oh! Yeah, sorry, man... obviously you won't be bothered about this one!"

Damn, Isaac *was* pretty downbeat for him. It's like he hadn't taken any anti-inhibition pills this morning making him rather more... inhibited.

I couldn't do Isaac's job, not the endless watching of 70's and 80's cop shows as that was the easy bit, but the gynaecology clinics.

I remember doing my fourth year speciality clinical attachments at medical school. Bearing in mind that, as a general practitioner, a lot of the cases you'd end up seeing would be mental illness, skin rashes, coughs and colds, so why on Earth we only had a month in psychiatry, two weeks in dermatology (or 'derma-holiday' as we'd rebrand it) and then *four* whole months in obstetrics and gynaecology, I do not know.

That's what midwives are for.

After that attachment, I'd delivered about fifty babies which was a huge privilege and though I did very much enjoy it, I also had to examine at least fifty vaginas.

But taking part in outpatient gynae clinics, with the commonly male specialty registrars or consultants and whether or not I was made to pop my fingers in and have a naive guddle around feeling for diseases that I'd never felt for before, was enough to put you right off the sexual aspect of the female form.

Indeed, after all that, gynaecology was the only final year medical school exam I was awarded a *Merit* for. Must've been doing something right!

Now it is certainly *not* a case of 'seen one, seen 'em all' because there was indeed a glorious variety. But like anything, you can have too much of a good thing. Or you might begin to visualise the not so good things when you least needed those images to make an unwelcome and unexpected appearance in the mind's eye.

I didn't need sudden visions of purulent discharges, matted hair, red lumps and malodorous, olfactory hallucinations when I was focusing on my own 'business' in hand, as it were.

I supposed that Isaac was better placed for that not to be a particular concern of his. But I did seriously wonder about his bedside manner.

Rob Banks sat down beside me with his usual morning tea and a bit of strawberry jam on toast as Isaac got up and slipped on his golden sandals to wander off at Nigerian speed[48] up to the gynae ward.

---

[48] In my own relatively limited experience, this was somewhat more laid-back than other nationalities.

"What you watching, Stud? Hey! *TJ Hooker*! I love this one, *Heather Locklear* is incredible in this!"

"Don't let Fi hear you talking like that mate! She'll have your guts."

"Ah, it's okay. She's cool. She kind of reminds me of Heather."

"Really?!"

"No."

"Idiot."

We chuckled like the naughty perverts we clearly were.

"Isaac's looking a bit down today for him. Hey, you still haven't been in my new car yet."

"Yes, I know mate, I'd still love to."

I liked my cars. My first car was a tiny, burgundy coloured *Fiat 126*, the lawn-mower. Mr Bignell would have loved it.

The problem with the *Fiat* was that you couldn't really get that much speed up, leaving only two things on the road worthy of an attempt at an overtaking manoeuvre. If you could position yourself correctly and find a decent downhill section of dual carriageway, you could slipstream a *Citroen 2CV* (equally underpowered) or a tractor and slingshot past them... in about five to ten minutes.

At least it stopped me speeding after I first passed my test. When you first pass, you tend go through a couple of distinct phases: 1. there is the sudden realisation that you're all on your own, you're scared and apprehensive and you 'pootle' along like a Sunday afternoon driver and 2. once you'd gained enough confidence and realised the extreme freedom you'd now gained, *Mad*

Max took over the wheel in all his over-confident and kamikaze glory!

That's when the accidents started to happen amongst the new young drivers. Their need for speed, especially for the lads, was a primeval instinct. But of course, you're invincible at that age aren't you?!

I did actually manage to spin my *Fiat* a full 360 degrees whilst taking a sharp right-hand bend once; well, it was dark and a bit icy and I was trying to keep up with my mate's gold *Vauxhall Nova* estate whilst on our way to a toga party dressed as Roman Legionaries... I *was* still at school. I missed every car parked on both sides of the road, came to a grinding halt and was met by an appreciative round of applause from a load of blokes stood outside the pub on the corner.

A near miss for the young gladiator, Maximus Gluteus Medius.

So, a progressive increase in the power of your successive cars was the best approach I thought. That way, you could gently increase your confidence in line with your actual competence to handle a more powerful vehicle. Anything more than a one-litre car when you passed your test was probably too much. Some of the road traffic accident carnage that we'd witnessed was a testament to the idiocy of the young male driving contingent in way over-powered vehicles.

"So how is the new 'beast' then, Rob?"

"It's amazing, Jace. It's a mid-engined, one point eight litre *Rover K Series* unit and really well balanced. Pretty decent acceleration too, nought to sixty in about eight seconds!"

"*MGF* you said it was?"

"Yeah, British Racing Green with lovely red leather seats and a soft top."

"You taken Fi in it yet?"

"Yeah, of course, a few times! Gear stick gets in the way though."

He stuck his tongue in the side of his cheek.

We smuttily wheezed like little boys again.

"What are you two girls giggling at?" Fi wandered in to the mess to fortunately only catch the tail end of our conversation.

"Oh, nothing. Just boy talk."

She ruffled Rob's hair in a very girlfriendy kind of way and not her usual authoritarian power-woman self.

Was she softening up? Perhaps it really *was* love!

"How's your revision going, Fi?" I wondered, given her vow of celibacy during exam preparation time.

"Oh, it's okay, when I'm not being distracted by *this* loser."

She stood behind Rob as he sat on the sofa and put her hands down the front of his scrub top to stroke his chest hair… well the couple of strands he did have anyway.

"Oi, less of that! Get a room you two."

"Next chance to do the final clinical part of the exam is not long before Christmas. Anyway, come on Nosey Parker, we need to go to the wards. Where's Dave?"

Dave's absence was clearly noticed.

"He took the morning off as annual leave to meet his parents for a nice North Indian breakfast. They're over for a couple of weeks from India. He's going to join us this afternoon."

"I couldn't eat all that spicy food for breakfast, it'd really give me gas!"

Rob rubbed his abdomen and pulled a face of pretend sickness.

"Yeah, a gas man with more gas isn't a good idea and you don't want to stink out the theatre when the surgeons are operating!"

"Well, you can blame it on the unconscious anaesthetised patient. They can't deny it!"

We fell about laughing again.

"Look children!" Fi interjected, slapping Rob and then me around the side of our heads.

Honestly, I wasn't *her* bloody boyfriend.

We spent the day in a relatively mundane way reviewing the patients and doing routine chores. Everything was mostly under control. I did miss Dave all afternoon as I had to hierarchically 'step down' and do all of his bloody donkey work.

I was far too senior for all that bollocks but when Fi says "do it", you just "do it".

"Where *is* bloody Davinder anyway? I've been doing *his* shit all day."

"I dunno, he hasn't bleeped us to tell us he was going to be late. Maybe he's caught up with Isaac to tell him how it all went."

BLEEEP BLEEEP

"Ahh, again, talk of the Devil and the Devil himself shall arrive... or bleep you anyway."

"Dr Manson..."

"Hey... Jayce... eet eez I-zak."

"Hey! Alright, man? Wassup?"

"Av, you seen Dev? Eez he okay?"

"Erm, no he hasn't joined up with us on the round this afternoon."

"Oh. Maybe he az been dee-layed."

"Don't worry, man, I'm sure he's fine. He's probably just having a challenge with his folks. It is a bit of a bomb shell he's dropping, to say the least."

Coming out of the closet, as Dave was planning to do, was going to shock his folks, especially as they'd probably already found him a future wife back in India.

"I am sure yoo ah-rayt."

Isaac put the phone down.

"Who was that?" Fi asked.

"Isaac. He hasn't seen Dave."

We hadn't seen Dave either. Where *was* Dave?

"Do you want to go and see if he's come back to the hospital, Jace? He'll have at least hung his duffle coat up in the mess and taken his white coat off the peg."

Yes, that was a good idea. Dave looked like *Paddington Bear* with that coat on... an Indian version obviously.

"Maybe he's checked in with Sister Sledge while looking for us on the ward round?"

"Yeah, she's probably collared him to do some of the tasks *you* were supposed to do, Jace."

"Funny. Okay, I'm going up to ward eleven then. See you in a bit."

"Okay. Laters, Jayce. Good luck!"

I walked on to Ward 11. Nurse Totten sat at the nurses' station next to Nurse Nightshade who had a mouthful of *Quality Street*. She was opening another purple-wrapped, hazelnut, milk chocolate one before she'd even swallowed the other ones. There was melted chocolate around her cheeks.

I caught Jessica's eyes and she just looked straight back down and carried on writing up her nursing notes.

Nurse Nightshade, without blinking, did not avert her direct, laser-cutting gaze and subtly stuck two chocolatey fingers up at me whilst sticking out an equally chocolatey and pierced tongue. A brown, syrupy dribble stretched slowly from her mouth and onto the desk.

Okay, I'm being ignored. Not important right now. I was on a mission.

"Dr Manson! And to what do we owe this honour? Twice in one day?"

Sister Sledge stood solidly before me with one eyebrow raised.

"Have you seen Dave?"

"Ah, yes, Dr Dewani. He did come up here not long after the patients had eaten lunch."

"Oh, good. Was he alright?"

"Well, I thought he'd gone back to join you on the ward round. He said that one of the other wards had run out of Actrapid[49] and a syringe driver for one of the diabetics."

"Right. Did he now?"

"Yes, he took the clinical cupboard keys. He did return them to me like the good boy that he is... not like you, *Doctor*, who took them home with you!"

"Nice," I was unamused. "So let me get this straight. He took insulin, a syringe driver... and the tubing too?"

"Yes."

---

[49] Actrapid is a fast-acting solution of human insulin used to treat diabetes and elevated blood glucose levels; one of the risks was hypoglycaemia if you gave too much.

"Shit!"

Was Dave trying to kill himself?!

An intravenous syringe driver of rapid-acting insulin would put him into a hypoglycaemic coma, dropping his blood sugar levels quickly. The chance of death would depend upon how long the low blood sugar had put him into a coma for... if that's what he's done.

Shit, if he's done this, he is a total wreck. Why, why, why?? Okay, I needed to get a move on. I'll try the mess again, I thought... on-call room would seem a good place to start. I know, the unused on-call room, the scene of Dave's accidental near exsanguination when we were trying to cure our hangovers!

"Sister, give me some fifty percent dextrose vials, a needle and some *Hypostop gel*? Quickly!"

We indeed moved quickly and grabbed the supplies to hopefully reverse Dave's stupidity.

I ran.

"Doctor?!" Sister Sledge called to me with a rare undertone of panic in her voice.

I looked back, the solid Sister Sledge looked somewhat ruffled.

Okay, if I'm lucky and I find him, he'll have about a 95% chance of a full recovery. The problem was, if I didn't and he did have the 'success' he clearly wanted, there'd be a fifty/fifty chance of death or permanent brain damage.

Any drug overdose was largely unsuccessful with only about 2% of people succeeding. It could also be a very harrowing way to die; take the popular Paracetamol overdose... it's cheap (not that that matters when you're dead), readily available, but it usually succeeded in knackering your liver resulting in you unceremoniously bleeding to death and without a hope of hepatic trans-plantation.

Shit, Dave, if you're gonna do it, jump in front of a sodding train or off a bridge[50]… but don't do it in front of an off duty doctor! I momentarily reflected.

I crashed into the mess carrying my kit. The mess was empty.

Everyone must still be on the wards or in theatres.

I checked the on-call rooms. They were all unlocked and open.

The unused one…

Locked!

"Dave!"

I banged on the door, fumbled with the handle, hoping he'd answer.

"DAVE!"

Fuckit. I don't go to the gym for nothing…

Grrrr… AARRGHH!!

Adrenaline-fuelled, I shoulder-barged the door open. The old, wooden frame splintered at the latch. I fell into the room.

"Oh! Fuck! DAVE, DAVE!! YOU UTTER, UTTER DICK-WAD!!"

Why didn't he come back to the ward round and talk to us… we're his friends!

Dave lay on the bed, sweaty and attached to the syringe driver which sat on the bedside table all neatly set up.

There was an entire empty bottle of *Bacardi* rum next to it. He'd obviously developed a taste for rum and

---

[50] The suicide mortality rate is about the same among male and female doctors and significantly higher than the general population.

this was *no* Virgin Mojito. The last time he'd had a double rum, he became practically unconscious. But a *whole* bottle?!

Okay... it *was* an airline miniature bottle... but that's beside the point. He must have still been very drunk.

For fkksake... look, he's put a bloody label on the syringe and written 'Actrapid' on it! He was a good lad, always labelling the syringes so you didn't get drugs mixed up but seriously, did it *really* matter right now?

Maybe he was hoping to be found? Smart boy.

"Dave, you knob-head!"

I pressed 'STOP' on the syringe driver, which had probably injected about half of the volume, and shook him hard. I could smell the alcohol.

No response, except for a trumpeting snore.

GCS? About 3. Airway? Open-ish. Pulse? Present and correct.

"Jeezus!"

I opened a packet of the *Hypostop* gel[51] and squirted it in Dave's snoring, open mouth and under his tongue where it would be absorbed quickly and start bringing his blood sugar level up and out of his life-threatening hypoglycaemic coma.

I started drawing up some 50% dextrose solution to directly inject into Dave's veins. He'd been courteous enough to cannulate himself with an intravenous line, which was a pretty skilful trick, to set his infusion going.

I disconnected it and started rapidly injecting the strong sugar solution.

---

[51] Hypostop is an essential emergency accessory for the treatment of potential diabetic coma, Glucogel is a flavoured, concentrated dextrose gel which provides a rapid increase in blood glucose level.

3 1 7

Come on, Dave, my little friend, my sidekick, my buddy, without whom my days would be very boring indeed. Plus, who would I pass on all my knowledge, coping mechanisms and other ludicrously crappy advice to? It would be like dying rich and childless.

Okay, I exaggerate.

Hang on… what's this?

On the floor, behind the bedside cabinet, there were several other empty glass bottles in a small pile.

I picked one of them up and spun it around to read the label.

'50% *Dextrose Monohydrate Injection*"

"What the fu…?!"

He's picked up the antidote by mistake. It must have been next to the Actrapid in the drug cupboard. Being so pissed, he can't have noticed.

Dave, you gloriously inept, idiotic Numpty! I slumped backwards on the bed next to Davinder, closed my eyes and listened to his Bombay Symphony orchestral snoring.

His act of actual breathing was a sitar to my ears.

Rather than a proper suicide attempt with insulin, Dave had succeeded in getting himself shit-faced…

… with one almighty SUGAR HIT!

Lucky, stupid bar-stard.

Chapter Twenty-Seven

Vorsprung durch Technik

Sweet Smell of Success

Dave's 'little episode' was particularly traumatic for our team. Everyone was shocked at what he'd done. Dave had silently put himself under a whole lot of strain and not properly shared his anxieties, and presumed depressive state, with anyone.

Dave's dad had been very angry and virtually disowned him for bringing 'shame' upon the family and accused him of wasting the opportunities that had been afforded to him.

Isaac took it particularly hard. He started attending his own ward rounds, going to his gynae clinics regularly and stopped watching *The A-Team* and *TJ Hooker*. He didn't give up *Starksy and Hutch* though.

Dr Bodman was very understanding and enabled Davinder to take time off work and seek some psychological help, with the support of a counsellor and his GP. He, of course, wouldn't be back for a while. Whilst he'd only got a bit drunk on miniature *Bacardi*, it still had to be put down as 'a suicide attempt by a junior doctor' and, naturally, taken very seriously.

This was tough for me too but it could have been a lot worse and the whole episode would need psychologically parking, along with the other psychological cars in my rapidly filling mental car park.

I was going to have to 'act down' as well as performing my own responsibilities. Where were we going to get a locum house officer from at such short notice?

This was particularly irritating as I was trying to finish my preparation for Professor Klein and arrange a proper face-to-face meeting; another priority faced some unwelcome competition.

My medical rotation was a coming to a close and I'd be unemployed if I didn't sort out a specialist training post in cardiology... or something.

Maybe I could blag starting another rotation and get some experience in the intensive care unit and in renal medicine, then I could just quit early when, or if, something better turned up. Those two specialities were always a bit scary but would be decent experience moving forward whatever I ended up doing.

Fiona came into the mess, this time with Rob and they were arm in arm. The Davinder episode seemed to have softened her persona even more and she was embracing the happiness she had discovered and publicly showed it off.

Well, they did look good together and were clearly in love... whatever that was.

"Hey, morning, Jace, how're you doing?"

The absence of Dave seemed to be having a lesser effect on her. I think she'd had experience of an attempted suicide by a colleague before.

"I'm okay. It's all a bit knackering without Dave."

"Well, I have some good news and sort of bad news."

"Oh right, here we go... what?"

"Well, the good news is, we have a locum house officer for our team."

"Oh, awesome! That's amazing! What's the bad news? Don't they speak English or something?"

"It's a final year medical student. They're doing their finals, they're at the pinnacle of their knowledge and they need the experience, not to mention the money, before they start their house officer jobs for real."

"Oh, a student…" I sighed a little but some help was better than no help at all, I suppose.

"It's Helena Mastromassaro."

I instantly perked up again as a brief flush of adrenaline entered my circulation.

"Oh… Helena, erm, that's good then."

The Greek goddess had returned to me from Elysium.

"Yes, Jace, she's the only one who volunteered. Apparently she enjoyed her experience of working with our team *so* much last time that she couldn't turn down this opportunity."

I smiled on the inside. She had definitely worked very well with me… and not just the once.

"It was Dr Bodman's idea, not mine," said Fi. "I'm sure you'll take good care of her, Jace… in a senior mentor sense!"

Fi pointed a firm and knowing finger in my direction as Rob smiled, gave her a big kiss on the cheek and went to put the kettle on. He briefly turned back around and, keeping a very straight, dead-pan face, gave a perverted 'pelvic thrust' in my direction behind Fiona's back.

I tried to keep a straight face of my own.

I rang up Professor Klein's secretary to arrange an audience with 'Die fantastische Welt von Oz!'

"Hello, it's Linda Lichfield, Professor McTavi… erm, Professor *Klein's* secretary speaking. How may I help you?"

Linda's voice was rather camp but also rather deep for a woman which made me wonder whether in fact she was in some form of sexual transition.

I explained my situation and, annoyingly, she offered me a window of opportunity.

"Oh, well if you can come up *now*, he's free."

Oh, shhhh-ouvlaki! I haven't prepared anything, I mean I had a few ideas in my head but...

"Erm, well, okay sure, I'll just check that my registrar can cover for me but assume she can and please tell the Professor I'll be there."

"Okay. See you soon, Doctor, remember... level nine."

Bloody hell. Well, this would make or break my career, I guess, but I suppose you've gotta take your chance when it presents itself.

"Fi... could you..."

"Yeeeees, I heard your conversation, Jace. It's okay, I'll be seeing Helena on the ward shortly so at least she'll get some proper teaching till you get back."

I didn't rise to the bait and just flashed her a fake smile.

Now I was getting nervous.

Level 9 was not only a long way to walk if you took the stairs, which I always did, it also felt like a genuine trek. Each floor I passed, the closer I came to a possibly life-changing career move.

The higher I climbed, the less people I passed. It was not unusual to pass a few physiophlamingos in their white tunics, blue trousers and trainers, trying their elderly or post-operative patients on stair therapy before they ventured back home.

By the time you got to about Level 7, they'd virtually vanished. There were no wards or clinical departments on Level 9 and I wasn't even sure if I'd ever been up there before. In fact, I didn't know anyone who'd ever been up there before.

The air was thinner and I was becoming rather short of breath. It was probably more due to anxiety and the fact that my legs were knackered rather than true altitude sickness.

Level 9. The Professorial Academic Unit. So it said on an ornate placard in gold-leafed writing. There was a thick, wooden door set in a grand, matching window frame to greet me.

Suddenly, everything began to look a bit more refined compared to the dated 1970's greyness that symbolised the rest of the hospital.

As I walked through the door, the subtle, sweet smell of pipe smoke tickled my airways. I found my way along a sort of one way maze of small corridors and discovered Linda.

"Hello, I'm Dr Manson here to see Professor Klein."

"Ah yes, hello, Doctor, we've been expecting you. The professor will be free shortly, please have a seat."

Yes, he was clearly a very busy man but he'd made time especially for me. In reality, I'd just got a bit lucky.

I sat down on an old, brown, cloth chair which resembled the on-call room chairs. Predictably, I sunk right through the centre of it as most of the springs had bust. A cunning and belittling trap!

So, things aren't *that* different up here then.

I flicked through a copy of *The Lancet* that was on a small table by the chair. One of the world's oldest and best known medical journals reminded me of the immense task ahead of performing medical research. I didn't really understand any of the stuff in the copy I'd picked up either, which made me even more nervous.

"The professor will see you now," Linda smiled at me. There were red blotches on her front teeth.

She looked a bit like 'Mish' *Moneypenny* from one of the old *Sean Connery Bond* films, only with much thicker, red lipstick, poorly applied eye shadow, black-rimmed glasses and I'm also certain that she/he was wearing a wig.

"Thank you, Mish Money... err, Linda."

I mean everyone loves a go at the Connery accent, don't they?

As I walked towards Professor Klein's office, the smell of pipe smoke strengthened.

Wow, his office was massive! All oak wood-panelled with a huge window overlooking the City... what a view! Who knew?

The professor, in a black suit with red waistcoat and gold buttons, sat at an enormous, dark, wooden desk on a huge, old-fashioned and almost regal-looking, red velour cushioned chair.

One presumed that the NHS did not provide such chairs as standard.

His greying-blonde hair was swept back on his head demarcating a rather recessive hairline. He puffed upon a large, brown pipe which was nestled in the corner of his mouth.

Honestly, give him a soft, white pussy to stroke and the scene would be complete.

It was quite a sweet smell and whilst I didn't really approve of smoking, I quite liked the smell of a pipe; it reminded me of my old pottery and sculpture teacher at school. No one cared about kids and passive smoking back then.

His eyes were a little blood-shot and they followed me over the top of his half-mooned glasses as I walked into the quiet room only to hear an old clock deeply ticking in the corner.

Jeez, who built this room, it looked nothing like anything that should exist in the NHS but yet, here I was.

He still said nothing but just nodded at a single seat in the middle of the room about five feet in front of his desk.

I took that as a *'hello, please take a seat'* or better still, *'I've been expecting you... Doctor Manson.'*

It all felt a bit weird and to be honest, he was quite rude now I think about it, acting all 'superior' as if I was nothing.

"Do you expect me to talk?"

"Nooo, Dr Manson... I expect you to die!"

Well, I guess in his eyes, I was a 'nothing'. My achievements through medical school, my life-saving successes and on-call war zone survival meant nothing sat here in font of him.

"Zo..."

His voice was deep and distinctly German.

"Vot kann Ich do fur Sie?"

Had Linda said nothing?

"Well, sir, I'd like to pursue a career in cardiology and I'm looking to do some research with a view to getting an MD[52]."

He shifted very slightly in his chair, took another puff of his pipe and a decent sip from his heavy-looking whiskey glass on the desk.

---

[52] M.D. - a post graduate academic research doctorate, Doctor of Medicine, requiring at least two years of work. Not to be confused with the standard first professional American graduation medical school degree; like Doogie Howser MD.

Shit, what *was* I doing here?

"Vell, ich might haff und project."

"Ah, oh, good... excellent!" I spluttered in pleasant astonishment.

I hadn't needed to share any of my ideas about rhubarb or indeed African Tree Frogs. I needed some good fortune.

"But, you vill need to prepare und Grant Application fur die Britische Herz Foundation."

He inhaled deeply on his pipe again and exhaled the sweet smoke of opportunity in my direction.

I breathed in that opportunity with equally sweet appreciation.

"So, what project would you like me to consider, sir?"

He took a large gulp of whiskey. The ice cubes rattled in the glass. The clock ticked more deeply.

"Vell... vee need to look... at zee effect..."

I held some more of the smooth, sweet smoke in my lungs for a few more seconds.

"...of statins on zee endothelium of zee coronary arteries in hyperlipidaemic, diabetic patients."

Okay, no rhubarb, no frogs... I could get into that.

"Okay, sir, I could get into that."

"Zehr gut! Ausgezeichnet!"

He sat back in his very comfortable looking chair and tried to relight his pipe.

Well, he did seem pleased, if perhaps just a little drunk. I hope he didn't have a ward round or the 'cath lab' later today. I think, him trying to manipulate wires and catheter tubes into someones arteries supplying their heart would not be too clever right now.

"Zo, komm und zee me again… ven you haff completed zee grant? Ist das gut?"

I heard the clock throatily tick in the background expecting me to give my answer. Time almost stood still.

I expected one of his henchmen, *Oddjob,* to appear from behind the curtains to make me accept this generous offer.

"Erm, sure. I'll keep in touch with you, sir, and let you know how I'm getting on."

"It vont be easy and you vill need to be very, very thorough. Great care must be taken. Okay, alzo, danke. Nice to meet you, Doktor… err…"

"The name's Manson. Jacen… Manson."

Remember my name, Professor… Ernst Stavro Blofeld!

I gave the professor a gentle reminder so as not to embarrass him.

Shit… it'd probably be easier to get the broomstick off the Wicked Witch of the West.

Oz, das Große und Mächtige.
Oz, the Great and Powerful!

Chapter Twenty-Eight

Sixth Sense

Not Quite Right

Everyone in the mess was at a very low ebb after the suicide attempt; it really brought home not only how fragile life could be, but also how it could potentially happen to any of us.

The signs could be cleverly concealed, especially by a doctor who has had some training in psychology or psychiatry. We also had the knowledge of, and potentially easy access to, some useful drugs that could make the experience quicker and hopefully more painless.

I hadn't personally heard from Dave but apparently Isaac had seen him and he was doing alright. Sadly, Dave hadn't since seen his parents who'd returned to India to cancel the wedding arrangements they had already put in place. I think his dad also thought that Dave had picked up a virus which had caused this 'sexual aberration' in the first place.

Isaac continued to keep a low profile and he was certainly far less manic but eternally grateful to me for saving Dave from an even greater sugar rush than he'd already delivered to himself. But there was nothing I could have done about his alcohol tolerance, or lack of it.

I hadn't heard from Jessica either since she'd so articulately delivered her 'joyful' news. I'd wanted to go with her to the hospital when she had the 'procedure' to show my support for her but she'd ignored my calls, so what could I do? I had tried her flat but either she wasn't at home or she just wasn't answering the door to me.

Why that hurt me, I wasn't sure. Was I feeling paternal? Maybe. It's not as if she was my ideal woman either, far from it. But somehow my warped emotions were deceiving me into thinking I probably liked her more than I thought I did. Maybe I'd attained some kind of saviour complex[53].

Jess needed help with her cigarette and Class A drug problem. She also needed a *'fucking'* dictionary but there was little I could do about that!

Derogatory, I know, but I think I was just generally pissed off right now; that was probably an understatement.

Did all doctors have this complex on some level? Was I actively seeking out girlfriends or friends that needed some particular help from me? I'd patch them up and then move on... like those classic US TV shows *The Littlest Hobo* or *Highway to Heaven*.

Whilst I couldn't be there for Karen when her mum died, it was because I was trying to help patients at work at the same time. I had spent the first few years of dating her trying to help her recover from some form of eating disorder and I was only just properly learning about that subject at medical school at the time. I wasn't her psychiatrist, I was her boyfriend; where does one begin and the other end when you're a doctor?

I'd heard via Sister Sledge, who'd heard from Nurse Nightshade, that Jessica had decided to change tack in her nursing career and started a new job on the cardiac intensive care unit. I suppose she could exercise her caring skills on those anaesthetised patients in drug-induced comas; they wouldn't answer back either.

---

[53] A messiah or saviour complex is a state of mind in which an individual holds a belief that they are destined to become a saviour or when an individual believes that he or she is responsible for saving or assisting others.

I was sure she'd also encounter Professor Kurt Klein, The Great and Powerful, if he made it down from the *Emerald City* or his *Bond* villain lair. He didn't do any cardiac surgery but he'd have to have some medical input into the post-operative patients she'd be tending to now.

Coincidentally, I'd also overheard Matt Dundee in the mess going on about some new, hot nurse with a weird, *funny accent* who'd started on the CICU.

"Jeez, mate, hev you seen thit new nerse on cardiac? She's got an amyzing sit of bazoomas bat oy theenk she's three bingers short of a barbie! Bit of a pricktease too oy theenk!"

Funny accent?! Drongo. He can talk!

That was all rich coming from him with his whiny, nasally destruction of vowels and his pointless upward inflections at the end of every sentence whether there was a question involved in it or not.

Fackin Iddee-it.

It did sound like he was indeed referring to Miss Black Country, Queen of Dudley.

Obviously, I could guess the way his dirty Antipodean mind was scheming. Did he know I was seeing her? Well, I wasn't actually *seeing* her, but I *was* seeing her.

He was the sort of bloke that wouldn't give two shits even if she was married and just see her as an even greater challenge with a more coveted prize for his arrogant surfer ego to polish and put away in his mental trophy cabinet… for another future lonely day.

I think I really was in a bit of a mood today (if you hadn't noticed). I could feel pain in the back of my throat, I was beginning to feel viral and it was getting more painful to swallow the ward chocolates and the great hospital canteen fry-ups. Maybe I was getting tonsillitis?

I'd been to the gym a couple of times this week and felt fairly strong but just really knackered and I was getting a bit short of breath very quickly. A fall in my usual performance at the gym often hailed the imminent arrival of a cold or the particularly loathsome man 'flu.

Fi had gone off on study leave to prepare the final push for her imminent exams and Dr Bodman had gone off sick with the actual 'flu. I suppose we were getting to that time of year.

I didn't see the point in getting a 'flu jab either as every time I got it, I got the damn 'flu.

A common complaint.

It'd super boost your immune system to cope with something like the top three or four viruses of the season and then you'd get sick from Ebola virus, Bird, Swine or bloody Aardvark Flu because your entire infantry of white cells and antibodies had been deployed elsewhere. If you're reading this under quarantine in 2020, you might even be sick from the coronavirus (COVID-19) or, more likely, sick of it altogether!

Helena and I, the remaining working members of the team, were reviewing Mrs P.G. Brown in the hospital canteen and enjoying a freshly baked *Otis Spunkmeyer* cookie with 'her'. Currently, my congested state was having its own personal war with my tastebuds. On top of which, this morning, Mrs Brown needed a full and thorough examination. Maybe Mr Tetley and Vanessa Caffay also need some special attention.

We were also discussing how Mr Clementine was *still* with us on the wards. He'd taken a turn for the worse. The first signs were him no longer telling us a terrible joke on every ward round. He'd started confabulating and getting more confused and forgetful. We'd done as much as we could from the medical point of view but I think his liver was really packing up and he probably needed a transplant.

Helena's bleep went off.

"Aren't you getting used to that yet?"

"Oh, I quite like it actually, it sort of makes me feel really important."

She unplucked it from her waist, smiled and examined the radiopager like it was a vital symbol of being a junior doctor.

"I'm sure that feeling'll pass once you're qualified, after maybe half an hour. It'll go off so often that you won't even have time for the loo. One day it'll go off when you're actually sat on the toilet and you'll just throw it in the bowl, before flushing, begging that they'd leave you alone!"

Here endeth another lesson.

"Anyway, you'd better answer that, it might be important."

She finished the last bite of her cookie and got up to answer the bleep from the wards. I couldn't help but allow my eyes to follow Helena as she walked away to answer the canteen phone. I think she knew it too because she seemed to roll her hips subtly more seductively than usual, as if to call out to me.

She came back to sit down after her conversation.

"Mrs Migginski's back. She came in last night under one of the surgical teams but they've written in the notes to say that maybe Dr Bodman's team would like to take over the care of 'their old friend'."

That was always a total-bastard thing to write in the notes and I hated it. Basically translated, it meant, "we've admitted this complex patient, found out that *your* team has seen her a total of maybe once, *we* can't really be arsed with sorting them out, so we'll 'politely' offer you the irrefusable opportunity, in writing (so it's part of the legal document that is the patient's case notes), to take over patient care and accept our 'kind and generous' offer."

I flubbered my lips letting out an exasperated sigh.

"What's wrong with her?"

"You took a biopsy from her a while ago in clinic and it came back as sigmoid colon cancer. She's had a bowel resection since then and apparently it hasn't spread, but the nurses just said that 'she's not quite right' now."

"So, nice and specific then."

We slurped the rest of our cold teas down simultaneously to signal our call to arms and stood up ready to hit the wards.

When the nurses say someone's not quite right, you had to take note. Ignore such non-specific remarks at your peril. Whilst things may be fine and stable from the bedside, sometimes the experienced nurse just 'knew'. You might not put your finger on it quite at first, but there was often that certain something, the sixth or indeed seventh sense.

We wandered onto the ward to be met by Student Nurse Alice Sharples. I hadn't seen Alice for a while and she had gained a certain air of confidence.

"Hey, Alice."

"Doctor Manson." She responded with an unusual professional formality... for her.

"Aw, why so formal, Alice?" I feigned grave disappointment and sadness.

"Oh, I'm sorry, I'm just trying to pretend to be as professional as possible to see if I can control my ridiculous habit of blushing all the time."

She blushed, revealing an abstract dermatological map on her neck and upper chest, this time of the Grand Canyon, I believe.

"Okay, well, good work so far… have you changed your hair?"

"Oh, Jacen, you noticed!"

She smiled very sweetly and flicked her new shoulder-length, and more professionally nursey, hairstyle at me. She looked a few years older and less like a frightened fluffy rabbit on a railway track with the 6.15 to London Paddington bearing down upon her.

Helena suddenly looked like she was harbouring an element of jealousy witnessing Alice's overt display of flirtation.

"Ahem… shouldn't we go and see Mrs Migginski, Nurse?"

Helena hijacked Alice's follicular fondling.

Ooo, two women simultaneously scrabbling for my attentions… I felt that I had to fantasise for a brief moment to make myself feel better.

Alice took us to see Mrs Migginski.

"She's not quite right… that's what Sister Sledge says. And I agree, she isn't."

I was, of course, delighted that not-yet-qualified Nurse Sharples concurred with the vast experience of Sister Sledge.

I sat beside Magorzata and did a brief examination. Nothing to find apart from the fact that she now had a stoma bag following her bowel resection.

"How are you, Mrs Migginski?"

"Oh, I'm okay, Doctor, I'm just tired. I'm fed up actually. My family think I'm a burden and want to put me in a nursing home. But I want to stay in my own home. My parents bought it when they came over from Poland and I won't be forced into selling it."

"It seems like we cured your cancer though?"

"Yes, Doctor, the bleeding's all stopped after the operation."

She had nonetheless become quite frail. She was looking better than when I'd seen her in clinic by putting on a little weight, but right now it seemed like she'd given up a bit.

"All her observations are fine, Dr Manson," said Helena, officiously perusing the observations chart and fluid balance sheets.

"Any pain?"

"No, not really."

Mrs Migginski's face had lost a certain energy and she didn't have that sparkle in her eyes that many elderly people still did, even though their bodies had become wrinkled, frail and wasted.

I did, however, detect that very faint, subtle, slightly spicy and musty smell in the air around her. I'd smelt this before on two or three previous occasions. It usually signified only one thing...

Death would be on the next train over and would probably have generously packed Mrs Migginski a small travel bag and purchased her a one way ticket to Rose Cottage[54].

---

[54] Rose Cottage is our euphemism for the morgue.

We walked back over to the nurse's station.

"So, Nurse Sharples," I thought I'd play Alice's game of professional formalities, "there isn't really anything for us to do right now but I'd just keep her as comfortable as possible. But, I sense that she's given up on her enthusiasm for life and suspect that she will no longer be with us tomorrow."

"Oh, really? But isn't there anything at all we should do?"

"How do you know that, Jace?" Helena echoed.

"Oh, it's the smell…"

And the fact that she's just *'not quite right'*.

Chapter Twenty-Nine

Starsky and Dutch

Lurching Backwards

So, my background work for Professor Klein was going fairly well. I was hoping to catch him again with a decent first draft of my grant application at the upcoming conference in Amsterdam. I'd only just remembered I'd booked study leave for it.

I had put all of the printouts of the relevant research papers and my notes that I needed in a nice, new, black leather briefcase that my dad had bought me for my birthday a few months before. They were accompanied by a clinical diagnostic kit and my new, engraved cardiology stethoscope in anticipation of my prospective chosen career.

My briefcase. It felt good and it looked the part. Despite the tough times in my personal life and at work, I was beginning to feel a touch of excitement again.

I thought that I'd pop over to Nurse Totten's once again to try and to get some relationship clarity. Although, I supposed that things were fairly crystal clear already, in all honesty. It did occur to me that she might not even have gone to the clinic at all for her 'procedure'.

I parked on the street just down from the 'hostel' that was Nurse Totten's lair. As I approached it, the usual personnel could be seen coming and going in their varied states of mental alertness. I passed by two of them on the pavement.

The big, orange door was closed. I knocked loudly. Slow footsteps caused the stripped wooden floor boards to creak.

Yet another stranger answered the door, he was about six feet five inches tall and you could have mistaken him for *Lurch* from the *The Addams Family*.

"YOU RAAAAANG?" I imagined that he should have deeply groaned his greeting but he actually said literally nothing. He looked just as pale as Lurch and also had a very prominent frontal bone to his elongated, thick skull with deep set eyes and a rectangular jaw. He'd obviously just inhaled a lung full of his long, fat roll-up cigarette and as he opened the door, he breathed it all out... directly into my face.

There was definitely more than just a dash of weed in that. Jeez! I tried to waft it away from my airspace.

Before I could ask him if Jess was home, I heard a window smash. I looked back down the street to where I'd parked to just see one of the weirdos I'd passed in the street moments ago, running off down the road.

Was he carrying my new briefcase?

I left Lurch... in the... err... lurch and ran back towards my car.

"Oh, for fucckkssaakke! You've *got* to be kidding me!"

I banged hard on the roof of my car with two tightly clenched fists. I think that I left a small dent. The car was quite flimsy anyway.

I'd stupidly left my briefcase on the passenger seat and the window was shattered all over the inside footwell and the seat. Of course, my case was now gone.

Stupid idiot.

Apart from my new stethoscope, the ophthalmoscope, tendon hammer and a pen torch from a drug rep (that's a medical drug company representative, not a cocaine dealer), there was nothing of particularly excessive monetary value, just sentimental value but, vitally, papers of utmost academic importance.

All that time researching and writing for that all-important grant application was now history.

I looked up at the sky. I think it's going to rain.

Oh, go on then, why not strike me down with a bolt of lightning as well?!

Piss.

Could my day get any worse?

Well, as it happened... yes... it could. Destiny, Torment and Utter-Bastard (yes, a double-barrelled name) were having a sodding field day with me.

My mobile phone rang. It was Mum.

"Hi, son. Are you alright? I haven't heard from you for a while and I was just thinking about you."

Mum had a habit of being able to do that. Her soft, beautiful and comforting voice was an elixir to my current, and indeed recurrent, despair.

I told her what had happened which made her news all the more difficult to deliver.

"Now, I don't want to worry you," whenever she started with this line, it was almost invariably especially bad news, "but Grandad has been admitted to hospital. They said it's just a little stroke and they're hoping he'll be home in a couple of weeks."

Great. That's all I needed.

"I'll drive up to see him, Mum, it's okay."

Grandad lived with Nana, who was also 'almost' *Mollie Sugden* in her heyday, in the north of England and about a five hour drive away. I'd need to take a few days of leave but only if Fi was back from her exam and only after the Amsterdam conference which was now booked, including my flights and accommodation.

All I really wanted to do was get in my car and go right now. But there was a smashed window to sort out first and I needed to call the cops to report this shite.

The police were as helpful as I'd expected. They took all the usual details and explained that it was highly unlikely that I'd get anything back but, given that there was nothing of any particular interest to a druggie, the thieves would surely just dump the bag and hopefully my research work would be retrievable.

I was kind of expecting them to send round *Starsky and Hutch, TJ Hooker* or the *California Highway Patrol* but better still, *Lieutenant Columbo*. I mean, surely there were fingerprints on my door handle to be dusted for, or samples of pubic hair to genetically test? They needed to take this seriously, goddammit!

"*And just one more thing...*"[55]

I was a victim of crime, *Lieutenant Columbo*.

So, the victim support officer came round to see me at my flat because clearly I now needed counselling, 'there, there, you're a victim of crime, there's nothing we can do to get your shit back because we're so understaffed and underfunded by the government that minor crimes like this can't have the resources thrown at them we'd otherwise like... unless you were murdered, of course, and then we'd take it a bit more seriously.'

I get the 'rationing of resources' argument in the public sector; we did it in the NHS all the time. But that didn't stop me feeling monumentally pissed off. Plus the victim support officer looked *nothing* like *Heather Locklear*.

---

[55] Lt. Columbo's brilliant trademark 'false exits' that wrong-foot all the murderers; after most informal interrogations with the murderer, Columbo leaves the scene, only to return a few seconds later with the opening gambit of "*just one more thing*" only for it to be the most important question that he "*forgot to ask*".

At least that might have taken the edge off it; I grasped weakly and desperately at the thought.

Both Fi and Dr Bodman were back at work. Dr Bodman's bout of actual 'flu had caused him to lose some weight, well a couple of pounds anyway, he'd boasted. Fi had done the final clinical part of her MRCP exam and was actually looking and feeling rather quietly confident. She wouldn't get her results until nearer Christmas time.

Rob was very glad indeed to have her back. By the sounds of it, he was reaping the benefits of Fi's recent release of exam pressure.

Poor Davinder was still off work but making some progress.

Dr Bodman, as usual, was supportive in allowing me to not only go and see my grandad but also to have some study leave for the cardiac conference in Amsterdam. He even told Helena that she should attend with me as it would be good for her education and continuing professional development.

As a student, she'd be able to attend without paying conference fees and, naturally, I'd be *more* than delighted to continually professionally develop her.

Fi didn't say anything as she knew that I probably needed the company and she was currently all about physical contact right now.

Helena was delighted at this suggestion when Dr Bodman had mentioned it to her on the ward round, much to the obvious disgruntlement of Student Nurse Alice Sharples who didn't at all feel that Helena should be accompanying me on her own.

Alice's stare bore into Helena, who in turn absorbed the stare, amplified it and reflected an even sterner one right back at Alice. Dr Bodman noted this stare-off and gave them both a special 'stare' all of his own... at the same time, without even moving his head.

Helena and I were sat on the small twin-propeller plane at the City Airport as the engines fired up. We were buckled in and I peered past her to look out of the window. The weather was looking a bit grim outside and Helena didn't really like flying... a bit like *BA Baracus* from the *A-Team*, only I couldn't just chloroform her and put her to sleep... well I could, but someone would almost certainly start asking questions.

She put her hand on my lap and firmly squeezed my thigh with some degree of aviophobia, although I did wonder whether it was just an excuse to fondle me.

I thought about my briefcase again. I still hadn't heard from the police and had resigned myself to having lost it forever. I'd have to start the work all over again and apologise to Professor Klein.

He wouldn't be happy and either send *Oddjob* to get me, drop me unceremoniously into a shark tank or slowly attempt to laser me in half, starting at the groin, the next time I went to see him.

The plane took off loudly. Helena grabbed my arm and pulled herself close to me for support. Of course, I was here to support her in any way I could.

I hated propeller planes too, I much preferred a decent jet engine; they just felt much safer than this wind-up toy we were currently sat in. But it was a relatively short flight to Amsterdam so we had to just put up with it and get pissed on the flight's miniature alcoholic beverage selection. Dave would have loved that! I spared a thought for my little buddy and hoped that he was indeed okay.

About half an hour into the flight and over all the loud engine noise, I thought I could hear the deep Germanic tones of Professor Kurt Klein, also on his way to the conference.

His voice seemed closer than I'd first thought. Would he even recognise me again? He was speaking actual German too.

I peered around a bit but couldn't really move much as the plane was so bloody small and there was only really leg room for Mr Bignall. This would be like Business Class for him.

Hang on... there in the seat immediately in front of me was the receding hairline of none other than Professor Klein himself. He was travelling in a slightly over-sized, pin-striped suit with matching waistcoat.

I could never understand people that travelled in suits on a plane. So uncomfortable. Were they just hoping for a free upgrade because they looked smart? I just travelled in comfy jeans, trainers and a hoodie sweatshirt. I didn't really like dressing like a doctor in public, especially when I was off duty. Some people did, as they felt more defined by their jobs than I did when out of work.

"Hey, Jace! Is that the new Prof Klein?" Helena asked, trying to raise her voice enough for me to hear her over the engine noise but soft enough not to be heard by him.

The professor must have overheard his name mentioned and he turned around and looked through the gap between the two seats in front of us. His eyes were still reddened and he smelt like he'd already consumed a few whiskeys in the departure lounge before boarding, aside from the full plastic glass, with the volume of at least three miniature *Johnnie Walkers* that he now held in his hand!

He was sharing a joke with two other German colleagues either side of him, Dr Helmut Fuchs and Dr Heinrich Winkler, his backroom staff of Clinical Senior Lecturers... *Happy Days!*

I sensed the pungent pong of power, infiltrating a cloudy cocktail of ethanolic breath and the faintest whiff of sweet, stale smoke on their clothes.

"Ah... Doctor Mmm... Smm... Nmm...?"

Okay, this time, he was getting *no* assistance from me, despite his slurring.

"Doctor Ham... ster is it?"

Okay, that's pushing it. I gave in.

"Manson, sir, Manson, Dr Manson... Jacen Manson."

"Ah, of course, yes, Dr Man... ster."

I'll give him *Dr Manster* in a minute.

"Ja, ich bin gewesen... erm... meaning to letz you know das der project ist nicht going to verk."

"Oh?"

My heart began to sink and the small pocket of turbulence we went through at that moment didn't help me.

Helena grabbed my arm again.

"Ja, vee have done zum verk, zum pilot verk und experiments back ins Germany on ziss und der resulten sind nicht gut."

Great, how long have you bloody known this for? You could have bothered to pick up the sodding phone!

"Entschuldigung! Zorry about it."

He took a large and condescending swig of whiskey, swallowed down my career, then turned back around and continued the jovial conversation with his two accomplices.

"What?!"

Klein, Fuchs and Winkler.

That pretty much summed up what I thought as well.

I looked at Helena, who had also heard what he'd said. She was sat in the window seat looking out, she put her hand back on my thigh and laid her head on my shoulder in silent consolation.

The professor... the Great and Powerful, had just shattered my career dreams in one aged, oaked, single malty instant.

Crap.

He might as well have lasered my balls off after all.

Chapter Thirty

High Tea

And a Nice Bit of Muffin

By the time we landed in Amsterdam and reached our hotel in The Hague, I was mightily pissed off for a decent handful of reasons.

I'd booked a twin room for myself, but after Student Doctor Helena Mastromassaro had been given the go ahead by Dr Bodman to come along, all the other hotel rooms near the conference centre had been booked up.

I, being the chivalrous gent that I am, offered to share my room. After all, it *was* a twin.

We got to the room to be joyously greeted by a large Super King Double bed.

"Ah, surprise. They seem to have… upgraded us."

"Oh, well I'm sure we'll cope, Dr Manson. But no touching."

A man's gotta do what a man's gotta do.

Helena flung herself on the window side of the bed in a show of ownership.

"Comfy is it?"

"Oh, the best!"

She shook the headboard a little. It didn't bang against the wall.

"Come on, let's go out for some food. I'm starving."

We checked out where the conference centre was and it wasn't far from our hotel so we went for an Italian dinner augmented by a nice bottle of *Chianti*. I think that we both needed to drown a certain level of our sorrows.

I did, at least.

So after a couple of glasses of our deep, full bodied, red wine with an aroma of cherries, Helena's inhibitions had reduced somewhat, not that it was going to take much.

"So, Jacen. Have you got a girlfriend then?"

I sensed she was leading somewhere with this. Some form of charade had commenced.

"Well, good question and one which I have currently posed to myself."

"Oh, why?"

Helena had one elbow on the white tablecloth and supported her chin on one hand whilst almost fully hiding behind the large glass of wine that she'd held up to her face with the other. We could hear soft, Italian operatic music in the background. Her face was dimly illuminated by the flickering of candlelight from our table.

"Well, I think that I've been dumped by my long-term girlfriend because we'd both forgotten what each other looked like and I was never there when she needed me, and… erm… I was sort of casually seeing one of the nurses who no longer acknowledges my existence."

And I did not mean Sister Kate Ellis in Casualty who loved to acknowledge my existence whenever she could get her hands on it.

"I just can't believe that." She smiled and gave me that consoling head tilt that women do sometimes to encourage me to keep opening up to them.

"Well, the nurse wasn't really my type and, to be honest, I'm not even sure why we were together in the first place."

I, of course, knew exactly why we were together and there were two fairly decent sized reasons.

"What about you?"

"Oh, I'm single, Jacen. Too early to settle down. I just want to have some fun."

She placed her wine glass on the table next to mine and brushed her little finger against the back of my hand.

Again, my astute reasoning had gained a further clue as to her possible intent, although I couldn't be absolutely sure. I was rubbish at this sort of thing.

"Oh and I think Student Nurse Alice fancies you!" She cunningly detracted from her own immediate feelings.

"Oh, I don't know about that," I lied.

You could tell that from a mile off what with her complex *Ordnance Survey*-like blushing reaction to embarrassment. I also quite liked Alice but I think she was probably too young for me... but not by much.

"Hey, so what do you think about *Robona*?" I hastily changed the subject before she probed me for any more skeletons, of which there may have been one or two.

"Well," she said, "I think they make a very handsome couple and they both seem so happy when I've seen them together."

"Yeah, bloody *Donald Duck* has really softened up *Queen Maleficent* hasn't he?!"

"Why do you call him that?" she laughed.

"Oh, just some nonsense about him buggering off to anaesthetic conferences in Orlando. We were pretending to be convinced that he made it all up just to do *Disney*, and one can't let a decent perpetual piss-take pass away now, can one? Plus, he still owes me a *Mickey Mouse* T-shirt."

We continued more small talk but it was clear that we should probably think about getting back to our hotel room given the obvious romantic tension between us.

Before that, and since we were away from work, we headed to a local late night coffeeshop.

Now, whilst smoking marjiuana in the Netherlands is illegal, you can buy cannabis over the counter in coffeeshops. Authorities generally tolerate it and may turn a blind eye to possession of under five grams.

There was no way I was buying weed to smoke though. Helena wasn't up for that either. We did decide on a nice cup of herbal tea and a chocolate muffin to start sobering up a bit and finish off the evening before heading back to our hotel room.

The conference would be starting early at about 8.00am so we had to be in some form of acceptable condition.

The smoky atmosphere from the other patrons inside was enough to get us both giggling, floaty and also somewhat more amorous. Although, I sensed that whether we'd inhaled the entire coffeeshop air space or not wouldn't have made any difference to the fact that Helena would definitely be trespassing onto my side of the bed later.

We decided on another cup of tea and another chocolate muffin each.

"Chocolate is never as good as back at home is it?" Helena took a big mouthful. "They're not like those nice, freshly baked, Belgian chocolate chip *Otis Spunkmeyer* ones at the hospital canteen."

"I agree. This stuffs a bit cardboardy and not really that sweet. Must be that fake, low fat chocolate. Bit flaky and gritty too. Maybe it's just got a high cocoa percentage?"

We'd both had dessert in the form of some homemade Tiramisu earlier but suddenly we were bloody hungry again.

"Come on, Jace, let's get out of here." She got up slowly from her chair and grabbed my hand to pull me up.

Erm, okay. Now where are my legs? I can't feel my legs!

"Helena, I can't feel my legs! I can't move!"

I mean, I knew that they were there and I could feel them if I pinched and poked them, but I couldn't actually feel them anymore as subscription-paying affiliated members of the Association that was otherwise known as my own body!

"*I* feel really funny too..."

She stumbled and fell against me. I reckoned that she exaggerated that clumsiness just a tad in order to end up sat on my lap with her arms flung around my neck and her head on my shoulder, again.

She breathed into my ear. I always liked the tingly sensation that it gave me.

The waitress came over with the bill when seeing us trying and failing to get to our feet and before we could do an inadvertent runner out of there without paying our dues.

We looked at the bill.

Special Tea x2

Space Cake x2

"*Special* Tea?" I squinted.

"*Space* Cake?!" Helena looked at me wide-eyed and cutely wrinkled her nose.

Herbal Tea?? Chocolate chip muffins??

"Those *weren't* chocolate chips, Jace..."

"That was *no* chamomile tea, Helena..."

We pissed ourselves laughing again.

"Better get a taxi back." She got to her feet and swayed a little.

"Oh my god, my feet feel like lead! I feel about ten stone heavier!"

"So... you're stoned then?!"

Cue, more ridiculous spluttering from what would normally be hugely unamusing word association.

I stooped over and manually picked up one thigh at a time using both hands and very purposefully, clumsily and quite slowly, walked myself out of the coffeeshop. Helena grabbed me and together we succeeded in making it to the door.

I don't think anybody in the shop really noticed us cocking about trying to get out of there, as they were all sat around in their very own private clouds of illegal, smoky ambience drinking their own special blend of loose-leaf high tea with it's own special kind of 'high'.

"Shit! My vision sure feels strange. It's like I can't focus on anything. When I look over there, then look at you, I see everything in between in super slow motion whooshing through my eyes like a huge, colourful, horizontal, blurry mess! With a big whoosh!... *WHHHOOOSHH!*"

"Like, how was it again?" Helena laughed.

"*WHHHOOOSHH!*" I whooshed.

We blurted out laughing all too easily again and fell against each other for balance and mutual bodily warmth, of course. It *was* getting cold.

Once we'd remembered where we were staying via what was written on our room keycard, we found a taxi to take us back.

I don't know about Helena, but I certainly couldn't remember exactly how we got back or how long the journey took. In fact, I think it would have taken about a single solitary minute to walk back if you had any sense of where you were, or indeed any sense at all.

I was beginning to feel a little nauseous now and the weird visual blurring, with heightened rainbow colours and probably a herd of pink unicorns, was not helping.

We didn't turn the lights on in the hotel room to minimise visual input which was now swamping our brains with so much information and without any form of natural filtration. Our senses had been dramatically heightened.

The last thing I recalled was not the silky smooth, naked form of Helena testing out the headboard for real but rather the tiny, red LED light that was dimly illuminated on the satellite box under the TV set.

That was the only visual input I could allow my greedy brain to receive in order to localise the rest of my body, prevent my head spinning out of control like a rowing boat in a giant whirlpool and avoid throwing up.

Vomiting would not be the most romantic way to spend the night and end an otherwise lovely evening.

So, I stared at the little, red light... all night. I intermittently gave each strained eye a rest by closing one and then opening the other to stare back at the light. My eyes alternated their night watch. I wondered, at the time, if I was also intermittently resting each cerebral hemisphere by doing this.

I don't know what Helena did after she took off all of her clothes, threw them on the floor and got under the covers, apart from feeling the pressure of her very cold, yet silky, naked bottom against the small of my back.

I obviously noticed that, whilst I kept religiously staring at the red light. My friend... the red light.

We hadn't closed the curtains and in the morning, the light came flooding into our room which fabulously illuminated the bare form of Helena, who was laid on her front near the edge of her side of the bed, softly snoring with her right arm slumped over the side and her thick, dark hair shaggily matted over her head and shoulders.

It was like she was at the end of my hallucinatory rainbow cuddled up to a cache of golden elven coins.

I must have fallen asleep and was also lying on my front, on top of both arms, neither of which I could feel. I rolled over and my heavy, numb, rubber arms flopped forcefully onto my face and chest with a thud. I tried to roll over again as the blood flow attempted to nourish my nerves again, restoring some sensation via a shivering, prickly, painful flood of neural re-perfusion.

I looked down at the floor over the side of the bed.

Why was it moving? The garishly patterned carpet was rippling with raucous waves like an ocean.

The whooshing, blurring vision persisted only now accompanied by the *sound* of crashing waves and the constant scrunching, tinkling sound of tin foil.

I wretched a bit.

What time is it? I can smell burning... and maple syrup.

8.23am it said on the bedside clock.

I don't think I'll be making the opening lectures. Nor would Helena, who was still softly and blissfully snoring and therefore breathing, and therefore very much alive.

Good.

She twitched… a myoclonic jerk that caused just enough force to dislodge the duvet that was already precariously covering her lower half; it gently slid over the side of the bed onto the floor.

The increasingly bright sunlight beamed through, bathing her blemish-free and beautifully bioluminescent body.

I really wished that I felt better. She would have been an excellent way to get up and start the day.

Is that a sparkly flying pixie? I swatted at the air.

Special Tea and Space Cake…

Chapter Thirty-One

Grandson and Doctor

Dastardly Discoveries

So, we did get to some of the conference in the end, which was all about heart muscle diseases, after the effect of the Space Muffins wore off. But on the whole, I think it was a little over Helena's head, academically speaking. She wasn't too bothered though, as it gave us both a chance to just hang out together and flirt a bit.

A welcome relief and an interim escape from reality.

I saw Klein, Winkler and Fuchs in passing but felt it best to just ignore them. Anyway, I was probably just an annoying itch to Professor Klein now that he had probably pissed the rest of my career down the aircraft toilet before disembarking.

As we wandered through to passport control back in good old Blighty, I checked my phone voice messages. There was one from the police.

"Good news, Dr Manson, we have recovered your briefcase and all of your things are still inside, except for the blue file which we found in a nearby skip. Please call us and we will send victim support to hand it over."

Oh, excellent. Police Constable 'NothinglikeHeatherLocklear' would be coming back.

Helena and I parted ways, for now. The previous night had left certain things unsaid and undone. There remained a certain 'tension' between us.

PC 'Locklear' did indeed return my case and a slightly dirty, but otherwise intact, file of research documents. Not that they were of any use whatsoever now.

The case itself had gained a little collection of needles and a few small syringes in the front pouch, some *Rizla* cigarette roll-up paper, a half-used packet of tobacco and remnants of white powder lining the whole of the inside. It was also a bit dusty but whoever took it had attached the shoulder strap back on to it. I'd taken that off because I never used it.

"Where did you find it?"

"Oh, in a drug squat. The large, old abandoned warehouse with the terrifying graffiti on the front wall."

The Council had concluded that it would be too expensive to convert the huge building into luxury apartments or even affordable housing; they couldn't raze it to the ground either because of the danger posed to the surrounding homes and businesses by the controlled explosions that would be needed.

I wondered if any of my medical equipment had been used. I'd have to thoroughly clean it later.

"Did you fingerprint it?" I'd hoped they'd passed the case to *Columbo* for his final verdict.

"No, not worth our time or money, Doctor. You've got it back now."

Fair enough, I suppose. My file was now redundant anyway thanks to bloody Professors Shite, Wanker and Fuckstick.

Yes, I was in a mood. Deal with it!

I needed to head up to see Grandad. So, after a rapid turnaround back at my flat, I got into my decidedly underpowered car to tackle the long drive up the M6.

Now, it can be strange being a doctor and going to hospital either as a patient or the relative of a patient. Sometimes you'd rather the staff knew what you did for a career to avoid the usual patronising, but generally necessary, translation from medical speak into man-on-the-street speak; or 'layman's terms', as we'd say.

The dumbing down of medical language.

If I knew that I was addressing a fellow medical colleague, it was much easier just to tell them how it was, which afforded the best and most accurate explanation and saved you from having to mentally convert everything whilst wondering whether you'd truly got your message across.

This itself is an art.

But at the same time, just being treated as a normal patient or just a relative was equally as valuable and sometimes more desirable.

I went to see Grandad and whilst I wanted to know exactly what was going on with him, I also wanted to just be his caring and concerned grandson.

The last few times I'd visited Grandad at home, I'd noted that he was getting thinner and I could begin to feel his ribs when hugging him goodbye. He'd always been a big and strong man.

Whenever I'd left, he'd started saying, "I hope I see you again, ay?"

"Of course you will, Grandad!" I'd tell him.

Before I went to the ward to see him this time, I spoke to one of the nurses in the relative's room.

"Ah, you're the doctor grandson then are you?"

So, my family had been bragging, but probably with understandable pride, which felt quite nice actually.

"Yes, for my sins. I hear from Mum that Grandad has had a small stroke but he'll be home in a couple of weeks?"

"Oh, well, I'll ask the registrar to come and talk to you. Here, I have his blood results back if you'd like to see them?"

She handed over a little pile of printed sheets clearly not knowing the interpretation of the numbers.

I'd been getting on with my revision for the MRCP too, admittedly and largely from extended toilet reading.

"Oh, shit! He's got Chronic Myeloid Leukaemia!"

"What, sorry?" The nurse looked surprised. "Oh, nobody told *us* that."

Nurses handover up here was not so detailed then.

Grandad had been pottering off to hospital on his own for a few years for check-ups for 'prostate trouble'. Well, that was believable. But it turns out he'd been seeing a specialist oncologist about his CML but didn't tell anyone in the family about it and he'd apparently refused any form of treatment.

But people with CML can live for years in remission[56].

It turns out that even the registrar hadn't realised yet about the CML.

I went in to see Grandad and he was looking and feeling fairly chirpy for him, albeit a lot thinner. Of course, he was absolutely delighted that I'd gone up to visit him.

He reminisced, as he often did, about his escapades during the War and reflected on his life and his family, especially his grandchildren. I was kind of jealous, not knowing if I'd ever have that.

I'd heard his stories before over the years, but it was always lovely to hear him recount them with such clarity and passion.

"What a life," he'd say, "what a life!"

---

[56] CML is often a slowly developing condition and treatment can keep it under control for many years. Modern therapy works very well and people can go into remission for many years; this is when the disease isn't active, you don't have symptoms and it doesn't show up in your blood samples. Generally 70% of men will survive >5 years after diagnosis.

But he didn't say it with remorse or any sign regret, but with a smile, a slight shake of his head in disbelief and a sense of fulfilment and achievement.

Well, the problem was, he wouldn't be coming home in a couple of weeks. Partly because of the blood results I'd seen and accompanied my own 'end of the bed' assessment of him. But also because he was 'just not quite right.'

I also very faintly detected that sweet, subtle, musty odour.

I think Death has boarded the train to the North. I hope it is delayed by leaves on the track or the wrong type of snow on the line.

I called Mum.

"You've got to come and see Grandad and bring Dad and bro."

"Oh, well, we will but I thought we'd come up next month when he's back at home." Mum was always Little Miss Procrastinator Extraordinaire!

"Erm, no Mum. This time, you have to listen to me and come up in the next day or so. Grandad won't be with us much longer, I think. Tell the rest of the family too?"

"Oh. Alright, son. We'll get our things together and come up later today."

I am so pleased that I did have that medical knowledge and made my own assessment on this occasion.

I still would have preferred to be just *grandson*.

I stayed with him for a few hours that day just chatting, mostly listening and sometimes watching him sleep. I read gossip magazines when he dozed off.

I reminisced about the times I'd spent with him whilst growing up. We spent time in his old garage making things like a little, wooden remote-controlled sail boat and a prototype wind sand-surfer. I also helped him sort out his tools, screws and nails out into separate glass jars. We'd watch Saturday afternoon wrestling on *ITV* together cheering on *Big Daddy* when he fought *Giant Haystacks*.

We'd then take Nana's cat out for a walk; the beautiful Siamese with shimmering blue eyes was too valuable to roam around alone on the streets so she had to wear this little, red velvet body harness on a lead. It was quite funny when you think about it. I've never ever seen anyone else take a cat out for a walk since! Although, she did refuse to go out without the harness after a while.

We'd pick up milk, pies for lunch and the *Daily Mirror*, pop in to visit his brother and then wander back home via the local pig farm. The pig farm always smelt of fresh tea, I don't know why.

Remember, elderly people are people who have led amazing and varied lives, they've experienced successes, failures, tragedy and tribulation. They have families and loved ones. They may have a decayed, physical shell but they have a full and fruitful core.

Stop. Listen. Respect. They were young like you once upon a time.

The ward nurses had started to unbox the Christmas decorations whilst I was there visiting.

Blimey, nearly that time of year already?

Time flies when the shit hits.

Chapter Thirty-Two

Need for Speed

Christmas Crap

The nurses, back in our hospital, were in full swing with putting up their Christmas decorations too. Doing the drug round, feeding the patients, changing the bed sheets and preparing bed baths would have to wait.

The only paperwork they'd be doing would be wrapping fake presents to put under the ward tree.

I was already monumentally pissed off this morning having got up late and then getting camera-flashed 'speeding' on the way in. I can't have been doing more than 35 mph but I suppose it *was* a 30 zone and in the cold eyes of the law, I'd duly broken it. More like a hairline fracture I would say.

Maybe I could try and get out of it by pulling another fast one and playing the 'emergency doctor' card. Although, that doesn't really wash with the authorities on the whole. In fact, the NHS spends hundreds of thousands of pounds and hundreds of hours each year in trying to appeal against speeding fines and to absolve the responsibility of paramedics speeding in their ambulances.

Automatic exemption on emergency vehicles? Tax payers' money well spent.

I know that Dr Johnny Winterson-Waring was speeding whilst on his way to work on the motorway. When the cops pulled up alongside him and pointed their finger at him to pull over, Johnny thought that he was quick-thinking and grabbed his stethoscope that was coiled on the passenger seat and dangled it at the cops through his side window.

"*I'm a doctor*," it symbolised, "*and I'm obviously in a hurry!*"

A gentle dingle-dangle minus the flashing blue or green lights, of course. Aside from that, being an orthopod, Johnny wouldn't have had a clue how to use his stethoscope anyway!

The cop in the passenger side of the pursuit car was equally as quick-thinking and with a broad, toothy smile, reflecting the full force of the law, he reciprocated with a friendly dangle of his shiny handcuffs back at Johnny. Needless to say, Johnny pulled over and was lucky to just get away with a caution that time.

They should have locked him up for the night, in my opinion.

I hadn't really slept much last night worrying about where on Earth my career was headed now that my research opportunity had gone up in whiskey-fuelled flames and pipe smoke.

I had no idea what Jess had decided to do with her pregnancy, as she wasn't answering my calls, and every time I went round to her place, Lurch answered and said nothing to me even though she wasn't at home - I mean, Lurch didn't even live there; I'd also tried the cardiac ITU but she was always too busy to come and speak to me.

I hadn't heard any more from Karen either and presumed that she just generally hated me now, but equally, I hadn't tried to call her either.

On top of which, Dave's suicide attempt was really playing on my mind... poor sod. I missed his ridiculously clumsy, yet entertaining, self; he was actually a very competent doctor with lots of potential and he'd almost clocked out of his career and his life far too early. He needed a bit of toughening up but he was conscientious and pretty smart. Plus, I missed the cheeky banter that we shared.

Trumping of all that, I was knackered, stressed and worried about Grandad and whether the family would all get to visit him before the end.

I knew that I'd seen him for the last time. As I'd left his ward and waved goodbye to him, my tears beginning to form, his smily face waved back at me saying, "Ta-tah, now, ta-tah!"

That would be my final lasting memory of him.

At least, perhaps, I could relax just a little bit at the hospital Christmas party tonight and try and take my mind off stuff. It always happened a little before actual Christmas as people usually started taking their annual leave to bugger off for the festive period.

Usually all the staff with families and loads of kids seemed to get their choices first and all of us singleton, childless failures were stuck doing Christmas Day, Boxing Day and any other day ending in 'Day'.

Helena, who was still locumming for Dave's time off for the moment, was up on the ward trying her best to be efficient and get all the results ready for the ward round. I think she'd turned up about two hours ago. Dave was always pretty reliable at that and he always had an answer to any question thrown at him by Dr Bodman.

Fiona ambled onto the ward, again looking decidedly happy, glowing and most probably in genuine love.

"Hey, Fi, you look positively radiant!" I balanced my finely annunciated words upon an imaginary blue velvet cushion and presented them to her with a subservient bow.

"Piss off, Jace!"

I mean, I *was* trying to pay her a heart-felt compliment.

"I'm *serious*, you do!"

"I can never tell when you're actually being serious anymore. But thanks anyway," Fi conceded, "plus, exam results are out later today... and I think I might be pregnant. Okay, let's get the notes trolley, Dr Bodman will be here shortly."

"Wait, hang on... you're *pregnant*? You can't just slip that one in!"

Unlike Dirty *Disney* Doctor Banks who'd clearly been slipping in a fair bit lately.

"Oh, well, it's early days anyway." She smiled a very broad and embarrassed grin which embellished her beguilingly, bedraggled beauty.

Things were really working out for Fi. I have to say that I did harbour more than just a pang of jealousy. Soon, I had to work up to my exams too but my relationship status was in absolute and utter chaos.

I felt like a honeybee sampling nectar from a dozen different flowers without really sticking to a favourite. I didn't even know where my hive was anymore.

"So, you won't be drinking at the hospital Christmas party tonight then?"

"Jace, our team is on-call tonight, haven't you read the rota?"

"Aw, *what*? You're having a bloody laugh. Really?!"

"Yep."

She popped the final 'p' between her lips as if to metaphorically prick my bubble of relative excitement with a tiny needle.

"Oh, for piss-sake."

Well, at least Helena was on with me too. She came over to us with the notes trolley.

"Morning, Dr Feelwell," Helena smiled, "you look well!"

"*See*," I said, "she's Preggers Plays Pop[57]."

I liked referencing the old children's programme starring the TV legend that was *Keith Chegwin*.

"Wow, congratulations, Fi!"

"Yeah, well, come on let's get going. Dr Bodman will have to catch us up."

"You'll be pleased to know, I'll be joining you today, doctors."

Sister Edna Sledge practically stood to attention. Her dark blue uniform was stretched tight and her knees and ankles were held tightly together again ready for action.

"Oh, fabulous. At ease, Sister! We have the oracle herself today. A rare pleasure."

"Less of your sarcasm, Dr Manson."

"No Student Nurse Sharples today?" I was more than a little disappointed not to have the aural pleasure of her dulcet Irish tones.

"Nurse Sharples is doing some of her nursing exams today."

There was a curtain around our first patient and I heard the annoying, nasally, nincompoop twang of none other than Doctor Johnny Winterson-Waring.

What was he doing on a *medical* ward? He'd be like a beached and hapless Beluga Whale[58]. He must be on-call for orthopaedics... great.

---

[57] Cheggers Plays Pop was a British children's game show shown on BBC1 from 1978 to 1986 and hosted by Keith Chegwin who was known as "Cheggers".

[58] The Beluga Whale adapted to life in the Arctic; it is all white and often called melonhead.

What a twonk. I kept my thought to myself.

Mrs Morag McPhlinket had been re-admitted overnight with another cold weather community-acquired pneumonia and, unfortunately for her, a recently hospital-acquired fractured neck of femur.

Her right leg was shortened by about six inches and externally rotated, a sure sign it was broken. She'd decided to throw herself out of bed in the early hours of the morning, presumably feeling disorientated in hospital and not in the midst of digging an escape tunnel.

"Well, Mrs Mc… erm… McPillking, McPhlingklent…" his posh pronunciation poppycock pulled her name apart. "I think we should probably do an x-ray just to check that your hip isn't broken."

Our team joined him behind the curtains.

"Of course it's broken, Dr Winkleton-Warning!" Fiona stepped in. "Perhaps you should just contact your consultant, Mr Branston, and get her prepped for theatre on the emergency list?"

She leant in towards Johnny and whispered in his ear.

"Stop pissing about delaying the treatment of this poor woman who is obviously in some discomfort and if *we* can't rehab her, she'll die in here and you know that."

Pale Johnny and his equally colourless demeanour allowed what remnants of pastel shades to drain away as his incompetence was confronted by our fearless (and pregnant) leader.

"Ahh, Team!"

The joyous, pomp and celebration of Dr Cleeve Bodman. He jigged flamboyantly onto the ward as if partaking in an opening night theatre performance.

He must have had some early patients up at The Tower and earned a couple of grand before the ward round.

"Good morning, Dr 'Bee'. You know Helena?" I reminded him.

"Ah, yes of course, the lovely soon-to-be *Doctor* Mastromassaro. I've heard a lot of positive things about your time with us. Thank you for your hard work during Dr Dewani's absence."

"Oh, thank you, sir."

Helena blushed a little wondering what I might have said to Dr Bodman about her.

"I'm sure you'll be looking for a job and a reference soon. I trust that you enjoyed the conference in Amsterdam?"

"Er, yes, Dr Bodman, it was very... educational indeed and Dr Manson really looked after me."

"Oh, I'm sure Dr Manson did!"

Dr Bodman gave me a smile and a wink, clearly with totally the wrong impression of me. At least I thought he was winking at me but then again, Dave wasn't here today.

Would I take advantage of a pretty, young medical student?

Sister Sledge must have marched away for a moment as she suddenly reappeared in 'double-time' and somewhat breathless following a brief and rare scuttle.

"Can I direct you all to Mr Clementine next, please? I think he's taking a turn."

A turn for the worse, one presumed.

Sister Sledge took Dr Bodman by the arm to divert the warfleet like a powerful, military tug boat.

Mr Peter Clementine was practically glowing in the dark with jaundice and he was semi-conscious, groaning and clutched his belly. No jokes for us today then.

"We've called the Liver Unit again about him, but at the moment they have no beds."

"Or livers!" I interjected.

Dr Bodman sat on the side of the bed next to Peter but he didn't say anything. He just observed the multiple bruises and petechiae that had formed on Peter's skin, his cachectic body and recurrently swollen abdomen.

We all knew the situation. He'd been given as much medical therapy as we could offer but he really needed a new liver. Alas, his long-term alcohol misuse had taken it's toll.

Peter's breathing was laboured and his thick respiratory secretions rattled in the back of his throat and reverberated deep down in the cavernous abyss of his lungs.

The Death Rattle, we called it.

"I think, Sister, we should set up a morphine infusion and try to make him more comfortable."

Helena let out a sigh. There's only so much you can do.

Mr Clementine would not be having Christmas this year. A piece of purple tinsel, that had been joyously sellotaped to his headboard, came loose, brushing gently against the side of his face.

Glad tidings we bring, to you and your kin... we wish you a Merry Christmas, forget about the New Year.

Back in the mess, we reflected on another ward round filled with very little good news. Some patients had begged us for 'Christmas leave' which was granted. But if you're well enough to go home for Christmas, then you're well enough to bloody stay there!

We were reaching that time of year when we were getting an influx of very sick, elderly people being attacked by the bugs of the season, whilst our own hospital computers were soon to be attacked by the imminent Millennium Bug.

The weather was getting frostier and Death came bearing gifts of Cold, Heart Attacks and Stroke.

Christmas was a time for cheer, but in our world, it was a time of sorrow and often tragedy that then shaped all the Christmases to come for the victims and grieving relatives.

I sat with Helena sharing a mug of sweet tea and Fi was cuddled up to Rob, who was now at the end of his shift trying to hand over some ICU tasks to Matt Dundee that he'd forgotten to mention earlier.

"Hey, Rob, I hear congratulations are in order you Dirty Dawg!"

"Yeah. Thanks, Jace, it's amazing."

He popped a hand on Fi's tummy in paternal pride.

"Aw, it's so sweet," cooed Helena, popping a hand on *my* thigh with some form of instinctive and primitive reflex.

My blood ran cold. Would I be ready for the pitter patter of tiny feet? Was Jess still growing one?

"Christmas Pardy t'noyt, mayt," Matt Dundee gloated.

"I'm on-call, cobber," I told him.

"Ah, that saucy Nurse Jessica Totten's going. Might have to barbie a sausage and give her a taste of 'Straya!"

Cocky bastard.

He clearly had no idea about my clandestine soirees with Jess and she clearly hadn't said anything to anyone but Nurse Nightshade, probably.

My blood couldn't run much colder but it certainly had a go at throwing me into an ice bath. I resisted from launching my fists of fury.

"You coming for a blast in my car then?"

"I dunno, Rob, I'm on-call today and can't really get out."

"Oh, go on Jace, he's been dying to take you for a blast in that," said Fi. "Go on, babes, take him down to have a look at it at least. I'll hold his bleep for a bit."

Fi patted Rob on the cheek and pecked him on the lips.

"Sod it! Come on then, Rob, let's go."

"Oh, good. Me and Helena can have some girlie chat then while you're gone."

"See you tomorrow after the on-call then, babes. After me and Jace have been for a spin, I'll go and pick up some food for a nice dinner and some non-alcoholic vino for you!"

Rob kissed Fi again.

It was very sweet, but I couldn't help but wonder how two doctors would make their relationship work. The challenges of staying together with perpetual exams, moving around from job to job, rotation to rotation with no guarantee that you and your partner could get a job in the same hospital or even the same region of the country, were ever present. As for getting consultant jobs in the same place? Forget it.

How would you cope with the simultaneous stresses that every day brings when both of you want to be grumpy and offload your troubles onto one another?

But then again, at least you could understand the nuances of each other's problems. The world of hospital life had to be experienced to truly appreciate the complexity of it.

"Bloody hell, mate! That is indeed gorgeous."

Rob had waxed his car up, buffed up the alloy wheels and the British Racing Green bodywork glinted in the winter sunshine. He flicked a button and the soft top opened up revealing the sumptuous, red-ribbed leather seats.

We both sat inside and inhaled the essence of British sports car.

"Right, listen to this..."

Rob fired up the engine and revved it up. The engine burbled and popped a little, and the sweet, intoxicating smell of fuel wafted delicately up my nostrils.

"Sounds great, man."

"Shall we hit the tarmac and give her a blast?"

Guilt stood alongside us feeling somewhat left out.

"Ah! Look, man, I'm on-call. I should probably... ah, fuck it! Come on, let's go."

We buckled up our seat belts and Rob sped towards the hospital car park exit almost hitting the automated barrier.

Guilt waved at me, frowned and tapped her watch. A further wave of guilt washed over me.

"Hey, look actually... I feel bad. I'd better get back in there, I shouldn't really leave the girls alone. Let's do it one weekend soon when we're both off and then we can go for a cheeky beer as well?"

"Yeah. Sure, buddy. You're probably right. You can't let my pregnant girl work too hard now!"

"Don't forget your groceries, darling, and tidy up the kitchen when you get home."

I jumped out and shut the door as Rob flashed two fingers at me, floored the accelerator, span and screeched the rear wheels streaking off down the road.

I coughed at the pungent smell and cloudy smoke of burning rubber.

I needed to upgrade *my* car.

Chapter Thirty-Three

The Magic Kingdom

Just a Pair of Socks

I met the others back in the mess to be greeted by a gift from Management appreciating the hard work of all the doctors during this Yuletide season.

Stood in the middle of the table where we'd sit and eat, when we actually had time to sit or indeed eat, was an entire, whole and unopened bottle of Sauvignon Blanc... not a bottle for each of us, but *one* bottle for all of us.

"*With thanks from The Management Team*" said the label attached to the bottle.

Now, okay, I get that we can't drink alcohol whilst on-call but we can take a bottle home to drink when we aren't on duty.

I thought about all the city boys and big businesses giving their employees Christmas bonuses whether the companies made a profit or not. If you were a chief executive and your company did badly, you could be sacked with a Golden Goodbye to massively plump up your bank account.

If you were a CEO sacked from your Trust in the NHS, you could be given a massive payout of taxpayers money, whether you'd fucked up or not; some, indeed, had literally done just that, having been involved in various hospital sex scandals.

In the NHS, you could even be re-employed after you'd already been sacked and benefit from another Golden Handshake and have your pension protected... that's really screwed up isn't it?!

One bottle of wine for all? You might just as well say 'Merry Sodding Christmas' and kick us all in the Festive Baubles.

An insult. It is most certainly *not* the thought that counts.

Nurses could earn double-time over the festive season for volunteering to work, whilst the junior doctors would be on half-time for *having* to work because your number was up on the rota. You might even find a porter on treble-time because, let's face it, who wants to do the crap they have to do over Christmas? So, incentive was needed.

Management sometimes forgets about the huge value of the porters. In a hospital, you need patient flow and if a journey from A to B is required, you need the porters and enough of them. They are like the hospital's public transport system. If there weren't any available due to understaffing, the Trust would end up inadvertently paying for a consultant or other senior doctor to ferry patients around in order to get things done such as urgent scans, interventional procedures or indeed surgery if they needed to be in theatre.

Why pay for a *Rolls Royce*, a *Bentley* or an *Aston Martin* to drive patients to *Poundland* when you can take the bus?

Failing that, patients would just need to wait and a traffic jam would be created.

"*Oh, but having our own department's porters is too expensive and we'll overspend on our department budget.*"

Okay, whatever. Nonsense.

"*One* bottle of wine! It's a bloody joke!"

"Don't sweat it, Jace. It's the thought that counts."

Fi's sarcasm oozed out of every pore and slowly dissipated to the floor.

"So, you girls had a nice chat? You're still here, so I'm guessing so."

"None of your business, Doctor," smiled Helena.

I guessed that my ears ought to have been smashing the fire alarms a few minutes earlier.

"So, you two getting on alright?" Fi enquired, her probing question clearly loaded with prior gossip about me and Helena.

"Um, yeah, why?" I played man-dumb as best as I could not wishing to giveaway the slightest sign of a feeling. Not that I would know what the slightest sign of a feeling should feel like.

"Oh, *nothing*, Jace," Fi's line of interrogation was thwarted by the Defence of Pseudoignorance.

BLEEEP BLEEEP

"Piss, it's Casualty."

Things had gone a bit *quiet* which was too much to expect for that to last.

Never mention the 'Q' word... always spells trouble.

"Hello, Dr Man..."

"Jace, that you?"

"Yes, Kate?"

"Yeah, it's me," she sounded anxious and a little out of breath.

"What's up?"

"Oh, we've just received a crash call from the paramedics. Involving another ambulance. ETA, five minutes. We'd appreciate your team's help if you don't mind."

"Yeah, of course, sure. Shit. We'll amble down now."

"Thanks, see you soon. I don't think it's a good one."

She hung up.

"Alright girls! We are up again. Casualty needs us. Trauma. Another ambulance involved in the accident. Helena? You up for it?"

"Yes, Jace. Bit nervous but yep, I'm ready."

She clapped her hands together exhibiting her tentative but obvious excitement. This would be another valuable learning experience.

"Fi, how're *you* doing? Stay here if you need to?"

"Jacen, I'm fine. I'm, like, ten minutes pregnant. I'm *not* quadriplegic."

"Okay! Just asking."

We ambled down to Casualty given that we probably needed to reserve some energy and the ambulances wouldn't yet have arrived. An occasional 'amble' can help to focus the mind and rehearse the imminent situation in your consciousness.

Take a deep breath in... and out... and in again... and out... control your thoughts, prepare for all eventualities, focus. Let the adrenaline flow through you... use it; you're going to need it.

In the resuscitation room, Dr Johnny Winterson-Waring was there already as part of the trauma team, chewing his nails in fear and pacing up and down. There would inevitably be broken bones to straighten. He rehearsed the Trauma Triage[59] system and primary survey to himself, knowing that he'd be a few levels down on the list.

Triage is repeated prior to transport away from the scene of an accident and again at the receiving hospital.

---

[59] Trauma triage is the use of trauma assessment for the prioritisation of patients for treatment or transport according to the severity of injury. Primary triage is carried out at the scene of an accident and secondary triage at the casualty clearing station at the site of the major incident.

The primary survey aims to identify and immediately treat life-threatening injuries and is based on the 'ABCDE' resuscitation system:

Airway control with stabilisation of the cervical spine.

Breathing.

Circulation (including the control of external haemorrhage)

Disability or neurological status.

Exposure or undressing of the patient, whilst also protecting from hypothermia.

Bloody hell, Matt Dundee? In black tie? He smells of alcohol.

"G'day, girls... that includes you, Jace!"

"Piss off, *Skippy*[60]. Why are *you* here anyway?"

"The Unit's short-staffed and they couldn't come down so they dragged me out of the party. I was just getting to third base with Jess as well."

Total muthaf*@£er!

My blood temperature went up exactly 63 degrees.

"Okay, boys put your toys and tackle away." Fiona reprimanded us before things escalated.

The resuscitation doors banged open.

Freya and Phil. Thank god, it wasn't their ambulance involved.

Freya looked entirely in control, although her golden hair had dried blood and flecks of what looked like

---

[60] Skippy the Bush Kangaroo is an Australian TV series, airing from 1968–1970, about the adventures of a young boy and his highly intelligent pet kangaroo; I was doing Skippy a disservice using his name in vain on Matt Dundee.

broken windscreen in it. Phil looked a bit puffed and like he was about to faint.

"Unknown male, probably late twenties, head on collision with an ambulance heading to another emergency call. Estimated combined impact speed of one hundred and forty miles per hour. Explosion occurred. Both paramedics critical, still at the scene. Airway secured, cervical collar in place. Tachycardic, hypotensive. GCS three. Probable pelvic and bilateral femoral fractures. Estimated forty-five per cent burns. Two large bore cannulas in situ and fluid resuscitation running."

Johnny perked up a bit in the corner.

"We found a donor card in his bag but you can't really read the details," said Phil.

"Shit, poor bastard, this doesn't look good. Doubt if the organs will be in any condition to use anyway."

"Oh my god, Jace. Do you think there's anything that can be done?" Helena's brain began discarding basic facts again.

They transferred our *John Doe* from the paramedic scoop board to the trolley.

Matt Dundee took the head end to maintain airway control.

Jesus, he's unrecognisable. His face and head were so swollen, blood and tissue fluid oozed from the burns, probable multiple complex facial fractures. I'd hazard a guess at a severe traumatic intracranial haemorrhage as well which would not be an easy one to recover from whatever the other injuries turned out to be.

Exposing the patient, a large seatbelt bruise across the chest and diffuse abdominal bruising. Probable severe visceral injury and haemorrhage. He'd be bleeding to death on the inside. It could be anything: liver lacerations, ruptured spleen, a torn aorta, ruptured iliac vessels from the pelvic fractures... the list could go on.

We were going to be fighting a losing battle with this one. But the paramedics had no choice but to deliver their 'package' to us.

"He's *CRASHING*!" someone shouted.

CARDIAC ARREST

I started chest compressions but there were so many broken ribs and probably at least two flail segments that it was proving futile.

ASYSTOLE

"Both pupils are fixed and dilated, Jace," Matt shook his head in resignation, "I'll bet there's a major intracerebral bleed as well, man."

I felt a sudden chill throughout my entire body as if I'd fallen through thick ice into a frozen lake. I could barely take a breath, I couldn't move and felt like I'd vomit.

The blanket covering the legs had slipped to the floor.

His socks were still on. I wretched badly.

Mickey Mouse on the left.

Minnie Mouse on the right.

Fi noticed at the same time. She went suddenly clammy and pale and collapsed to the floor.

Helena caught her fall and eased her to the ground. She crouched down beside Fi and cradled her head, amidst all the commotion.

Johnny grabbed a cardboard kidney dish and threw up.

Matt, still in his suit, leaned against the back wall next to the oxygen supply and slid slowly down to the floor, wide-eyed. He also knew.

"Who is it?" Freya said.

"It's Doctor Banks," said Sister Kate.

"Oh my god!"

I put my arm around Freya and led her out of resus.

I'd almost gone out with Rob in the car earlier. I *should* have gone with him. I *could* have told him to slow down. But it might've been *me* here too. But Fi is pregnant. They're both happy and in love. But he's going to be a dad.

The Magic Kingdom has fallen.

Chapter Thirty-Four

Aftermath

We are Family

To say that the mess was a sombre place the following day, was quite simply an understatement. Although there was an unspoken togetherness and a camaraderie that, whilst always present amongst us, was amplified with great emotional clarity.

Despite our varied specialities and our spectrum of seniority, we were all in this together. We were a family of squabbling, stressed brothers and sisters. The incessant cheeky banter was set aside.

Life for us was refocused, re-calibrated and catalysed by an event of apocalyptic proportions.

One of our own was gone and in the most horrific way.

Fi didn't return to work, of course. I didn't know when, or indeed *if*, she would come back.

Her exam results came back though. She passed, unsurprisingly.

Dr Fiona Jean Feelwell MBChB... MRCP.

I sat quietly with Helena on the sofa in the mess, we were both clearly deep in our own thoughts.

Matt Dundee was back in the intensive care unit with his other anaesthetic colleagues who were also struggling to cope with the loss of Rob, which was made more difficult by the fact that they were treating people even more on the brink of death everyday.

Breaking bad news to relatives when you've recently lost friends or family of your own was more than just a challenge.

Davinder turned up that day, not to work but to see everyone and show his own support. Dave wasn't yet back to full mental fitness but he wanted to see his real family. Us.

We didn't share much conversation but there was an unspoken, reciprocated respect and gratitude.

Dr Bodman told us not to bother with the ward round today and that he'd do it alone so we could be with our junior doctor siblings. But we couldn't really leave him alone as he was a bit dappy without us, plus the fact that he probably hadn't inserted an intravenous cannula or taken blood from a patient for twenty years. I was certain that he wouldn't be able to use the hospital's archaic computer system either... too modern for him.

The ward and intensive care nurses all took it hard. Rob was the archetypal 'nice guy'. You couldn't help but love him.

Grandad died that day. Dad rang to tell me. I expected it to occur soon anyway. The day couldn't really get a lot worse. The 'good' thing was, that all my family managed to get to see him before he passed away and said their goodbyes and he was surrounded by those that loved him at the end. I'm glad that I was at least able to ensure that happened.

My mind was beginning to shut down and I felt my mood tumbling lower and lower. I got up off the sofa and went to sit on the side of the bed in the on-call room, exhausted.

My consciousness was beginning to fail and my thoughts were beginning to become slow, clouded and irrational. What was the point? Why bother? I don't see a way out of this. I have no-one. It'll all just turn to shit anyway.

I carried a small pocket *Swiss Army* penknife on my keyring. I took it out and looked at it. I opened one of the blades and held it over my wrist. Tears began to flood my eyes and flow down over my face as the world began to slowly close in on me.

I felt like I was walking in the dark along the edge of a cliff in the driving wind and rain with the violent, black waves crashing upon the massive, craggy rocks hundreds of feet below; it would be so easy to stop struggling and just let my feet slip from underneath me.

Just gracefully fall backwards into the blackness. Spread out your arms and look up to the sky in desperation but with a final relief.

Just disappear.

I turned my head slightly and caught a glimpse of my forlorn face and crumpled form in the mirror above the sink.

What are *you* doing? You're no better than the patients you end up having to treat and get frustrated at for trying this sort of thing. Dave was here not so long ago and what did you call *him* for doing it?

Who's going to find *you*? Who's going to miss *you*?

"*Son, you are here for a reason.*"

At that moment, the calming, soft elixir of my mother's voice echoed around inside my mind as if there were no other voice in existence. My conscious self seemed to float above me with ethereal beauty and looked down upon my breaking shell with hurt and regret.

Stop! Just… STOP!

Our lives needed to go on. People needed us. We had other patients to help, lives to save, diseases to cure. We had to comfort the ones that could not be cured.

We had families that loved us, that supported us, that nurtured us. My family gave me these wonderful opportunities.

BLEEEP BLEEEP

I snapped out of this out-of-body trance and collapsed back into the real world. I became aware of the knife and quickly put it away.

"Hi, Dr Manson here?"

It was Karen. I felt a wave of love flood back into my emptying mind. I don't remember everything she said after that, except:

"I'm thinking of starting a career in medicine."

Epilogue

Fiona didn't return to work for over a year. She had her baby, Robert Michael Jr. Whether his friends would end up calling him *Mickey*, only time would tell. She didn't go back into medicine as a physician but changed her career path to become a radiologist; I approved, it was the future. Plus, all the junior doctor rotas were being changed to include regular weeks of night shifts. No thanks, I know what happens.

I finally passed my MRCP exams but after the huge let down by Professor Klein, who incidentally forgot all about me needing a job; he later advertised a locum cardiology registrar job without even bothering to let me know. I found out that he'd offered it to someone less experienced than me even though they were the only one at the interview. So, I decided that I'd do a stint on the intensive care and renal units for a few months.

Maybe radiology *was* the way to go but I'd need some time off to think about it. I'd have to study for the FRCR[61] which would be a gargantuan task and I hated exams, so maybe not.

I took a year off work to reflect, when I say 'off work', I decided to go freelance and work as a medical escort... no, that did not involve galavanting around

---

[61] FRCR - Fellowship of the Royal College of Radiologists

and partying with yummy, lonely middle-aged women whilst dressed as a doctor (not a bad thought though, there's got to be money in that!), but it was for an aeromedical company. I'd travel the world picking up sick or recovering British tourists and escorting them safely back home to Blighty. It paid okay, I stayed in top hotels, ate good food, but it was tiring and not especially challenging, plus I didn't really like turbulence.

I also took four months off on a total holiday and travelled around South America with a backpack.

Nurse Totten didn't keep the baby. I had no say in the matter but to be honest, I had no idea whether it might have been mine or Matt Dundee's. That was probably a close shave anyway. I couldn't imagine a lifetime of contact with her, it would've been a nightmare.

I think Davinder sorted things out with his family, well, as best as possible at any rate. Although, I'm not sure whether his relationship with Isaac lasted that long. There's only so many times you can watch the *A-Team*. Plus Isaac would drive anyone bananas.

Nurse Alice Sharples qualified, eventually, but she ultimately gave up nursing to become a pharmaceutical representative and just did a few Casualty shifts for some extra pocket money. A lot of nurses became reps; it paid better, you didn't have to put up with a truck load of shite *and* you got a company car. A shame really, as she would have made a great ward sister one day.

In fact, Freya did the same thing having realised that dealing with catastrophic trauma was not doing her mental stability any good. I bumped into her again a few years later but that's another story.

Karen did indeed change career and she became a doctor, ultimately deciding upon general practice. I think she was spurred on by her mum's illness and her own personal battles. I can't believe she did it but I wondered if she'd experienced anything like the things I went through whilst we were together. In some ways I hoped she did, but in others, I really hoped she most certainly did not.

Helena qualified from medical school with distinction, obviously. In a lot of ways, I regret not pursuing a relationship with her. She was attractive, smart, funny and we kind of clicked. But we went our separate ways eventually, as many medical relationships did, as she'd managed to get a rotational job elsewhere in the region. Surprisingly enough, she eventually decided to become a radiologist too.

Believe it or not, my attentions were later turned, and for some time at that, by a 'physiophlamingo', the almost forbidden of all fruit! It must have been their mating season. I'm not even a rugby player anymore. Again, a tantalising tale for another day as 'phlamingos' are certainly much more than meets the eye, especially this one.

So, the German territorial dominance within the hospital persisted for a few years until the inevitable materialisation of the medico-military might of the Italians... that's what they thought anyway.

The friction between the clinical world and the academic sphere continued. Professorial careers were created or destroyed by the fight for multimillion pound research grants and high-powered academic journal publications. A cut-throat and clandestine business in the NHS, a fight for ultimate control and a battle for national financial rewards.

MAXIMILIAN VAN DEN BOSS

Like I've mentioned before, 'Publish or Perish' is their mantra. Stop at nothing, steamroller anyone, steal ideas and pass them off as your own, take no prisoners. That's where the political 'fun' and intrigue began; corruption, manipulation and protection.

As for me, I'm not telling you what I ended up doing but I am still doing it and I am actually still enjoying it. Suffice to say, that if you do find yourself contemplating entering the medical world... get some clarity first.

Honestly, you just couldn't make it up!

Acknowledgements

I'd like to thank 'Montel' for his beautifully creative book cover design and for learning a little about the electrocardiograph whilst doing it.

Huge thanks to the lovely Jacqui for her time and patience in her initial proof-reading of my scrawl.

I am very grateful to the handful of family and good friends that took the trouble to read and critique my cerebral vomit for the first time, only to wonder where it all came from.

I'd like to thank my friend Dr 'Frank', counsellor and psychotherapist for his immense support when I needed it the most.

"Perhaps write down some reflections," he said.

90,000 words later...

About this tome, it was remarked by my girlfriend that "all blokes should come with a manual" and "I probably would have dumped you if I didn't understand a bit of what you went through" - I'm not sure how helpful those comments are, but I suppose they hold a grain of truth. It's a work of fiction anyway!

I thank my dad for his unwavering support of my education and medical career to date; he finally told me he was proud of me. Although, if he knew the half of it, I wonder whether he would have let me be a doctor in the first place. Perhaps he shouldn't read this?!

Finally, I am eternally grateful to my mum for everything. She died suddenly over two years ago which ultimately precipitated this cathartic cerebral download.

"Son, you are here for a reason."

If you are a doctor, or even if you're not, remember that.

About the Author

Maximilian van den Boss is the pseudonym of a consultant in the National Health Service in the UK. He trained in the system and after qualifying in the mid 1990's became a physician for several years before changing his mind... a few times. He is now a respected specialist in his field of practice and he has published extensively in the medical literature in the form of research papers and book chapters. This book is rather different.